Giant in the Valley

L. Faulkner-Corzine

Giant in the Valley

Edited by Tom Siebert of Kingdom Projects
Cover Art and Design by Linda Hamil

Bible references are from The Holy Bible:
King James Version
New King James Version
New Living Bible
New International Version

Dedication

To my husband Gary: Thank you for your long-suffering patience in hearing it all, just one more time—and then, just one more time again—and again! Thank you for your generous encouragement, constant support, and wonderful ideas! Most of all, thank you for introducing me to my heavenly Father, and my Lord and Savior, Jesus Christ. Finally, thank you for being a godly man, for your Christian witness, and for your integrity, strength and courage—you are my hero!

To my dad, Ed Faulkner: Though you're in heaven now, I still must thank you for planting the seeds for this book! Beginning with my very first memory: my hands clasped tight around the saddle horn, and short legs curled over the swells of your saddle. I can still feel your right arm holding me safe, and see Stormy's mane flowing in cadence with each stride, as her ears framed the mountains. I owe to you my appreciation of horses and leather and hay. You taught your daughters about honor, hard work, and consideration. As you so often said of others, you were: a "prince among men!"

Special thanks to:
Jake, Lindsay, Michelle, Mike and Velma Corzine,
Gayla Amaral, Tonya Gibson, Pam Jones,
Jan Knigge, Sandy Mathis and Ann McKinney

Dear Lord Jesus: Please bless this book!
May it be entertaining so readers will turn to the next page.
May it be inspiring so they will turn to You!

TABLE OF CONTENTS

PART ONE

PROLOGUE

"God helps the righteous and delivers them from the plots of evil men." Psalm 37:40

Summer, 1865 - Denver, Colorado

Her golden eyes reflected in the window glass as she watched and waited in the dark. Finally, she saw it: the quick strike of a match, a bare wink of flame, and then it was gone. Quietly, she slipped from the house like a shadow, and made her way to the secluded arbor in her back garden.

The man waiting for her was dirty and saddle weary. Dressed in dark buckskins, he wore a double brace of pistols and his boots bore heavy Mexican spurs with long, sharp rowels. His grizzled face looked even more fierce in the moonlight. Brazenly, she met his cold gray eyes as he glared at her from under the wide brim of his hat.

Taking the thick envelope she placed in his outstretched hand, he cursed her and grumbled, "I'm callin' it quits—ain't doin' no more jobs fer ya. Done workin' fer a woman!"

His disdain meant nothing to her. Instead, a sly smile played about her rosy lips and her eyes flashed with a look of evil anticipation. Moving closer, her velvety voice became animated as she whispered, "If that's what you want. But remember? You still owe me! You promised you would help me—and then—you would bring her to me—when the timing was right. Well—my sources tell me that, he won't be able to protect her much longer. And—if things continue as planned, that worthless little *mistake*...will be delivered right into our hands!"

Then her dark-rimmed, golden eyes sparkled as her countenance turned from malicious to venomous, as she hissed:

"It's going to be...almost...too easy! It's only fitting—after all, she ruined my life...my dreams. And now...I'm going to turn her life...into a nightmare!"

Chapter 1
Omen of Hard Times

"We have dreamed a dream, and there is no interpreter of it. And Joseph said to them, Do not interpretations belong to God?" Genesis 40:8

Late Summer, 1865 - Booneville, Missouri

Augusta awoke with a cry of alarm, her breath coming in fearful gulps. Her golden eyes fluttered open, just as the first blush of dawn crept through her bedroom window.

"No...not again!" she begged. "Please, no...it can't be happening again."

Hiding her face in her pillow, she longed to wish away this nightmare—and the omen that she knew it to be. For the dream she'd just awoken from—wasn't new; it had tormented her before, and each time something terrible happened—usually to someone very close to her. It was like watching a runaway team of horses thundering right for her and knowing that she could neither stop them nor step aside.

Maybe it's only a dream this time; maybe nothing will happen.

Sitting up she wrapped her arms around herself and rocked back and forth as she gazed around her cozy attic room. She'd always felt safe here, with the flowery wallpaper and thin white curtains that billowed from the window like full sails on a ship. Here she could pretend that all dreams were sweet and that bad things never happened. The calming scent of lilacs drifted in through her window, even as her thoughts drifted back, remembering her dream. It was the same vision that had stalked her sleeping hours for many of her sixteen years. It was a wonderful dream—in the beginning. She would be racing a magnificent silver-coated horse, across a flower-strewn valley. Always, a majestic mountain stood in the distance, beckoning to her, like an old friend. It began as the kind of dream, fairytales were made of, but then suddenly her joy would turn to terror, as without warning she would find herself alone—in a dark, cold pit. There was never a way out and more often than not—there were snakes!

A shudder shook Augusta's small frame, and she raked her fingers through her dark curls, as if she could disentangle herself from the dream and what it might mean to her and to her father.

"It's nothing!" she insisted. "Probably just my melodramatic Irish roots showing out."

With an unladylike groan, she kicked off her bed covers, hurried to the washstand, and spoke to her reflection: "Listen here, Augusta Colleen O'Brien, doesn't every one say that you're much older than your sixteen years? Well, prove it! Only children are afraid of nightmares!"

Augusta bent over the basin, gasping as she washed in the cold water. This morning, at least, she was thankful for the shock to her senses. Then, as if to prove to herself that she was not afraid, she began whistling the liveliest tune she could think of as she brushed her long hair and dressed for the day. Still, in spite of her pretense, the uneasiness clung to her like a burr. The dream meant hardship—it always had. Augusta could not help but believe that something bad was about to happen. She just didn't know. What would it be—this time?

Bull O'Brien placed one boot on the bottom step as he called up the stairs, "A.C., darlin'! Are ya comin' gal? We've got a business to run, ya know!"

He chuckled at the loud Irish tune his daughter was attempting to whistle. Then he smiled proudly when she appeared on the landing.

"I'll be right down Papa!" she called. Augusta had her boots in one hand, and quickly sat down on the top step. "Just let me put these on!" she grunted as she pulled on one boot and reached for the other.

Then, giving her father an imperious look, she scolded: "Papa, I thought you weren't going to call me…A.C. anymore!"

Gazing up at his only child, Bull barely heard a word she said, for his thoughts had taken flight. *O'Brien, just look at her! She's so fine and sweet...ya must do all ya can...to keep her safe!*

Not wanting his daughter to read his thoughts, which the little scamp was prone to do, Bull quickly turned away from his tender thoughts and put on the air of the hardened ex-cavalry man that he was.

"Listen hear, gal," he growled. "Fer the hundredth time…it pleases me to be callin' ya A.C. because it suits the way ya are when we're workin' together! So, A.C. it is. And I'll be hearin' no more about it!"

The man ended his statement with a hard slap on the baluster to make his point.

However, when Augusta blinked down at him, he softened his voice saying, "Besides, I don't know why ya mind it. I think it sounds grand!"

"All right, Papa." Augusta gave in; she always did. Her bluster was just that. She was strong willed but no match for her father. Shaking her head she trotted down the stairs and threw her arms about his neck. "You call me A.C. 'cause it sounds like you might have a son helping you, and not just some silly girl!"

Augusta said the words teasingly but there was a wound there and they both knew it.

Bull gave her a hardy squeeze, then he asked: "And what would I be wantin' with a son? Name me a lad that rides as well as you? Or has yer sweet way with a horse now?"

Augusta smiled and rolled her eyes as her father linked arms with her.

"And furthermore…" he continued as he walked her to the front door, "can any of them boys train a colt by day and then of an evenin' put a fine meal on the table? Or bake an apple pie that fairly melts in yer mouth? No, they cannot I say! So why, me darlin' A.C. O'Brien, would I be wantin' with a son? When I'm blessed as can be with a dotter like yerself. And that, me girl, is the truth of it!"

"Oh, Papa!" Augusta smiled and shook her head, then she mimicked her father's thick accent. "You have a true gift of Irish blarney! And that, Papa…is the truth of it!"

Laughing she skipped out the door, jumped off the porch steps, and then walking backwards, she taunted: "Race ya' to the livery, Papa!"

Not expecting to be taken up on her challenge, she took off like a gazelle towards the barn. Bull watched his daughter with a troubled look clouding his face as she gracefully slipped out of sight.

Oh, darlin'! Please don't be gettin' mad at your ol' papa now… fer I don't think I could bear it!

Chapter 2
A Guest for Dinner

"Dear friends, do not be surprised at the painful trial you are suffering, as though something strange were happening to you. But rejoice that you participate in the sufferings of Christ, so that you may be overjoyed when his glory is revealed." I Peter 4:12&13

Leaning back in his chair Bull patted his stomach with a contented sigh, "It's just as I was telling ya this mornin'; we sold two horses ya trained, and now at the end of the day, ya put a fine a meal on the table."

For a long moment Bull toyed with his coffee cup, then with forced nonchalance, he added: "Ya'll be makin' a fine wife!"

As if stunned by his own words, he quickly changed the subject and asked, "And what now…will, uh, will we be havin' fer dinner tomorra?"

"Wait, Papa…" Augusta scoffed. "Me? A fine wife? I'm never getting married. And even if I wanted a husband, which I don't, how would I get one? You don't allow me to talk to men and you have certainly made it clear to every man in the territory, not to talk to me!"

Augusta shook her head as she dried the coffee pot then set it back on the stove.

"Remember last month? You punched that poor man—and just for saying I looked too pretty to work in a livery."

Bull frowned and grunted, "Huh…that scoundrel, he'll know next time not to bother a fine lady!"

Now it was Augusta's turn to humph. "Fine lady … A.C. O'Brien? Barn cleaner, horse trainer?"

Looking truly offended, Bull responded vehemently: "And isn't a lady, what I've been raisin' ya to be? And I want to know—what's for dinner tomorra?"

"Dinner? I thought you were going to tell me you…found me a husband!" Augusta teased.

Bull choked on his coffee and sprayed it half way across the table.

"My goodness, Papa, are you all right?" she asked as she pounded his back.

Finally, when Bull was able to get himself under control, he responded, "I...I'm fine. Don't be fussin'."

Clearing his throat again, he tried once more. "Dotter—I'm wantin' to know—what's fer dinner tomorra?"

Augusta was puzzled, then it dawned on her what this was about.

"Oh! I almost forgot—your friend is coming in on the stage tomorrow. Well? How about a nice stew and a batch of fried cornbread?"

Bull looked horrified. "Heavens, no!" He blurted out. "I want the best dinner ya know how to make! This man is me good friend, Timothy Grainger, from Boston—don't ya know! We should have a fine roast with all the trimmings and a couple of big pies fer dessert."

It was then that Augusta noticed her father was suddenly pulling at his collar and his face was flushed.

"Papa, you aren't yourself tonight. Are you feeling poorly?"

Concern showing in her honey brown eyes, Augusta gently touched her father's forehead.

"You don't seem feverish."

"Ah, nonsense, gal," he hissed. "I'm excited. That's all! I served under his father, Colonel Grainger. Later, we became friends, and I've known Timothy and his twin brother, Tytus, since they were both...knee high to a short duck. And...I want to welcome the man in a proper way. He's a fine man, educated in the law—don't ya know! I want ya to do things up right, the way Missus Drew has taught ya."

"Papa—are you worried, that this Boston dude might look down on us?"

"No—not a bit of it!" Bull assured his daughter. "Why, Timothy is a prince among men. I know ya'll think a lot of him, just as I do. And I want very much, fer ya both to become good friends!"

"Why, Papa?" she asked. "Isn't he still planning on heading west come spring? He'll be far away helping his brother run their ranch in Colorado."

"That's all true—but I told ya, Grainger lived most of his life in the city. I promised ya'd help him choose the right stock, the proper harness, find a good wagon and oh, well you know—whatever he'll be needin'."

"You want *me* to help him?" Augusta questioned. "But you're his friend Papa."

"Dotter, ya know I have no patience fer that sort of the thing! Surely, I can be trustin' ya to help Timothy—without steppin' on the man's pride. Ya can do that for me good friend! Can't ya now?"

"I suppose I can Papa, if you like."

"That's me girl!" he said with a wink, "And—um—by the way—did ya finish that green dress now?"

"Almost—" Augusta shrugged, "I didn't think there was any rush—why?"

Not understanding this turn in the conversation she added: "I keep telling you and Missus Drew—it's too fancy!" Augusta groaned, "I can't imagine ever wearing it."

"Well now, I can imagine ya wearin' it!" Bull said in a tone that allowed no debate. "And I'll be askin' ya to finish it tonight. And be wearin' it tomorra—when ya greet our guest."

Augusta sighed and reluctantly nodded her head, knowing it was no use to argue. Still, her father's behavior troubled her.

"Papa, you look like it's been a hard day; why don't you go on to bed?" Then with a little sigh she added, "As it happens, it seems I have a bit of sewing to do tonight."

Rising up on her tiptoes, Augusta kissed her father's cheek then watched with concern as he shuffled down the hallway to his bedroom. As she turned to climb the steps to her room, she felt uneasy. Bull O'Brien had always been known for his powerful military bearing, his brisk no nonsense manner, his quick purposeful stride. Augusta realized that she hadn't seen that powerful step of his in a long while. Her father was growing old...and...it frightened her!

Chapter 3
Bull O'Brien

Train up a child in the way he should go: and when he is old, he will not depart from it." Proverbs 22:6

Barrett McDuff O'Brien, known by one and all as "Bull" from his early days of breaking mounts for the U.S. Cavalry, was neither large nor tall. And yet if you asked anyone in town to describe him, they would have said Bull O'Brien is a big man. For O'Brien carried himself with the confidence of a general leading an army. His "can do" attitude and bullish way of getting things done made him a force to be reckoned with, and yet, Bull O'Brien was ever the gentlemen. The man had an infectious personality and a smile that rivaled the sun breaking through on a cloudy day. He was a distinguished looking man, with sky-blue eyes, high cheekbones, and a square jaw; and though he hadn't a hair upon his head, he boasted an impressive handle bar mustache of snowy white.

When Bull O'Brien walked down the street, women tended to look after him and men stepped aside. The O'Brien Livery was well respected, and Bull himself was a celebrated horseman; he had an uncanny eye for quality, and an extraordinary gift for breaking and training even the most stubborn mounts. And on the day he discovered that his daughter had inherited the O'Brien way with horses, his chest had filled with pride!

But tonight as he lay in his bed listening to the soft whir of the treadle wheel, he felt a strong pang of shame, not in Augusta—never in her—but in himself. His darling girl was obediently finishing her gown, just as he had demanded, even though she didn't understand its import. Bull could always count on Augusta to do whatever he asked. And knowing this was partly why he couldn't sleep. How much more *should* he expect from her? Augusta had worked hard for him all day. And now, at his request, she was up in her attic room, sewing away. He could imagine her dark curls falling over her shoulder as she bent her head over the rich green material. He listened to the rhythmic *ra-ta-tat-tat* of the needle as it thrust in and out of the shimmering fabric. Before long the clatter of the treadle came to a stop and he heard light footsteps moving overhead, as she changed into her night things and washed. Next came the light squeak of the ropes holding her mattress, and after that—silence.

"Oh, for the clean conscience of the young!" Bull thought to himself as he rubbed his chest.

His mind was pestering him with guilt and uncertainty over the series of decisions he had made. It was no use! Bull threw off his covers, padded down the hallway, then wandered into the kitchen. Then, as he always did on nights when he could not sleep, he poured himself a glass of milk, stole some cookies from the jar, then began his ritual of pacing round and round the kitchen table, thinking back on the life he had shared—with his little girl.

Just before Augusta's ninth birthday, O'Brien was forced to become both father and mother to his daughter. It had been a daunting challenge for a man like him to raise his girl to become a proper lady. However, Bull was very opinionated about the gentler sex, and being an ex-military man, he believed in having a strategy. He could not abide the spoiled, simpering females he'd known in the South, but had equal disdain for some of the Western women, who could sometimes be brutish and crude. No—Bull O'Brien's daughter must grow up knowing how to be useful in this world, and yet, still be a proper lady. For this, Bull O'Brien perfected his line of attack.

After speaking to various townspeople for help, he diligently set about arranging for his daughter's "education". To accomplish his plan he utilized the barter system; for two hours every afternoon Augusta was sent to the town café owners, Wes and Emily Tylane. She was to help in any way she was able, and in return, they were to teach the young girl to cook, serve the guests, and stock a proper kitchen.

On Tuesday and Thursday mornings, Augusta was sent to the town dressmaker for sewing lessons. Mrs. Amelia Drew was an elegant widow woman who had been reared in New York society. She was not only to teach the young girl to sew but also instruct her about *all things proper*. Though Augusta was not overly fond of sewing, she loved Mrs. Drew, and she not only learned to make clothes for both men and woman, but she also memorized the older woman's countless rules regarding manners and etiquette.

On the whole, Bull's scheme worked amazingly well, for Augusta was a lonely child but she was also a pleasant little thing and she wanted nothing so much as to please all those around her. And since neither Mrs. Drew nor the café owners, Wes and Emily Tylane, had children of their own, they readily took to O'Brien's proposal and found themselves looking forward to Augusta's visits. Mrs. Drew doted on the young girl as if she were her own granddaughter, always sewing pretty clothes for Augusta, especially proper, split riding skirts, with embroidered vests and ruffled blouses. The townsfolk often jested that Augusta O'Brien was the best-dressed stable boy east or west of the Mississippi. Emily Tylane became Augusta's dearest friend and the nearest thing to a mother she would ever have. Even when she wasn't needed at the café, the young girl would sneak to the back door of the Dutch oven for a treat and a visit with Emily!

The rest of Augusta's time was spent in her father's shadow. Bull chose not to send the girl to school; instead, he gave her lessons in reading and ciphering himself. And when she displayed a natural aptitude with numbers, it wasn't long before she took over her father's simple bookkeeping system.

Augusta worked hard learning all the many things that would please her father and her teachers. But what she loved best of all were the horses at her father's livery! Augusta could catch even the most cantankerous horse with ease. And if she asked them to stand, they would not move a muscle. If she asked a horse to lower his head so that she could bridle him—he would lower his head! The sight of a small girl handling the big animals so sweetly and so well was entertaining to the townsfolk. And Bull soon learned that his little girl, was good for business.

The only time Augusta grew impatient with her father was when he constantly admonished her to "behave like a lady". Augusta would often sigh in frustration, asking, "Papa, exactly how would a 'lady' shovel out this stall?"

Bull would not be deterred, however. In his truest Irish brogue, he would shake his finger and say,

"A.C., darlin', it doesn't matter what ya do—but ya'll do it—like a lady!"

Chapter 4
The Prince Among Men

"He grants a treasure of common sense to the honest. He is a shield to those who walk with integrity." Proverbs 2:7

Augusta rose from her bed just as the hall clock chimed for the fifth time. An hour later she was washed and dressed with coffee boiling, bacon frying, and flapjacks sizzling on the griddle. Hearing the snoring coming from her father's room, she covered his plate and pushed it—along with the coffee pot—to the back of the stove to stay warm, then quietly, she slipped from the house. Later, as she slid the livery door open, she was greeted by a raucous chorus of nickers and stomping hooves.

"My goodness!" she said, laughing. "You all carry on so. You'd think I never fed any of you."

Augusta's chores began each day at the crack of dawn: breakfast for her papa and then she served up breakfast for the horses at the livery. The number of horses varied: some they rented out, some were being trained for sale, and others they boarded, like the horses owned by the doctor and sheriff. Today there were twelve, and she always started with her favorites! And the one she loved most of all was her father's stallion, Quest!

"Hey there, Q, my man!" she crooned. "Got my morning kiss?"

It was a daily ritual. The sleek animal stretched his graceful ebony neck over his stall door, allowing his mistress to place a quick kiss on his velvety muzzle. His obedient response earned the high-strung stallion the privilege of being fed before all the others. The first time Bull O'Brien had seen his daughter take such a risk, he demanded she never do it again, for stallions are prone to bite! Then, while Augusta was making her argument, the younger Quest turned and snapped at the girl. Quick as a wink, she doubled her small fist, and down it came, right on the end of the stallion's tender nose. The surprised animal flung his head and squealed. Patiently, the girl coaxed him back to her, only to have the beast test her once more, and of course down came the small fist. Tirelessly, she would call him back.

"Come on, boy." she cajoled. "Stop this nonsense—we all have to learn our manners—I had too!"

Bull had trained horses all his life and watched with pleasure as Quest finally allowed the girl to kiss the tip of his nose. Augusta of course immediately rewarded him with praises and handfuls of grain.

Quest became the sire of choice for horse breeders throughout the county. Morgan's were a fairly new breed, and his bloodlines were noteworthy. His sire had been the well-known Black Hawk, direct grandson of Figure, the first stallion of the breed named after the breeder and owner, Justin Morgan. Quest was a magnificent animal, possessing the powerful muscles and graceful lines one might see sculpted in marble or fashioned in bronze. His gleaming coat was the darkest ebony with golden modeling about his muzzle, ear tips, and flanks. A perfect white star graced his forehead, then tapered down, ending in a snip across his muzzle. The markings resembled a star on a quest, hence, his name. There was a special kinship between the stallion and the girl, and they trusted each other. So much so that if Quest took a disliking to someone, then without hesitation, Augusta would too.

The next horse Augusta fed had been her first—a bay mare named Kippy. At thirty-one the mare was ancient, and blind in one eye, but she was still sound and very gentle. Augusta gave riding lessons every Saturday morning, and the mare was perfect for inexperienced riders. The other horses were methodically cared for as they waited in their stalls. And when they finished munching their food, Augusta turned them out to a large paddock, just behind the livery. Smiling, she watched them "feel their oats" as they cavorted around the corral; sometimes, she even joined them in their play. When one of the younger horses called to her with a beckoning whistle, she laughed and called back: "Sorry, Skeeter. No time to play with you today!"

Instead, she tied a scarf around her brown curls and went about the business of cleaning each stall. She neither loved nor hated the chore; it simply had to be done. While she worked she planned out her day. She tried to ride Quest every morning; he could get awfully ornery when she missed even one day. The thought troubled Augusta. Her father used to ride quite often, but lately he never felt up to it. And then Augusta's thoughts turned to Max and Molly. She was determined to have the matching buckskins trained both to the harness and the saddle by spring, hoping to sell them to a family going west with the wagon train.

Oh, bother! That dude is coming tonight. Papa's making such a fuss. I can't believe he asked Emily to come fix my hair! And making me wear that fancy new dress, just to serve dinner? It's all so silly!

Augusta didn't have time to ponder the situation for long, as suddenly the livery door swung wide open.

"A.C., darlin'!" Bull shouted as he stormed towards her. "Why didn't ya wake me?" He chided, "I'd have done the mornin' chores!" Bull frowned, and yanking the scarf from Augusta's hair he grumbled, "We've got company comin'! And here ya are lookin' like a Teamster and smellin' like the barn!"

Augusta rolled her eyes. "Papa! I clean the stalls every morning; they don't get that bad. And I bathe every afternoon before dinner."

With her hands resting impatiently on her hips she chided, "You're making us both as nervous as a long tail cat in a room full of rocking chairs! And for what?"

Augusta traded the pitchfork in her hand for the scarf in her father's and blew out a breath.

"Your friend might not even show up for dinner tonight. What if he's too tired after all his traveling?"

"Ah, don't be worrying over that me girl. He'll want to see *you*...you and me...uh, us both, first thing!"

When Augusta gave him a suspicious look, Bull raised his eyebrows and pinched his daughter's chin. "You just be sure to be a proper lady and have yer finest dinner on the table when Mister Grainger arrives. Fer the man will dine with us tonight—ya can count on it. All you need do is—make sure it's perfect!"

❧❧

"PERFECT!" Augusta hissed, as she dropped the lid back over the pot. It had been—hours earlier! Now her perfectly cooked carrots, juicy roast, and fluffy rolls were orange mash, a brown brick, and rocks! Word had been sent hours earlier that the stage, along with Grainger, had arrived on time!

"Where can that man be?" she hissed. "Oh, blast Papa's Boston dude!"

And, oh, how she wished she could run and hide! As far as Augusta was concerned, the stranger deserved this meal for being so late! But her father was going to be furious—and not with his friend but with her!

Then she heard the knock on the door and Augusta's stomach suddenly dropped like a lead weight.

"Now—you're here!" she groaned. "A gentleman should either come on time *or not at all!*"

She toyed with the idea of not answering the door.

Papa's still checking on that mare. I'll just say I didn't hear him knock. Because I was—?

"Ooooh, dad-blast old friends anyway! It's no use; I'm not a child. I can't exactly hide under the bed."

When the knock came the second time, she pouted for another moment, then sullenly went to the door.

She glanced in the hallway mirror as she swept past it, and as it had the first time she looked, her grown-up reflection surprised her! It shouldn't have; she was seventeen after all, or would be in two months. But Emily had put her hair all up in curls off her neck, and in the stylish new gown she felt quite... womanly! The dress had turned out well: it was a luscious emerald green, with black velvet collar and cuffs, and a wide black sash at the waist.

When the third knock came Augusta ordered herself to quit stalling! She pinched her cheeks and braced herself for what she knew would be the worst evening of her life! Then, slowly, she opened the door.

He was such a surprise! She knew her mouth had dropped open and that Mrs. Drew would not be pleased. It was *very un-ladylike,* but she couldn't help it. In her mind she had created an image of what "Papa's friend" would be like. She was prepared for a serious older man, pale in color, slightly bald—just a dull Boston dude; but the man standing on her porch was not at all what she'd expected. To begin with, he was grinning at her with straight white teeth. His smile lit up his eyes and one deep dimple. He was thin and tall, very tall, and... very handsome. He was dressed in a dove gray suit with a gray derby hat and he carried a black cane with a silver tip. Definitely a man from the big city and, yes, he was older than she, maybe twenty-seven or eight—but that was not *too much older,* she decided. He had thick short-cropped hair, the color of ripe wheat. His eyes were a deep shade of cobalt blue and they sparkled with merriment or perhaps, she wondered, a bit of mischief? The irritation she had harbored for this man only moments earlier vanished like mist on a sunny morning. Augusta felt instantly drawn to this smiling stranger. And the tender expression on his face made her feel as if...*they* were old friends!

"Mister Grainger?" Augusta finally managed to ask. At the sound of her voice the man's grin grew even wider but when he said nothing, she added: "You've come a long way—won't you come in?"

Augusta suddenly feared the man might be mute; he seemed not at all inclined to speak. Feeling more and more perplexed over his silence, she found herself rambling.

"I am s-sorry Papa's not here. He, uh, he just went to check on a colicky mare; should be back—soon."

Still the man kept staring at her, smiling gently but saying nothing. She continued self-consciously, "I'm...I'm his daughter, I'm..."

"You are the lovely Miss A.C. O'Brien!" the man finally uttered.

Augusta smiled at the sound of his voice, for it was a warm, buttery, baritone.

Reverently, he said: "I can't tell you how I've looked forward to finally meeting you!"

He slipped the hat from his head and stepped over the threshold while he continued to speak. "I feel as though I already know you so well from your father's letters."

Augusta was filled with relief that the man could talk, but then his words made her shake her head. "Oh dear," she said wincing, "If you know me from his letters, well then, you don't know me at all, sir! You see, Papa hails from both Irish and Welsh stock. A combination...that often leads to wild exaggeration! In other words my father is a master of BLARNEY! Especially concerning his only child."

When Timothy chuckled, she responded with mock irritation: "And that rascal never let me read any of your letters. Of course, he's told me about you and your family, and best of all, he's given you his highest praise."

Augusta lowered her voice, and imitating her father's Irish brogue, she quoted: "Timothy Grainger is a *prince among men!*"

The man bowed in response to her compliment, then with a twinkle in his eye, he replied: "That was kind of him to say. However, Miss O'Brien, by your own account, your father's kind words about me—couldn't those too be just more of that, um, famous Irish blarney?"

Suddenly, his countenance grew serious as he asked, "And what was that—you say you've never read any of my letters?"

"Nary a one," Augusta said with a shrug. "Sometimes, Papa would tell me something you said, but…"

Augusta stopped when she saw a very definite shadow pass over the man's clear blue eyes. He quickly recovered, however, and said simply, "No matter—it's just good to be here and finally meet you, Miss O'Brien or—may I call you A.C.?"

Augusta rolled her eyes. "Papa calls me A.C. because it sounds a bit less feminine than Augusta. Mostly, I think when he'd rather not admit to having his daughter as his business partner."

Then she shrugged and added graciously, "But I certainly don't mind if you prefer it."

Timothy held up his hand. "Oh no! If that's the case, you certainly look much too beautiful this evening to be called…A.C." He suddenly colored and said: "Pardon me, please. I hope you don't mind my being so bold, Miss O'Brien?"

Augusta found herself blushing. She'd always laughed at girls who behaved foolishly around men, but suddenly she felt warm and tongue-tied herself, until finally she gathered her wits and replied: "Not at all. Thank you for the compliment." She punctuated her words with a curtsy, then added, "Miss O'Brien seems so formal. Our families are old friends. Would it be proper to call me Augusta?"

"Only, if you call me Timothy!"

The two were smiling at each other just as Bull O'Brien burst through the door.

"Well, now, if it isn't Mister Timothy Grainger himself, standing in me parlor. And it's about time too!" Bull entered the room like a hurricane coming on shore. The older man was nearly beside himself with delight as he beamed his broad smile on the couple; then, rubbing his hands together he exclaimed,

"Isn't it grand? Us all here together at last! I do apologize that I wasn't here to introduce you two but I suppose ya both managed to figure out who ya both were… right?"

While Timothy and Augusta exchanged amused glances, Bull slapped the younger man on the back.

"Aw, that's fine!" he chuckled, then turning to his daughter, he said: "Well now, I'm sure our good friend is about to expire from starvation. Please—tell me dinner is ready!"

Augusta's hand flew to her throat, "Well...Pa—pa...you see it's just that..."

"Darlin', ya've been at it all day! Now is dinner ready or not?"

Augusta wished to talk privately with her father but in his excited state she knew...he wouldn't listen.

Instead, she muttered, "Almost. I'll call you." Softly, she added, "It's as good now as it will ever be."

Augusta contemplated confessing the whole fiasco and suggesting they dine at the Dutch Oven. But then—everyone who was used to having her serve their food would see her bedecked like a queen. She just—couldn't face the jesting she would no doubt receive.

As soon as Augusta disappeared into the kitchen, Bull pulled Timothy to the opposite wall of the parlor.

"Good to have you here, lad! Well now, tell me? What do you think of her? Quite a beauty—eh?"

Timothy smiled and nodded, "In every way sir—but I have to tell you—I am very disappointed!"

"Here, now!" Bull sputtered. "Disappointed? In my A.C.?"

"No sir, of course not!" he stammered as his face grew red.

"But your daughter has no idea of our agreement or why I am really here—does she?"

It hadn't been a question, and Timothy allowed the irritation he was feeling to lace his voice. "She told me she has never read any of my letters. Not a line I wrote to you, and so I gather, sir, she has never read any of the letters, I wrote to her?"

Bull frowned stubbornly and replied: "No sir—she has not. I didn't want her hurt if ya decided not to come. Or if ya changed yer mind."

The two men were squared off at each other when Augusta peeked into the parlor and announced,

"Dinner's ready—*such as it is.*"

But when she saw the odd demeanor of the two men, she asked, "Is something wrong?"

Bull quickly schooled his features, then he slapped Timothy on the back and said, "Nothin' wrong, darlin', but ya've got two mighty hungry men here to feed!"

As the two hungry men headed into the dining room, Augusta could only hope they would be too busy talking over old times to look at, or especially—to taste—the disaster she was serving up. Her only other ploy was to take some advice Mrs. Drew had given her: *Never call attention to a less-than-perfect meal by apologizing, she had warned; instead, a good hostess distracts her guests with lively conversation!*

So, before the men could even settle into their places, Augusta immediately began firing questions with the speed of a Gatling gun. She asked about Boston, the train, the stagecoach, traveling west, Colorado, Indians, rustlers, and ranching. Her plan was working; Timothy had scarcely been able to take a bite. Unfortunately, her father wasn't so easily sidetracked; instead, he scowled at the unappetizing dishes and cautiously tasted each one. Then, to Augusta's utter mortification, he threw down his fork.

"Timothy, my friend," he fumed, "I must apologize for this shameful meal—it is quite intolerable!"

Then he turned to Augusta and demanded, "What happened, darlin'? Never have ya done s'poorly!"

When Augusta bit her lip and seemed to turn three shades of crimson, Timothy came to her defense. "Now see here, Bull, there is no need to go on so. This is a better meal than any I've had in weeks!"

Augusta smiled at her guest's attempt to come to her rescue, but she held up her hand to stop him.

"Please!" she begged. "I appreciated your kindness. Really I do—but, Papa's right!"

She spooned up a dollop of thick lumpy gravy and rolled her eyes.

"This would be best used to—mortar a brick wall, I think? I owe you both an apology—I am sorry!"

Augusta gave a little shrug, and as she shook her head, explained. "I'm used to putting dinner together in such a hurry. Today I started dinner way too early and then I tried to keep it all warm. I stirred and I stirred and..."

Augusta wrinkled her nose as she took Timothy's plate away. "If you'll come again tomorrow night, I bet I can make you a meal that's actually fit to eat!"

Timothy grinned. "I'll be here, even if you serve up mashed cactus and fried skunk."

Augusta turned quite serious and waved a hand over the contents of the table, saying, "Why, Mister Grainger, that's what tonight's dinner was—mashed cactus and fried skunk. Would you care for seconds?"

Timothy threw his head back and laughed while Augusta shyly stood to her feet. "Gentlemen," she said, demurely, "there is a silver lining in tonight's menu. Once you've taken an apple pie out of the oven—you simply leave it alone. So, what would you both think of a dinner-size piece of apple pie with thick slices of cheese on the side and piping hot coffee to wash it down?"

With a shrug of her slim shoulders she added, "Not a typical dinner, perhaps, but it could be worse! And—I could serve it in the parlor—if you like?"

Bull stood and kissed Augusta on the cheek. "Well now, that's one silver linin' that suits me just fine! How 'bout you, Grainger?"

"Oh yes," Timothy agreed, "I've never turned down a piece of pie in my life—apple is my favorite!"

While Bull chatted away in the parlor, Timothy mused about his first dinner with Augusta. It hadn't gone too badly, well, except for the food. He kept thinking how she had taken his breath away when she opened the door and how he'd acted like a nervous schoolboy. The tintype Bull sent didn't do her justice. He smiled to himself thinking of the mess dinner had been. Most young women would have burst into tears and run from the room. And Bull certainly hadn't spared her feelings. But despite the humiliation, Augusta had openly accepted the fault, laughed about it, and then done what she could to salvage the situation and proceed on a happy note. So far at least, she was proving to be all that her father had promised and, possibly, quite a bit more.

Timothy's thoughts melted away when the lady herself entered the room. He couldn't keep from staring, as she moved gracefully into the lamplight, making her dark curls shine and bathing her smooth complexion in a soft glow.

Bull, however, was watching Grainger, pleased as punch by the look of infatuation on the man's face.

Gracefully, Augusta placed the tray in front of the men and poured out the coffee.

"Timothy," she asked, holding the spoon in her hand, "I saw you take sugar in your coffee—may I?"

"A.C., where are yer manners?" Bull nearly shouted. "Do ya call a man ya just met by his first name?"

Augusta straightened so quickly she knocked over the sugar bowl; humiliated, she lowered her eyes to the floor. Normally, she would speak up for herself, but her mind went blank with embarrassment.

"I assure you the girl does know better!" Bull blustered. "I apologize—it's just that she's…"

But Timothy was quick to cut him off, and said congenially, "Bull, in your absence *Miss O'Brien* and I were obliged to introduce ourselves. She of course greeted me as *Mister Grainger*. However, since our families were such *old friends*, we deemed it *proper* to use each other's given names."

When Timothy finished his explanation, Augusta gave him an appreciative nod, and was rewarded by a quick wink of his eye as his dimple creased one cheek.

Bull made a few muffled apologies, then quickly turned his attention back to the pleasure of dining on his daughter's famous spiced apple pie, served with mellow cheese and hot coffee. And despite Augusta's earlier humiliations, she soon found herself enjoying the evening.

Timothy proved to be a skilled storyteller, regaling the O'Briens with one tale after another of his adventures thus far. Augusta found herself riveted to the man's account of his train ride from Boston with the widow Samson and the antics of her six children and their dog named Fred.

"Actually, we had the most fun trying to sneak Fred back into the passenger car from the freight car!"

"You helped them?" Augusta asked.

Timothy, smiled sheepishly. "Well—I probably shouldn't admit that," he said with his eyes sparkling. "But it did keep the children entertained! And there was a new adventure every time the train stopped."

Augusta laughed, intrigued by this man who seemed to find delight in just about everything.

Later on, the stories changed from past travels to future plans. Augusta smiled as her father sat on the edge of his chair, his blue eyes shining while Timothy spoke of his plans to take up ranching with his brother in Colorado. She was equally inspired by his description of the majestic mountain range, thrown down like a gauntlet across the grasslands; and the huge ranch with thousands of cattle and hundreds of horses. Even his description of his brother's home seemed fascinating. He called it a hacienda!

When Timothy stopped to sip his coffee, Augusta asked, "Is your brother raising a big family on his ranch—as well as horses and cattle?"

Timothy's face turned solemn. "That's what he had hoped to do!" He paused for a moment then continued, "He built the place for his fiancé, a lovely southern belle. He worked on it for three long years to make a home out of the wilderness, then he sent for her. He was so proud of it, but she looked the place over, declared in unworthy, and then left him flat!" In a somber tone he added, "Sadly, Tytus has given up on marriage; he thinks life there is too rustic for the kind of woman he'd want for a wife and mother to his children."

Just then, Timothy leaned towards Augusta and stated seriously, "But I don't agree with him! I just think he picked the wrong girl. I think the right woman could make a home there and love it!"

Augusta ran her finger around the rim of her coffee cup while pondering his words, completely unaware that the two men in the room were all but holding their breath.

Desperate to know what was going on in Augusta's mind, Grainger blurted out, "I would very much like to know, Augusta, what a woman like you, for instance, would think of it?"

Augusta was somewhat startled when she realized both men were watching her so intently. Feeling terribly self-conscious, she gave a little shrug. "I'm hardly the one to ask," she explained, taking a hesitant peek at her father she added, "I do try to be *a lady* but..."

Bull was quick to interrupt. "And what are ya, if not a lady?" he demanded. "Let me finish, Papa."

Turning towards Timothy, she continued, "Papa has made *sure* that I know all a lady should know! But the truth is—despite all I've learned—I'd rather be out training a horse or mending tack, than doing needlepoint in the parlor. So, you see, *my* opinion would be of little worth."

Timothy's face took on a very tender expression as he said, "If you don't mind my saying so, Miss Augusta, your being able to train horses and mend tack, and enjoy doing so...well, that makes you a versatile woman—but no less a lady! Please, tell me what you think?"

"Well, the ranch sounds quite appealing to me," Augusta stated thoughtfully. "Especially, the hacienda! It's built like a fortress, because it's a wilderness home. And yet—it sounds—wonderful!"

21

"Aye now, that it does!" Bull added with his usual enthusiasm. "Must be a grand place to live! Can ya imagine wakin' up with those beautiful mountains all about ya? And all those horses? And wouldn't it be grand to have a stallion like Quest to cover the mares sired by Echo! What fine colts those two bloodlines would make."

Augusta turned towards her father, her golden eyes flashing. "Papa! I know you gave Echo to Colonel Grainger but you're not thinking of giving them Quest too—are you?"

Her fury fell first on her father but then her suspicious gaze turned towards Timothy. The man was quick to put up his hands and shake his head, dissuading her fear, though her blazing eyes intrigued him.

Still, it was for Bull to put her mind at ease and he was quick to do so. "Heaven's no, gal!" he groaned. "Why that beast loves ya as much as—well, almost as much as I do!"

Augusta put her hand to her throat. "Goodness, Papa! The way you said it, you frightened me!"

"Nah, Quest goes only where you go," Bull assured his daughter.

"I guess it was silly of me—you would no more give Quest away than you'd give me away!"

She didn't notice the exchanged glances between the two men, for just then the upstairs clock began to chime. Gracefully, Augusta rose to her feet.

"I'm afraid I must excuse myself, gentlemen. I have a few chores to do."

When Timothy stood as well, she smiled and offered her hand.

"It was a pleasure meeting you, Timothy. I apologize again for dinner, but you will join us tomorrow?"

"Yes, if you promise—no more fried skunk," he teased.

With a chuckle he drew her small hand to his lips, brushed a light kiss across her fingers, then added: "Actually, I can't remember an evening I've enjoyed more. You are a lovely hostess and your apple pie was perfection. I am already looking forward to our next meal together."

Bull stood and gave Augusta a kiss on the cheek and then she bid both men goodnight.

Weary from her long day, Augusta quickly changed into a work dress then tackled the messy kitchen. While she filled the sink with hot water and soap, she found herself smiling at what a surprise Timothy Grainger had turned out to be, his handsome face and dimpled grin floating into her thoughts. She'd never been friends with a man before, never wanted to be—but this man—he wasn't like anyone she'd ever met. And he seemed determined to be her friend too, not just her father's.

Augusta was suddenly reminded of that evening's disaster when she grabbed the last pot to wash. "Eewww," she groaned, as she looked down on all the ruined food she'd scraped into it. Grimacing, she carried it to the backyard and dumped its contents. As she returned to the kitchen, Augusta was surprised to find her father waiting for her. She gave him a guilty grin then said, "I feel sorry for the hungry raccoon or stray cat that happens upon our dinner scraps tonight." With a giggle she asked, "Do you think I should leave a dish of bicarbonate of soda for them as well?"

"I think ya should be ashamed for treatin' poor defenseless animals with such cruelty!" he quipped.

Augusta frowned and put her hands on her hips.

"Speaking of shame," Augusta huffed, "what a mess tonight was! At least I tried not to embarrass you—Papa. I wish you'd shown me the same courtesy. You humiliated me all evening!" Augusta mimicked her father's words, "'A.C., where are yer manners?' Papa, what got into you tonight? You've never spoken so harshly to me before—and in front of company no less!"

"Ah, and don't I know it," Bull said in surprising agreement. "And—and I'm just that sorry fer it too!"

Quickly turning away he rubbed his hand over his face. For in truth, Bull wasn't sorry at all. On the contrary, he was quite pleased that his well-placed insults had brought Timothy so quickly to Augusta's defense. The lad hadn't even seemed to realize that Bull was helping him become his daughter's champion and soon he'd be much more!

Augusta narrowed her eyes at her father's deadpan expression, then handed the man a dish towel.

"And what's this for?" he asked.

"Penance!" Augusta retorted, as she handed him a platter to dry.

"All right, but tell me now," he demanded to know, "what d'ya think? Ya like the man now, don't ya?"

Still scowling, Augusta took her father's chin in her wet soapy hand and said, "Oh, no you don't, Papa—you're not changing the subject!"

Bull twisted away. "Ah—yer getting me all wet! And the subject is Grainger—do ya like him?"

Augusta shook her head and laughed as she washed out the sink.

"Yes, Papa, he's very nice! Why didn't you let me read his letters? He seemed…upset that I hadn't? You can tell a lot about a person by the things they choose to write in a letter. Can I read them now?"

"Hah!" Bull huffed as he absentmindedly rubbed his arm. "No need—he's a prince among men."

Rolling her eyes, Augusta untied her apron, then noticed her father pacing in a circle around the table.

"What's the matter, Papa? You only march around the table when you're worried."

Bull abruptly turned to face his daughter then blurted out his pent-up words before he lost the courage: "Augusta, we're going west with Timothy." Swallowing hard he added, "We'll be leavin' next spring."

"What's this?" Augusta was shocked at first, but then her expression softened with understanding. "Oh, Papa, I saw the way you looked when Timothy spoke of the ranch. That was once your dream."

She took the broom and began to sweep the floor, knowing she must be careful of her father's pride.

"Papa," she began guardedly, "the livery is doing well just now. And we have to think of your health."

Augusta put her hand on her father's shoulder. "Neither one of us want to face it but—you aren't as strong as you used to be—and we have good ole Doc right here next door, and…"

"Listen, gal." Bull held up his hand. "I've a lot to explain. Ya might as well know—what's done is done!"

"And—what is it you've done Papa?"

Slowly, O'Brien rubbed his chest, then raising both hands to his head, he rubbed them briskly over the top of his bald head. Augusta tensed; her father's familiar gesture was not a good sign.

"Timothy said I should have told ya—and he was right—I see that now."

"Timothy knows something…I don't?" Augusta asked. "I'm your daughter and we're partners!"

The old man held his hand up again. "Please, darlin', hold yer tongue. I'm awful weary…just now."

"All right…" she complied, but a chill of foreboding knotted in her stomach.

Bull sighed as he pulled up a kitchen chair then nodded for Augusta to sit down beside him. A gnawing ache was spreading down one arm, and he scowled as he worked to rub it away.

"I love ya, gal. And I've done me best to raise ya proper, and to prepare ya fer this world. I made ya grow up fast, been hard on ya at times...fer...well, I knew I might not be around to see ya grown."

Augusta bit her lip and laid her hand on her father's. Bull acknowledged her gesture, then continued, "Darlin', what's done that cannot be altered is that I've sold the livery and the house. The family that bought the house won't arrive 'til spring, so we can stay here 'til the wagon train leaves."

Bull took in his daughter's confused look then quickly added, "As I was sayin', we're goin' west with Timothy. But first...you and he...will be married! He and I have been discussing this fer quite some time now. He has been courtin' ya by mail. But I thought it best to keep his letters from ya. Just in case the man changed his mind, I—I didn't want ya hurt."

Bull gazed at his stunned daughter, hoping to explain, but he felt as if he'd just cut off his right arm.

"Ah, darlin', it's just that ya seemed so young when he and I first spoke of it. And I didn't want ya thinkin' about marriage until the man himself was here. He thinks I was wrong!"

Bull muttered and rubbed his head again, then his arm, and then his chest before he went on. "But the plain truth is...I'm not well! And I want this done as soon as possible. But, darlin', we've all made sure it would be a nice weddin' fer ya! Missus Drew's been correspondin' with a fancy dressmaker in Boston. They made sure Timothy brought a weddin' dress ya'd be proud of and a trunk with everythin' a bride would be wantin'. That's why he was late getting here tonight. He took yer trunk of weddin' things to Missus Drew's house first."

Bull stopped to wipe his face again, he looked down, and frowned as he muttered, "All right now—ya can speak yer piece."

Augusta felt like a bucket of cold water had been dumped on her head. What was she supposed to say?

"I thought we were partners? And you think some nice wedding clothes will make me agree to marry a stranger—a man I just met a few hours ago?"

Suddenly, she shot to her feet and began marching around the table, just as her father had done earlier. "Papa, how could you? And 'who all'—besides Missus D.—is party to this betrayal?"

25

Augusta made another circle around the kitchen table, then she glared at her father. "You've sold the house and livery? And given me no say? What does being partners mean to you?"

Bull could not have felt lower. Augusta sounded so wounded. He had to make her understand.

"Listen, gal! Being a father is more important than being a partner." He added with a groan, "I know, sayin' it out loud, it all sounds dreadful, even to me own ears. But I'm not sorry! I did it to protect ya, to keep ya safe! I raised ya to be a lady, and I found a gentleman worthy of ya! That's what papa's do!"

O'Brien dabbed at his face with the bandana and stated more firmly, "Timothy Grainger is a fine man—a well-propertied man! Together you two can have a good life! Ya may not know it yet—but I've done good by ya!"

Staring into her father's eyes Augusta shook her head in disbelief. "I had *the nightmare* again, Papa!" Augusta's chin quivered as she stumbled over the words. "I knew something bad was bound to happen. But I never imagined that you could betray me like this!"

Bull grimaced, both at Augusta's words and at the violent pain that surged through his body.

Augusta was too upset to notice her father's ashen face; she shook her head and paced around the table. "Papa, I'll be seventeen in two months. I'm grown enough to make my own decisions! I won't marry that man!"

"It's done, gal," he moaned, feeling shaky and weak. "There's no goin' back—the deeds are signed, the funds are under Grainger's name—without him, ya'll have nothin'. I knew that's how it had to be."

Augusta was furious! Angrily, she swiped away the tears, her golden eyes filling with hurt and confusion.

"Papa, you'd leave me with nothing? You've always said we were partners; this is like stealing from me! I will not marry that stranger—and I will not let you BULLY me—Bull O'Brien! Not anymore!"

Augusta turned and ran up the stairs to her room, but before she reached the top step, she heard a loud crash.

"Papa?"

Chapter 5
A Promise for Papa

"Listen to your father, who gave you life." Proverbs 23:22

Augusta waited in the hallway outside her father's bedroom, feeling as if she had been caught in a cyclone. She tried to make sense of all that had happened, all that was said, but all she felt was guilt!

What have I done? I know better than to argue with him—to make him angry!

She covered her face with her hands. Losing the house and the livery, even having to marry a stranger and go west—none of it seemed important now. The only thing that mattered was for Papa to be all right. Yes, he was often bull-headed, demanding and difficult. But then he could also be so very gentle. Her papa was all she had! How could she have forgotten about his heart? How had she been so foolish?

When the doctor arrived, he had insisted she wait in the parlor, promising to call her if things changed. But when Augusta found Timothy waiting there, staring into the fire, she couldn't abide being in the same room with him. Silently, she fled to the porch off the kitchen, jumped off the back steps, and hugged herself as she walked into the darkness, allowing her tears to fall unchecked.

Above her, the night sky was ablaze with stars as they scattered across the heavens, while a sliver of a crescent moon glowed high overhead. The peaceful evening should have helped to calm her—but instead it made her angry. On a night like this, the sky should be churning with dark clouds and lightning. A hard rain should be falling—just as hard and fast as her tears. It seemed cruel somehow, that this night of all nights should show itself with such clarity while everything about her world was so completely out of kilter.

Standing with a cool breeze brushing across her hot cheeks, she searched the sky, as if she might see beyond its inky blackness. Is there more out there, she wondered? More than just earth and sky? She felt so alone and so very vulnerable.

Finally, she whispered one word: "God?"

The word was spoken so faintly that it might have been mistaken for the rustle of leaves. Then she mustered all her courage and spoke into the night once more.

"God—are You really up there—can You hear me? Do You know or even care what's happening down here?"

Augusta waited to see if He would answer her, notice her. She had never been sure how prayer worked. There had been a childhood friend once—she had spoken of God. And her friend's mother had read them stories and prayed to God as if He were a friend. But no one else she ever knew—knew God.

Still she had to try, and she whispered again into the night, "Don't take Papa away! He's all I have! I've lost everyone else…"

Suddenly, she was filled with doubt. She had lost everyone else—why should God stop now?

"Why did You let me be born? I know I was a mistake—why did You let it happen? I've never had a mother to love me—Papa is all I've got! And…You are going to take him—aren't You?" she challenged. "Why do You keep punishing me? Is it You that sends that nightmare? What have I done?"

Augusta waited for an answer as she stared up into the night, her golden tears glistening in the moonlight. She whispered again into the dark, her voice childlike and heartbroken. "Papa's so sick. I can't live if he dies. If You know all things, then You know that's true! Please, I'll do anything You ask. I'll marry that stranger—I'll go west! Please God, just make him well."

As the hour grew late a chill evening breeze blew against Augusta's slight frame. She rubbed her arms as a shudder passed through her. The night air blew the soft curls from her forehead and dried her tears. Slowly, she walked back into the house, and tapping lightly on her father's door, Augusta peeked inside. "Doc," she whispered, "how's Papa?"

Dr. Mitchell rose from his seat beside the sleeping Bull O'Brien and motioned for Augusta to step into the parlor. Timothy turned from where he stood by the window, his face clouded with concern as he took in Augusta's beleaguered appearance and tear-stained cheeks.

"How is he?" he asked.

Dr. Mitchell gently led Augusta to the settee, but when he noticed the tall stranger, Augusta said stiffly, "Doc, this is Papa's friend from Boston, Mister Timothy Grainger. Mister Grainger, this is our good friend, Doctor Samuel Mitchell."

With that bit of formality done she turned to the white-haired doctor and asked in a no-nonsense voice, "You must be honest with me Doc—how bad is Papa?"

Dr. Mitchell took out a handkerchief from his pocket and dabbed at his brow. "Frankly," he said with a sigh, "I've been warning Bull for the past few years to expect something like this. I'm afraid his heart is very weak. I wouldn't allow him to talk much, but he's restless and agitated. I've given him something to force him to sleep. But he must stay calm or this episode will repeat itself!"

The doctor then turned his full attention to Timothy, and giving him an appraising look, he took off his spectacles, breathed on each lens, then methodically wiped them clean with his handkerchief. Finally, the doctor put his spectacles back in place and said gravely, "Mister Grainger, I know all about you. I have understood you to be a great deal more than just Bull's friend. Is that not true? He has told me all about his arrangements for you and Miss O'Brien here."

Augusta breathed a sigh of relief. Dr. Mitchell loved her like an uncle; surely he wouldn't approve of this nonsense. He would never think it right to force her into marrying a stranger!

"Oh, Doc!" Augusta said before Timothy could speak. "You can talk to Papa. Reassure him that this is all nonsense. Mister Grainger is a good man, but we don't even know each other!"

Augusta turned to Timothy and said, "You're a kind and reasonable man. I never saw any of your letters and Papa never mentioned any of this. It's impossible for me to marry you!"

Before Timothy could respond, Augusta turned back to the doctor again. "And, Doc, it doesn't make sense for Papa to have made all these drastic changes! Won't you help me get the house and the livery back? I'm perfectly capable of running the livery alone."

Dr. Mitchell gently lifted Augusta's chin, and looking intently into her honey-colored eyes he said, "My sweet girl, I know how upsetting all this is to you. But it appears it's you I must give a talking to." With care, the kindly old doctor took Augusta's small hand in his and smiled. "You know, Augusta, Becky and I love you like a daughter and we're delighted your father has made such an excellent match for you!" Nodding towards Timothy he added, "I can assure you—this man—is a fine fellow!"

Timothy looked away, feeling uncomfortable that the doctor felt the need to campaign on his behalf.

"Now," the doctor continued, "I understand what a shock this must have been to you. But, I have to tell you, after this episode—your father's afraid that he's running out of time. He feels that you two must marry—not just soon," the doctor cleared his throat then added gently, "but uh...tomorrow!"

Both Timothy and Augusta looked to be dumbstruck.

"I know, I know—I caught you both by surprise, but quite frankly, it's a wise decision. And I have to say—I agree with Bull!"

The doctor took in Augusta's pale face and said to her, "He needs to see you taken care of. And besides, a happy occasion like a wedding might actually be good medicine. It could possibly even buy him a bit more time!"

Augusta blinked up at the doctor; she opened her mouth but said nothing.

Timothy saw the desperation in her face and lowered his eyes; he wanted nothing so much as to marry Augusta Colleen O'Brien. He truly believed he could eventually win her heart, at least once she got to know him. What a terrible night this had been for her, and it kept getting worse. He had met Augusta, just a few hours ago, and yet in this brief time he had found her to be gracious, humble, and strong!

Throughout the long journey from Boston he kept warning himself that no woman, let alone a sixteen-year-old girl, could possibly live up to Bull's bragging—or to be honest—his own infatuation with that one picture of her. However, instead of being let down, he realized that in the past few hours he had seen Miss A.C. O'Brien quite probably at her lowest ebb, and he found himself more smitten than ever—and even more certain that she was God's choice for him. He was sure of it!

Still, he could not help but have pity for her; after all she was being warred against in her own parlor.

Augusta could only stared at him in confusion. "Surely sir," she whispered, "this cannot be what you want. We mustn't upset Papa but there has to be some other way."

Sheepishly, he gave her an understanding smile and shrugged, "Augusta, I know that I am a stranger to you, but you aren't to me. I'm sorry things have turned out like this. But I came to marry you. I plan on courting you and I promise to work very hard to win you. But in my heart I believe God wants us to marry. And this is perhaps your father's last request. We must marry!"

Chapter 6
World out of Kilter

"Children, obey your parents in all things: for this is well pleasing unto the Lord." Colossians 3:20

Augusta awoke the following morning, curled in the chair beside her father's bed. When she heard voices coming from the kitchen; she checked to see that her papa was resting peacefully, then quietly, slipped from the room.

As she stepped into the kitchen, Augusta was surprised to find both men sitting at the table, amiably sipping cups of hot coffee over plates speckled with the remnants of biscuits and bacon.

She strolled over to the older man, gave him a hug, then said sleepily, "I had no idea you were here, Doc."

"Haven't been here long. Peeked in on you and Bull about an hour ago, found you both sleeping. My sweet Becky sent me over with the food—but I made the coffee! Grainger here said he only knows how to boil water."

The white-haired man chuckled—he was about to make a jest about Grainger's one talent coming in handy for the couple's first child—but he coughed instead, then mumbled, "She was happy to help!"

Augusta nodded. "You have the best wife in the world, Doc. You'll thank her for me—won't you?"

Dr. Mitchell looked at the young woman with an appraising eye as he answered, "Certainly! And—uh—you don't look as stiff as I thought you would... after spending a night in a chair!"

Augusta exchanged glances with Timothy. "No—I'm—all right."

The truth was that Timothy had checked on her every hour all through the night. At two a.m. he found her rubbing a stiff neck.

"If you won't let me take your place," he had whispered, "then at least take a stroll around the house for a minute. I've got hot water on the stove. You'll feel better after you've washed your face and hands—then hold a hot cloth against your neck a while—believe me it will refresh you. It might even ease that headache you've got!"

Augusta looked skeptically at the man. *How did he know how she felt?*

Though Timothy didn't hear her unspoken question, he answered it anyway: "Trust me—I know exactly how you feel. My mother was quite ill from time to time. I've spent many a night just as you are doing now. You'll probably be spending tomorrow night in the same way and you won't be any good to your father if you're so stiff you can't move."

Timothy gave Augusta a half smile then gently lifted her by the arm and led her to the door.

In the kitchen Augusta found a washcloth and towel laid out beside the pan of hot water; she did just as Timothy suggested and the small respite was a comfort to her. She made herself a good cup of tea, not that nasty herb concoction of the doctor's, and headed back to her father's side once again, feeling replenished and strengthened.

However, as she entered her father's room, she saw Timothy's head bowed, his hands clasped tightly together. He wasn't speaking but he had such an impassioned look on his face that Augusta had to ask, "What are you doing?"

Timothy looked up at Augusta and shrugged. "Same thing I guess we've both been doing all night, praying for healing," he whispered.

Timothy glanced affectionately at the old man, who had always seemed so invincible, but now looked small and vulnerable in his bed.

"He's quite a man—isn't he?"

Timothy gave Augusta one of those gentle smiles that made his whole face radiate with kindness. Quietly, the two traded places. Augusta hadn't meant to say anything but found herself whispering, "Thank you."

As the hours chimed through the night, she couldn't help but think of Timothy waiting in the parlor, praying for her papa. He assumed she was doing the same, and she had tried to! But Timothy wasn't fumbling in the dark when he prayed, the way she had earlier. She was still wondering if there was a God, while Timothy seemed to know!

There was such a sense of peace about this man, and she longed to know what that felt like.

Augusta was suddenly brought back from her thoughts as the doctor stood and asked, "Why don't you two stay here while I look in on Bull? I'll see how that ticker of his is doing after a good night's sleep."

Dr. Mitchell paused at the door, then he turned back and inquired, "Augusta, did your father say anything—about the wedding?"

Augusta covered her face with her hands, and with her words muffled, she said, "Yes...Doc...I gave him my promise."

Timothy nodded his agreement, and said, "We have no choice but to put Bull's mind at ease. Tell him we both agreed to have the wedding today."

Augusta sighed as she sat down in one of the kitchen chairs. Her look of defeat was hard for Timothy to bear. He longed to pull her into his arms—but since she would not have welcomed his comfort, he poured her a cup coffee instead. Remembering she liked only a dash of milk, he fixed it accordingly and placed it before her. When she turned away from him, he said, "We left you a plate of food warming in the oven—be happy to bring it to you." Then adding with concern: "You need to keep up your strength."

Augusta scowled at him then mumbled. "I don't eat breakfast." But she pulled the steaming cup towards her and took a tentative sip. When she found it to her liking, she scowled again. His kindness felt like salt on a fresh wound. Suddenly, there were a few things she wanted to ask this man.

"Mister Grainger," she began, "didn't you think it odd that I never answered any of your letters?"

Timothy shrugged. "Yes, it did concern me but I..."

Augusta was too angry to listen; instead, she interrupted with another question. "This isn't the Dark Ages. What did you think my reaction to all this would be? Or were you just relying on my being young and foolish?"

"No, of course not! I thought there would be time to court you, and I..."

Timothy stammered but Augusta was already speaking again. "And look what this has done to Papa!"

Augusta was too upset to stay seated any longer; she sprang from her chair and paced the length of the kitchen. Suddenly, she stopped and threw her hands in the air. "What's the matter with me? I have a dozen hungry horses to feed!"

With a loud groan she headed for the back door. "We'll have to talk later—after I've done my chores."

But Timothy stepped in front of her and said calmly, "It is all right, Augusta—you needn't worry." He explained: "The doctor told me that—uh—Sammy the blacksmith's son said that he'd feed the animals from now on. Since they own the livery, and most of the stock, they said they might as well start doing the work and..."

Suddenly, Timothy froze as he watched the expression on Augusta's face. "I—I'm so sorry Augusta—I assumed you knew."

This was just something else Bull had failed to tell his daughter.

"Anyway," Timothy sighed sympathetically and continued, "they didn't want you or Bull to worry! They also promised to take especially good care of Quest for you!"

Nodding, Augusta breathed out a long sigh and leaned heavily on the kitchen table. "So, Smithy bought the livery."

She was not looking at Timothy, and not really speaking to him, as the words tumbled from her mouth.

"I didn't even know about the sale, until last night. I didn't know much of anything, as it turns out! I didn't know the business I was supposed to be a partner in had been sold out from under me. I certainly didn't know my house wasn't mine anymore."

Finally, she turned towards Timothy and said sadly, "I didn't know I was getting married today—and I know almost nothing about the man I am to marry."

Augusta dropped into a chair; it was very un-lady like—Mrs. Drew would be mortified—but she didn't care.

"Well, I guess my life as I've always known it is over! Done and dusted, as they say."

She looked so sweet and vulnerable. Timothy sat down beside her and said tenderly, "Augusta, I know it sounds like an archaic idea, but your father and I really did and do mean well by you. I wish you'd read my letters—you'd know me if you had. And you'd know that you'd never have anything to fear from me, and that we two could have a wonderful life together! You think I'm a brute right now and, normally, I would not be the kind of man to hold anyone to an agreement made between two other parties. But ... "

Timothy leaned towards Augusta and spoke with the utmost sincerity, "You may not believe this but...I am in love with you! And, I believe in time that you..."

Timothy suddenly stopped; he never would have believed that fire and ice could come from the same set of eyes! But the look Augusta gave him could have melted an iceberg and frozen the deepest sea.

"Sir," she hissed, "you do not know me and if you did—you would not love me!"

Timothy reached to touch Augusta's hand but she yanked it away.

"I'm sorry," he muttered. "I know it sounds crazy but your father sent me a picture of you and Quest. The moment I saw you, I knew you were the woman God meant for me to marry! Which is a lot to say because that's the one thing I thought I would never do!"

With a sheepish smile, he added, "I know a lot about you. Perhaps, as you say, some of what your father wrote was Irish blarney. But in just these few hours with you I've seen what kind of woman you are!"

"In these few hours? What could you possibly know about me?" she demanded.

"Well, your father said you had a bit of temper." Timothy shrugged his shoulders. "And—when you were riled—you're as stubborn as a mule! There was no blarney in that statement!"

When once again the fire and ice from Augusta's eyes rained down on him, he added gently, "I learned for myself that you bake the best pie I ever tasted!" He studied her a moment then he continued. "Your father told me how all the townsfolk love you as if you were their own. And as soon as I got off the stage and asked where you lived, people were telling me how everyone respected the O'Briens and how—Miss Augusta was the nicest girl in town: how pretty, how sweet, and that she rides like an angel."

Augusta stared at the floor and shook her head while Timothy spoke; there was a strange mixture of emotions running through her—anger, confusion—embarrassment.

Timothy watched as moisture filled her eyes then he added with a tender smile: "When you opened that door last night—you took my breath away! Oh, I know it's hard to believe but in the past twelve hours of being with you, I am more determined than ever to have you for my wife!"

Augusta looked at the man in disbelief. "Mr. Grainger," she said with exasperation, "the past twelve hours have been absolutely dreadful!"

Timothy gave her a tender smile and said softly, "It is because they were absolutely dreadful—I'm more sure than ever! I've watched you endure a night full of embarrassment, betrayal…and then as if those things weren't enough, the evening ends with the fear of losing the most important person in the world to you! I've seen you handle all of this trauma with strength and poise and grace!"

Timothy ran his hand over his jaw then proceeded to explain: "Augusta, it would be dishonest to say that I wasn't pleased to be marrying you today. But,

I promise you—I'll be a good husband. I know we can have a happy marriage, given a little time. And I want you to know that…I'll wait. I don't expect anything from you but to be allowed to court you and spend time with you. I don't want you to worry that I am going to pressure you in any way. You can take all the time you need."

"You'll wait?" Augusta asked, as she blinked up at the man in confusion, then she brightened. "Do you mean we'll just pretend to get married today?"

"No, we'll have a real wedding today." Timothy's face colored a bit. "But I'll wait for the real marriage between us to begin. I'm leaving the timing of that up to you."

Augusta sighed and gave Timothy another blank stare; she hadn't any idea what he was talking about. Feeling defeated, Augusta shook her head then wearily began busying herself with clearing the table. Timothy folded his arms and leaned back, balancing his chair on two legs, thinking that this was a glimpse of what married life would be like. A lifetime of watching Augusta, she was so sweet and…

Abruptly, Augusta spun around and faced the man who had turned her life upside down—as a sudden understanding seemed to flash upon her like lightning!

Timothy nearly fell over backwards as the young woman glared at him then hissed, "Wait! I think I understand now—how all this mess came about."

"I know why you didn't marry a girl from Boston. Because those women are show ponies and you needed a work horse!" Augusta crossed her arms as her mind reasoned it all out. "Of course, Papa told you that Missus D. was teaching me all things proper, so maybe I'd pass your brother's inspection. And I'm sure he added that I could cook for a café full of people or a ranch full of men!"

Augusta's temper flashed with indignation as she pierced Timothy with her golden eyes. "I've been on the auction block and didn't even know it! I'm sure Papa told you that I could clean barns during the day and sew my own clothes at night! I'm surprised you haven't asked to see my teeth!"

Augusta kept her voice low, but she was in a fine rage as she stepped closer to Timothy.

"And that's just how you two went about this, isn't it?" she demanded. "A buyer and a seller—exchanging letters. Papa says you're looking for a nice filly to take west? Well, I have one that'll do—she's young and strong—and does what she's **told**! And what is your reply—SOLD!—you say. Without even a bye-your-leave." She shuddered once, then added, "And why should I have a say in it? After all, I'm nothing more than chattel—only exchanging one master for another!"

Augusta was storming back and forth around the kitchen table as Timothy watched with rapt attention. Each time she glanced at him, she found him staring at her intently, with an inscrutable look on his face. She wanted to shame him—make him admit his guilt or at least try to deny it—but the man said nothing.

In truth, Timothy did feel guilty, believing at least in part that he deserved her scolding, even though her conclusions were completely wrong. Still, he held his tongue, having been told that women felt better if allowed to vent their anger. Actually, he would have been disappointed had she wept or pouted like a child. Instead, her golden eyes flashed with passion and fire, and he knew he'd never known a woman to be more intriguing than A.C. O'Brien was to him just then. Her skin was like cream with her high cheekbones all flushed and rosy. He loved the way her long brown curls spiraled down her back, almost touching her small waist. He drank in the sight of her: expressive eyes and full lips as she articulated her grievances. And yet, if she'd known him better she would have changed her strategy. This show of temper simply made him all the keener to have her for his own—for Grainger was a man who delighted in a challenge and had a rare gift for optimism. Doctors had told him that he would die young! So at an early age, Timothy established the philosophy of making the most from every day, every opportunity—whatever it was! Even when his health improved, his philosophy remained the same. Timothy gazed at A.C. O'Brien and saw his future; she was full of life, brimming with vitality, passion, strength and character. Oh yes—making a happy marriage with his reluctant bride was going to be the greatest and most enjoyable challenge of his life!

Augusta suddenly stopped her scolding. It was having no effect on the man anyway; then an idea came to her. Bull had influenced all of her friends to think well of Timothy. And yet, didn't she deserve to have at least one unbiased opinion of this man? Smiling shrewdly, she remembered that she still had one friend who had not heard of Timothy Grainger. And this friend—could be counted on to give her a wholly unprejudiced point of view. Augusta surprised Timothy when she stalked to his side, took hold of his arm, and then pulled him to his feet.

"Come with me, MISTER GRAINGER. There is someone I'd like you to meet."

She gave no hint as to where she was taking him, but Augusta frowned when Timothy reached down and plucked an apple from the basket on the floor.

Augusta quickly exchanged her frown for a smile, and in a strained voice she said, "You don't want that—it'll spoil your appetite. I'll gladly fix whatever you like when we get back!"

Timothy was instantly suspicious, but said politely, "This will do." He muttered, "Besides, you won't have time—we have to get ready for the wedding."

Augusta stiffened, glaring at him as if the word "wedding" was a blasphemy of the worst kind.

Timothy said no more as he absentmindedly polished the apple on his sleeve, all the while wondering, *what was she up to?* She'd been giving him a good dose of—*what for*—then suddenly, as sweet as her famous apple pie, she offered to fix him anything he liked? Oh yes, she was up to something, he grinned, and he couldn't wait to see what it was.

A short time later they were walking under the large sign, that read: "O'Brien Livery". As they stepped inside, Timothy heard someone whistling in the back stall, and assumed he was about to be introduced to the new owners—Smithy or his son, but just then Augusta called out.

"Don't mind us, Sammy, just here to check on Quest!"

Timothy allowed his eyes to adjust to the dark barn, then he reached into his jacket pocket and withdrew a small pen knife. He followed Augusta to the large box stall, his excitement growing, for he was about the meet the mighty Quest. He recalled showing the tintype of Augusta and her stallion to a friend; the man had taken his time, and when he gave it back to Timothy, he had smiled and nodded approvingly. "Those two make quite a pair! There's a quality about them—both of them!"

Timothy thought of that statement as Augusta pointed towards her stallion and explained slowly, "Except for Papa, this is my best friend. Mister Grainger, this is Quest!"

She didn't walk to the animal but stepped aside and waited for Timothy. The man from Boston sensed a trap or at very least—a test!

Quest snorted at the newcomer; he didn't like strangers as a rule, and he'd never seen this man before. Nervously, he circled the inside of his stall, his head in the air, sniffing the unfamiliar scent; then he lowered his head and blew a warning while he pawed at the floor.

"Easy now, Quest," Timothy said evenly, taking one small step towards the stall door. But the stallion tossed his head, then looking at Augusta, he whinnied loudly. When she didn't respond, he became even more restless, stamping and circling, blowing and snorting

"Your friend seems a bit agitated—shouldn't you greet him?" Timothy asked calmly.

"No!" Augusta retorted. "If you want to be a part of my life you need to prove yourself to Quest."

Augusta was surprised when a smile spread across Timothy's handsome face. The man wasn't at all put off by her challenge; it was plain to see he welcomed the idea.

"You are absolutely right, Augusta."

Remembering the apple in his hand, Timothy began rubbing it slowly against his lapel. He purposely relaxed his stance, and then turning slightly away from Quest, he continued to speak in a low and gentle voice.

"You like apples, big fellow?" he muttered softly. "Of course I only share with my friends."

Augusta stared at Timothy. This was very similar to the way she would approach a high-strung horse for the first time, allowing the animal to accept her presence rather than forcing herself on him.

With her curiosity piqued, she watched the greenhorn from Boston with a little more interest.

Slowly, Timothy sliced through the apple, then with a grin he offered the first piece to Augusta. "Care for a bite, Miss O'Brien?" he asked.

Augusta narrowed her eyes and shook her head. Timothy bowed to her politely, then put the slice of apple into his own mouth and chewed. The sleek stallion sniffed the air and pricked his ears forward. He could smell the sweet scent of apple and he watched closely to see what this stranger would do with it.

Timothy looked up at Quest, and with his voice still low and calm, he said: "Well, boy, you are just as fine as your mistress is beautiful."

He kept talking in that easy way as he methodically sliced another piece from the apple, all the while nonchalantly inching his way closer and closer to the stall door. When he was just barely beyond the animal's reach, he stopped again, and once more, offered the slice to Augusta. Slightly irritated she waved him off. Again, Timothy bowed and gave her one of his closed-mouth grins, causing that impish left dimple to crease. Then he slid the thin slice of apple right from the knife's edge into his mouth. Around the bite, he said reverently, "Ah, Quest, I'm looking forward to seeing your mistress ride you!"

Although he kept his attention on the stallion, he turned slightly and gazed at Augusta so tenderly that she took a step back and her hand fluttered to her throat. His gaze lingered a moment longer. "The townsfolk tell me that you two are really something to see!"

Timothy's voice was deep and tranquil, and the spirited stallion was quieting down. He no longer circled his stall but leaned his head towards the man, sniffing the air, his ears pricked forward, as he listened to the deep rumble of the strangers' words. The stallion murmured in reply, breathing in the scent of the man, but it was mingled with the scent of his mistress and the tangy aroma of his favorite treat. Finally, Timothy held out the apple and stepped towards the dark stallion, who was now eager to make friends.

"Here you go, old man," he said. "If you are in the mood to bite down on something—how about this?" Timothy winked at Augusta then added, "Instead of me!"

The sight of the powerful stallion bowing his head and gently nibbling away at the apple pleased Timothy—almost as much as it irritated Augusta. He continued to hold the apple lightly with his fingers, until only the core was left and then it too disappeared into the horse's mouth. While Quest munched sloppily on the juicy apple, Timothy ran his hand up the stallion's forehead, giving it a good rub. As his eyes scanned the animal's sleek lines, he continued to speak softly. "Yes sir, old man, you do not disappoint—you're the best of the best, aren't you boy?"

When Timothy glanced at Augusta, he found her staring at him with her eyebrows knit together in a frown, not quite believing what she had just seen. Quest had not even attempted to bite Timothy. Worse still, the big oaf was even now pushing playfully against this stranger's arm, wanting either more apple or just more of this man's attention. Quest had never taken to anyone so quickly.

Augusta was mystified: *How had this Boston dude charmed her grumpy stallion?* She always trusted anyone Quest trusted—but she hadn't expected this!

Timothy grinned at Augusta as he took his handkerchief from his pocket and wiped his sticky fingers. "Well, Miss O'Brien—did I pass your test?"

"Test?" Augusta asked innocently.

Timothy just shook his head and blew out a breath, wishing he could put Augusta's mind at ease.

They stared at each other a moment then suddenly Augusta's face went pale. "Oh, no! I suppose it's up to me to make the arrangements—I guess I have to find a preacher and ... "

Timothy gently touched Augusta's arm. "I'm sorry—that's something else you should already know but—Doc told me he spoke to the preacher this morning. He also asked the Tylane's to pick up your wedding trunk and bring it to your house. The wedding will be this afternoon at two o'clock. Doc said that's when your father would be at his strongest. He said mornings and evenings were the hardest on his heart patients."

Once again Augusta felt like a pawn on a chess board. Through gritted teeth, she asked sardonically, "Doc didn't happen to mention when my patience would be at its strongest—did he?"

Timothy grimaced, his kind, blue eyes trying to convey his understanding. "I am so sorry, Augusta. I wanted our wedding to be wonderful, not traumatic! I promise to make this all up to you someday!"

Augusta ignored Timothy's words. She shook her head sadly and drew close to her stallion.

"Hey, boy," she whispered as the big horse leaned his head over the stall door. Augusta rubbed her cheek against the hollow of Quest's muzzle and slowly ran her hand down his sleek neck.

The great animal suddenly became very still; he murmured to her gently, not understanding and yet he seemed to sense the sadness in the young woman's heart.

Augusta lingered only a moment, then swiping away a tear, she turned to Timothy.

"I want to spend as much time as I can with Papa."

With that said, she straightened her shoulders and left the livery with Timothy staring after her.

Chapter 7
The Wedding

**"Therefore, what God has put together let no man separate."
Mark 10:9**

Emily frowned in concentration as she curled a shining lock of Augusta's dark hair around her finger. Mutely, Augusta studied their reflections in her dressing table mirror, and for the hundredth time she wished that she and Emily were scrubbing floors or even peeling onions just now—anything but this.

The silence in the room was so loud it gave Emily a headache and broke her heart at the same time. The O'Briens were as dear to her as any kinfolk. When she and Wes had opened their café that morning and realized the town was all a-flutter over Bull's illness, and the news that he was insisting Augusta be married that day—Well!—there was nothing for it. Emily, that redheaded spitfire from Tennessee, threw off her apron and grabbed her husband by the arm.

"Westin Tylane!" she demanded. "You put a sign on that door, 'Closed fer the day!'"

When Wes opened his mouth to speak, she didn't know if it was to agree or protest, but she cut him off.

"Now, Wes," she hissed, "we helped raise that lil' gal! She needs us, and we are *not* gonna let her down!"

An hour later, Emily was bustling into Augusta's small attic room, and in her wake was the elegant Amelia Drew. The older woman was already explaining to all who would listen that though this was a hastily put together event, it was still to be done beautifully and in a proper manner. Wes, being wise to the ways of these women, mutely followed behind, huffing under the weight of the large trunk.

When Augusta saw her three dearest friends invading her tiny domain, she swallowed down mixed emotions. She was touched by their loyalty and friendship, and though she loved all three of them dearly, a wound festered within her—for she knew that each of them had at least played a part in what she viewed as a conspiracy against her.

Wes wisely made a quick exit, leaving the three women to stare at each other. Mrs. Drew, however, was one to face things head on. Cupping Augusta's chin in her hand, she spoke in a solemn tone, "We all love you, dear, and though you may not agree with what's been done—it is for the best. And we are here to help you!"

With that said, the older woman gave Augusta a quick hug, then immediately busied herself with unpacking the wedding trunk. Emily was next to draw Augusta into a loving embrace. Then, in hopes of defusing the tension, she picked up the hair brush and began chatting away, as if nothing were out of the ordinary.

Knowing her friends loved her, Augusta's anger was quelled for the moment, when another emotion took her by surprise! A sudden onslaught of melancholy overwhelmed her.

If Papa's outrageous plans go unchecked, we'll have to say good-bye! Wes is as dear as any uncle—and Emily? What would I do without my sweet, funny redhead? She's been like a mother and best friend combined! And Mrs. D—she's always so proper but she loves me and I love her! How could I ever say good-bye to them?

"Hey now, darlin'!" Emily soothed, "Quit yer frownin'." Smiling into the mirror she gave Augusta's shoulder a squeeze. "I'm makin' ya as purty as a houndog on huntin' day!"

Though the redhead kept up her banter, she was secretly wishing that things could have turned out as planned. Timothy was to have courted Augusta and won her heart. Still, Emily well understood Bull's insistence: the world could be a cold and dangerous place for a pretty young woman.

Augusta drew Emily from her musings, when tongue and cheek, she looked into the mirror and remarked, "Well, at least I know why you've been sharing all those stories about how your father arranged your marriage to Wes. And how you two started out as strangers but *finally* learned to get along!"

Emily's forehead creased into a frown. "Oh darlin'—please say ya ain't mad at me. And what I said was that; though we wed as strangers—it wasn't long 'til the two of us fell in love!"

With an impish smiled she added, "As fer us gettin' along? Well now, that's a whole notha' thing!"

43

When she saw that Augusta was not amused, Emily became more serious: "Sides, ya know yer pa ain't been doin' good. We didn't want nothin' bad to happen, if he—well…"

Taking in Augusta's beleaguered expression Emily continued; "Ya know we all love ya, and we'd try our best to help ya—but with Grainger ya've got a real future!"

Gazing up into Emily's reflection Augusta shrugged her shoulders and gave her a weak smile.

"I know you meant well." she groaned. "But I don't understand why it was kept a secret? If I'd known I might not have upset Papa—I'm usually so careful with what I say, but I got so angry and hurt!"

Augusta dropped her head in her hands and moaned, "When he told me everything and that I had no say—I lashed out—I caused this attack. If he dies…?"

Emily bent down and put her cheek against Augusta's while she gazed at her young friend in the mirror. "You listen to me. You ain't to blame! And that little hissy fit of yers didn't cause this! Yer pa knows you inside 'n out—why he told us from the beginnin' that when you found out about all of this—you was gonna be as mad as a cat in a bath! You didn't say one word yer pa wasn't expectin'. And you can get riled again if you like—but we all think he's done the right thing!"

Augusta pushed away from her friend. "Emily—shame on you! How could you possibly agree with how this has turned out?"

Emily lifted Augusta's chin with one finger, and spoke her mind: "Girl, you need to understand—a woman alone in the world, finds herself with few choices. And most of 'em ain't too purty! Yer pa done a good thing. And just in time, too, in my way a-thinkin'."

Augusta opened her mouth, but stopped from voicing her arguments, as Mrs. Drew came gliding into the room, bringing with her the scent of roses and a long ivory-colored veil. Her handsome oval face was flushed from climbing the stairs; still, she looked every bit the aristocrat she was born to be. Augusta had grown up wishing to be as likable as Emily and as elegant as Amelia Eloise Langstrom-Drew.

The woman was the heiress of a wealthy family in New York. However, after eloping with a poor school master, she was promptly—disinherited. Nevertheless, she spoke of her marriage as a happy one, though childless. When

Augusta had come to town, she'd filled a void in Amelia's life—she was the child of her heart. The woman had little money but gave what she had to give: her talent for sewing and gardening, her knowledge of what was proper and ladylike, and all her love.

Wistfully, Augusta watched Mrs. Drew cross the room, always the picture of graceful beauty. Even with her cheeks moist and rosy from steaming the wrinkles out of the wedding gown, not a hair of her thick snow-white braid was out of place, as it regally circled the top of her head, like a crown. Her gown was a soft blue-gray satin, matching the color of her eyes, which—Augusta noted—seemed a bit misty.

"Augusta," the older woman cooed, "just look at this!"

Amelia was glowing with pleasure as she brought the ivory veil closer for Augusta to see.

"Isn't it lovely?" she whispered. "Venetian lace. The finest I've ever seen!"

Emily and Augusta exchanged glances; lace was lace as far as either of them were concerned.

"Well now ... " Emily drawled. "Never heard of that before—sure is purty though. Huh, Augusta?"

The reluctant bride-to-be gave an insipid nod and shrugged her shoulders. All she knew about today was that her life was never going to be the same. She had agreed to this wedding, but she viewed it like a dose of medicine. Yes, she would swallow this bitter pill, but only for her father's sake.

Stoically, Augusta stared into the mirror, as the delicate veil was draped over her head and settled gently around her shoulders. Next, Amelia held up a wreath, and even Augusta was struck by its beauty. It was fashioned from three braided cords: two cords made from the same satin as the wedding gown; the third from the lace. Sprinkled lightly across the wreath were dainty clusters of silk orange blossoms.

"And this," Amelia added softly, "this delicate creation goes over the veil, to hold it in place."

When Mrs. Drew saw the tears filling Augusta's eyes, she mumbled something about checking on things down stairs, while poor Emily groped for something to say.

"It's gonna be fine!" she assured her young friend. "Ya know I talked to yer fiancé this mornin'. He sure is good lookin' and he's got the sweetest smile and ... "

45

"STOP!" Augusta demanded, then she softened her tone. "I'm sorry Emily, but—don't you see how frightening this is? Papa's sick and I don't care a whit about that stranger—sweet smile or not! On top of that I've never once given a thought to being married. I know most girls dream of it—but not me!"

Speaking to Augusta's reflection, Emily asked: "So, what were ya gonna do...when ya got grown?"

Augusta rolled her eyes and raised her palms into the air. "Papa told me I'd be running the livery. I just needed to be a good horse-woman and a good bookkeeper. He made sure I could cook and sew if the livery failed. But we never talked of marriage—or family."

Emily's eyebrows went up. "Yer pa never said, 'yer gonna make a fine wife or mother someday?'"

"No, not ever!" Augusta hissed; then she blew out a breath. "Well, that is, not until the last night!"

Just then the hallway clock chimed once, and Augusta shivered as her face turned a ghostly white.

"But in exactly one hour I'm getting married—I barely know what that is—and to a stranger, no less!"

"Ohhh, darlin'," Emily exclaimed with a wince. "It wasn't supposed to be like this—the plan was fer ya to have time to court and all. It seemed romantic! Kind of like a fairy tale: a rich, handsome man comes with a trunk full of fancy do-dads. Then, he whisks his bride away to live happily ever after out in the west."

Suddenly, Emily had a thought. "Hold on now! Ya ain't been alone with the man much, but ya ain't truly afraid of Grainger, are ya? He hadn't been mean to ya, has he?"

Augusta scrunched up her face and shrugged her shoulders, "Nooo—-" she groaned. "I wish I could say he had." Rolling her eyes she added, "What I find disagreeable about Timothy is his resolve to marry—me! And other than that major flaw in his character, which, by the way, all my friends seem to share, Mister Timothy Grainger has been considerate...charming...gentle... and...nauseatingly kind."

Augusta drug out each word as if they were an insufferably long list of flaws.

"So, gentle and kind—hey? Why ya poor little dear—forced to marry rotten ol' Prince Charmin'."

"Not Prince Charming," Augusta corrected. "Remember, Papa calls him a 'prince among men'!"

Augusta's thoughts went back to the man she was to marry. After a bit of pondering, she couldn't quite believe the things she'd accused him of that morning. However, she was still too confused to know what to believe. Glancing back into the mirror she asked, "Emily, why would a 'prince among men', marry a girl like me?"

Augusta touched her face. "My nose is too long, my eyes are too close, brown eyes and brown hair. I'm uneducated, didn't even finish the early grades of school—so why me?"

Carefully, Emily arranged a few wispy curls around Augusta's forehead to frame her face, "Oh, ya silly goose," she chided, "there's nothing plain about ya! Yer hair's the color of mahogany and yer eyes have shades of pure gold! And that skin of yers?" Emily touched Augusta's cheek with the back of her hand. "Feels like satin and looks like peaches and cream. And when everyone sees you today, they're gonna swear the—Queen of Sheba's come to town!"

Augusta's expression was impassive as she whispered, "He treats me like I am the Queen of Sheba. But—Emily, I am a simple girl that cleans barns and rides horses. I accused him this morning of bartering for me like a workhorse in a sale barn. I don't really think I believe that but...this whole thing still doesn't make sense. Timothy's handsome and rich—he has a definite way about him. I bet he's the one person in the world who could have talked Papa into delaying this wedding, but he wouldn't even try!" Augusta turned to Emily. "I met him yesterday, and this morning—do you know what he said? That he fell in love with my tintype and knows me through Papa's letters. Ever heard of such nonsense?"

Emily raised her eyebrows. "Augusta, my sweet, the truth is—a man wants his wife to enjoy the kind of future he sees for himself. Otherwise, they'll both be miserable. Grainger sees his future in the west on a big horse and cattle ranch. He don't want some city gal; he needs to marry somebody like—A.C. O'Brien! A woman who happens to love horses. That ain't nonsense! And I don't doubt the man fell in love with that tintype! Fact is, half the town stops what they're doin'—just to gape at ya, when ya ride Quest of a mornin'. Yer dressed in one of them embroidered ridin' skirts and vest, with yer long hair fallin' down yer back. Ya sit so tall and straight on the big flashy stallion. Yer quite a pair—both of ya! And besides," Emily hissed, "No smooth talker's gon-

47

na change yer pa's mind about yer gettin' hitched today! Now—be honest—Miss Augusta Colleen—if Grainger backed out of this weddin', or did anything to upset yer pa—ya'd either be holdin' a shotgun on him yerself, or chastisin' him 'til he cried Uncle—and *you* know it!"

Augusta could think of nothing to say, mostly because Emily was right. Reluctantly, she admitted, "I suppose... neither of us could or *should* say no to Papa. It's just—how could he say he loves me? He doesn't know me. And he's got Doc and Missus D. and Wes and—YOU—all wrapped around his little finger!" Augusta groaned, "I feel like you all are just, throwing me to the wolves."

"Darlin', it's not like that!" Emily sighed then headed for the door. "I've gotta go help Missus D. bring up your dress." Suddenly, Emily stopped. "Wait, bet ya'd feel better if your grumpy old stallion voted yea or nay! Wes'll take Grainger to meet that ol' boy. If Quest bellows like a banshee and takes a hunk out of him, why then...What's the matter? Thought ya'd like my idea."

The enthusiasm in Emily eyes faded when Augusta scowled at her suggestion and shook her head, "I liked the idea, very much," she groaned. "This morning—when I had the same thought."

Then with a look of surrender Augusta added: "You might as well just get my dress. My grumpy old stallion and my *fiancé*—have met!"

Emily stood with her hands on her hips ... "AND?" she asked.

Augusta toyed with her veil, while under her breath she muttered, "Quest—that big fat traitor!"

Emily bit back a smile. "Don't tell me—that big turncoat slobbered all over the prince among men?"

Augusta blew out her frustration: "Of course...like all my friends, he just *loves* Timothy Grainger!"

Emily's eyebrows rose to the ceiling, "Well, no reprieve from yer best pal! Eh?" Shaking her head she muttered, "I'll go fetch yer dress."

⊰≫

Slowly, Augusta opened her bedroom door and stood for a moment on the upstairs landing, taking in deep breaths, trying to compose herself as Emily squeezed her hand and Mrs. Drew sniffed back tears.

Moments earlier the women had stood in wonder, gazing into the oval floor mirror as the last button was fastened and the flowing skirt was smoothed into place over the crinoline and petticoats. Augusta had suddenly been transformed when she stepped into the exquisite ivory wedding gown. Could this be the same impish creature, the little girl who loved horses and whistled off-key while scrubbing dishes and pulling weeds? Suddenly, like a butterfly, she had emerged as a woman with grace and beauty.

The gown was simple perfection on Augusta. The color was as unique as the young woman herself: it was a deep ivory with a hint of blush in the hue and it accentuated Augusta's chocolate-brown hair and creamy complexion. It was styled with a high collar at the nap of her neck then the neckline dipped lower. Modesty was maintained with a delicate netting that spread across her bodice, then tapered down to Augusta's small waist. The skirt was gathered in a series of rows on either side, held with tiny clusters of silk orange blossoms. The sleeves were fitted to the top of the shoulder then the fabric fell gently down until it billowed softly to be gathered again at the wrist, with more miniature blossoms. As she turned to her friends and smiled serenely, the metamorphosis was complete; the girl—was now a woman.

Trying to keep her voice steady, Amelia straightened Augusta's collar while she mused, "You know, I…had a lovely necklace when I was a debutante, haven't missed it or even thought of it in years, but I wish I had it for you today! No matter—you—look like an angel my dear!"

Emily suddenly dropped to her knees beside the trunk and began tossing sheets of tissue over her head.

"I'm just gonna give this trunk one more look-see! If she needs somethin' it's bound to be in here."

Just as she spoke, her fingers brushed across something cool and smooth to the touch.

"See—what'd I tell ya? she exclaimed as she held up the carved jewelry box and slowly opened it.

"They didn't forget a thing after all. And oh, my stars—will ya jes' look at these bead!"

Mrs. Drew raised one eyebrow and reached for the box. "They aren't beads my dear—they're pearls!"

Augusta frowned. She'd made it known that she thought the trunk presumptuous on Timothy's part. Everything in it had been too luxurious. Like magic, each time they needed something, from her unmentionables to her dainty satin shoes, they had found it in the trunk—in her size, smelling of lilac. Her favorite scent!

"Stop scowling, Augusta!" Mrs. Drew scolded. "I know you think he's putting on airs; but I assure you—the man is not being considerate or generous—just to irritate you!"

While Emily stifled a smile, Amelia quickly fastened the necklace around the bride's throat. Then in her grandmotherly way, the older woman cupped Augusta's face in her hands, and said: "Augusta, over the years your father— and your friends here—have all shared what we could to help you become the woman you are today. You're a little bit of all us—strong and capable! So our advice is: keep your eyes dry...your chin high...and embrace your future!"

⋈

Augusta pondered Mrs. Drew's words as she took her first step down the staircase, but as she glanced back at her two friends, she found they couldn't follow their own advice; their eyes sparkled with unshed tears.

When the desire to cry overwhelmed her as well, she reminded herself of how her father disliked weeping women. Anger had always been her best weapon against tears, so with each step she recalled her least charitable thoughts regarding Timothy and his motives. When she finally reached the bottom step, she realized that she no long wanted to weep. No—now she could have gleefully walked up to Grainger and quite effectively—put this man in his place! Regretfully, she remembered the other behavior that was guaranteed to upset her father, even more so than tears—and that one thing was—failing to behave like—a lady!

Timothy was the first to look up and behold Augusta gracefully descending the stairs. The others turned the moment they heard the man's deep intake of air and saw the expression on the groom's face. It changed from wonder to a smile of admiration. With amused glances the other guests followed the man's gaze until...they too gave a collective sigh. They were used to seeing this young girl pouring coffee at the café or cleaning barns or riding horses. She had always been a pretty little thing! They had not, however, expected to see her like this; not as a beautiful woman of elegance and poise!

As Bull O'Brien watched his daughter, his chest swelled with pride, while Timothy was certain that a portrait of Augusta was forever being etched into his memory.

When the bride reached her father's side, and bent to kiss his cheek, her friends saw how close to the surface her emotions were; but then instantly, they saw her straighten and school her features. They were all so proud of her when she turned and graced everyone in the room with her sweetest smile—everyone, that is, but Timothy. Somehow she managed to welcome each guest, all the while ignoring her groom entirely! She focused instead on the preacher. Holding out her hand to the older gentleman, she said graciously, "Good afternoon, Reverend Hawkins. Thank you for performing the ceremony today."

Timothy was impressed with her calm demeanor and tried to get Augusta's attention, hoping to give her a look of encouragement, but her eyes seemed locked on the preacher's shiny silver tie pin. Suddenly, the groom realized with amusement that his bride's plan was to treat him as if *he* were not there! Possibly, that she wasn't either!

Unaware of the undercurrent of emotions, Rev. Hawkins smiled broadly at the handsome couple. He knew only that the ceremony had been moved up due to the father's poor health. Clearing his throat to let everyone know he was ready, he began by saying: "Well, now, Mister Grainger, if you would please, take your bride's hand."

Augusta's look of somber tranquility quickly turned into a frown. She'd never held a man's hand before—other than her father's. She knew it was childish but she did not want to hold Timothy's hand! Instantly, her rebellious eyes flew to Emily. The redhead knew exactly what the problem was. Pressing her lips together, she sternly nodded her head, as if to say: 'O for pity sake, let the man take yer hand!'

Augusta took a deep breath, then begrudgingly held out her hand, mortified when it shook visibly. Quickly, Timothy took it and held it firmly in both of his. Then he surprised Augusta when he leaned towards her and whispered, "There has never been a bride more breathtakingly beautiful than you are right now, Augusta!"

His softly spoken words were meant to calm her, but they had the opposite effect. Augusta didn't know how to respond. Not wanting to look at him, she stared at the preacher instead, but when he grinned at her, she frowned and looked down. That's when she saw her small hand entwined in Timothy's larger one. Suddenly, she felt dizzy and her heart seemed to be pounding with every tick of the hallway clock.

Oh, why did he have to say that? I'm angry at him and I am going to stay that way! He probably wants Quest more than he wants me! I'll undo this marriage...just as soon as Papa gets well.

As the ceremony continued she managed to at least appear serene, by pretending she was watching someone else going through this ancient ritual. She could hear herself repeating the words the preacher told her to say, but the sound of her voice seemed foreign. She looked down at one point while Timothy placed a gold band on her finger. As if from a distance she heard the reverend say the words, "I now pronounce you man and wife!" Adding forcefully, "And what God has put together let no man separate!"

The words made a cold shiver run all through Augusta's small frame. He might just have well have said, *"You're trapped, young woman—there will be no escape!"*

Augusta hadn't taken the ceremony seriously, even though she hoped that seeing her wed would make her father well! But the way the preacher talked, it seemed no matter how she had taken it, this getting married was serious business. Still, she planned to continue behaving as if her husband did not exist!

Glad to have it over she turned towards Wes and Emily, but when her new husband refused to release her, she glared at him and tried to yank her hand away. Quickly, the preacher reached out and gently guided her back to Timothy's side as he whispered, "The ceremony is not quite finished yet, my dear."

Addressing the guests in the room, Reverend Hawkins said boldly, "Ladies and gentlemen, it is my pleasure to introduce Mister and Missus Timothy Grainger!"

When Bull grinned and began to applaud the other guests joined him. Then the preacher said something that Augusta thought Emily or Mrs. Drew really should have warned her about—for his words hit solidly in the pit of her stomach, as he cheerfully announced, "Mister Grainger, you may now *kiss* your bride!"

For the first time since the ceremony began Augusta actually looked into Timothy's face. He smiled gently, his blue eyes full of understanding. While her eyes turned from honey-colored terror to sparking flames of golden fire. In an instant her expression and stance went from wary to mutinous!

Hawkins, unaware of the sudden mêlée taking place between the bride and groom, repeated his request: "Sir, you may kiss your bride!" With a happy chuckle he added, "In fact—I insist on it!"

A few nervous coughs and side-ways glances ricocheted around the room as Timothy slowly leaned towards Augusta, and she stubbornly moved out of his reach. Augusta's expression was insisting, even demanding, that her groom think of a way out of this particular part of the ceremony.

Timothy straightened, as he realized what a difficult position Augusta had been placed in! He was a more-than-willing participant—she was not! With a tender smile Timothy gave his bride an understanding nod, then taking both her hands in his he said, "Missus Grainger, if ever a woman looked like a queen on her wedding day, it is you."

He then gallantly bent down on one knee and said sincerely, "As—uh, Prince Albert said to Queen Victoria when he was pronounced to be her husband, 'You, lady, are the queen of my life and my heart. I'll take no kiss from your lips today but shall endeavor to earn them from this day forward!'"

With that said, Timothy lightly touched his lips to Augusta's fingers then stood to his full height. He released her with a wink and one of his deep smiles, producing a dimple in his left cheek.

Augusta blinked up at the man—this husband of hers—had understood! For a moment she forgot her anger and found herself returning his kindhearted smile. However, she couldn't help but wonder. *It was a kind thing to do. Of course, I all but screamed that he better come up with something—so he did! But was it kindness or was he just humoring me—like when he gave Quest the apple?*

As the ceremony ended, subdued congratulations were given to the young couple and the ever-weakening Bull O'Brian. Augusta forced a smile as she leaned down, allowing her father to kiss her cheek.

"Papa, you really should rest now!" she whispered.

When she straightened she was surprise that Timothy was already flanking one side of her father's chair while Wes took the other. The two men settled O'Brien comfortably back into his bed, taking as much care of the man's body as they did of his pride.

Chapter 8
Passing the Torch

"About! these commandments I am giving you today. You must teach them to your children and talk about them when you are at home or out for a walk; at bedtime and the first thing in the morning." Deuteronomy 6:6-7

While the sun and moon traded places, Augusta remained at her father's bedside, refusing to leave. Bull's quiet patience was telling, for at any other time, he never would have allowed anyone to fuss so—but there came into the man's spirit a kind of *knowing*: this was a battle…he was going to lose. And so he savored this time with his daughter, cherishing her soft words and gentle comfort.

Augusta, however, clung to the hope that she and her love could tether her father to the world of the living. Hour after hour, she bathed his face, stroked his hand, and once again—she tried—to pray.

"Please God … " her heart cried, "don't take him. He is all that I have left!"

As if from somewhere within…came a gentle rebuke. *You're not alone—you have a husband now!*

"No!" she denied, rejecting the notion, even as she recalled Timothy's kind face and his vows to honor and protect her. Suddenly, other unwelcome thoughts came flooding into her mind.

Remember, you made vows too! And—what God has put together let no man separate.

This inner turmoil hounded Augusta, until she finally fell into a troubled sleep. Just as the night was creeping slowly to dawn, Bull rallied and opened his eyes. His expression grew tender as he watched his child. Oh, how like an angel she had always seemed to him—especially while asleep! A great burden had been lifted as she and Timothy were pronounced man and wife. He was almost at peace now; he had just one more thing to do before he could finally rest easy.

"Augusta!" he whispered. "Hey, me darlin' girl!"

Still clothed in her ivory wedding gown, she sat up in a rush, with her hair tousled and eyes cloudy. "Papa? Are you all right? Should I get Doc?"

"I'm as good as I'll ever be, just wantin' to talk to ya awhile—ain't that all right?"

When O'Brien licked his dry lips, she helped him to a drink of water, and said gently, "Of course we can talk, Papa. But you're so very weak and sleep is good medicine."

"Ah, yer all the medicine I need. Ya look like an angel in that weddin' gown. I'm glad ya kept it on. It pleases me to see ya lookin' so grand!"

Augusta bit her lip as she watched her father stop to catch his breath before he could continue.

"Now I've got some things to be tellin' ya, and ya must be strong and brave—just as ya were this afternoon. Oh, I know darlin'—twasn't an easy day fer ya, but ya did me proud. And I must ask ya to draw again from that strength that's within ya and let yer ol' papa be tellin' ya...good-bye."

Augusta's eyes filled with tears, as she shook her head, then said softly, "Not...good-bye Papa, just good night...surely."

Bull's sky-blue eyes became misty in spite of himself. He attempted a lop sided grin, saying: "Ah, gal, even when ya were a little might, ya had a feeling fer things. Now is the time to be honest, and ya know as well as I, it's good-bye fer us. Ya know that—don't ya now?"

Augusta nodded her head slowly, answering, "Yes—I suppose I do."

Bull frowned as a silent tear slid down Augusta's face. It was no exaggeration that the man hated tears and he feared they'd both be weeping if he wasn't careful. Suddenly, a sparkle came into his blue eyes. "I was proud of ya today," he added softly, "fer many reasons, one being that ya didn't give yer poor husband a sound thrashin'—when yer papa wasn't lookin'. Darlin', ya came down those stairs in a fury, then pretended the man wasn't even there."

When Augusta looked shocked, Bull gave her a weak smile and shook his head. "Ah, no matter, ya fooled all but me—we always could read each other! And, well, I know ya ain't thankful for that man. But ya'll never find a better one. We had us a talk, while ya was gettin' dressed and—he reminded me of some important things I've failed to do. He shamed me good 'n proper, he did."

"He shamed you?" Augusta hissed. "Who does he think he is to shame a man like you? Why, you are the most respected man in this territory? And he's just a—a—"

"Easy...now...ya best be watchin' that Irish temper! And I'll be thankin' ya to let me finish! While ya was gettin' dressed, the man was kind enough to sit with me, and he ... "

Bull stopped, his hands shaking as he stroked his thick mustache then continued, "Darlin' ... the man prayed for me. It's been a long time since I heard a man pray like that. Twasn't pompous or flowery, but sincere and earnest. It was a strong man's prayer, and one from his heart, praying for God's healin'—of this heart."

The old man tapped his chest and smiled. "The reason I said he shamed me is, for it was then that I realized that yer ol' papa has neglected to teach ya the most important thing!" he exclaimed, as he reached for his daughter's hand.

Bull drew in another deep breath and went on, "And that neglect makes me a poor father indeed."

"No, Papa." Augusta soothed. "Why, you are the best papa in the world. You've been father, mother, teacher, and friend! You taught me to ride horses, and made sure I could sew and cook and ... "

Leaning closer, she tried to add a playful note as she whispered, "You even tried to teach me how to clean barns like a lady!" Augusta shrugged. "Granted, you may have failed at that!"

A flicker of a smile crossed the man's pale lips, as he nodded and said, "Perhaps so...but what I failed to teach ya about—was God! Ya know so much, lass, but less than nothin'...about our Lord Jesus. I've failed to tell ya that He loves ya dearly and that He died fer ya!"

Bull slowly took in a number of deep breaths to regain his strength, while Augusta looked perplexed.

"You know about God and about Jesus, too?" she asked. "I've always wondered if God was real but..."

Augusta stopped mid-sentence when she saw the pain etched on her father's face and tears well up in the corners of his eyes. Bull O'Brien hit his chest with his fist and said bitterly, "Ah darlin', I was so set on ya knowing so many things. I've known about God and Jesus all me life, but failed to tell ya about them. Can ya ever forgive me?"

The anguish in her father's face alarmed Augusta. "It's all right, Papa!" she soothed. "All this talk is hurting you. I want you to rest now."

"Nay—darlin', I've waited too long as it is—I've a sacred trust to pass down to ya. My Irish mama, yer own dear Granny O, she taught me an old Irish prayer, and I should've taught it to ya, and more besides. But I hadn't thought of it in years—not until I heard the prayer of that good man of yers today."

Bull drew in a deep breath and with a trembling voice he recited:

"God be in my head, and in my understandin';
God be in my mind and in my thinkin';
God be in my eyes and in my seein';
God be in my tongue and in my speakin',
God be in my heart and in my lovin';
God be in my hands and in my doin';
God be in my ways and in my walkin'."

"Augusta, that was just how twas with yer grand-parents. God was in everythin' they said and did! And though ya couldn't have told it by me. That's how I was raised and how I began me life! In me tenth summer, I understood that Jesus Christ died on the cross to save me from all my sins. Twas then I asked Him to forgive me, and to come into me heart. I told Him that He'd be the Lord of me life...fer all me days...."

Bull's chin quivered and a tear rolled down his cheek. Augusta tenderly wiped it away before it reached his bristly white mustache.

"I've never once told ya that—have I gal? No...I know. I never did."

"Why not, Papa?"

"Aww...darlin'," he said, rubbing his head. "Anger—it's a terrible thing! And the devil uses our anger against us with great effect! I got angry and I stayed that way. I was angry at yer mama for goin' away. And I was angry at God for lettin' things happen the way they did. I told God that he should a done better—and that neither me nor mine would follow him ever again!"

He sighed as his brows knit together.

"As if a mere man has any right to fuss at the creator of the world! But that's what I did."

Bull suddenly raised hopeful eyes to shine into his daughter's sweet face.

"But, darlin', when I watched ya walk down that staircase today, I was that proud of ya and I wished I had some treasure to give to ya! It was then I remembered Timothy's prayer, and that of me mother's—and it got me thinkin'. Faith in God...that's what my parents gave to me. Mama used to say twas like passin' a bright torch down from one generation to the next. She always warned that it took just one careless person to let that torch burn out. Then generations could be left in eternal darkness!"

57

Bull shook his head, years of regret lining his face.

"I'm the one, Augusta—I'm that one careless fool that let the torch go out. I didn't even try to pass it onto ya. I just buried it in a bitter heart and there it died! But darlin' girl, I am re-lightin' that torch fer ya tonight! And I'm trustin' ya to carry it onto the next generation!"

Bull could see the bewildered look on his daughter's face; he patted Augusta on the hand and said, "I know ya don't really understand what I'm talkin' about—do ya? But yer husband...does. He's a fine Christian man; ya ask him about the Lord, and he'll show ya the way."

Augusta nodded and gave him a tender smile—but he was right—it all seemed so confusing.

Drawing in another shaky breath, Bull tapped his daughter's nose with his finger and said, "Now promise me ya'll be a good wife! And that ya'll be listenin' to all the man has to say?"

"Oh, Papa, let's not talk about him. I'm worried about you! Tell me what to do to help you get better?"

Bull O'Brien managed one of his famous smiles that always seemed to light up any room, but his voice was unusually soft as he looked into his dear daughter's face. "Now, that's just like me A.C.—get on about the task at hand, right? But I've finally made me piece with God. So don't ya worry about me—and I needn't worry about *you*—no more; we're both in good hands."

Suddenly, Bull felt so weak he knew it was time he bid his child goodbye, but what he said was: "I'm awful tired now, darlin'. If ya don't mind, I'll be sayin' good—goodnight to ya. And always be rememberin', me girl, that yer papa loves ya!"

Augusta watched her father drift off to sleep, still clinging to his calloused hand. She was married now and Papa had made his peace with God. Did that mean he was content to leave her? How could that be—when she still desperately needed him?

Chapter 9

A Sad Good-Bye

"My flesh and my heart fail; but God is the strength of my heart and my portion forever." Psalm 73:26

Augusta numbly took Timothy's arm as he slowly led her towards the cemetery. Barrett McDuff O'Brien had been a well-respected man throughout the region, and mourners had come from far and wide to bid farewell to the fine old gentleman.

Still, when Augusta arrived at the graveyard, she was amazed at the large crowd that had gathered and was touched by their presence. To honor her father, she kept her chin up and back straight, maintaining her poise as she stood steadfastly by his grave, while those in attendance stopped to give her their condolences, and with them, a mention of some special memory.

Reverend Hawkins delivered the eulogy and prayed over her father's grave. Once again she felt as if she were watching from afar. This was something that happened to other people; surely, this sad event had nothing at all to do with her. It couldn't be Papa's grave she was standing over. Words were spoken, songs were sung, but they floated past her like morning midst rising off a distant lake. Everything seemed so strange—yesterday this same preacher was congratulating her and now he was giving her his condolences. This man of God spoke of eternal glory, that being absent from the body was to be present with the Lord. Yes, she hoped that was true, the words were meant to comfort her, and in part they did, but they also angered her. For hadn't she begged God not to take her papa? Yet, when she had awoken that fateful morning, she found herself curled up on the floor beside his bed, still clutching his hand, a hand that had become cold and lifeless. God had stolen him away from her. One look into his pale face had told her that her papa was no longer residing in that body. Her father had done something he had promised he would never do—he had left her. That was the one thing Augusta had feared most, all through her life—and now it had happened. He had gone away to a place where she could not follow.

Never before had Augusta felt so completely alone! Her friends were all very kind, but they were not who she needed right now. And then there was Timothy! This man...this...husband she was connected to all the sudden. Wherever see turned, he was there, hovering close by, solicitous and sympathetic. Why didn't Timothy Grainger understand? He was an interloper, a greenhorn—he didn't belong! She resented the man's very presence; each act of kindness only served to un-nerve and irritate her.

Most of all, Augusta did not want to return to her father's house—*with Timothy*. She was even bold enough to ask Mrs. Drew and Emily if she could stay with either of them, almost begging them like a little girl. She had maintained such dignity and composure all through the service. But now that only her closest friends remained, she yielded to her anguish. Staring into the faces of the two women who were the closest to her in all the world, she pleaded, "Please don't make me go home with that man!"

Emily and Mrs. Drew pulled the girl into their arms and held her as she wept. However, when her tears subsided, their answers had not consoled their young friend. Mrs. Drew dabbed the tears from her own eyes and then Augusta's, and said softly, "Sweetheart, you are Missus Timothy Grainger now! You are a married woman and your place is with your husband. Especially while you are grieving...he will be a comfort to you...if you let him!"

Then Emily added, "Missus D's right! It's time ya go on back home. Yer grievin' fer yer pa and it's all right to have yerself a few good cries, but after awhile ya got to try to do yer best—and be a good wife. Okay, darlin'?"

Augusta frowned and turned away with a look of defeat. It broke Emily's heart to see her young friend so forsaken. Softly she whispered, "You listen to me—we all still love ya! And ya can—still come to visit us—any time ya like!"

A sudden idea came to Emily, so she quickly added, "Darlin'—ya need to—stay busy! Ride that ol' Quest a bunch! Get back into some kind of routine; if ya can't sleep then just get up and bake pies. The Dutch Oven will buy any pies Timothy don't eat!"

With that said, Emily gently pushed Augusta towards her husband. Timothy nodded his thanks to this insightful young redhead, then tenderly led his bewildered wife back to the home they now shared.

Chapter 10
Getting Acquainted

"Submit to one another out of reverence for Christ." Ephesians 5:21

While Timothy made himself comfortable in what had been her father's bedroom, Augusta all but barricaded herself in her small attic room. And for a girl who thrived on being out of doors, this self-imposed prison made her grief even harder to bear. All there was to do was stare out her small window and pace the floor. But there was no lovely view of flowers or landscape, and her little room wasn't even as large as Quest's box stall. Finally, in the dark hours before dawn, Augusta made herself a promise: *I am not going to spend one more miserable minute this way! I'm not afraid of that greenhorn—I have no need to hide. No more of this—I'll do what Emily said. I'll get back into a routine—I'll stay busy!*

The following morning, before the hallway clock had struck its fifth and final chime, Augusta had bolted from her bed. Before it could chime again, she had washed, dressed, cooked breakfast, and was quickly making her way to the livery. At first, the idea of cooking breakfast for Grainger galled her. But then she assured herself that cooking in the morning had always been part of her routine and she needed to fill her day with as many tasks as possible. Also, she knew that Emily and Mrs. D. would both chastise her if she didn't feed the man. Of course when she learned that Timothy was considerate enough to wash the dishes and clean the kitchen, she found a perverse pleasure in leaving a bigger and bigger mess each morning. After all...if she needed to stay busy...he might as well too!

Augusta's intent was not only to—stay busy—but to avoid her husband whenever possible. In the mornings she helped at the livery. The place had never been so clean, or the tack so well organized, and Quest's coat shone like polished ebony from all the extra grooming. Augusta's afternoons were spent with either Emily or Mrs. Drew. Still, when evening came, her friends were faithful to "shoo" her home to prepare dinner for her husband. But even though she cooked a dinner for two, she still stubbornly pretended that she ate alone. When Timothy tried to make conversation, Augusta would either leave her food untouched, which worried her young husband, or she would pick up her plate and take it upstairs to her room.

Weeks passed, and busy or not, both Timothy and Augusta were miserable. He longed to comfort his wife, and she longed to be comforted—but not by him! Augusta wanted her father back—and her husband gone!

For his part, Timothy had never prayed so hard in his life. The more aloof his wife became—the more determined he was to win her. Sometimes, the only thing he knew for certain was that he would never leave her, no matter how high she built the walls around her heart. Finally, he decided patience might not be a virtue after all; they couldn't go on like this—it was time he pushed back.

⚜

Augusta skipped the shovel over the ground in one quick motion. As she dumped the contents in the wheel barrel, a tall shadow fell over her. She felt the familiar flutter in her stomach, then spun around to find her young husband, watching her. At least, he didn't look quite so much the Boston dude; he wore a white shirt and gray trousers, with tall black boots and a straw hat. And yet there was still something rakish about the man and his presence unnerved her. Augusta frowned at him then returned to her work.

"I'm here to collect that promise you owe me," he said coolly.

Augusta glanced back over her shoulder, "I've made no promises."

Timothy's eyebrows lifted; he thought to remind her of their wedding vows, but instead he said: "Actually, it's more a promise your father made me—on your behalf. He said you'd help me get ready for the wagon train. You know…help me choose the stock, buy harness, and supplies—all of it!"

With her hands on her hips she muttered sarcastically, "You're an intelligent man; you bluffed your way into Quest's good graces. I'm sure you can manage well enough—you don't need me."

Timothy put one boot on the lower rail and leaned over the top of the fence.

"I wasn't bluffing with Quest," he said earnestly. "He just knew he could trust me and so can you!"

"You bribed him with an apple!" she hissed.

Timothy chuckled. "I shared my apple. He and I get along because we both love the same things!"

Augusta gave her husband a wary look. "What things?" she scoffed.

Timothy bent forward, his eyes locking with Augusta's golden gaze, and said slowly: "Oh…apples…I guess…" Looking down, he added softly, "among other things!"

Timothy's warm expression made Augusta uncomfortable; quickly she changed the subject.

"Actually—we do need to talk. I'd like to ask you something."

Timothy's face turned serious. "You can ask me anything, Augusta."

Defiantly, Augusta blurted out, "Can Christians lie?" Then in a lower voice she added, "Papa…said you were a Christian."

Though Timothy had hoped to share his faith, her question and the anger he heard in her voice worried him. Hesitating a moment he said, "Well…God wants us to tell the truth, but we can choose to lie. He gives us all free will, but lying grieves God and hurts my conscience—so I always try to be truthful."

Just then, the old mare Kippy sauntered up to Augusta and nudged her hand. Absent-mindedly, she scratched the mare's soft ears while she glared up at Timothy.

"All right—so be truthful with me now!" she demanded. "In fact let's both tell the truth! Admit that you're really here for Quest." She dared, "Then I can tell you, that you can't have him. And if I hear one more time that you fell in love with my picture…I…I think I'll be sick."

"That's ridiculous," Timothy groaned. "You think I married you for your horse?"

"Don't you dare talk down to me!" she ordered. "I'm not as gullible as you seem to think."

"Augusta!" Timothy sighed. "You must believe me when I…"

"No!" She held her hand up to stop him. "I recognize the heavy hand of Bull O'Brien when I see it. And maybe you did think you were doing an old friend a favor by marrying his poor little daughter. It wasn't a bad bargain. You were getting a fine stallion and a young girl with lots of work in her. It makes sense, I suppose."

Timothy shook his head. "No! Nothing you've said makes sense! But I understand—you're upset—you're grieving."

Augusta's eyes blazed with golden flames as she hissed, "I don't want your understanding or your pity. I want you to undo this mess. You're a lawyer—surely you can fix this mistake!"

At the start Timothy took any conversation with his bride as a good thing. Even though she wasn't making any sense, she still had a right to vent her frustrations. He even reasoned that being a victim of her anger was better than being a victim her silence. And, she was awfully pretty like this, so alive, so radiant, with eyes flashing and cheeks flushed. But when she called their marriage a mess? It shocked him just how much it had hurt.

"Mess?" Timothy questioned. "This marriage is certainly not yet what it should be...but...it's not a mess nor was it a mistake."

Suddenly, resenting all the barriers between them, Timothy gripped the top rail of the fence and vaulted over it. He wished only to be a little closer to her—to somehow—make her see his sincerity. But when she stepped back with fear in her eyes, he kept his distance. Then he shrugged and muttered sadly, "Well, at least I know why you see me as the enemy."

The two were silent for a long while. Timothy pondered all he knew of Augusta along with what she had just told him. How was he going to make her see that she had been wrong about him and her conclusions? Keeping his voice gentle he said, "Typically, I do not like to mention this, but my brother and I are both wealthy men. Quest is magnificent, but then so are a good many other stallions. Augusta, we could easily afford to buy fifty high-quality stallions that would suit the needs of the ranch, and not think about it twice. And the ranch has an excellent cook—as well as a number of strong men that do the work. So, please understand that I did not marry you for Quest or because you are young and strong!"

Augusta raised her head defiantly, "There are precious few stallions like Quest—and you had to marry me for a reason, and I'm just a plain girl. I don't understand!"

Timothy smiled, "You've never been plain to me, Augusta!"

When she rolled her eyes at him, Timothy blew out a breath and tried again to explain. "Your father and I never discussed Quest and the Bar 61, until after I had asked to court you! And it wasn't just the picture. It was also all the other things I was learning about you. And, yes, your being accomplished in a number of ways was appealing to me."

Augusta continued to stroke the old mare's back, all the while frowning and shaking her head.

"Listen to me." Timothy begged, "God takes first priority in my life. But after God, the woman I choose to be my life-long companion is of the utmost importance. Marriage is sacred to me, and quite frankly a blessing I thought I'd never have. It may sound odd, but when I saw your picture, I felt that God was telling me that woman was to be my Eve. And when you greeted me that first day, that same feeling hit me again, and I think...I think you felt it too. Something special happened between us that night."

Timothy smiled gently when Augusta dared a quick glance into his face.

"It wasn't fair that your wedding day was forced upon you—I understand that. But that doesn't make our marriage a mess or a mistake. I'll never forget how proud I was when I looked up and saw you coming down those steps. You were exhausted, not to mention scared and *angry*. But despite it all, you were so beautiful, so full of grace and courage. I felt humbled to be marrying a woman like you!"

Augusta worried her lower lip, her heart beat wildly in her chest, and she was confused all over again. All her reasoning as to why this man wanted to marry her didn't seem so logical any more.

They both stood silent, running their hands down opposite sides of Kippy's back. The old mare stood perfectly still, enjoying the attention and perhaps—knowing that she was needed. When Timothy's fingers accidently brushed over Augusta's, she jumped back, feeling suddenly like she'd swallowed a hot coal.

Timothy smiled and his look was heartbreakingly tender when he said gently, "The simple *truth* is, I am in love with you! And now that I've married the woman of my choice, all I want to do is make you happy...and for us to be together. Ah, let's go west Augusta—let's help my brother run our horse and cattle ranch. Tytus may have given up on marriage but...I never will!"

When Augusta suddenly looked trapped and miserable he softened, saying, "You would love living on the ranch. But if you refuse to go with me, then we'll just..."

Augusta quickly brightened then finished his sentence, "We'll just annul the marriage, and I will stay here while you go west alone."

Timothy let out a sigh. "No!" he insisted. "If you want—we'll stay here—but as husband and wife. You want me to tell you the truth? My brother and I have dreamed since we were ten years old of running a big ranch together. But you're more important. If you want to stay, we'll stay."

Timothy ran his large hand threw his thick blonde hair then straightened and said, "You don't have long to decide though. Doctor Mitchell's new assistant will be moving into the house come spring. If we don't go west, we'll have no place to live! I'll try to find a place close to town, so you can give riding lessons on Saturdays. And I can always put out my shingle and practice law."

Augusta hadn't expected this. "What about your dream to be with your brother?"

"I would love for that to happen!" Timothy puffed out a weary sigh then continued, "But my dreams are no more important than your happiness!"

The man softened his stance and leaned close to her, and in almost a whisper he said, "I hate the way things have turned out—my plan was to court you, sweep you off your feet!"

Just then his blue eyes sparkled, and he gave her that impish grin that made butterflies dance across her skin.

"Trust," he went on to say, "is a difficult thing for one person to give to another, and that's what I'm asking from you."

When Augusta looked down, Timothy boldly lifted her chin. "Please hear me!" he begged. "I will be your husband until death parts us. Whether or not… you ever choose to be my wife."

Timothy's eyes were as dark as sapphire, and they spoke to her young heart of his deep sincerity.

"Please," he whispered, "All I'm asking of you…is to give us a chance!"

Augusta couldn't speak; finally, the truth seemed all too clear, Miss A.C. O'Brien had needed someone to blame for her heartbreak and loss. And there stood Timothy Grainger, an easy scapegoat. After all the man had come to change her life! To move her away from all her friends. And yet, Augusta reasoned, wasn't change the rite of passage for most girls as they became women? After all he was only asking for a chance."

Slowly, Augusta gazed up at this tall husband of hers. She had tried to ignore his handsome looks and gentle ways, his patience, and even his sense of humor. She had, in fact, ignored everything that was good about Timothy Grainger. Still, she was not ready to admit defeat. Begrudgingly, she muttered, "I suppose it wouldn't hurt to get to know you…a little better…before I make up my mind."

Then, raising one eyebrow, she took a long look at the man standing before her, "Well, at least you didn't wear your *derby hat* today! But tell me now, just how *green* are you?"

Timothy's face lit up. He didn't mind her sarcasm; she was going to give him a fighting chance!

"Green as in 'greenhorn'?" he asked with a shrug. "I don't think of myself that way, but you're the expert. I could be a downright menace to the town, if someone doesn't take me in hand and teach me what I need to know! Besides," he added, "it's boring around here. We'll stay if you want Augusta but just think about going west!" His voice became animated when he added, "Just imagine, a trek across open prairie would be akin to a voyage across the sea! And I think a bit of adventure, right about now, might do us both a world of good!"

Augusta wasn't ready to agree with Timothy on anything, but when she thought of it, a bit of adventure did sound good. However, what she said to the man was... "All right, we'll start with a riding lesson—and it begins right now."

Grabbing a halter, she fastened it around Kippy's head, and nodding towards the horse, she said cynically, "Lesson number one:

THIS—IS—A—HORSE".

Chapter 11
The Way

"Jesus said, I am the way, the truth, and the life: no man comes to the Father, but by me." John 14:6

The following weeks were so much improved that it felt like a holiday to Timothy. Augusta still grieved for her father, but it no longer consumed her every thought, nor did he hear her crying herself to sleep at night. And though his wife still had not accepted their marriage, he took hope in the fact that she was at least trying to get to know him.

Things between them were at their very best when they were on horseback. When they were out on a ride together, Augusta was truly the A.C. O'Brien her father had described in his letters! She was confident, capable, bright, and beautiful!

As for Augusta, the problem was that while she stubbornly fought to maintain the wall she'd built between herself and her husband, it was becoming more and more difficult, for every day she realized that the man was simply too fine to ignore. He was too handsome, too amusing, too kind—she couldn't help but enjoy the time they spent together.

So, while Augusta struggled to kept their relationship from progressing to that of husband and wife, Timothy remained undaunted; daily, he wore away at her defenses. He even managed to find dozens of subtle ways to court his wife. In the morning she would open her door to find a bouquet of flowers awaiting her and another on the kitchen table. Whenever they had a long day of riding he would buy their dinner at the Dutch Oven. One morning Augusta walked into the tack room to find that Timothy had polished her saddle and bridle, and purchased a fine new saddle blanket she had been admiring from the general store.

Little by little the young bride's barricades were being worn away. As the days grew colder, Timothy kept Augusta from escaping to her attic room by luring her to sit with him by the fire, keeping her spellbound with stories about interesting places he had been to and people he had met. Impressing her greatly one evening, as he humbly admitted to having hosted a party for Abe and Mary Lincoln in his home when the man had been running for president! Each evening seemed to slip by so quickly as they talked, finding they agreed on many things. Augusta's favorite topic was always horses—Morgan horses, more specifically, but also Arabians. Her interest was piqued when Timothy read her one of his brother's letters telling of the spotted Appaloosas, bred by the Indians, and his desire to purchase some Arabians for the ranch.

One fall evening after the two had enjoyed a particularly long ride, they sat lazily by the fire in the parlor, enjoying slices of Augusta's luscious cherry pie. The ruby-red filling was encased in a golden, sugary crust that was so delicately crisp and buttery that the cook's cheeks were blushing nearly as red as the cherries by the time Timothy finished his outlandish praises. They both chuckled over his foolishness, then settled back to savor their dessert, all the while sipping from steaming mugs of hot coffee swirling with fresh cream.

Augusta leaned back in her chair and sighed, feeling better than she had in months. It had been a lovely long day in the saddle, topped off by a quiet and pleasant evening. Her thoughts drifted idly by when Timothy excused himself, but she stiffened noticeably when he came back carrying his Bible. In spite of what she'd promised her father, she really did not want to know God any better just now. Hadn't she prayed to God, with all the sincerity she possessed, begging Him to save her father? And then, hadn't she awakened to an empty shell where once her dear papa had been? No, she didn't care to know God any better—not now—maybe never.

Timothy was saddened by Augusta's hardened countenance but not perturbed, he smiled patiently, as he sat down beside her and said softly,

"Like you, I've loved horses all my life, but when I was a sickly, city boy," he added, giving Augusta a slight grin, "my health wouldn't allow me to do much about it. So, I'd look out my window and watch all the horses going by. Believe it or not, Boston has some fine, high-stepping animals! One day I began to wonder what, if anything, God's word said about the horse. This morning my Bible fell open to the page where I'd written down some verses, and I thought I'd share them with you."

Augusta shrugged her shoulders and nodded. "All right," she said blandly.

Timothy ignored her obvious lack of interest and began fanning through the pages. "Well now, here is one I thought you would find interesting. This is in First Kings: 'And Solomon had forty thousand stalls of horses for his chariots, and twelve thousand horsemen.'"

Augusta pondered that for a moment then smiled. "Timothy," she asked skeptically, "Do you realize—that figures out to be about three and one-third horse for every man? Tell me—" she teased, "exactly where do you put the saddle on a third of a horse?"

Timothy narrowed his eyes and frowned. "I won't respond to your poor jest. But...you—uh, you figured that awfully fast. Is that right? You hardly even took time to calculate it!"

"I've always liked figures and sums," she said with a shrug, "and Papa hated bookkeeping...so...." Then she added wistfully, "It was a waste of time for me to learn to run a business and keep the books."

"Learning is never a waste of time!" Timothy chided, then added excitedly, "And if we go west, my brother would love having your help! The Bar 61 has extensive contracts with the U.S. Army, not only for cavalry mounts but beef cattle as well. Ty hates the hours he spends with his ledgers. None of your many talents need go to waste, not in training horses or keeping books."

Timothy grimaced slightly and then added, "Of course, that is, *if* we end up going west! By the way that decision needs to be made soon. In the meantime I have been looking for a place. Haven't found anything near town. I've even offered to buy back the livery and the house but no one wants to sell."

Augusta didn't know what to say; she had been avoiding talk of her going west and avoided the idea that she was now tied to this man and to his future. Wanting to change the subject, she asked, "Did...um... you find anything else about horses in your book?"

Timothy smiled over her sudden desire to hear scripture, as opposed to talking of their future together.

"Yes, actually," he said eagerly. "I'll read you my favorite; it's where God is speaking to a man named Job. Now, Job was an honorable man, who had always been obedient to God but suddenly he was beset by hard times. Finally, one day he asked God the question many of us ask at one time or another—why me? God answers Job by reminding him who is in charge of the universe. This is what He said to Job:

"Did you give the horse his strength or clothe his neck with a flowing mane? Do you make him leap like a locust, striking terror with his proud snorting? He paws fiercely, rejoicing in his strength, and charges into the fray. He laughs at fear, afraid of nothing;

he does not shy away from the sword. The quiver rattles against his side along with the flashing spear and lance. In frenzied excitement he eats up the ground; he cannot stand still when the trumpet sounds."

Timothy read the words with passion in his voice then he closed the Bible and said, "I like those verses because they remind me to walk humbly before God and to value the magnificence of His creation! And to remember that God is in control, and when I don't understand something, to know that—He does—and that's all that matters."

Augusta stared into the fire a moment then said, "Papa told me that he'd spent the last few decades of his life angry at God." She looked up at Timothy and asked, "What about you? You've been ill most of your life and separated from your father and brother. Why do you believe in a God that would allow illness and heartbreak?"

Timothy turned to the woman he was falling more in love with every day, silently pleading for God to give him the right words. He so wanted her to understand, and to share his faith.

"Augusta," he began slowly, "the Christian life isn't about God providing happy endings. It's about God and the devil waging war over who wins our souls, for now and for eternity. But because God created us with 'free will' we get a say in who wins the battle!"

Augusta pondered his words. "It's more than that for you, though—isn't it? You seem to have a closeness with this God of yours."

A thoughtful expression crossed his face. "That's true now—but it wasn't always that way. Tytus and I always thought of ourselves as two halves of the same person; we couldn't believe our parents would separate us. And for a time we were both filled with a childish rage—against them—and at God!"

Augusta nodded; now that was something she could understand—rage against God.

"So, how did you ever get over it?" she asked.

Timothy leaned his head back and smiled. "God placed two special people into our lives; their names were Joseph and Natty May!"

"And who were they?" she asked.

"They were slaves, Augusta—Grainger property," he said stiffly.

Timothy took in the stunned look on Augusta's face and explained: "Natty May was the cook and Joseph, her husband, was a groomsmen and trainer for our stables. I don't honestly know what would have become of my brother and me if it weren't for those two. They were more like parents to us than our own father and mother. They loved us, and were constantly telling us that God loved us even more!"

With a frown Augusta muttered, "It's hard to believe in a loving God when bad things happen."

Timothy nodded his understanding. "That's true," he said gently, "and I stayed angry for a long time, then finally—I saw what folly my anger was, and so did your father there at the end. We need to remember that God sees around every corner and from a perspective we can't even imagine. Yes, bad things happen and always will, because we live in a sinful world where sinful people have free will. That combination leads to chaos and heartbreak. But when we trust in God, He can bring good out of evil, joy out of heartbreak, order out of chaos, and love out of hate."

Augusta was still perplexed. Slowly, she shook her head and said softly, "What you're saying is that He doesn't take away the problems but instead sees us through them? Still, even that seems a bit fanciful—like a—"

"A story?" Timothy asked.

When Augusta shrugged, he nodded and said, "Well, you're right. The Bible is a book of stories. But—the stories happen to be true! The Bible contains the account of how the Creator of the universe chose to be loyal to the mankind he created, even though mankind chose to be disloyal to Him. It's a story of how the very first man and woman on earth sinned by choosing to disobey God, and in so doing they destined all mankind to eternal death and separation from our Creator! But even though God can't live in harmony with sinners, He loved his creation too much to spend eternity without us. So, He provided a way to mend our broken relationship!"

Puzzled, Augusta asked: "If we're all sinners and God **can't** live with sinners, then what could He do?"

Timothy turned to her and said earnestly, "It took the greatest sacrifice of all time! The Bible says: 'For God so loved the world, that He gave His only begotten son, that whoever believes in Him should not perish but have everlasting life.' You see, Augusta, God rescued us from our own disobedience by sending to earth His obedient, sinless Son. Jesus was both God and man and He had two missions to complete: First to live as a man in perfect obedience to God; and second, since the penalty for sin is death, He had to willingly die and take onto Himself the punishment for the sins of all who would believe. He was beaten and crucified for us! You see, all of mankind is under the death penalty for sinning against God. The sentence is to be carried out the moment our earthly bodies die, then our souls will serve out an eternal prison term in hell! But God made it so that all the sins of every believer could be placed upon Jesus Christ when He died on the cross. He suffered not only a physical death but the eternal death and hell for all of us! All of us who would believe, that is!"

Augusta had never heard this before; it was a lot to fathom, but it touched someplace deep within her.

"It is a story, Augusta." he continued gently, "a profound story, but a very simple one. The only thing Jesus asks of us is to believe, confess our sins and ask Him to forgive us. He waits patiently for us to invite Him into our hearts and make Him the Lord of our lives—that is what makes a person a Christian!

Augusta shuddered then she wrapped her arms around herself as if to ward off a sudden chill.

"I'm confused though—how can you pray to someone who is dead?" she asked.

"Because the story doesn't end at The Cross!" Timothy smiled. "Jesus suffered death, hell, and the grave for three days. And on the third day He conquered death and He came back to life. Jesus is alive right now, and He longs for each of us to invite Him into our lives!"

Timothy touched Augusta's hand gently and said, "Now that you know the way, it's up to you to choose. Your father chose your husband, Augusta, but only you can choose your God."

Augusta's eyes were glassy when she asked softly, "And that's the way? Papa told me to ask you."

Timothy nodded then quoted, *"Jesus said, 'I am the way, the truth, and the life: no man comes to the Father, but by me.'* Augusta ... " he whispered gently, "you could pray right now and ask Jesus to come into your heart! Would you like to do that?"

Augusta felt like a tug of war was raging inside her heart. Desperate to escape the battle inside her she bounded to her feet and snapped out her answer.

"No! No, I'm sorry ... but I'm...just not ready."

She felt so strange; it was as if she could feel the tender eyes of God himself watching her, gently beckoning to her. The uneasiness grew until she couldn't stand to be in that room another minute.

Heading for the door, she muttered something about wanting to go for a walk. When she turned to see the saddened look on Timothy's face, Augusta lightened her tone and spoke softly. "Listen, you've given me a lot to think about—and I will—in the meantime, will you walk with me?"

Timothy understood her confusion, and was heartened by the invitation, so with a smile he said: "It is a very beautiful night, and…I don't think I'd mind…being your escort."

As they stepped outside Timothy offered his arm and was pleased, and a little surprised, when she took it. The night air was crisp and clean, and they filled their lungs, while drinking in the beauty of the evening. Augusta couldn't help but think of how big God must be as she gazed up at the vast canopy above them. She felt so small and insignificant compared to the endless sky, bejeweled with a million sparkling stars, and a dazzling full moon. How could it be, she wondered.

I can believe a mighty Creator made all of this. It's too perfect to be otherwise. But how could such a mighty God want to lower himself to care about someone like me?

A cool breeze teased the curls that framed Augusta's face as she stared up to enjoy the night sky.

"It takes my breath away!" she sighed, nearly tipping over backwards as she gazed up at the heavens.

"Easy now—you keep doing that and you'll wind up on your backside," he teased.

Then Timothy gently put his arm around her shoulders to steady her, and said, "I've got you now! Go ahead—star-gaze to your heart's content."

Augusta chuckled then leaned her head back; the light touch of Timothy's arm around her and the nearness of him was all it took to quicken her heartbeat. Normally, she'd have moved away from him but she didn't want to hurt his feelings—she'd been rude enough. At least that was what she told herself.

As they slowly returned to the house Timothy took fleeting glimpses of his pretty young wife. She seemed even more lovely in the moonlight; it cast a soft glow over her smooth skin, and whenever she looked up at him, her golden eyes sparkled like the stars overhead. He was making progress with his reluctant bride. And yet he found himself longing for more, and was having to remind himself what a patient man he had always been. They'd been married for nearly two months and every day he lost a little more of his heart to a woman who continued to keep him at arm's length.

As they reached their front porch, Augusta sat down on the top step and pointed to one specific star. "That's my favorite—that one right there by the moon. It shines the brightest!" she added dreamily.

Timothy gazed down on his enchanting young wife; she was at times so stubborn and unyielding and at other times so soft and womanly, and then like tonight, so like a little girl—innocent and guileless.

"I believe that's Venus!" he said, his voice low. "When I was in New York, I found a book that is all about stars and constellations. If you like...we can bring it out here tomorrow night?"

"Yes—I'd like that," Augusta agreed, then said: "So, now I know that you've been to New York. And you told me you have also been to Washington and Georgia and Virginia and Maine and ... umm...Connecticut? You said you've been there too, right?"

"Yes ... " Timothy said with a slight chuckle. Keeping one foot on the ground, he easily stretched his long leg and settled the other foot onto the top step of the porch next to Augusta. Then leaning towards her he said, "I am not what you'd call...well-traveled," adding humbly, "just been up and down the eastern coast." Then, in that relaxed way of his, he said: "My greatest adventure has been coming here to find you!"

Augusta's heart caught in her throat. She did not want to talk about their relationship, or what it might mean for her future; she preferred trivial subjects. Pretending a calm she didn't feel, she suggested wistfully, "I know Timothy— let's play the 'What If Game'!"

Remembering the idle game she and her father used to play on nights like this, and without waiting for his reply, she asked the question her father always began with: "What if—you were the master of your destiny and could have anything in the world exactly the way you wanted it! What would your life be like—right this minute?"

Augusta hadn't looked at Timothy while she asked her question, but stared at the stars, with a bright twinkle in her eyes, waiting for the man's wonderful imagination to spin out some fanciful yarn. But when silence followed, she looked up at him, and found him gazing down at her with such tenderness and longing that heat rose to her cheeks and her heart quickened.

"Timothy?" she said, with a shrug. "It's just a game ... "

The man nodded slowly and gave her an understanding smile. Then he leaned close and whispered, "I know ... " His voice was husky and very controlled when he added, "but Augusta, I've told you before, I really do try to be an honest man and you're not ready to hear my answer, not to a question like **that!**"

At Augusta's bewildered expression, Timothy gave her a wink and said: "Goodnight, my beauty, I'll pray that you sleep well—and that all your dreams are sweet!"

Augusta said nothing as Timothy went into the house. And yet, her heart seemed to keep rhythm with his footsteps as they echoed down the hallway. Finally, he stopped outside his bedroom door. Augusta held her breath, for there was a long silence, as if he might be thinking of returning to her. Then she heard him step inside and quietly close the door.

Chapter 12
Dinner at the Dutch Oven

"You have put gladness in my heart." Psalm 4:7

"All right Max, you scoundrel—" Timothy chuckled. "I'll scratch your ears before I go."

The man could barely get the bridle off the tall buckskin, for the horse was playfully pressing his large head against his chest.

Watching their antics, Augusta smiled and leaned against the fence, her arms lazily folded over the top rail, her chin resting on her arms. "You love every minute of this—don't you?" she asked softly. "Working with the horses, I mean?"

Timothy grinned, his blue eyes twinkling. It had been another long day in the saddle. The couple had finished training Max and Molly to the harness, then they worked on breaking the matching buckskins to the saddle as well. And although Augusta was loath to admit it, she and Timothy made a good team. Greenhorn or not, he was wonderful with the animals; he had a light hand and good instincts.

"I like it!" the man admitted. "My friends would laugh, I'm tired and dirty—and I—feel wonderful! Is that crazy?"

Augusta laughed and slapped the dust from her riding skirt. "Yes—but I know exactly what you mean." With a wistful look she added, "Papa used to call it 'a worthwhile weary'. It's a deep contentment that comes after a long day in the saddle, when you feel like you've accomplished good things! You're filthy and you ache all over. But—somehow it's a good ache!"

Timothy smiled his agreement. "A worthwhile weary? I like that!"

"I still can't believe how well you're doing." Then impishly, she added: "For a city boy, that is."

"Well—it's probably because this city boy happens to have a good teacher."

"Nope, that's not it." She said humbly, "I tease you about being a green-horn but actually you have an excellent way with animals. You have a gentle touch…and…the horses respond to it."

Her tender confession was eclipsed when Augusta's stomach growled loudly, causing her to blush then giggle. "Excuse me, that wasn't very lady-like—was it? I can't even imagine what the proper ladies of Boston do with the likes of me?"

With arms akimbo, Timothy took a long slow appraisal of his wife, causing her blush to deepen.

"In my opinion," he said grinning broadly, "there is not one lady of Boston that can hold a candle to you!"

Praise always seemed to fluster Augusta so Timothy took pity on his blushing bride and quickly added, "Besides, my stomach has been growling like a grizzly bear for the past hour!" Then with a mournful look he added, "And—you've been working me so hard I scarcely throw a shadow anymore."

Augusta rolled her eyes and gave a light chuckle. "Well, sounds like we better go feed you!"

Fastening the latch on the corral gate, she began describing that day's special at the Dutch Oven. "Emily said they'd be serving venison stew, cornbread, and apple pie! Will that suit you?"

Timothy patted his stomach, as they headed for the café. "Right down to the ground!" he groaned. "I hope they've got plenty. I want three bowls of stew, a pan of cornbread, and one whole pie all to myself! I swear my appetite has doubled since I left Boston."

Augusta smiled at Timothy's enthusiasm, then took an appraising side-long glance at the man walking beside her. The sleeves of his white shirt were rolled up high on his arms, showing bronze skin and tight muscle; his long legs were clad in khaki pants and knee-high brown leather boots. His tanned face made his eyes more penetrating and all the bluer. She watched as he lifted his straw hat and finger-combed his thick wheat-colored hair. All in all, Timothy Grainger was a very handsome and compelling man!

When Timothy caught Augusta staring at him, he flashed her a white smile and winked, only to have Augusta blush and quickly turn away. He wished he knew what his bride had been thinking. He prized these new relaxed moments they shared; the teasing and banter had been more than enjoyable. Still, he wanted to learn everything he could about this woman. As they strolled towards the place that had been such a big part of her life, he said, "I've always been intrigued by the way your father went about your education. Having you work at the café to learn to cook, then assist Missus Drew so you could learn to sew and garden. Actually from what I gather, your days spent with Amelia Drew were as beneficial to you as attending an eastern finishing school."

"Well—that's Papa for you! He always had his own way of doing things. Still, even though I worked hard, all my teachers were very good to me, and I owe each of them a great deal. A side benefit to working at the café was that you get to learn a lot about people! You know... folks come into a café...for more than food...sometimes they're more lonely than hungry!"

Timothy smiled, his wife had a tender heart, then he laughed when Augusta grimaced and made a face.

"You know what the worse thing was about working at the café? Hands down—*peeling onions*!"

They both chuckled as they entered the café and seated themselves at their favorite table. Glancing around, Timothy frowned. "Speaking of onions—that scent is pretty strong right now. I don't see Emily or Wes. Wasn't a new girl supposed to start helping out today?"

Augusta gave him a knowing smile. "Yes—poor thing," she said, with a shudder. "I'm sure that's why the place smells like an onion wharf."

When Timothy looked confused Augusta whispered in a conspiratorial voice, "You can always spot a new worker when they serve your dinner with red-rimmed eyes."

Timothy frowned. "Are the Tylane's that hard on their help?"

"No!" Augusta giggled. "Well, yes in a way—you see *onion duty* is serious business as far as Wes is concerned. If the new girl doesn't quit after cutting onions all day, he figures she'll stick around long enough to teach her the more important things. Like how to fry up the perfect steak. And if she pleases Wes—then and only then—will Emily teach her how to bake a pie. The Dutch Oven is famous for perfect steaks and great pies!"

Timothy laughed. "You must have passed the onion test—because your steaks melt in my mouth. And your pies? Not even Natty May could bake a better pie!"

Augusta's heart gave a little flip. She didn't know why his praises should affect her so, but they did!

A moment later Wes brought them that day's special, and Timothy bowed his head and thanked the Lord for the food and for the pleasant day spent together. She was used to it, but lately when he prayed she felt God watching her—beckoning to her. His eyes seemed sad, maybe because, she still hadn't trusted him.

They enjoyed a comfortable silence while they ate, then Augusta touched the napkin to her lips. "I meant what I said, about you and the horses! *You* shouldn't have any trouble on the trail!"

Timothy set his fork down and nodded, trying not to show the pain over the meaning of her words. *He* wouldn't have any trouble on the trail, not **they** wouldn't have any trouble.

How can she still be expecting—or even hoping that I'll forget my vows and go west without her?

Augusta took a sip of coffee while she contemplated what Timothy needed to know next. "You really should learn about guns! That's one thing Papa never taught me, but Wes could teach you!"

Augusta thought for a moment then added, "Actually, I want to learn too! No matter where I end up living—I should know how to protect myself."

There she goes again, he thought, alluding to the idea that our lives are going in separate directions.

Clearing his throat Timothy spoke up, "Augusta, we won't be needing Wes. I've purchased all the weaponry and ammunition required by the wagon master and more, in fact. And you're right—you should learn too!"

With a roguish grin he added, "But I'll be the instructor this time—been looking forward to it."

Augusta blushed at the look the man was giving her but she felt skeptical about what he was claiming.

Although he'd proved to be quite capable in everything he'd tried so far, guns were something else.

"Timothy, you don't even carry a gun. They're dangerous, and we need someone with real experience."

The man responded to her words with one raised eyebrow. "Augusta, I am proficient with every weapon I brought!"

When she gave him a skeptical look, Timothy boldly gazed back at her, his blue eyes sparkling. "Why don't we settle this tomorrow?" he challenged. "We'll go out to that steep ravine by the creek. We'll set up a few targets—take a few shots." Grinning impishly he added, "It's beautiful there! We'll pack a picnic lunch and make a day of it!"

Augusta worried her lip; she didn't quite like the sparkle in Timothy's eye. They had been sharing meals and working together. But this sounded too much like a romantic outing—and she wasn't sure if that was such a good idea.

When they walked into the kitchen to tell the Tylane's goodnight, the place looked as if a bomb of dirty dishes had just exploded! Emily looked exhausted but she smiled as she called over her shoulder,

"Goodnight, you two! Will we see ya tomorrow?"

"Where is Hazel?" Augusta asked. "I thought she would be in here helping you. Was it the onions?"

"Well—" Emily sighed. "Guess the answer to that is, yes and no; she was here most of the day. Doing real good too! Course this being her first day—Wes had her on onion duty."

Augusta couldn't help but glance up at Timothy—they shared a sly smile before she asked, "Was it too much for her? Did Wes fire her? Did she quit?"

Emily wiped her brow with the back of her sleeve. "No ma'am, that little gal's a hard worker. Never complained or fussed but by the time she finished cuttin' up a mountain of onions, she was near blind with tears, on that very last onion—wouldn't ya know—she cut right into her finger! Had to send her off to docs to get stitched up. I told her to go on home and come back in the mornin'. I think she'll work out fine."

The weary redhead tried to sound optimistic as her blue eyes gazed around the kitchen overrun with dirty dishes, pots, and pans. Again, she wiped her brow with the back of her hand and groaned, "Think I fed the whole town today. But I ain't complainin'—our cash box got fed today too, ya know!"

Emily gave a half-hearted chuckle and turned back to the dish water.

The couple exchanged another glance—then quietly Timothy smiled and said in Augusta's ear, "I'll go help Wes clean up in the dining room. When we're finished, we'll come help in here."

Augusta mouthed a silent *thank you*, then began rolling up her sleeves as she walked towards the steaming water on the stove. Emily started to frown at Augusta then an instant later she sighed, "Oh darlin', I'd say I don't need yer help! But ya know how I hate to lie!"

Augusta looked her friend over as she clucked her tongue like a mother hen. "Emily, your ankles look like tree stumps. I bet you haven't been off those feet all day!"

Still shaking her head Augusta guided her friend to a chair by the work table. "You sit here, I'll do the washing…while you dry…all right?"

Emily lifted her skirts, grimacing at her swollen legs while Augusta began dumping handfuls of flatware into the wash pan, then poured steaming hot water over them.

The redhead let out a loud yawn, and then smiling, she propped her feet up on the another chair. "Ya know…I've always liked you…Augusta Colleen. But never so much as I do right now!"

Augusta smiled as she dropped handfuls of clean forks into Emily's dish towel. The older woman gave each utensil a cursory swipe before tossing it into the box marked FORX.

"Hey darlin'," Emily asked. "Ya know we haven't had us a good talk in ages. So, tell me, hon', how's married life?"

Augusta frowned and kept scrubbing. "I don't know," she shrugged. "I suppose it's fine. Not much different than living with Papa—I guess."

Emily laid her dish towel down and gave Augusta a puzzled look. "I hope to shout! Don't tell me ya still haven't noticed what a fine hunk a' manhood yer married to?" The redhead glanced over her shoulder adding, "Now don't ya dare tell Wes I said that—I think he's pretty fine himself, ya know!"

Augusta smiled, then added coolly, "I guess Timothy's handsome; he has been very nice to me."

Though she wouldn't have told Emily, she often thought Timothy was too good looking; it disturbed her, somehow. And—it was in the man's nature to be kind; she hadn't even had to ask him to help Wes.

Augusta set a tray of glasses down before Emily to dry, then she noticed the puddles on the floor.

"Now don't worry about this—I'll mop up before I go!"

"I'll let ya!" Emily said with a weary chuckle then added seriously, "and dinner's on the house!"

"We'll take it!" Augusta said with a tired giggle of her own. Concentrating on scrubbing an especially sticky plate, she said slowly, "Emily—I'm still having nightmares. It's embarrassing, because I cry out in my sleep, and Timothy comes right into my room and wakes me up. I know he should not see me

82

in my nightgown but he just barges in and I don't know what to do. I'm glad he wakes me up! But then, there he is, *standing over me!* It's humiliating, and I don't know how to stop it."

Augusta was surprised when a frowning Emily was suddenly standing beside her—with arms akimbo.

"Did I hear right?" Emily huffed. "That Timothy comes into YER room when ya have a nightmare?"

"Yes! Isn't it awful? He marches in as bold as brass. I know he just means to help—but ... "

Augusta stopped short, her eyebrows knit in confusion when Emily turned her around to face her.

"Augusta, my sweet," she said gently, "I know ya weren't prepared fer all the blows life has dealt ya lately. And I know yer young—but ya ain't that young! Timothy is yer husband, and husband's sleep in the same room and in the same bed, I might add, as their wives! That's marriage! I know he said he'd be patient, but my goodness, girl! It's time ya let this marriage begin for real! Okay, darlin'?"

Augusta frowned and pushed her friend away while her eyes sparkled with frustrated tears. "Emily! I didn't know what Timothy meant when he talked about waiting. And I don't know...what you mean about letting the marriage begin? My parents never shared a room. All I know of men is what Papa and Missus Drew taught me. To always be a proper lady around them and never ever let them dally with you! *I never was even quite sure what 'dally' meant.* But Missus Drew always said men should never see a lady's unmentionables. When we hung them up to dry, she made me hide them behind the sheets. So, if a man shouldn't see undergarments hanging on a line—then he surely shouldn't see them on you! And if that is true, then a man should not be standing in your bedroom or sleeping in your bed! I'm just doing what Papa and Missus Drew taught me!"

Feeling angry and embarrassed, she turned her crimson face back to the task of scrubbing dirty dishes.

While Emily could only shake her head.

"Well, I'll be. You really don't have a notion about any of this ... do ya?"

When Augusta's chin began to quiver, Emily patted her back and spoke softly. "I'm sorry darlin'. It's not yer fault! Missus Drew probably thought I was telling ya the things a girl needed to know and I thought she was."

Emily was just pulling Augusta into her arms for a motherly embrace, when they heard male voices heading towards the kitchen.

Embarrassed that she'd been crying, Augusta quickly turned her back, frantically swiping away her tears.

Without a word Emily hurried through the swinging doors before the men could enter.

"Well, now boys … " she said, taking each man by the arm. "I wonder if you two gents would do me a favor?" Gracefully, she turned them to the stairs that led up to the Tylane's private quarters. "Tim, I've been just desperate fer some girl talk with yer wife. How about you men go upstairs and put yer feet up. And hey, Wes, why don't ya teach this ol' boy to play some poker? It's just not proper for a man to go west and not know how to play poker."

When both men gave her a befuddled look, Emily winked and put a finger to her lips.

Timothy and Wes exchanged glances, assuming this was one of those things they were probably better off not knowing. With a shrug they headed up the steps with Emily calling after them, "Much obliged boys!'

With that done Emily drew in a deep breath, straightened her shoulders, slapped a smile on her face, and returned to the kitchen. Somehow, she must explain the ways of the world and marriage to a very confused young bride.

Chapter 13
A Good Day

"Live happily with the woman you love through the fleeting days of life, for the wife God gives you is your best reward." Ecclesiastes 9:9

Timothy wore a wide grin as he slapped the reins, and Max and Molly trotted out of town.

"Breathe in that air, Missus Grainger—it's golden and sweet. Just like Emily's apricot preserves."

Augusta rolled her eyes at the man's inexhaustible good humor. And yet—she couldn't deny that—it was a delicious day, with every tree and bush, a painter's pallet of autumn colors: lemon yellows, corals, crimsons and golds, made even more brilliant against a sky of sapphire blue.

Timothy, following Augusta's gaze, adding: "Perfect day for a picnic, don't you think?" Giving her a nudge he asked, "What's the matter—why so serious? Come on—tell me what those clouds overhead look like to you?"

Augusta sighed—and gave a little shrug. "Well…they look like…a bunch of…big white clouds?"

When Timothy looked down at her with narrowed eyes, she frowned up in concentration. "All right! They…really do look like…a bunch of boats!"

"That a girl!" he chuckled, happy that he'd drawn her into his game.

"But they're not just boats! They are an armada of sailing ships, headed to the Spice Islands!"

Timothy threw his free arm around Augusta shoulder's and gave her an affectionate squeeze.

Augusta couldn't help but giggle; once again Timothy had broken down her wall of reserve. Still, she was finding it hard to relax around the man. She hadn't been able to stop thinking about her talk with Emily, nor could she stop herself from blushing. Especially now, as she sat beside her handsome husband, feeling intensely aware of his warm presence, his strong arm brushing against hers, his clean scent of shaving soap. She made a point of looking away each time he glanced down at her, which only served to pique his curiosity, making him want to look at her all the more.

Timothy couldn't imagine what was wrong! At first he assumed she was upset that he hadn't invited Wes. But she wasn't acting angry—just ridiculously shy, which made no sense at all. The day before had been wonderful; they had worked well together and talked all through dinner. But after her visit with Emily, she had been as nervous as a cat all the way home. And she'd acted oddly all morning.

Then, as if to add to his confusion, Augusta surprised Timothy when she suddenly blurted out, "You know, you are absolutely right! It really is a wonderful day for a picnic!"

When the man cocked his head at her suspiciously she smiled and explained, "I just remembered—I haven't been on a picnic since I was a little girl…and…I loved it!"

What she didn't add, but had decided just the same, was that it was pure foolishness to let worries and fears paint a black cloud over such a fine day. Nope, today—she was going to enjoy herself!

Soon her excitement rivaled Timothy's as they followed a trail that ran along the top of a high ridge and looked down over a lazy winding creek. A gentle breeze teased the air as they drove the wagon down the steep hill and into the secluded little valley.

Together, they made quick work of hobbling Max and Molly and unloading the wagon. Timothy chose a shaded spot near the creek that would put the sun at their back. Smiling, he looked to his wife. "Well now, what do you think—will this do?"

Velvety brown eyes took on a dreamlike quality. "Ohhh, yes, it certainly will! It's perfect!"

Timothy laughed, pleased to see that whatever had bothered his wife earlier seemed to be gone now! Augusta was suddenly a bundle of delight, as she gazed around the lovely meadow. It was shielded by the steep ravine that followed the bend of the creek. Ribbons of shining water sparkled in the sunlight, as they bubbled over thick beds of stone, making the water sweet and as clear as fine crystal.

Impatient to begin the adventure, Augusta laid her hand on a gun case. "Shall we shoot first?"

"Oh-oh no, that picnic basket comes first!" Timothy insisted as he shook out their blanket. "No food—no lesson! Besides we'll...uh...shoot better on a full stomach!"

Augusta wasn't convinced—but—then—her own stomach grumbled, so she decided not to argue.

Timothy laughed and teased, "I heard that!"

Augusta ignored him as she unpacked their lunch: fried chicken, pickles, biscuits with butter and honey, ginger bread cookies, and apple tarts. Pouring them each a glass of lemonade she asked, "You made that up about shooting on a full stomach—didn't you?"

"Yes, ma'am!" he admitted. "I'm hungry. However, had you burnt the chicken—I might have diplomatically added that...no one can shoot straight... after...eating poultry!"

Still smiling he said, "Let's thank the Lord for this feast...and that you didn't burn the chicken!"

He grabbed Augusta's hand, bowed his head reverently, and began to pray: "Lord, we can't thank You enough for this beautiful day and for this glorious place to have our picnic! Every blessing, large or small, comes from You. Please keep us safe as we work with the guns today. And please, Lord, bless this food and the precious hands that prepared it. In Jesus' name, amen."

Timothy released her hand with a wink, grabbed a chicken leg, and bit down with a groan of pleasure.

Augusta couldn't help but wonder about this man who had suddenly overtaken her life. Timothy—he was the gentlest man she'd ever known, and at the same time, strong and masculine. He loved to tease and yet he truly revered and loved God. He went from teasing to praying and then back to teasing again. Most people reserved God for the serious or sad times but God was given a seat of honor in every part of Timothy's life. The relationship this man had with God intrigued her, almost as much as it puzzled her.

Swallowing his bite, Timothy lifted his chicken leg in a salute. "Mmmm, Augusta—perfection!" Then pointing towards the ravine, he added, "We'll set our targets against that sandy embankment. That way no stray bullet will get away from us."

Curious about Timothy and his knowledge of guns, Augusta found herself asking, "Papa told me that your mother raised you—so who was it that taught you about guns?"

Timothy gulped down a full glass of lemonade before he answered, then a tender smiled lit his face. "His name was Baker—Simon Baker. My father saved his life when they served together in the military. When mother and I left Georgia, he insisted on escorting us, then he stayed on as my tutor. But, he was also protector, friend, and a devout disciplinarian! All in all, he was like a father to me."

Timothy added the last description with tender eyes, as he gazed over the meadow, then said wistfully, "Baker was quite a man—tough as a boot. He taught me that all wisdom comes from seeking God out and studying His word."

Shrugging his shoulders he added, "Baker believed every man should know the art of self-defense, so he taught me about guns and shooting. He also taught me about fist-de-cuffs—and fencing."

Timothy suddenly flashed his playful white smile at Augusta and teased. "If you shoot well today, I'll teach you how to fence tomorrow. Or maybe we could box a few rounds!"

Augusta giggled; he never said what she expected. Then, looking longingly at the creek, she muttered, "Actually...I'd rather you teach me how to wade in that creek over there."

Timothy gazed over at the shimmering water. "Mmm, it does look inviting, doesn't it? But I'm afraid I can't teach you—I've never been wading."

"Well then—I'll teach you. I've only been once—but I guess that makes me the expert!"

Timothy smiled as he watched Augusta lick a bit of honey from her finger, then close her eyes as she savored its golden taste. Trying to get his mind back on the task at hand, he teased., "Hey, I thought today was about shooting. Do you want to be a swimmer or a gun fighter?"

"I don't recall saying I wanted to be either!"

Then she batted her eyelashes, which made Timothy laugh, as she added brazenly, "Then again—maybe I'll just be both!"

"Explain that?" he insisted with raised eyebrows, enchanted by her playful mood.

"First," she said with her golden eyes sparkling, "you teach me to be a sharp shooter. That should take, oh, thirty minutes or so—"

When the man's eyebrows went even higher Augusta gave him her most captivating smile. "Then, we'll have all afternoon to do what's really important—play in that lovely water!"

Timothy couldn't look away, and had to remind himself to breathe. So much of Augusta's life had been about work. But today she was a carefree enchantress, all sunlight and fairy dust; her dress, a bright yellow and white gingham, showed off a youthful hourglass figure. Her thick mane of dark curls fell like a waterfall over slim shoulders—nearly touching her waist. She was as sweet as a mountain stream and bright as a new penny. Suddenly, Timothy knew—this woman owned his heart. That knowledge was sobering: what if after all his efforts she never learned to love *him* in return? Watching her was sweet torture as she leaned back, closed her eyes, and tipped her face to the sun, her rosy lips curving in a blissful smile.

Timothy allowed himself another moment to drink in the sight then forced himself to stop acting like a besotted schoolboy. He lowered his voice to a soft growl and muttered, "Well, if I've only thirty minutes to turn you into a sharp shooter—we'd better get to it!"

Holding up a revolver he began the lesson with a wicked grin,

"THIS—IS—A—GUN."

Augusta only rolled her eyes, but Timothy was pleased when she suddenly, leaned closer and her eyes sparkled with interest.

Each gun came in an elegant wooden case, lined with green velvet. They were embellished with carved brass fittings and even bore his initials "T.D.G." emblazoned on the stocks.

Augusta became especially curious when she noted the initials on two of the guns.

"Why do these two have 'A.C.G.' rather than 'T.D.G.' carved in them," she asked. "Who's—'A.C.G.'?"

Timothy thought she was jesting at first, but when she seemed sincere, he shrugged and said, "I—uh, had those made just for you Augusta—A.C.G. stands for Augusta Colleen Grainger"

"Those are mine?" she asked.

Augusta wasn't sure what to think; these guns had been special orders, just for her. He'd certainly taken for granted that she would marry him. But was this an insult or a compliment? It didn't feel like an insult.

Timothy was unaware of Augusta's thoughts or of her sudden scrutiny of him as he continued.

"Naturally, my hope is that these guns will be for hunting—but we must be prepared for any eventuality. For myself I brought my .50 caliber Remington

89

Creedmoor—it has a double trigger. If handled properly it can be very accurate at a great distance, but it's much too heavy for you."

He let Augusta feel it's weight, then picked up another revolver. "I'll also carry this—it's a .44 caliber Dragoon."

Augusta watched as he carefully returned both guns to their carrying cases. He started to pick up another gun from the blanket then hesitated for a moment. "Also...there was something you said yesterday.. I think you should know—I am never unarmed."

He reached under his vest and pulled a derringer from a concealed pocket. The weapon looked diminutive in his large hand, then he tucked it away and added, "And, of course, I'm almost never without my cane!"

"Your cane?" she asked. "I hadn't thought of that as a weapon exactly, but—."

Timothy's lips curved into a faint smile as he picked up the cane, and with a quick flick of his wrist, the handle shot up, and with his right hand, he slowly withdrew the hidden rapier. As his eyes met Augusta's he said modestly, "Baker wouldn't allow me to leave the house alone...not until I was on...quite friendly terms with this."

With practiced ease he slid the weapon back into its discreet scabbard. Timothy looked into Augusta's eyes again and said humbly, "I am not an expert on weaponry, but what I know will serve us both well enough."

Augusta's breath caught in her throat; she'd thought this man a typical Eastern dude—a greenhorn. But she was coming to learn that there was a great deal more to Timothy Grainger.

The man held up the two weapons with her initials and said with excitement, "I hope you'll like these! They're much lighter than mine and I believe you will find them easy to handle—once you get used to them. If we go west, the wagon master insisted on everyone having a hand gun and long gun. For your hand gun—" He held up the revolver, adding, "I bought you a .36 caliber Navy Colt."

Augusta nodded mutely; he really did seem to be serious about allowing this decision to be her choice.

"And for your long gun," he continued with pride in his voice, "I was able to get you a brand new model. It was a special order sent to me straight from the New Haven Arms Company. It's an 1866 Winchester! I know it's only 1865 but I have stock in the company and I wanted this gun specifically for you! It only weighs nine pounds! It's called a 'Henry Rifle'; it's a .44 caliber rimfire."

Timothy opened a box of bullets and showed Augusta that the end of the bullet was stamped with an 'H' for Benjamin Tyler Henry, the man who developed the popular 'Henry Rifle'.

Timothy suddenly took a deep breath and looking directly at Augusta as he said solemnly, "Now, my beauty, pay close attention—keep your finger off that trigger until you mean to shoot, and don't ever point a gun, even an empty one at *anything or anyone* you don't intend to kill! It's too easy to shoot someone by accident. On the other hand if you waver in the face of an enemy, he will take your gun away from you and use it against you! Do you understand?"

Augusta looked up at him with wide, almost-frightened eyes. "Isn't that a little extreme? How could a gun be dangerous if it's empty. It can only kill if you pull the trigger and IF you aim correctly."

"NO!" Timothy's deep voice came out sounding severe. "Even when you're cleaning the gun, even if you know you took out every bullet, you must still treat it as if it were loaded and dangerous! People die every day from somebody pulling a trigger when they didn't **think** the gun was loaded. They may not have meant to do anything wrong but their victims are still wounded—or worse—dead!"

Timothy's blue eyes bore into Augusta's and he said again, "I won't teach you another thing until you promise to take this very seriously!"

Augusta nodded, and recognizing the sober nature of what they were doing, she gave him her silent promise.

Timothy relaxed and nodded. "Good," he said. "Let's get started."

Augusta liked watching him load the pistol; every movement was confident, fluid—purposeful.

"Since we're about to shoot, I'll put a bullet in every chamber," he explained. "But normally, we'll keep an empty chamber for the hammer to rest against, so if you drop it, it won't fire!"

A flicker of doubt worried Augusta when Timothy placed the gun in her hand for the first time.

"Oh my!" she remarked. "It is lighter than yours but—it's still a little heavy—isn't it?"

Timothy assured her she would get used to it, then patiently he showed her how to use the sights.

"Now if you ever have to face an enemy, you'll aim at the center of the man's chest—then fire."

Timothy took in Augusta's horrified look. "I know," he said, grimacing, "But if you have to protect yourself from man or beast, that's what it comes down to." His words were gentle but firm. "If we go west, we may have to fight for our lives. In the wagon train people rely on each other to stand up and fight if necessary. And if we go, that last stretch to the ranch will be just you and me—we'll be relying on each other!"

Augusta nodded—she hadn't made up her mind—not about Timothy or what her future held. Still, she needed to be able to protect herself, whether she had a husband or not.

"For now," Timothy said patiently, "just get the feel of it…we'll concentrate on accuracy later."

Augusta aimed, and then pulled the trigger. Although Timothy had warned her, she really wasn't prepared for the ear shattering noise or—for the gun to buck so violently in her hand. She also wasn't prepared for how crestfallen she'd feel after completely missing the target.

"I missed that whole thing?" she groaned. "I didn't even get close—did I?"

Timothy just smiled. "It may take a bit longer than thirty-minutes—so please—try again."

Augusta nodded and pulled the trigger—but when the dust cleared the target remained untouched.

"It's not possible that the bullets aren't coming out—is it?" she questioned.

With that, Augusta turned the gun towards herself and Timothy, thinking to peek down the barrel. This set off a chain of events. Immediately, Timothy knocked the gun upwards and away from them. The sudden motion startled Augusta, whose hand jerked reflexively, causing her to pull the trigger. The gun roared and pitched in her hand while the *wild* bullet exploded into the sky!

Augusta was instantly horrified! At first she couldn't speak—then she began to stammer. "Oh—oh—oh no, Timothy! I—oh no! I didn't mean to shoot, I—"

Alarmed and embarrassed, her eyes filled with tears, as she began to shake. "Oh, Timothy, I might have killed you!"

The man blew out a shaky breath then drew her into his arms. "Augusta—whew!" he groaned. "That was a close call—for both of us!"

He let out another loud sigh then said, "Actually, I'm almost glad that happened. You see now how easy it is to shoot someone, even yourself—accidentally?"

Augusta, did indeed realize how foolish she had been. In fact, it took her a while before she could make herself touch the gun. But when she shot again, she still missed the target—every time.

When she finished her last shot, Timothy reached for the pistol. "Why don't you rest for a minute and let me shoot a few rounds. It might help if you watch me."

Standing tall, legs braced apart he fired; and as the dust cleared, there was a hole in the target, dead center.

"My!" Augusta exclaimed. "That's what they call a bull's eye—isn't it? Could you do that again?"

Timothy laughed and shook his head. "Augusta, you do wonders for my ego! Well," he said with a shrug, "let's see if I can."

In quick succession he shot five more times. Now there were six holes in the very center of the target.

"Bull's eye every time!" she praised. "Is that what you mean, when you say you're on friendly terms with something? You said that about your rapier too—what else are you on friendly terms with?"

Timothy winked, and with a grin he added, "Lots of things! I'm a... very...friendly man, Augusta."

For some reason the way he turned that dimpled grinned on her with his blue eyes sparkling and golden hair shining in the sunlight—a barrage of butterflies begin to dance inside Augusta's young heart.

And though Timothy looked the picture of composure—the way his wife returned his gaze made a sudden warmth creep up his neck. He had finally impressed his wife. He had never cared about impressing anyone before, well, except possibly Baker. He felt embarrassed to admit it but—more than anything, he had wanted Augusta to look at him just like that—and finally she had! Of course his ability had come as a shock...that stung a little...but...still...it felt good.

When Timothy suggested Augusta brace one hand with the other, she did much better. And although she never made a *bull's eye,* she did hit the target more often than not.

When Augusta seemed fairly comfortable with the smaller gun, Timothy handed her the long gun, "I want to see how you do with the Henry. It holds seventeen shells. I want you to feel comfortable with both weapons, but—the Henry will serve you best! You, my dear, and this rifle—" Timothy paused and grinned broadly, "need to be on the *friendliest of terms!*"

Augusta felt the butterflies dance again; what was it about this man's smile? She forced herself to at least appear unaffected as she lifted the rifle. Once again, it was heavier than she'd expected. Her arms were already feeling tired, and why, oh why, couldn't she keep the rifle barrel straight? The slightest breeze seemed to blow it off course.

"Oh, bother," she huffed, lowering the gun. "You've gone to so much trouble—what if I can't do this?"

"Nonsense!" he said, with a teasing smile. "You'll learn...because...I'm a very good teacher!"

"That might be!" she muttered. "But what happens when a very good teacher has a very poor student?"

Timothy thought for a moment, rubbing his hand over his jaw, then he added nonchalantly, "I could help by steadying the gun—just until you got used to the weight, if you wouldn't mind?"

Relief lit Augusta's face; she hated the idea of failing at anything. Smiling her agreement she said, "Yes, please—if you help a little, then I'm sure I'll be able to do it by myself, once I get used to it!"

Hesitantly, Timothy placed both hands around her small waist and tugged her back against him. Suddenly, both he and Augusta seemed to have need of air, for they each drew in a steadying breath.

Augusta's eyes grew wide; she hadn't thought about how he would help her. But—those pesky butterflies came rushing back in full force. He placed his right arm around her, holding onto the rifle barrel. Gently, he pushed the stock tightly against her shoulder and with his left arm he helped her hold the gun in position. Augusta found herself utterly surrounded by Timothy's embrace. It became clear now why he had asked if she would mind. They had never—ever—been this close!

Along with the butterflies came a sudden quickening in her heart. Timothy must be feeling it, too, for she was certain that she felt a steady drumming against her back. There was silence for a moment, then slowly Timothy began giving her instructions. Augusta found it impossible to concentrate at first, then

finally she began to—not relax exactly—but to…listen at least and then to…
enjoy! She had to admit, this was nice! His white shirt sleeves were crisp and he
smelled of shaving soap and something else—spicy—yet still very masculine.
All that combined with Timothy's deep voice, and the feel of his breath—warm
against her neck—made for a strange mixture that both calmed her and thrilled
her at the same time. His words were repeated many times over: "Take a deep
breath and hold it…line up the two sights…steady. Now, gently—squeeze the
trigger."

If she did anything at all right he would praise her. When she fumbled,
he would say, "That's all right; now you know not to do that again. See, you're
learning something every time you fire."

They continued like that until they'd shot every bullet, then Timothy
straightened and lowered the gun.

"You need to rest for a little while!" he said gently. "I can feel you trembling!"

Augusta let her arms fall to her sides and blew out a disgruntled sigh. "I'm
used to throwing saddles all day—why can't I seem to do this without your
help?" she fumed.

"Hey, don't be discouraged," he soothed. "You really are doing fine!
You're a strong woman, but not used to holding your arms like this." Gently, he
pulled her back against him. "Come on, lean back and relax."

Augusta closed her eyes, breathing in sunshine and fresh air. The muscles
in her arms throbbed and she couldn't even think of moving away. It shouldn't
feel so natural to lean against Timothy—but it did.

Slowly, he rubbed his hands up and down her arms, then bent close to
her ear and breathed her in. "Mmm, you always smell so good! But it's not lilac
today—it's new—what is it?"

Augusta could feel his warm breath against her neck. *And, oh, how the butterflies danced!*

Timothy's unexpected closeness and this sudden intimacy made Augusta
feel wary and a bit—giddy. Shouldn't she be shocked and push him away? That
seemed silly; hadn't she been thinking the same about him? Just because he
voiced what they both had been thinking didn't make it improper—did it? Augusta wasn't sure, and after Emily's talk the night before, she was more confused than ever. How should she behave? This man was, her husband…but…she

still wasn't sure if she wanted him to be? Suddenly, she recalled that Timothy had asked a question—and it was a simple one at that.

"The scent? Um, y-yes, it is—n-n-new." Angry that she was stammering, she took a breath then said, "I just tried a new soap—to wash my hair. It was scented with lemon verbena."

Augusta let out a sigh. *Goodness, but she was relieved to have gotten that said. She even thought proudly that she sounded quite nonchalant, well, there at the end anyway.*

Timothy chuckled and rubbed his nose in Augusta's dark curls and breathed deeply, "Mmm. I like it!"

Now—Augusta knew that she should move away. Then she reminded herself that she needed to rest first—so that, she could continue her lesson! It wasn't as if she were allowing Timothy to rub her arms because she liked it—no—it was just to help her circulation! But to keep Timothy from misunderstanding, she quickly turned the topic back to shooting. "Timothy—" she asked. "What if I can't master this? I'd feel terrible if I had to give up!"

As if it were something he did every day, he wrapped his arms around her tightly, and held her close.

"Then don't give up!" he whispered. "Augusta, there isn't a thing in the world you cannot do if you set your mind to it. This is your first lesson—don't be so hard on yourself."

Augusta had just decided to accept his encouragement when he stole her breath away by brushing a kiss against the crook of her neck.

All at once a thousand tiny sparks of pleasure leapt from where his lips touched her neck, then slid all the way down to her fingers and toes—and on their way down they collided with the butterflies. What is happening to me today—she wondered? She certainly hadn't expected a shooting lesson to turn out like this! And how could such an innocent little touch race through her like a wild mustang? She was sure of only one thing—she mustn't—ever—allow him to do that again!

Their marriage hadn't really begun, at least that is what she'd taken away from Emily's little talk. They really weren't married yet and she was certain—well, fairly certain—she didn't want to be!

Feeling Augusta suddenly stiffen in his arms, Timothy released his hold and announced, "Well, I think you've rested enough for now—and you *are* doing better! So, let's get back to it."

As if nothing at all had happened, they both resumed their previous stance. However, before Augusta had time to think, Timothy swung the rifle to the left, slid his hand over hers, and together they pulled the trigger. The gun roared and bucked, but this time, when the dust cleared, a large snake the color of fall leaves lay dead in the sand, no more than fifteen feet away.

"Good girl!" Timothy praised.

"But I...I didn't do anything! I...just—"

Augusta stammered and shook while Timothy ran to examine their kill.

"A copperhead!" Timothy called to her. "Good thing we shot him before we went wading! Wouldn't want to find the likes of him hiding in our boots."

Timothy sauntered back to the blanket where Augusta stood shivering; he stopped short when he realized she'd turned a ghostly white, and was obviously fighting tears.

"Augusta? What's the matter?"

"Sss—snakes! I...do not...like—**snakes**!" she stammered as violent tremor shook her body. Rubbing her arms as if suddenly freezing, she looked about, asking: "Do they come in pairs? Could others be nearby?"

Timothy smiled gently and squeezed her hand. "Don't worry. I'll scout around—make sure it's not a family reunion!"

Not appreciating his humor; Augusta grabbed his arm. "Please, let's just go home!"

"Hey, now, what about our plans to go wading?" He tweaked Augusta's chin and said in a soothing voice, "I'll look around, make sure it's safe—and then—we are going wading! Besides, life is an adventure, my sweet, whether we stay here or head into the wilderness. It's no life at all if you let things like this spoil a perfectly good day."

Augusta knew he *was* right! But her fear of snakes ran awfully deep! When Timothy declared the area serpent-free, Augusta tried to laugh it off, but her voice betrayed her. "Sorry to be such a c-coward. It's just that in my nightmares, there are always snakes and—"

Timothy's gaze was sympathetic. "I know. I hate that you have so many nightmares—"

"I'm sorry," she said with a blush. "I don't mean to wake you...it's just that they're so ..."

"Terrifying?" he finished for her. Giving her a quick hug he added, "Well, I think we should fill the rest of this day with happier things to dream about. Don't you?"

Augusta nodded and gave him a weak smile. *Oh, to only have happy things to dream about.* Finally, she relaxed enough to finish her shooting lesson. It was still difficult but finally when she knelt on one knee, she found she could handle the gun much better.

"See—that's good—you found a way to handle both guns!"

But Augusta blushed again when he added with a roguish grin. "I have to admit, it was a lot more fun—when you needed my help!"

As soon as the guns were put away Timothy was the first to dip one large toe into the creek.

"Now, my girl," he said, grimacing over the cold water. "Since you're the expert—what are all the pleasures of wading in the creek? Smithy's son called it a 'crik'—which is it?" he teased. "Creek or crik?"

Augusta frowned and thought for a moment. "A proper Bostonian should definitely say creek! However," she added wryly, "out here in the country, most folks would say—'this here's a crik!'"

Timothy laughed as he watched Augusta splashing noisily through the water. As she came close, she gathered her skirts in one hand, then reached out with the other and touched the dimple in his cheek.

"I wonder why you don't have two of these?" she asked. "Only just the one. It makes you look very—I don't know?" Her eyes suddenly sparkled. "Yes, I do, it makes you look mischievous!"

"Mischievous?" Timothy asked innocently. "That can't be—I'm a proper Boston dude—remember?"

Augusta groaned and rolled her eyes. "You aren't at all what I expected."

She tossed a handful of multi-colored leaves onto the water, then watched them sail away.

"Papa told me all the things he *thought* would impress me—that you were sophisticated, well-read, a real gentleman, trained in the law, don't ya know! But do you know what I thought?"

Timothy frowned, "Hmm? I—don't think—I want to know..."

Augusta laughed. "I'm sure you don't. I thought you were...about as interesting as a bowl full of dust!"

When Timothy grimaced, Augusta giggled. "I try to be honest too, you know. Anyway, that's what I thought. And I can tell you—it was quite a surprise when I opened the door and there you stood, grinning at me like a jaybird!"

Frowning down at her he grumbled. "Jaybirds don't grin. And I resent being compared to dust!"

Augusta bit her lip to hold back her smile. "As I was saying," she continued as she looked up at him, "your eyes had that twinkle, like they do right now. And then—I saw that one impish dimple. I told myself don't you be fooled, A.C.! Despite what Papa told you—that man—can be a rascal!"

"How could you think me dry as dust and then conclude that I'm a rascal? And all that time Bull was supposed to be bragging about me. The plan was for me to walk in and you would swoon at my feet!"

Timothy put a hand to his heart. "All your papa's well placed blarney—wasted!"

"No! You're not listening," she said with arms akimbo. "I'm saying the real thing turned out to be better than the blarney. You're a strange one all right—Timothy Grainger—but you are better than a bowl full of dust! And I kind of like that you're a bit of a rascal. It's entertaining!"

With that last remark, Timothy grinned, wiggled his eyebrows, and made a grab for her.

Augusta evaded him and called over her shoulder as she trotted down the stream. "You...are also incorrigible...from head to heel and back again!"

The two had a wonderful time as they splashed and talked their way up and down the creek bed. Timothy had never been happier. Suddenly, Augusta stopped mid-stream and smiled up at him, "You know, you still haven't answered me? How did you end up with just this one dimple?"

Timothy grinned. "I was born with two! But one was on me and the other on my brother!"

At Augusta's puzzled expression, Timothy chuckled then added, "If you ever meet my brother, Tytus, then you'll know two of us—each with one dimple!"

When Augusta's eyes shone with interest he continued, "You see, we're an unusual set of twins. Typically, twins look exactly alike or completely different. Our faces are almost identical, but while I have light hair and blue eyes, Ty has dark hair, and very dark eyes. We're both the same height—but when we stand side by side you will find that he has a dimple on the right and I have

the one on the left. When we look at each other it's like looking into a mirror."
Amused, he added: "Fascinating—don't you think?"

Augusta thought it was! The story had brought up other questions about
the mysterious twin brother, but before she could voice them, Timothy was
pulling her down the stream. They played in the wet mud as it squished between their toes, while a soothing breeze clattered through the autumn leaves
and tousled their hair. They marveled at how the lemony sunlight shimmered
over the water, debating whether it looked more like a thousand tiny mirrors or
yards of shining silk winding through the meadow.

"Bet your feet are getting pruny!" Timothy declared. "Should go back
soon—don't you think?"

"So...what if they are pruny?" Augusta retorted. "I'm certainly not ready
to leave!"

Timothy smiled. *What a sweet, feisty little thing she was at times.* He couldn't
resist, grinning from ear to ear, he reached down, and scooped her into his
arms.

"Show me those little toes!" he demanded.

"No!" she squealed. "My toes are none of your business! I'm sure it's not
proper!"

"I'll just hold you until you show them to me," he insisted as he calmly
walked down the creek.

"You'll give up before I will. Besides, I'm awfully heavy—better put me
down."

Timothy's grin grew broader. "Hah! You're light as a feather. I could carry
you all the way back to town—in fact, I like that idea—and that's just what I'm
going to do!"

Abruptly, he stepped out of the creek and headed towards town, with
Augusta laughing and wriggling to be free.

"You can't do that... what about the horses?" she asked.

"They can carry themselves back into town!"

Augusta giggled. "You are definitely a rascal. And no more picnics for
you—you don't behave well!"

Timothy stopped; his look turned serious as he gazed down at her. Then
his deep voice rumbled, "But—I like the way *we behaved*!" he said sincerely.
"All day—I liked everything about today, especially my lovely companion—she
was the best part."

Augusta stared at Timothy; surely he was jesting. Dolefully, she lowered her eyes and spoke softly, "Your companion was not lovely. She's as plain as a mud pie...brown hair...brown eyes. And she almost shot you—then panicked over a dead snake. The day would have been ruined—if not for you."

Timothy squeezed her gently then growled in his low voice, "I said she was lovely—and that's what I meant! You're not plain, Augusta—don't even think it." When she shook her head sadly, Timothy spoke again, his voice sounding deep and rich, "It was the things your father told me about you that first caught my attention! But, when I saw your picture, I was fascinated by all those dark curls that frame your pretty face. And when I finally met you and looked into those honey-colored eyes—if I hadn't already been smitten—that would have done it!"

Still holding her close Timothy swayed slightly, making Augusta feel like a branch in the wind.

"Please—put me down," she asked breathlessly. "Surely, you're getting tired of holding me by now."

Hugging her closer he whispered, "I'll never get tired of holding you or looking at you Augusta. When I look into your eyes, it's hard for me to look away. There's nothing plain about them; the outside rim is so dark but inside they're honey-colored and green—and gold! Your eyes captivate me!"

Augusta gave an impatient smirk and squeezed her eyes shut. "Might as well put me down now—you've nothing to look at!"

"Hmm, I'm not the only rascal around here. I'll just look at the rest of your lovely face—and it is lovely! I don't think you realize it. Your lashes are long and thick, like butterfly wings resting on soft pink cheeks. And oh—my!" he chuckled. "Right before my eyes those cheeks are growing even pinker— why they're nearly crimson!" he teased.

"Tim—o—thyy..." Augusta groaned and wriggled to be free. "You're being awfully silly—for a grown man. Please, stop all this foolishness—put me down."

"Nope." he said coolly, "I'm a firm believer in enjoying the moment and— this one's a beaut! Besides, I've decided that you need to be held—at least until you realize just how 'un-plain' you are. So, you might as well quit squirming and let me finish."

Augusta squirmed anyway, but when he only laughed and tightened his hold, she finally gave up.

"Now, where was I?" he asked. "Ah, your nose—it's straight, slightly rounded at the tip, perfect! And freckles—I hadn't noticed before. Of course I've always heard that a woman with freckles is stubborn, hard headed, a real little imp! But—it's still a lovely nose."

When Augusta scrunched up her nose and stuck out her tongue, Timothy laughed out loud.

"See, you've proved my point...and once again...led me to the next item on the list...your mouth!" Timothy's tone suddenly became slightly husky as he said, "You have a lovely mouth—I mean, smile—a wonderful smile! Your lips are so soft and full and..."

Augusta's eyes fluttered open, for the timbre in his voice suddenly made her want to see his face.

"Your smile—" he continued, "it's like a tonic to me. When you smile at me I feel ten feet tall!" Timothy shrugged his shoulders. "And maybe you've guessed—I'm just a man—in love with his wife!"

Guilt stabbed Augusta's heart; he loved her and how many times had she frowned when she could have just as easily smiled.

Timothy stilled and drew in a breath when Augusta's expression became tender, and she laid her small hand against his jaw. She'd thought him handsome all along, with his strong face, golden hair, he had the kindest blue eyes she'd ever seen, even when they twinkled with mischief. She ran her thumb over his thick mustache, remembering how it had tickled her neck. His face was very masculine, his nose and mouth were straight and firm, and his jaw was strong and angular. And then...there was that...one dimple; she smiled softly and traced it with her fingertip.

Timothy slowly leaned forward and touched his forehead to hers and in a husky voice he asked, "Augusta, my sweet...do you have...any idea—how much I want to kiss you right now?"

Blinking, she moved her gaze to his lips then to his eyes that were now a deeper shade of sapphire blue, intense and serious. With a naïve innocence, she breathlessly whispered, "Nooo?"

Her doe brown eyes were soft, as her mouth formed an 'O', as if in a pout. Strange, but she couldn't seem to make herself pull away—instead she ran her fingers lightly over his lips, and once again she felt the butterflies dance.

This was all the invitation Timothy needed. He took possession of Augusta's sweet mouth in one bold move, knowing full well that he couldn't have stopped himself if he wanted to. When the tiniest sigh escaped Augusta's throat, Timothy instinctively deepened the kiss, and felt like a man who'd been given the key to Solomon's treasure, for his reluctant bride—was kissing him back!

Something profound took place with that kiss. The barrier she had built between them began to crumble.

The kiss denied on their wedding day had finally been given. To Timothy it felt like a sweet benediction, sanctioning their past vows and future promises. With that kiss came a quickening in both their hearts as the autumn breeze swirled about them and seemed to carry them over the tallest trees to some secret place known only unto them.

When they finally drew apart, they were breathless and more than a little stunned by what had just happened. But when Timothy saw that Augusta's expression was troubled, his heart filled with compassion. It was if by kissing him, by letting down her guard, she had betrayed herself.

He could read her pain so clearly; and wanting desperately to comfort her, he said, "It's all right my beauty—I'm not pressuring you. It was a good day and a beautiful way to end it. That's something you need to know Augusta, even when you're grieving—there is no shame in having a good day. And that's what it was—wasn't it? A wonderfully good day!"

Later, as they drove silently towards town, Augusta pondered all that had taken place. And it wasn't just the kiss, although that was something she'd definitely had to think on! But something else had happened! Her life had turned a page; unexpectedly, she realized that, though her father was dead, she wasn't— she was still alive! It shouldn't have been a revelation—but it was! All her life she'd felt that if her father died, her life would end too. She had felt guilty for living, ashamed that she could still laugh or smile or care. Something about today had freed her of that burden of guilt. Timothy had understood when he said: "There's no shame in having a good day." She was still uncertain about almost everything, but she hadn't betrayed her father...and perhaps at least...that was one nightmare...she could escape.

Chapter 14
A Dream. A Nightmare.
A New Beginning!

"When my father and my mother forsake me, then the LORD will take me up ... Wait on the LORD: be of good courage, and he shall strengthen your heart: wait, I say, on the LORD." Psalm 27:10, 14

The mare's silver coat glistened like a diamond in the sun, the shining mane fluttering in cadence with each graceful stride. Horse and rider joyfully raced across the valley floor, as if born on wings, they drew closer to the tall stony peak, centered in the range of purple mountains. The peak stood like a benevolent giant, soaring miles above timberline, spreading its arms protectively across the valley. The stony features of the mountain were lightly dusted with snow, making it appear to have a stubble of a white beard over a lined and craggy face. The lower knolls and foothills gave the appearance of muscular arms spreading off into the distance. Laughing with delight, she headed for the mountain, urging her horse across a field blanketed in a rainbow of wild flowers.

Without warning everything changed—one moment both horse and rider had been soaring like eagles over the meadow, thrilled by the beauty around them. Then in the next moment they were tumbling head over heels, with flailing hooves digging into the ground and thrashing into the air. In the next instant she found herself alone, a prisoner in a cavern of shadows. Gone—were the horse, the meadow—even the mountain! Instead, she was surrounded by high stone walls. Then—imagined or real, the walls seemed to convulse as the air was filled with the sickening rhythmic melody of snakes!

Terror gathered in her throat; she tried to scream but couldn't. She clawed at the walls but they were as smooth as glass. Just when she thought she'd go mad—she saw it—it began as a tiny flicker, only a pin prick of light as if seen through a dark cloak. She stared until her eyes burned, afraid to blink, lest she lose this fragile hope! Her heart throbbed as the flame grew, until finally, wonderfully, there was a blaze as bright as sunlight, looming just above her. Then, as if coming through a fog, a man's hand pierced the darkness. It was pitifully scarred, belonging to one who had known great pain and yet to her it was beautiful. The hand reached for her and she latched onto it like the lifeline it was, and without delay, she was being lifted like a feather, up and away and out of her prison of stone. Then as soft as a breeze gliding over satin, she heard her name.

"Augusta," the voice said with great tenderness, "don't be afraid." Again it repeated: "I am with you—don't be afraid!'

Suddenly, there was a different voice calling to her, "Augusta, wake up, honey! You're having another dream."

She felt her body jerk—and believed she was falling back into the pit. She stiffened and cried out.

Timothy shook her gently, "Wake up! You're all right now; you're safe! Please honey... wake up!"

Gradually, as Augusta was able to focus her eyes, she recognized the calming fact that she was in her own bedroom; a soft breeze was coming through her window and damp curls were being stroked from her forehead. Timothy had pulled her into his arms and was rocking her gently; slowly, her body began to relax. *It was the dream—again.* Augusta swiped at her tears, embarrassed that she had been crying in her sleep. Still, it was comforting to cuddle closer into the arms that held her tight. She lay her head against Timothy's chest, and was instantly soothed by the sound of his steady heartbeat and the vibration of his deep masculine voice speaking words of comfort.

"You're all right, honey—you're safe!"

Augusta patted his arm. "Yes ... of course I am."

Fully awake, she felt embarrassed. She was safe now, but she wasn't ready to be alone—not yet. Timothy had awakened her before, but he'd never stayed before. Never before had he held her so possessively. The other times he had broken the nightmare's hold, then left her alone in the dark. But this, she had to admit, this was so much better! It was dreadful being alone after a nightmare like that, but awfully nice, being wrapped up tight in Timothy's strong arms. She recalled how easily he had picked her up and carried her from the stream. Then she remembered his kiss: the thought was like a spark to dry kindling.

Heat flooded her body and colored her face—and for once, she was thankful for the darkness.

Neither spoke for a long while. Augusta thought her fears had passed, until Timothy moved to lay her back on her pillow—and a fresh wave of panic surged through her.

"Please don't go!" she pleaded as she clutched at his arm. "Not yet!"

He smiled, the kindness in his eyes instantly calming her again.

"I'm not leaving—this is where I should be."

Their eyes met, glistening in the dark, as he turned to lay down beside her. Pale streaks of silvery moonlight brightened the room and bathed their faces in a soft glow, as they recognized that something of import was passing between them.

"Augusta," Timothy whispered tenderly, "my dear—sweet wife."

Wife—he mused, that simple word tasted like honey on his tongue.

"Sweetheart, I know you are lonely and you're scared. You have nightmares nearly every night. I hurry to your room, wake you, and then you send me away, and I hate leaving you alone in the dark."

Augusta felt miserable and more confused than she'd ever been. She had come to care so much for this man. But what about the nightmare? It always seemed that the people closest to her were the ones to suffer. No, she told herself, it just wouldn't be fair to Timothy—she must not accept this marriage.

"Augusta," Timothy insisted, "your father wanted me to be here for you and I believe that's what God wants too! Maybe you don't think much of me now...but...in time..."

Augusta had to interrupt him; she couldn't allow him to think she had a low opinion of this good man.

"No, Timothy! I doubt that there is a better man on earth than you! But it's still better that we separate. The truth is—I was a mistake on the day I was born and every day since. Hard times follow me; that's why Papa trapped you into this marriage. And I want to set things right before something bad happens!"

When Timothy looked baffled, she turned her face away and said, "We're only husband and wife on paper—I understand that now—about how a marriage really begins and this one hasn't. And it never will!"

106

Her words were emphatic, then her body flooded with embarrassment as she realized she was still clinging to Timothy. "And I shouldn't be doing this," she muttered as she roughly pushed away from him.

"It was a mistake not to have kept my distance from you. Today's picnic was a mistake. I never should have agreed to it or allowed you to kiss me!" Lowering her eyes, Augusta said softly but firmly, "You should go back to your own room now. I appreciate you waking me up—but please—go."

Moving to the far side of the bed she turned her face away, adding, "I said I'd give you a chance—and I have—but I've decided it's time to have this marriage annulled."

Timothy leaned back against the headboard and folded his arms across his chest. "Augusta, I am not leaving this room! Not until we've talked this out. You've mentioned annulment before and you know how I feel about it! Besides, I don't believe you're being truthful with yourself. What about the past few weeks? Our long rides and evenings together—they've been wonderful! Every day we've gotten a little closer. This day wasn't a mistake—it was wonderful! We enjoy being together—we're good together."

In her heart, Augusta knew he was right, but the nightmare always meant trouble, and she didn't want Timothy hurt.

"I'm sorry," she whispered, "but my life, this day, this marriage—they were never meant to be—they were all mistakes."

"Augusta, please, explain this to me—how is your life and our marriage a mistake? I know you're troubled—you lost your mother at a young age and now your father...but..."

"My mother isn't dead!" Augusta blurted out. "Or maybe she is—I don't know!"

Timothy frowned in confusion. "Please, Augusta, trust me enough to tell me what this is all about."

Augusta was silent for a long while. Timothy even wondered if she would refuse to speak, but when she did her voice was small and void of emotion. "I suppose I do owe you an explanation. You see, something happened when I was a little girl. One day the teacher sent me home early because I wasn't feeling well. I could hear my parents raised voices before I even opened our front gate."

Augusta paused and stared out the window, her eyes fixed on something in the distance, but Timothy could tell that in her mind's eye she was seeing herself as that little girl from so long ago.

"It was a week before my ninth birthday," she continued. "I was afraid Mama was angry because Papa said he might buy me a new saddle. Mama never thought I behaved well enough for presents. Anyway, whenever I heard them arguing I was to sit on the front porch until they'd finished. I'm sure they had no idea I was there because that day they were in the parlor with the window to the porch wide open. At first I didn't even listen, until I heard what my mother was so angry about."

Augusta's words trailed off and she suddenly became very still until Timothy gave her a gentle nudge.

"It's okay," he said. "What did you hear?"

Augusta swallowed and blinked up at Timothy. "You know, in all these years Papa and I never told the truth about this, not to anyone—not ever!"

The man put his arm around her and gave her a gentle squeeze. "Probably past time you did—so, go on."

Augusta nodded then continued sadly, "Mama said, 'I insist you get rid of her!' I thought she was talking about Papa's new brood mare, but then she said, 'I knew from the moment the doctor put that child in my arms, that she was a terrible mistake. I can't wait for Augusta to leave for school in the morning, and I dread her coming home. And it only gets worse. Yesterday, her teacher came by and told me I needed to spend more time with her—on her studies. Well, I won't do it!' Then Mama's voice changed—it sounded so hateful—and I'll never forget her words! 'I don't care what you do with her;' she said. 'Kill her, take her out somewhere, and lose her. I hate her and if you don't get rid of her—I will!'"

Augusta grew silent and Timothy felt sick. He gently ran his hand down her arm and asked, "So, what does a nine-year old child do when they hear something like that?"

"When she told Papa to...kill me and that she hated me...I was so scared...I jumped off the porch and ran. I didn't choose a very wise hiding place. I ran straight for our barn, threw my arms around Kippy's neck, and cried like the world had just ended. And that's what it felt like."

Timothy gave her a questioning look. "Old Kippy? The same one I had my first lesson on?"

"The same!" Augusta sniffed, then added: "She's seen me through a lot of tears. Anyway, that's where Papa found me. He took one look at me and knew I had heard it all. It was the strangest thing. I instantly stopped crying. Papa

108

looked so stricken. He held his hand out to me and said. 'Let's take a walk, child.' Papa had a small bundle under his arm and when we headed towards the train station—I knew—Mama had won—and that he was going to get rid of me. I don't think I was ever a child again after that day and I remember being very solemn when I asked, 'Where are you sending me, Papa—will I ever see you again?' At first, he just stopped and stared down at me. When he realized what I had just asked him, he dropped to one knee and hugged me tight. He explained he was just taking me to a friend's house—that I was to come straight home after school the next day and we'd never be apart again!"

"What happened the next day?" Timothy asked.

"Well, I never saw my mother again. I came home and found Papa packing the few things Mama hadn't taken. We left the next day. He wanted to go farther west, like your brother, but this was as far as our funds would take us. When we settled here, Papa decided we would tell everyone that we lost Mama, just before my ninth birthday, and that was the truth."

"You see, Timothy, I'm that child—not even a mother could love. My parents might still be together if it weren't for me. Papa might even still be alive, were it not for me and all the heartache I brought him. I am a mistake! My own mother hated me, and I often felt I had to earn Papa's love—to be worthy of his sacrifice. I was still slow in school when we moved here, so that's why Papa had to come up with his own plan to educate me. I worked hard to please him—I learned to train and sell horses, cook and sew. But I never could make up for what he had lost—it was never enough."

Timothy pulled Augusta into his arms and for a long time he held her close.

"I wish you didn't have memories like that," he soothed, "but that's partly why you're so strong. And you listen to me: how your mother felt—does not make you a mistake! It was her thinking that was flawed—not you!"

"No!" Augusta argued. "God should have never allowed me to born—it was a mistake!"

Timothy gently kissed the top of Augusta's head. "The devil likes for us to believe that kind of lie. He wants us to hate God and hate ourselves because we are God's creation! But, I promise you, God does not make mistakes!"

Augusta looked up at Timothy in frustration. "Then what happened in my life?"

Timothy answered with a shrug. "Oddly enough, the same thing that happened in mine!"

"Yours?" she asked. "Papa told me you were reared by a doting mother!"

"I was!" he agreed. "Augusta, God doesn't make mistakes but people make them on a grand scale. Your mother's mistake was not in having you. Her mistake was in not loving you! And both of my parents made the same mistake."

Augusta looked up at Timothy, disbelief in her eyes. "Both your parents? What do you mean?"

Timothy nodded and shrugged. "It seems we have more in common than either of us knew. You see, on the day my twin brother and I were born, the doctor made a big mistake. Again, God didn't make a mistake but that doctor sure did. He told my mother that the stronger twin robbed the weaker one of nourishment and that the weaker child, which was me, would probably die! It was unreasonable but my mother took an instant dislike to my brother. She handed him over to a wet nurse, Natty May, the slave I told you about, then she devoted herself entirely to saving my life! On the other hand my father acted as if I was already dead. He announced that he had one son, namely Tytus! So it happened that Tytus had a wonderful father and no mother, while I had a loving and kind mother, but never had a father. We all lived together until Ty and I were ten years old—together yet separate. Finally, Mother and I moved to her family's estate in Boston, while my father and Tytus remained on the plantation, in Georgia. I told you about Baker—he was father's friend but didn't like how he treated me. I think that is why he stepped in the way he did. Still, I have to admit that I bore hard feelings toward my father for many years. Then one day Baker read me a passage from the book of Isaiah and God began really speaking to me—about a lot of things."

Augusta was puzzled. Timothy said God spoke to him through the Bible; it seemed a very strange thing to her, but she held her tongue and listened.

"The verse asks, 'Can a woman forget her nursing child, that she should have no compassion on the son of her womb?' Then the verse goes on to answer the question, 'Even these may forget!' Don't you see, Augusta? God knew that some parents would be flawed. They could and would do the unthinkable. Turn away from their own children. But God doesn't just leave us with our own sad truth. God gives us His own promise when he added the following verse, which says, 'Yet I (God) will never forget you. Behold, I have engraved you on the palms of my hands.' Just think of it, Augusta. No matter who may reject us—we are loved intimately by God!"

Timothy had his arm protectively around her; pulling her closer he added, "We were both rejected by a parent but we are not mistakes and I know that God has a plan for us!"

Augusta gazed up at Timothy. She couldn't fool herself any longer. She was falling in love with him—and in loving him, she feared for him. And she knew that staying with her could be dangerous.

"Timothy, you need to understand something—this nightmare I have. It isn't just a bad dream—it's an omen. It has always meant that something terrible will happen—not usually to me, but to someone close to me. It's a warning that you should stay away!"

Augusta waited for Timothy to scoff at her fears, but instead, he said seriously. "I believe we should pay attention to signs and dreams. And if you feel you are being warned of danger to come, then my place is beside you. For better or for worse—remember?"

Leaning close to her he whispered, "Something bad may be coming but something good happened between us today. Let's not talk about ending our marriage. Let's talk about beginning it—for real And regardless of what lies ahead, we'll see it through together!"

Timothy slid the back of his hand, slowly down her cheek. "Please Augusta, give me your trust! We can have a happy marriage!"

Augusta had never heard Timothy sound so vulnerable. Suddenly, a womanly instinct as old as Eve spoke to her heart. *You know this man: his love is genuine! He's all that Papa had said he was—a prince among men, a man of strength and integrity.* She turned her head to look up at him, and saw that he was clenching his jaw, nervously awaiting her answer.

"I haven't wanted to trust you, Timothy Grainger," she said softly.

Nodding, he looked down at her. "I know—but—I wish you would."

Taking his hand in hers Augusta slowly ran her fingernails down his palm. "I've tried just about everything to keep from loving you," she admitted, "from anger to bad manners. Nothing seems to work. I didn't know you could fall in love, even when you were determined not to."

A slow grin spread across Timothy's face as he deciphered Augusta's words.

"This isn't how I thought this talk would end. But I want to be your wife—if you're sure you want me?"

"Oh Augusta!" Timothy groaned, then he laughed out loud with relief. "How can you ask me, *IF* I want you?"

Augusta could see the tender passion in Timothy's face and it made her feel self-conscious and nervous. Timothy bent to kiss her… but before he could she blurted out: "You know what Papa kept saying after Mama left?"

Timothy's smile was full of understanding; his wife had finally declared her love, in a very round-about way. But now, she was the one feeling vulnerable. It didn't matter; he could be patient awhile longer.

"Your father was a wise man—I'd like to hear what he had to say."

Augusta cleared her throat and mimicked her father's Irish brogue: "'We'll not mourn over yesterday's tears, fer if we do, we'll only be missin' today's blessin's!'"

Timothy grinned at the accent but then the meaning of the words sank in. "I like that! It's good advice for the two of us!"

Again he leaned in to kiss her, but once more Augusta held him back.

"Timothy," she said with a grimace. "I am sorry for the way I acted on our wedding day. I'd never even held a man's hand before, and I just couldn't allow a stranger to kiss me. But, I did appreciate what you did!" She paused for a moment then asked, "But I've been very curious—may I ask you about something?"

Timothy rubbed his chin over the top of Augusta's head, feeling the silky texture of her hair.

"Right now," he sighed, "you could ask me for a king's ransom and you would have it! Ask away!"

Augusta gave a little giggle. "I don't want a king's ransom. But, my question is about royalty."

With her golden eyes sparkling she asked, "What you said about Prince Albert and Queen Victoria—were you telling the truth about that?"

Timothy leaned back, a deep chuckle rumbling from his chest. "Well—to be honest—I have no idea what good old Albert said to his bride that day."

Augusta frowned. "Thought you always try to tell the truth," she teased.

Grinning, Timothy pulled his wife close, tweaked her nose, and then explained: "Augusta, there were a number of truths I was dealing with on our wedding day. First, never have I seen a bride that was more beautiful than you! You took my breath away!"

Timothy kissed Augusta's forehead tenderly, then he looked down at her with a broad grin. "The second truth was that never have I seen a bride more determined not to kiss her groom!"

Augusta covered her face with her hands. "I know … I'm so sorry—I just couldn't … "

"It's all right, Augusta!" Timothy chuckled as he pulled her hands away from her face. "I'm not chastising you," he said. "But I had been looking forward to our first kiss and I was hoping to make it memorable, not traumatic! So, when the reverend insisted I kiss my bride, I knew I had to think of something. I don't know why Albert came to mind but I was sure happy that he did!"

Augusta stared dumbfounded at her husband. "So, you just—made it up?"

Timothy grimaced. "It seemed like a good idea at the time!"

Augusta laughed. "Yes! It certainly was!"

Her expression turned sheepish when she admitted, "You don't want to know what I would have done if you had tried kissed me that day!"

Wrapping Augusta in his arms, Timothy whispered, "Oh, I knew! You'd have kicked me in the shins the moment your papa wasn't looking! Right?"

"How did you know?"

Timothy gave her another squeeze. "It was written all over your face! But I didn't mind—and our first kiss was worth waiting for! Wasn't it?"

"It was…" Augusta agreed shyly. "And…I have just…one more thing to say to you … "

Timothy smiled, wondering how long it might be before Augusta relaxed enough to allow him to kiss her again. However, he was happily surprised when he heard what it was that she had to say: "Mister Grainger," she said with a wondrous smile, "you may now kiss your bride. In fact—" she added, "she insists on it!"

Timothy drew in a deep breath, and was pleased when Augusta boldly returned his adoring gaze, her expressive golden eyes telling him all he needed to know. This moment had been well worth the wait—he wanted to promise her again that he would protect and cherish her. At that moment it seemed there were no words worthy of his feelings. Timothy lowered his head and kissed Augusta's tear-stained cheeks, first one side then the other. He drew in another deep breath, looked again into Augusta's dewy brown eyes, then took possession of her soft mouth, gently covering her lips with his. Slowly, Augusta's hand came up to touch his face then she moved her fingers until they curled around his neck, and tangled in his hair. When Timothy heard Augusta's contented sigh, he instantly deepened the kiss. Suddenly, they both were caught up in a sweet passion, where all worries and fears were swept away. These new feelings went beyond anything either had ever imagined. As Augusta responded to the tender ardor of her husband's embrace, the woman hidden within awoke and blossomed. In one instant she felt as if she was bathing in a liquid fire, and the next, that she and Timothy were being swept away to some secret place, unique only unto them. Each embrace—a precious gift—knowing that neither had ever shared this intimacy with anyone else.

As moonlight shimmered through the window, their marriage truly began. Never were kisses sweeter nor passionate embraces more ardent. And just as God himself ordained, on that special night, the two became one, and so they began their journey, that matchless adventure, as husband and wife.

Chapter 15
Getting Ready

"A wise man will hear and increase in learning, and a man of understanding will acquire wise counsel." Proverbs 1:5

Once Augusta and Timothy truly began their marriage, it was as if all the disjointed pieces of their lives suddenly fell into place. They immediately began preparing for their journey west and spent their days like two happy children at play. Augusta's fears vanished as did her terrifying nightmares, and in their place, came dreams—dreams of an adventure crossing the Plains—dreams of horses and cattle and of ranching in the West. The only concern that troubled Augusta was the thought of leaving her friends behind. Then, one day answered prayer in the guise of an energetic redhead rushed like a whirlwind through Augusta's back door.

"Oh, darlin'!" Emily gasped as she ran inside. "Just wait 'til ya hear what's happened! Ya won't believe it—ya just—won't believe it!"

"Emily!" Augusta chided, "Catch your breath and what is it—I won't believe?"

With her blue eyes sparkling and a grin as wide as the Mississippi, Emily threw her arms around Augusta then released her and fell dramatically onto the closest kitchen chair.

"It's a miracle—a gen—u—ine miracle!" she huffed. "And it all started when a dandy of a New York lawyer came into the café this mornin'! He asked fer the house special, a cup o' coffee, and directions to the home of Missus Amelia Langstrom-Drew. 'Course I saw him there m'self, so's I could stick around and make sure he wasn't up to no good."

"Well, was he up to no good? What is this all about?" Augusta fussed.

"Just hold on—I'm getting there! Ya know Missus D.'s pa died awhile back and then she told us that her mother passed on last year."

When Augusta nodded, Emily raced on with her story.

"Well, this lawyer; he's got thick white hair, looks real dig—ni—fied, dresses real fine, and he's kind a handsome and..."

Augusta impatiently shook her friends arm. "Emily, I don't care what he looks like—what did he say?"

"I said I'm gettin' there! Ya know I got ta tell things m'own way! Anyway—the lawyer, he says to Missus D., 'I don't know if you realize it but you were the only heir to the Langstrom for-tune and estate. You have inherited two brownstones, and the mansion, Mosslet Way, along with all other family assets!'"

Emily shook her head. "Seems even though her parents were spittin' mad at her when she married, they never got around to changin' their will. Turns out, our sweet little friend and town seamstress—who's barely been makin' ends meet—is a bloomin' millionaire! The way things stand now—you and Tim won't be the only ones packin' up for a big adventure!"

Emily stopped long enough to fan her face with her apron, then a happy glow spread across her face.

"And, as it happens," she added softly, "the Tylanes won't be left out! Missus D. don't want to go alone! She has no family—and well—she wants to claim Wes and me as her own."

Augusta quickly squeezed her friends hand, "Oh. Emily that's—"

"Hold on now," the redhead interrupted. "There's more! It's kind of a private thing but ya know we've lost three young'uns. I never have carried one past six months. Missus D. said she'd take me to one of them specialists and maybe—if I didn't have to work s' hard or be on my feet all the time—well, maybe? Anyway—Lord willin'—we just might have us an heir fer the Langstrom-Tylane estate some day!"

At that, Emily and Augusta fell into each other's arms, allowing the tears to flow unchecked. They were just mopping up the evidence of their joy when in came Timothy, Wes, and Amelia herself.

There was much laughter as the miraculous story was told and retold. The news spread through town like wild-fire! It seemed the most beloved citizens of their sleepy little hamlet were leaving. Nothing would ever be the same; the livery was under new management and now the Dutch Oven was up for sale. The Tylane's would be sorely missed—Wes with his kind easy-going ways and Emily with her bright smile and quick wit, not to mention their cooking! Amelia Drew was another town favorite; and with her departure, they would lose their best seamstress plus the refining influence she had on all the female population. And then, of course, they would all miss watching the pretty young

A.C. O'Brien riding down the street on her fine stallion. Everyone had even grown fond of her young husband, Timothy Grainger.

Although the townsfolk already mourned the loss of their favorite citizens, it was a comfort to this small group of friends that they each had a special adventure of their own to look forward to. It also took a bit of the sting from their good-byes—but just a bit, for the good-byes still had to be made.

Things moved almost too quickly for Mrs. Drew and the Tylanes. The Dutch Oven and Amelia's little cottage sold in less than two weeks. Unlike the Graingers, they needn't delay their journey east waiting for good weather or the prairie grasses to grow deep. Suddenly, there was nothing for it, but to head for New York, and begin their new lives. And so, it was a somber group that walked towards the stagecoach one chilly morning. Augusta linked arms with Mrs. Drew on one side and Emily on the other. They huddled together as Timothy prayed, beseeching God, not only to give them all safe journeys, but to guide each of them in the new challenges that lie ahead.

Still, Augusta just couldn't seem to bid them a final good-bye. She would hug Emily then Mrs. Drew, then Wes, then—start all over again. Finally, Timothy leaned down and gently whispered, "The driver insists on leaving now, my darling—we must let them go!"

The driver cleared his throat. "Got a schedule to keep, ya know!"

Augusta forced a smile as she helped Mrs. Drew into the coach, then hugged Emily once more before Wes helped her up. As tears streamed down her face Augusta hugged Wes, then whispered in his ear, "Promise you will take extra good care of yourself and—all four of you for that matter!"

Wes frowned as he muttered: "All four?"

When Augusta nodded towards Emily; the man blushed so that even his neck turned crimson. Emily had shared her precious news with Augusta just that morning.

Wes grinned then leaned down and kissed Augusta's cheek. He and Timothy clasped hands while they slapped each other on the back. The driver, impatient and weary of all the sentiment, lifted his whip and the team began to move out. Wes had to catapult himself inside the coach or be left behind.

Augusta didn't even try to hide her heartache, and Timothy held her close while she and Emily and Mrs. Drew waved their handkerchiefs at each other until the stage was completely out of sight. And yet, as much as she hated to see her friends leave, it was a relief to have these painful good-byes behind her.

The following months sped by in a flurry. Augusta became nearly as excited as Timothy as they gathered supplies and prepared for their journey. When they heard that the man who would be leading them west was the well-seasoned wagon master, Caleb Wolf, they were even more encouraged. Timothy studied the man's letter of instruction with nearly the dedication he gave his Bible. Although he felt sure he had followed it in every detail, Timothy pulled it from his pocket and read it again, just to make certain.

Mr. Grainger,

You'll need six stout horses and the harnesses to go with them. Horses—not mules, not oxen. Indian's favor mule meat and no ox has ever outrun a war party. Two teams will pull your wagon, the third is for the remuda to trade out with or add when the trail is rough. Sell your fancy clocks and harpsichords, or they'll be used as firewood along the trail. Buy the best built wagon you can find and even better wheels or you will find yourselves a foot. Wagons are to be fitted with a double osnaburg cover; boil linseed oil and beeswax, and coat them both generously!

Each wagon will need: 2 water barrels; everything else must be bagged. 400 lbs. flour, 1 bushel cornmeal, 60 lbs. pilot bread, 20 lbs. rice, 150 lbs. bacon packed in bran, 10 lbs. coffee, 5 lbs tea, 1 bushel dried beans, 1 bushel dried fruit, 50 lbs. sugar, 5 lbs. saleratus.

Bring a variety and goodly quantity of medicines and bandages. Whiskey drinking will not be tolerated on the Wolf Train. However, if used as medicine, you may bring two jugs. Bring Laudanum—if you can get it.

Pack: 1 small sheet metal stove, 1 Dutch oven, 1 cast-iron skillet, tin plates and cups, 1 handgun with gun belt, 1 rifle, 1 shotgun, plenty of ammunition; powder and shot, and a bullet mold. All clothing must be sturdy. Pack extra shoes and the material and leather to patch or replace as needed.

Good shots are expected to hunt. Good cooks are expected to invite me to dinner.

Caleb Wolf, Wagon Master

Augusta hid her smile when Timothy returned Wolf's letter to his pocket; he didn't need to look at it—he could recite it from memory.

"We're pulling out tomorrow, Augusta! It's finally here and now that it is—I can't believe it!"

Augusta nodded wearily, as she lay encircled in Timothy's arms. They both knew they should be sleeping. Mr. Wolf had warned everyone to prepare for an early start, and a hard first week. He had also told everyone that he hated to "burn daylight". Still, thoughts and emotions crowded out any hope of sleep.

They had said all their good-byes: to Smithy and Sammy, to Doc and Becky Mitchell, and to all the children Augusta had given riding lessons. Augusta had even said good-bye to Kippy and the other horses at the livery.

On Timothy's part, it wasn't only excitement that kept him from finding sleep. He'd been feeling guilty. Finally, he let out a very uncharacteristic groan and broke the silence. "There's something I've been meaning to talk to you about."

Timothy frowned up at the ceiling, trying to say this so as not to upset his wife, but to prepare her. "I've been a little worried that I haven't told you enough about Tytus. The past few years he's become a hard man…hardest of all…on…women, I'm afraid. Not physically, but you know that our mother rejected him, and his fiancé rejected not only him but his ranch. He's become very judgmental regarding the fairer sex."

Augusta rolled to her side, and stared at Timothy. "I know all that—what are you worried about?"

"Well, because of my health I had assumed I'd never marry. Then after Savannah, Ty decided he would never marry. He has looked forward to the two of us brothers running the ranch together. But the Bible says, 'It is not good for a man to be alone. You've made me so happy, and I want that for Tytus too!"

Turning towards her he lifted her chin and gave her a thorough kiss; then he winked at her and said, "We need to show Ty that he's been a fool to give up his dreams for a wife and children. He would still make a good husband and father. He just needs to find the right woman. More people move west every year: God's bound to have someone for him. At first I didn't tell him about you, because he's so suspicious of women and I wasn't sure if I could get A.C. O'Brien to stay married to me!"

Augusta smiled, "Well, Miss A.C. O'Brien is now quite happy to be Missus Grainger!"

Timothy grinned. "That's good to hear, Missus Grainger! And I want you to stay happy. And I want Ty happy too. He's a good man, Augusta—when he's not being hard headed and—stubborn."

"Timothy, it sounds like he'll be determined to hate me—even before he meets me."

"I honestly don't know how he'll react. He can be intimidating. But I don't want him to accept you for my sake. His heart won't heal until he meets a woman he can respect."

When he saw the worried expression spread across Augusta's face, he quickly added, "I have faith in you. If anyone can tame that beast—it's you!"

Augusta shook her head. "Why did you wait until now to tell me all this?"

Timothy smiled as he twisted one of Augusta's soft curls around his finger. "I don't know—we've been having so much fun, I guess. Besides, I have told you that Ty had been hurt. How he worked like a man possessed for three years preparing for Savannah's arrival. He even named the ranch, the Bar 61, because that's the year their life together would begin. But—when she saw the place—nothing was good enough for her, including Ty. When she left, it seems, she took all his hopes and dreams with her. It's been five years, but he's still prickly on the subject. The only good that came out of it was that Ty insisted she bring with her the two slaves I told you about: Joseph and Natty May. Father sold them to Savannah's family because Ty was so close to them. Of course Ty freed them the moment they set foot on the Bar 61. Anyway, a few years back Joseph wrote me that Savannah had brought with her expensive bolts of fabric. Natty May was to have sewn window curtains and made cushions. However, when Savannah saw that Ty had built them a hacienda, not the Georgian plantation house like she'd expected, she said it would be like putting a silk dress on a mud-hog. After Savannah left, Joseph wrote me that Natty May started in on the curtains but Tytus wouldn't hear of it and had everything stored in a back room. Natty May died soon after, and no woman has lived on the place since. The only part of Ty's dream that remains is for me to join him. Just we two brothers working side by side."

Augusta shook her head. "Sounds like things are going to be messy at first, aren't they?"

"Probably—but people can change and my brother needs too. And I believe your presence will help him do that."

Augusta shuddered. "You're expecting an awful lot of me!"

Timothy turned where he could look into her eyes. "No—" he assured her. "I'm only expecting you to be yourself—ride horses, sew curtains, bake bread and pies. Be that sweet and sassy A.C. O'Brien-Grainger I've come to adore!"

Augusta groaned and shrugged her shoulders. "And...if your grumpy brother never likes me?"

"He will!" Timothy insisted. "Tytus just needs to meet a woman who was meant to be a Grainger. Meant to be a rancher's wife. But—you will need to stand up to him! Let him know that you are just as much a partner in the Bar 61 as I am! I did write him. I just wish I'd sent it sooner—so he could have, a little more time, to get used to the idea."

The late hour was finally catching up with Timothy; he stretched and yawned before adding, "And then of course you have an ace up your sleeve."

Augusta was suddenly very curious. "What ace is that?" she demanded.

"Surely you remember all those extra jars of cherries, not to mention all the sugar, cinnamon, and spices I insisted we pack! Tytus Grainger has the biggest sweet tooth of any man I've ever known. With that in mind I have stocked your arsenal—with the weapons my brother has no defense against!"

"And what exactly would those be?"

"Cherry pie—cinnamon rolls—and sugar cookies!"

Chapter 16
The Santa Fe Trail

"We prayed that God would give us a safe journey and protect us, our children, and our goods as we traveled." Ezra 8:21

Spring—1866

The first few weeks on the trail were both exciting and exhausting. There was a sense of pride as the pioneers passed through towns and villages as they headed westward. The curious would watch from porches and barn lofts as the long line of wagons rolled by, no doubt speculating if these travelers were headed for fortune or folly. As for the sojourners themselves, there seemed to be two distinctive and opposing opinions that prevailed among them. The men took on a bit of a swagger, proud that they had finally acted on their dreams, pulling up stakes to boldly face the unknown. While at the same time, apprehension settled upon the women. Most of them had faith in their men, believing they'd do their best to provide. Still, they knew the burden of making sure that the food and clothing lasted, and their families stayed healthy, fell upon the women. They found themselves praying with every mile, that the supplies so carefully packed would hold out until they could be replenished. They knew precious little about what lay ahead, and what they did know, seemed harsh, barren and lonely. Of course, this was the mystery of the pioneer couple. The siren call of the great unknown seemed to kindle a fire in a man's blood, while it chilled the hearts of their women.

Collectively, the women kept one eye on their children and the other on the distant horizon, watching for one of the scouts to come riding back in a cloud of dust, giving a warning of danger ahead. At those times the woman and children would stay close to the wagons, keeping the few milk cows and remuda of horses as close as possible.

After months on the trail the rigors of this journey had changed everyone. For some, they became leaner, harder, and stronger, while others grew weaker with each passing mile. The journey was most difficult on the very old and the very young. For most, this excursion for its own sake quickly lost its luster. What drove them on was the anticipation of that illusive pot of gold at journey's end! For some, it was the literal hope of gold, either dug from the mountains or dipped from the streams. They dreamt of rich claims, and easy living. For others it was the vision of golden wheat, waving waist high on their own land. As for the women, they dreamt of the golden flames coming from a real fireplace, in a real house, where their families would be safe and warm. They longed for a roof made of wood not canvas, one that did not leak when it rained and a home that did not sway when the wind blew. For each traveler it was their own hope and vision that gave them the courage and strength to rise each morning and face the challenges of another hard day. After all, they had been warned by their wagon master, Caleb Wolf. As was his custom, that first morning before the first wagon pulled out of Missouri, he had gathered them all together and told them plainly that each and every journey west exacts its own price.

"I can promise you folks two things," he had began.

"One, this journey will present you with hardships beyond anything you have ever experienced. The other is that some of you standing here will die along the way. Some of you will not make it to whatever destination you call the promised land. There will be breakdowns; it may be you, your wagon or, your stock. A breakdown means that you'll be forced to set down roots wherever your hardship occurs. I cannot say who will make it and who will not. That— thankfully—is in God's hands, not mine."

His steel gray eyes searched the people gathered around him then he added, "If you change your mind at this time, your money will be refunded, and no one will think ill of you."

The wagon master had walked away, allowing the group to consider his words as they made their way back to their wagons. An hour later he returned riding his appaloosa stallion, leading the way out of town—and not one had stayed behind.

Timothy prayed every night that this wagon train would escape Wolf's sad prediction. And for the first few weeks, though the trail was often rough and the days long, nothing major happened. Then tragedy struck the Wolf train when six-year-old Betsy Darkin was kicked in the stomach by one of their horses. The gentle mare had responded to the bite of a horse fly and the little girl had simply been standing in the wrong place. They had no doctor and it might not have helped if they had. In less than an hour, the little girl died in the arms of her heartbroken parents. Overwhelmed by grief and blinded by rage, Betsy's young father grabbed his rifle and shot the horse that had killed his little girl. It wasn't until after the child was buried and prayed over that the Darkin family realized that they no longer had enough horses to pull their wagon. Though others offered to lend them one of their horses from the remuda, the family declined, deciding in their sorrow to build their farm there beside little Betsy's grave.

The reality of Caleb Wolf's prophecy settled into the travelers as they bid the Darkins good-bye. He had told them every journey exacts a price and now they had understood how great the cost could be. The journey weighed more heavily on everyone after Betsy's death. It seemed that one challenge was conquered only to be faced with another and then another. First came the relentless rains. From them came the never-ending series of mud holes. And then of course—when they arrived at the next creek or river, they would find the waterways swollen and angry. Each mile seemed to test the strength and fortitude of both man and beast.

When they reached the vast open prairies, and the winds came and dried the ground, they were grateful. For it also dried their wet clothing that chaffed their skin. However, they soon learned that the prairie wind was a force all its own, that it too could be dangerous and deadly. This was a wind that not only dried their clothes and the mud holes, but it also dried the watering holes, it ripped the canvas wagon tops, and parched their bodies. The wind was a parasite—sucking the life from everything it touched.

The bright spot of each week was Sunday. Mr. Wolf insisted the wagons halt on the Lord's day, and that was a blessing for everyone. This was greatly appreciated by those who wished to worship on Sunday, but soon everyone saw the wisdom in giving their teams and themselves a day of rest! Timothy and a few of the other men took turns reading scripture, then sharing what those verses had meant to them. Among the travelers there were two men who played guitars and one of the older women who played a mouth harp. They sang hymns after the scriptures were read, but quite often another impromptu singing would start up around sundown to round out the day. Still, the Sabbath wasn't entirely a day of ease; for broken harnesses had to be mended and clothes washed—if water was available—and both people and their stock had to be fed. But it was a time they all looked forward to and needed!

Finally, the day came when the Wolf train arrived at the Cimarron Cut Off. There was a nervous tension that filled the air, and more good-byes to be said. For this was where the Wolf train would split in two; most of the wagons would head south, crossing the Cimarron Desert bound for Texas, while still others continued all the way to Santa Fe, New Mexico. This group of wagons would be led by Tres Sanchez, Mr. Wolf's top scout. The Graingers, along with five other wagons would remain with Mr. Wolf and head up into the Colorado Territory.

Wolf led the smaller group for they were more vulnerable. From the beginning, they had prepared themselves for skirmishes with Indians, or possibly even rustlers or bandits. However, thus far they'd been spared attack, partly due to—that old adage—safety in numbers. So far nature had been their worst adversary. But now that the Wolf train numbered only six, they must be even more watchful for enemies that walked on two legs and rode on four. As each mile brought them closer to their destinations, they reminded themselves to stay vigilant, or they might just be the ones Caleb Wolf had spoken of—those who would not make it to their journey's end, their promised land, or even to the end of the day!

Chapter 17
The New Passenger

"Children are a gift from the LORD; they are a reward from him." Psalm 127:3

Timothy knew that coyotes would soon be calling up the morning sun—but for now—all was still in the moonlit hours before dawn. So, he stepped quietly, as he carried two buckets of water through the sleeping camp. As he approached their fire his eyes met Augusta's, mirroring the concern they both felt as another heartbreaking cry came from the young woman inside the wagon. Without a word he poured the fresh water in the heavy pot while Augusta stoked the flames.

Ian and Rachel Kelly had become close friends. Being the only married couple with no children to look after in the evenings, the four had struck up an instant friendship. And yet their commonality was to be short lived, for Rachel was even now struggling to give birth to her first child.

At first the young woman bravely muffled her cries but the last few pains were so severe she couldn't help but scream. When Augusta heard her friends anguish, she threw herself into Timothy's arms.

"If I can't stand this—how can she?" Augusta asked as she wept. "I'm sorry. But, I don't want to have a baby—I don't."

Timothy held her tight, and brushed his cheek against her silky hair. Never had he felt so helpless. He didn't know how to comfort his wife—for he was deeply shaken himself. He had heard that while in labor, a woman walks through the valley of the shadow of death...this night—he knew it to be true! His heart went out, not only to poor Rachel, but to Ian as well. The frightened young husband was beside himself and Timothy couldn't help but wonder how any man could bear to see his wife suffer this way.

Knowing the only one that could help, Timothy pulled Augusta close, then bowed his head, praying, "Lord, please have mercy on Rachel and the baby! We ask that this child come into the world safely and soon. Thank You for sending a mid-wife just when Rachel needed her. We see Your hand of mercy in all of this. Please let all these tears soon turn to joy—and we will praise You for it!"

As if on cue a soft mulling came from inside the wagon. It was followed by a strange croaking cackle as the old mid-wife called out: "Praise the Lord, young'uns—ya got yerselves a fine boy!"

❦

Augusta sighed as she put the last cook pot away and laid her dish rag over the back of the wagon to dry.

"I just can't get over…the difference a week can make! Exactly seven days ago, Rachel was in agony and Ian was terrified—*we all were terrified*. And now John Patrick is thriving, Rachel is mending quickly, and Ian is as proud as a peacock. They are the happiest little family I've ever seen!"

Timothy grinned at Augusta's surprise. "Children are a gift from God; it doesn't always turn out this way but this is how it's supposed to be."

Augusta smiled, but there was a sadness in her eyes. She picked up the baking she had set aside.

"I'm going to take these biscuits to Rachel, and see if she needs any help. You don't mind—do you?"

Timothy shook his head, hoping a walk would ease the tension he saw in his wife's face.

"I don't mind—as long as you've made enough for me too!" he teased. "Besides, I think a visit with Rachel will do you good. I'd come with you but I need to get this harness mended."

"Don't worry—I'll be gone for a while—after I check on Rachel, I want to stretch my legs a bit."

Augusta patted his shoulder then turned and walked away. Her words turned bitter in her mouth, for she wasn't telling the truth. She didn't want to walk—she wanted to sleep. She'd been so tired lately and that wasn't like her. Her Boston 'greenhorn' was thriving on this journey. He seemed to grow stronger and more handsome with every mile; his arms were becoming thick and muscular, his skin bronzing in the sunlight, his blonde hair becoming even more golden.

Why aren't I thriving too? I wasn't even feeling completely myself before we left home. Something's not right. What if—I'm? I know Timothy wants children…the way he stared at me the other day when I was holding John Patrick…that tender look. Rachel said she forgot the pain when her baby was put into her arms. But, I'll never forget what Mama

127

said: "The moment they put that child in my arms—*I knew she was a mistake!" Oh Lord, what am I going to do? I just can't have a baby—I just can't!*

Augusta was torn from her thoughts when five-year-old Sarah Burns ran to meet her.

"Missus Gusta!" the girl called, as a riot of red curls floated about her head in a wild tangle.

"Gots a flower fer ya! It's the best—est one. I want ya should have it!"

"Oh, Sarah," Augusta said, smiling as she knelt down before the little girl. "That's awfully sweet of you…but since it's so special…don't you want to save it for your mama?"

"Nope, I already gave her another best—est one!" she said, then pushed the flower into Augusta's hand.

Augusta chuckled. "Well, it's beautiful! Thank you, sweetheart!"

She hugged the little girl and kissed her cheek before she ran away in search of more pretty flowers. When Augusta reached Rachel's wagon, a strange feeling came over her as she watched the new mother tenderly gazing down at her sleeping child.

When Rachel noticed her standing there, she smiled as she took the biscuits. Then, in her smooth Virginia drawl she said: "I am much obliged—for these! Why—this mornin' the babe wouldn't allow me a minute—to fix Ian's breakfast!"

Rachel knew all about Augusta's fears; she also knew her friend needed to face her fears.

Making a shooing motion with her hands, Rachel said insistently: "I believe you have an impo'tant visit to make. I am not goin' to let ya put this off anotha' minute! Now go—and talk to her—she'll put your mind—at ease."

Rachel's black hair fell over her shoulder as she bent to lift the baby from his cradle, then with an amused look she added, "And—if it is as I expect, I will allow John Patrick to be the one—to teach you all about—changin' a dirty diap'r."

Augusta ignored her friends teasing and walked away, feeling more frightened than ever. As she passed each wagon, she reminded herself that life was a challenge for everyone. Regardless of the variety of hopes each wagon and family represented, none of them knew what lay ahead. Did their futures hold joy or sorrow, life or death?

Finally, Augusta came to the wagon belonging to the mid-wife. Timothy had been right—her joining the wagon train just when Rachel needed her had been God's hand at work! And perhaps God had sent this woman to help her as well.

Timidly, Augusta approached the woman as she sat by her camp fire. She hadn't remembered her being such an odd little thing, and was finding it hard not to stare. Her face was as round as a full moon and crisscrossed with lines, like a dry desert. She wore a dress made of flour sacks cut into squares and sewn together like a patchwork quilt. At the hem of her skirt was added a good six inches of flaming red ruffle. Peaking from beneath the ruffle were a pair of men's trousers tucked inside two unmatched boots. And yet despite her unusual attire, there was something about this woman that reminded her of the fashionable Amelia Drew. At first Augusta thought it was just the way the old woman wore her hair: all pulled into a thick braid, and coiled about the top of her head, like a crown of polished silver. But it was also in the way the little woman held herself; she was small but regal. Then Augusta looked into her eyes and saw a pair of the most intelligent, bright blue eyes she had ever seen. And like Timothy, the old woman had a definite look of mischief about her. Augusta instantly thought of her father's stories, about the impish little folk who seasoned his tall tales of his beloved Emerald Isle. Augusta smiled to herself; Timothy would love this! She would return to him tonight and tell him she had gone for a walk, and along the way, she had met the Fairy Queen!

"Pardon me?" Augusta asked shyly. "I'm sorry I…uh…I don't remember your name?"

The old woman gave Augusta a toothless grin and said with a shrug: "Folks has always called me Aunt Sis," she answered with a chuckle. "Ma and Aunt Eulla was healers. They jes' called me Sis. But—when I begun healin'… folks didn't reckon Sis twas respectful like. So they started in callin' me—Aunt Sis—been goin' by that handle pert' near all ma life."

With another gaping smile she nodded her head, and added sweetly, "I shore 'member you, Mizz Grainger, and I'm plum tickled to see ya, deary—been spectin' ya."

"Expecting me?" Augusta mumbled. "I didn't even know I was coming—not for sure—it's just that…"

Augusta shrugged self-consciously as the old woman's sea-blue-eyes seemed to study her. She couldn't help but wonder if this "Aunt Sis" wasn't some kind of a Fairy Queen after all or possibly even an—angel? Timothy had read to her about entertaining angels unaware, and the woman had appeared just when needed.

As if she could read Augusta's thoughts, the old woman spoke up, her voice both soft and raspy. "Rest easy, Mizz Grainger. I ain't nothin' but an old woman," she soothed. "And a friend! If ya'll allow it? I been wantin' to thank ya, 'n yer husband, fer helpin' with the birthin' t'other night!"

"We didn't do much," Augusta muttered. "But your joining us when you did was certainly a miracle!"

"Well—us healers ere a strange lot, 'n folks don't always take to us. 'Cept when they's in pain."

A penetrating light came into the old woman's eyes as she stared at Augusta, then she said slowly, "We healers…have a kind of knowin'…reckon it's 'cause we see so many tears. There's a heap to learn 'bout a body from their tears."

A tremor passed through Augusta; she was fearful of what this old woman might be seeing in her.

Suddenly, Aunt Sis clucked her tongue, with her thin lips curling in, she patted the smooth rock next to hers beside the fire and said: "Come 'n sit—deary. I'll just fix us some tea—and—we'll have us a little talk."

Warily, Augusta sat down, tightly clasping her hands together to keep them from shaking.

"Well now—" Aunt Sis began softly, "d'ya know there's somethin' special that comes into a woman's eyes when she's with child? Oh, yes! I can always tell."

Augusta's heart began pounding in her ears as the old woman took her youthful hand in hers and said, "Ya've had a notion…fer quite a while…haven't ya? But being as young as ya ere…ya just couldn't believe it had really happened to *you*? Ain't that right?"

Augusta stared into the fire, but found herself nodding as tears filled her eyes.

Aunt Sis gave her hand a gentle squeeze. "Now—now—ya mustn't be afeard. This is glad news! And yet I see terrible worry in those sun-kissed eyes a your'n. So—why don't ya jes' tell this old auntie all about it, honey. Tell m' everthin'."

Augusta looked into the sweet face of this woman and found such kindness there that before she realized what she was doing, her whole life story was pouring from her lips. She told of her mother's rejection, her father's death, and her sudden marriage to Timothy—and now—this new fear of what was happening inside her.

"I'm ashamed," she sobbed. "But this is not glad news for me—I don't want it to be true." With her face turning a thousand shades of red she admitted, "I haven't had a monthly since my father died. I thought maybe I couldn't have a baby. I know I'm wicked to think it but—to me that was glad news."

Augusta groaned miserably. "I haven't been sick—not a day. But I haven't been myself either. Even before we left home I—felt *different* somehow."

Augusta tried to school her features to behave like a grown woman should, and not as a frightened child, even though that was how she felt.

"And what makes it worse," she added, "Timothy and I are going to live on a big ranch, where I'll be the only woman for miles and miles! Having a baby right now—it's just not possible—I can't do it!"

The old woman's face was a picture of serenity as she prepared the tea, quietly listening to Augusta cry out her fears. Then, as daintily as Mrs. Drew would've done, she filled two tin cups with the richly scented brew and presented one to Augusta.

"Now, ya drink every drop a this," she ordered, then said gently: "Ya've seen yer share a storms, sure nuf! A...course ya already know the best way to make it through life's storms. Twas a blessin' to hear yer man praying outside the Kelly wagon. God gives strength to his children. So, we'll pray and the Lord'll do the rest!"

The old woman's words pierced Augusta. Once again she was aware of God's sad eyes looking into her heart, waiting for her to ask Him in. She wasn't a child of God—Timothy was. Is that why she struggled so, because she still hadn't made things right with God?

Suddenly, Augusta was distracted from her thoughts when the old woman pulled a small tin from her pocket. Carefully, she opened it, revealing a reddish brown powder, and Augusta was instantly intrigued.

"Care fer some snuff, deary?"

Augusta was shocked. Mrs. Drew had told her no lady would ever do such an unwholesome thing. "Humm...n—no thank you," she said politely but still she watched with unabashed curiosity.

"Well—I know—some say it ain't fittin' fer a lady!" Aunt Sis readily admitted, even as she pulled a small twig from her pocket.

Augusta noticed that the end had been chewed and frayed out to make a little brush. She dampened the brush with her tongue then dipped it daintily into the powder. As Augusta looked on with wide eyes, Aunt Sis grinned her toothless grin and passed the little brush back and forth over her gums. Leaving Augusta to wonder if this wasn't why...the old woman had no teeth!

A few moments later, as if Augusta's sensibilities hadn't been taxed enough, Aunt Sis asked graciously, "Would ya hand me that can over yonder, deary? I'll be needin' to spit—directly!"

Augusta bit back her startled smile and did as she was told. It was then she concluded that Aunt Sis probably was not an angel. And fairly certain that even impish fairy queens would never spit into a cup!

When the old woman finished her little ritual, she turned to Augusta with a grin, saying: "Now, young'un, I'm gonna tell ya m'secret to a life well lived! Trust in the Lord, no matter what! When the Lord sends ya good times— thank him! For all blessings come from God and God alone!"

Taking Augusta's small hand in hers, she stared deeply into Augusta's face. A shadow seemed to fall over her expression for a moment and then the old woman whispered gently, "Hard times'll come, deary—they always do. To some—perhaps more'n others. There's nothin' fer it, but to roll up yer sleeves'n say, 'Lord, I'm a-trustin' ya to get me through this!' And—He will!"

Augusta gave the old woman a questioning look. "And—what about the baby?"

"Ah! Nothin' to worry about there!" she continued, now speaking strictly as a mid-wife. "Mizz Grainger, yer built jes' right fer having young'uns. Don't foresee ya havin' a bit of trouble. So don't ya be frettin'. Ya'll do jes' fine. Rest— and a peaceful heart—twill be yer best medicine!"

⊱≈⊰

Augusta tossed and turned in the narrow confines of the wagon, while the dream tormented her. Once again, she was enfolded in utter darkness— trapped in a prison of stone. Then she heard the rattle of snakes, and felt something brush against her foot. She stiffened and screamed, "Nooooo!"

"Augusta!" Timothy called, gently shaking her, his deep voice penetrating the nightmares hold.

"Honey, it's all right—wake up! Augusta, wake up!"

Her golden eyes fluttered open to see Timothy's profile silhouetted in the dark. "Oh—Timothy..." she panted as she clutched at his nightshirt, "I was so afraid—."

"I know darling—I know! It was that bad one again—wasn't it?" he asked.

Augusta didn't want to speak of it. She was exhausted and knew Timothy was too and that he needed his sleep.

Still, she couldn't quite catch her breath and her pulse raced. She hadn't had that dream in months, had hoped she'd never have it again. But now that she had, oh, now that she had—what could it mean?

She patted Timothy's arm. "We can talk about it tomorrow," she whispered. "Go back to sleep."

Timothy held Augusta close, not wanting her nightmare to return. They lay like spoons with his arm curling around her. Suddenly, Timothy jerked away. Something had thumped hard against his arm. Augusta tried to move away but he pulled her close and placed his hand lightly on the same spot. He was rewarded with a strong—kick! Augusta turned to face Timothy, and even in the dark, there was no mistaking, that she knew—that he knew!

"Augusta?" he asked with a grin. "I've known or at least suspected for quite some time now. Isn't there something—you'd like to tell me? I think I've waited long enough, don't you?"

His smile disappeared, however, when his wife buried her face in her pillow and began to sob.

"Hey, my beauty," he whispered. "Why are you crying? Is—something wrong?"

Through muffled sobs Timothy was able to decipher a few words like: "baby's okay" and "scared!"

His tender heart twisted as he listened to his young wife stutter and sob. Still, he couldn't stop thinking;

My child—mine—and it just kicked me!

Gently, Timothy took Augusta's face in his hands and wiped away her tears with his thumbs, then said. "I take it you went to see the mid-wife on your walk—and she confirmed what we've suspected?"

Augusta nodded, then drew in a shaky sob. "I didn't know you suspected too."

Timothy shrugged. "Well, I have, I even wondered sometimes—if I'd have to tell you!"

Then his voice grew pensive when he asked, "The mid-wife didn't say anything was wrong? Did she?"

"No," Augusta groaned, then sniffed indignantly. "She said—I was built—for childbirth."

Timothy gazed tenderly at his frightened young wife and sighed in relief. "Thank God for that! Did she say when we should expect this amazing event?"

Augusta frowned, her eyes still brimming with tears, her words still shaky. "She wasn't sure, because I…" Augusta felt the warmth creep up her cheeks. "Well—for lots of reasons plus the fact that I'm so long-waisted. Aunt Sis says babies hide in long-waisted women. And I'm not ready for this *amazing event*. I don't know how to be a mother," she cried.

"Augusta, you have good instincts!" he chided. "And children love you— you're wonderful with them!"

Augusta wiped her eyes with the sleeve of her nightgown and frowned back at her husband. "Timothy, you had a father who couldn't love you and I had a mother who couldn't love me. What kind of parents will we be?"

When Augusta tried to roll away from him, Timothy wouldn't allow it; instead, he tightened his hold.

"Augusta … " he soothed, "I'll tell you what kind of parents we'll be. We will be the kind who know better than to ever reject our children! We will love and teach and nurture them!"

He gently lifted her hand to his lips and kissed it.

"We are not our parents. I couldn't be happier about this. And now, tell me the truth, weren't Saturdays your favorite day of the week, because you spent all day giving riding lessons—to children!"

Augusta stared up at Timothy; he was right, she had always loved children. Her mother, on the other hand, had never liked her or any other child.

Turning to her husband, Augusta's eyes filled with concern as she remembered the nightmare. "Oh, Timothy, the nightmare! I find out for sure that we're having a baby and then comes the omen. It's a warning—it always has been! What if it's about the baby?"

"Nonsense," he growled, "you've been upset—it was just a dream, Augusta!"

"Don't tell me dreams mean nothing! We've been reading about Joseph in the Bible and his interpreting dreams. Timothy, I've told you not to discount this nightmare! I had it before Mama left us, before my Granny O' died, and before Papa died. And then I kept having it until the night I said yes to you! When I didn't have it again, I assumed it was because my giving myself to you had made things all right again. But now?"

Augusta clutched at Timothy's arm. "Why did I have it tonight, just after hearing about the baby? Something bad is coming Timothy—I know it!"

Timothy wanted to calm Augusta's fears but the Bible did speak of dreams foretelling the future. Just because he didn't want this dream to be prophetic— didn't mean that it wasn't.

"All right——" he said softly, "you've never described this dream to me— can you tell me about it now?"

Augusta hesitated only a moment, then she began by telling Timothy how wonderful the dream was—at first. The joy she felt as she rode a magnificent horse, across a flower-strewn valley, and of the mountain that loomed in the distance like a giant. She tried to explained that the mountain was more than what it appeared to be. How in her dream it seemed to be beckoning to her to come home, where she belonged.

Then Augusta's demeanor changed as she told of how the dream suddenly became a nightmare. How the horse disappeared and she found herself in a deep, snake-filled pit.

"That's usually when I wake up screaming, or you wake me up."

With Timothy still holding her close Augusta added thoughtfully: "But sometimes a man comes and rescues me—not you—someone in the dream itself. At first it's so dark but then, suddenly, when I look up it's like sunlight right above my head! Then I see a man's hand reaching out to me. It's always the same man, because I recognize his hand. It's terribly scarred." She continued sadly, "And yet it never frightens me. Even though the scars are shocking, his hand is—beautiful somehow. I never see his face, but his hand is always the same and so is his voice!"

Timothy blew out a sigh. "My word, Augusta, that's quite a dream! What does he say to you?"

"In the most tender voice you could imagine. He says, 'Augusta, I am here—don't be afraid.'"

Timothy let out a low whistle and ran his hand over her face. "Augusta, I don't know how to interpret dreams, and yet—it would seem to me—that the giant mountain waiting for you at the end of the valley might represent God!

After all He's the one that watches over us and sees us through the valleys of our lives."

He pulled Augusta closer then continued: "If this dream is prophetic, it may mean that there will be great beauty ahead but also hardship and sorrow. And then, Augusta, when you described the one who saves you, the bright light and his scarred hands—that can only be Jesus! I think God may very well be speaking to you through this dream. I believe God is asking for you to trust Him. He wants to stay near you through the challenges to come!"

She pondered his words then whispered, "So all this time the dream was a warning, but also, it was Jesus asking for me to come to Him?"

"Augusta—I'm sure of it. Listen, my love," he added softly, "you've been saying you weren't ready to give your heart to Christ. But now, don't you think it's time?"

Augusta nodded her head. "I've been so stubborn. For months I've felt like He watches me with sad eyes. But—what do I say to Him?"

Timothy smiled gently. "Just talk to Him, darling. Invite Him into your heart."

Augusta took Timothy's hand, and with bowed head and halting words she began to pray: "Lord Jesus—all these years—I've been angry at You for this dream. It still frightens me, but I know somehow you've meant if for my good. Please Lord, forgive me for my sins, for my doubts, and stubbornness. Please make my heart right with You. I believe that You are the only son of God, that You died on the cross for my sins. Thank You for all You've done for me—and please—I ask You, Lord Jesus, come into my heart, forgive my sins, and stay with me forever!"

Augusta sniffed back her tears then continued, "And please Lord, bless our baby. Help us be good parents. May Your will be done in our lives. In Your name, I pray. Amen."

❧

The following days and weeks passed with Augusta feeling as if a thousand-pound weight had been lifted from her shoulders! Like a deer panting for water she had an overwhelming thirst for God's Word. Every free moment she spent reading Timothy's Bible, then she would pummel both Timothy and Aunt Sis with her many questions.

Augusta's accepting Christ as her Savior did not change her circumstances. She still faced all the things that had frightened her: she was still pregnant, her childbirth would come without help from a mid-wife or doctor, and she would still be the only woman living on a ranch full of men. Her new faith didn't take away her problems, but it gave her the courage to trust God to deal with them. She was like a ship in the middle of the sea. She was still just as vulnerable to all of life's storms, but now she had Jesus as her anchor and navigator. He would see her through whatever lay ahead.

Determined not to dwell on her fears, Augusta found spending time with Aunt Sis both distracting and an education unto itself. The old mid-wife knew how to recognize and use healing herbs as well as how to find sources of food, such as: roots and berries and plants that grew wild along the trail. Augusta filled her journal with these bits of wisdom. They varied from how to soothe a colicky baby to...how to dress a bullet wound...to how to stitch up a cut using a hair from a horse's tail. Aunt Sis also spoke often of childbirth and child rearing since that was uppermost on Augusta's mind.

Timothy marveled at how Augusta was maturing each day, how her faith in God was giving her a renewed strength. And yet he knew she sometimes still struggled with her fears. He couldn't blame her, for he too prayed constantly for Augusta to have a speedy and safe delivery when the time came. He even shared his concerns with Aunt Sis, and the old woman became even more determined to do all that was possible to prepare the young couple for whatever might come their way.

Chapter 18
More Good-Byes

"But I have promised you, You will possess their land because I will give it to you as your possession, a land flowing with milk and honey." Leviticus 20:24

The wagon master, usually so self-assured, looked ill at ease as he held his hat in one hand and the reins of his stallion in the other.

"Mister and Missus Grainger—it's been a pleasure."

The older man's face was the same color and texture as the leather buckskins he wore. His forehead was banded by a white line of skin that rarely saw the light of day. Caleb Wolf had lived a hard life and not even he knew how old he was, although the grey in his temples suggested a man in his autumn years. He was quiet by nature and frugal with his words—but he'd grown fond of this couple and was finding it unusually difficult to bid them farewell. Though Wolf had led a dozen wagon trains down the Santa Fe Trail, this was the part of his job he hated the most When those in his charge split off from the main group and headed towards their own destinations. He preferred leaving folks safely in a town or fort, but that wasn't always practical. He didn't know if it was his Welsh or his Indian blood, speaking to him, but he had an uneasy spirit about the Grainger's leaving his protection.

"Folks," he said, "I know you both are wise enough to keep your wits about ya. The last stretch of any journey is the most dangerous. Don't let your guard down, and *almost home* don't mean you're safe!"

Timothy nodded his agreement, then the two men shook hands. Timothy was surprised when the stoic ex-buffalo hunter reached up and gave his shoulder a fatherly squeeze. The two had enjoyed their hunting trips together and the wagon master had come often to the Grainger's campfire.

"Thank you again, Caleb," Timothy said firmly. "Remember you are always welcome at the Bar 61. And sir..." he added softly, "should you ever need anything, don't hesitate to call on the Graingers."

With a fatherly expression, Wolf turned towards Augusta. "Ma'am I shall miss yer cookin'! But mostly—" he added softly, "I shall miss yer smile!"

Augusta impulsively kissed the old man on the cheek, making his white forehead turn a bright crimson. His lips tipped slightly, then he stepped away and slapped his hat forcefully back onto his head.

Timothy helped Augusta onto the wagon seat, turned once more to shake the older man's hand, then he too climbed up beside his wife.

With no more words worth speaking Caleb Wolf mounted his horse and hollered, "Lead wagon—move out!"

Timothy clucked and slapped the reins, with Max and Molly as the lead team, pulled their wagon away from others. Tytus had long ago given his brother directions to the ranch. He was to leave the wagon train at the Big Sandy River right where three large boulders stood sentinel, like three kings, he had called them. The map had them travel for about two miles west by northwest from the three kings. Then, they were to follow the old Indian trail until they came to the 'Twin Brothers'. That was also the name Ty had given the two large flat-topped hogbacks that marked the entrance to the ranch.

"Head straight between the brothers and keep going," Ty had written. "Before you know it you'll be at the ranch grounds of the Bar 61."

This was a bitter-sweet time. Timothy's eyes shone with excitement; just another week and he and his twin brother would be reunited! Augusta however, swallowed back her tears. They were leaving friends again. They had celebrated and suffered with these fellow pioneers. They had welcomed babies, and they had prayed together over lonely graves. It was doubtful that they would ever see any of these people again—not this side of heaven anyway. Augusta and Rachel had cried themselves out the night before; and yet, there was nothing for it. Their destinations had been settled before they began. The time had come for the Graingers to leave the Wolf train, and head towards their own promised land.

As difficult as it was to say good-bye to Rachel, it had been even harder for Augusta to part with Aunt Sis. The dear old woman had come to their wagon just before daybreak. Her bright blue eyes were misty, as she handed over what looked like a large canvas bedroll.

"This here's yer birthin' bundle, deary," she said softly while her chin bobbed up and down with each word. "Done got it finished fer ya last night."

The old woman squeezed Augusta's hand. "Now, honey, don't ya be a frettin'. 'Member all I told ya 'n jes' trust in the Lord!" Chuckling softly, she patted Augusta's rounding belly and added, "You too, lil' darlin'!"

Augusta felt like bursting into tears; she hugged the old woman and whispered, "I don't think I can do this—without you!"

Aunt Sis took Augusta by the shoulders and spoke in a firm voice, "YA CAN and YA WILL! Now deary … " she continued more gently, "The good book says, worry 'bout nothin', pray 'bout everythin'! Stay close to God and He'll stay close to you."

With that Aunt Sis turned quickly towards her own wagon but not before Augusta saw a tear make a winding rivulet down the deep creases of the old woman's leathery cheek.

Chapter 19
Bushwhacked

"My command is this: Love each other as I have loved you. Greater love has no one than this, that he lay down his life for his friends." John 15:12-13

"Timothy, please," Augusta sighed, as she straightened herself in the wagon seat, "stop asking me if I'm all right, I promise you I'm...just...FINE!"

"Augusta," Timothy urged .... "you are not, fine! You haven't looked me in the eye or spoken a half a dozen words since we left the wagon train—and that was seven days ago. I know it nearly broke your heart to leave Rachel and Aunt Sis. I want you to talk to me! Yell at me! Scream at me if ya like!"

Augusta shook her head then turned her face away, looking off into the distance.

"Whoa!" Timothy pulled hard on the reins. "Augusta," he added gently, "it's all right to cry. I know you are angry at me for taking you so far away from all that's familiar! I hate that Aunt Sis couldn't come with us or that we couldn't go on with her...but..."

"No, Timothy..." Augusta couldn't allow him to continue. "I'm sorry I've worried you. I am scared and I am nervous—but I am not mad at you. I just haven't felt like talking—what is there to say?"

Determined not to cry; Augusta even attempted a smile but knew Timothy was unconvinced. Still, she would have succeeded in not blubbering all over the man—if only—he hadn't pulled her so tenderly into his arms. That did it! The flood gates were open and the next thing she knew she was stammering and sobbing out all her fears, all the same worries that he had heard a thousand times before. It was just that now every mile brought the things she feared closer and closer!

"Timothy," Augusta hiccupped, "I'm so sorry! I just don't understand myself anymore. I never used to be like this—I feel like I'm always losing my battle with tears and all sorts of silly emotions!"

Timothy tweaked her nose. "Then stop fighting the battle and you won't lose!" he advised gently.

"Let it out! You are overdue for a good cry. And I understand—you're already lonesome for all your women friends, aren't you?"

His understanding her so well, coupled with his gently spoken words, brought on a second flood of tears. When he thought he had heard the last sniffle he lifted her chin and kissed her. "Feel better?"

Augusta smiled and nodded. "As a matter of fact," she said with another sniff, "I think I do!" Augusta blew her nose, took in a deep breath, and searched the horizon; then she patted Timothy's arm. "Come on," she said. "It can't be much farther now!"

"That's my girl!" he said, giving her his broadest grin. "We—are—almost home!"

A few hours later their excitement grew when they spotted the two hog-backs in the distance. The ones Ty had referred to as the 'Twin Brothers'.

Augusta hadn't known what a hogback was; finally, she got to see for herself.

"Timothy!" she said with surprise, "they looked like two small mountains, whose tops have been sliced off, to make them even."

When Timothy nodded and let out an impatient sigh; Augusta touched his arm, "I know—" she said sympathetically. "Close…but still too far away!"

He gave her a wink. "You are reading my mind! You know, if we push the team a little, we could get there in a few hours—what do you think?"

"I think, the horses are just as anxious to be free of this wagon as we are!"

Timothy could only chuckle. "I know what you're looking forward to—a hot bath in Ty's fancy bathing room! And sleeping in that soft feather bed I've promised you."

Augusta laid her head against Timothy's shoulder and hooked her arm through his. She could feel the cords of muscle working as he drove the teams. They chatted about all the changes that were in store for them in the following days and weeks and years to come. The sun was high overhead, and though the trail seemed fairly even, the altitude was increasing and the horses were working up a lather.

As the trail curved around an outcropping of boulders, Timothy guided the horses under some shade trees then pulled back on the reins. "Ty mentioned this place on his map. There's a natural spring here—we can water the horses and freshen up a bit."

Timothy wiped his brow with the sleeve of his shirt. Then he gave Augusta a roguish grin, adding, "Maybe, we could even go wading?"

Augusta frowned at her husband. "Mister Wolf told us to keep our wits about us. And you know very well that you do not behave when I take you wading, if you remember?" Augusta teased.

"Oh… I remember!" he grinned, "Best day of my life!"

Their banter quickly stopped when suddenly the horse just in front of Timothy dropped dead in his tracks, along with the report of a rifle. Immediately, the other three horses began rearing and pulling, flinging their heads from side to side and trying desperately to free themselves from the harness. But the leather was strong, and the weight of the dead horse and the even heavier wagon held them fast. Augusta was frozen in shock, but Timothy threw himself in front of her. Using the momentum of his own body, he scooped Augusta into his arms and carried her with him, over the side of the wagon. Before she knew what was happening Timothy had her safely on the ground and was grabbing his gun from under the wagon seat.

Their attackers were two men on horseback. They were coming fast and shooting wildly. Timothy aimed his rifle at the larger of the two men and fired. The bullet struck the man in his right arm, and with a cry of pain, his gun spun from his hand. He might have fallen from the saddle but for his younger partner who helped him ride for cover.

At the back of the wagon, Augusta heard Quest squealing and pulling against his rope to get free.

"Quest!" Augusta called. "Easy boy—I'm coming!"

"No!" Timothy ordered. "Take cover behind those boulders. I'll get Quest!"

As a wild shot whizzed over their heads, Timothy took her arm.

"Wait, Augusta!" he whispered as he handed her his rifle. "Take this and once you're behind those boulders, try to get off a few shots. Keep them busy while I get Quest and some more ammunition."

Timothy hurried towards the back of the wagon, while Augusta awkwardly made her way around the boulders. She picked a spot to shoot from and quickly squeezed off two shots. The bandits returned fire, ripping a hole through the canvas top of their wagon.

From the bushes Augusta heard cursing, "Stop that, ya dunder-headed-fool—you'll hit what we're here for!"

So that's it, she thought. *They want Quest.* Then she heard the low rumble of Timothy's voice.

"Easy boy—eezzee," Timothy soothed as he approached the horse, who was wide-eyed with fear. He reached up and stroked the stallion's sleek neck. Quest stopped pulling but his eyes were still wild, his nostrils flaring. Timothy kept up a low dialogue with the horse, as he crawled into the back of the wagon. Working quickly, he swung the bag of ammunition around his neck, stuffed two revolvers in his waist band, and grabbed another rifle; then, slowly, he eased himself from the wagon. When both he and Quest appeared behind the boulders, Augusta breathed a sigh of relief.

"Thank God you're safe!" she groaned. "But...now...what do we do?"

Timothy pondered their predicament: with one horse dead—they were trapped.

"I'm praying that we're close enough to the ranch for someone to hear all these shots and come see what all the ruckus is about! Beyond that, there are only two men out there and I've wounded one of them. The other one looks to be young and scared! At first he was throwing shots in every direction—now he's not shooting at all."

Augusta stared at Timothy suspiciously. "What are you planning?"

Timothy's expression was unlike any she had seen before. He looked—dangerous! But he spoke gently, saying, "I'm planning on you keeping them worried, while I circle around behind. I want you to shoot the rifle and then the pistol. Make them think we are both firing at them from these boulders."

Timothy shook a box of bullets he'd brought from the wagon.

"I should be able to get in place once you've used these up. I'll come at them from the left, so keep your aim to the right of those scrub oaks."

Augusta's eyes grew wide. "No, Timothy—isn't there any other way?"

"Augusta, it would be impossible for us to cut a dead horse out of the harness, and try to escape. We know one man is badly injured; they may try to make a run for it! But if we let them go, they may send other scoundrels to finish what these men started. The wisest thing—is deal with these two—on our own terms!"

With that said, Timothy pulled her close and gave her a long kiss, then he smiled down at her. "This'll be a great story to tell our baby one day!"

When Augusta gave him a tremulous smile, he added more seriously: "Listen to me! If you think something's gone wrong then I want you to get on

Quest and ride for the ranch! Don't try to help me on your own. Just find Ty and don't come back here unless he's with you!"

Augusta's eyes filled with tears. "But the baby—I shouldn't ride—"

Timothy grabbed her by the shoulders and gave her the most intense look she'd ever seen. "The best way to take care of our baby," he said earnestly, "is to keep yourself safe!"

Then he wrapped his arms tight around Augusta and closed his eyes. "Lord," he prayed, "we're in a lot of trouble here. Please protect Augusta and the baby. And please send us some help! In Jesus name."

He breathed an "amen", kissed Augusta soundly, then before she could say a word, he slipped out of sight. Augusta stifled a sob, as she aimed her rifle beyond the scrub oaks and pulled the trigger.

✄

The wounded man leaned his back against the boulder and cursed the one that shot him!

"Pup…" he moaned. " Tear yer shirt off—see if ya can stop this bleedin'."

The boy's stomach lurched; he'd seen a lot of terrible things in his fifteen years, but the sight of the sticky red fluid pulsing from the older man's mangled arm made him want to run. He forced himself to swallow as he tore off his only shirt and wrapped it tightly around the bloody arm.

"Looks awful bad, Jasper! Yer bleedin' like a stuck hog!"

"Hah! Feels a heap worse than it looks!" he groaned. "Seen anything of that worthless boss of our'n?"

Still feeling sick, Pup shook his head. "Nope—maybe he got shot too!"

Jasper's face contorted in pain. "That'd serve him right fer tellin' us that Boston dude wouldn't be no trouble! Said it'd be like takin' candy from a baby and we'd both get what we wanted: him the girl, 'n me the horse!"

Shuddering painfully, Jasper stared down at his arm, while beads of sweat rolled from his ashen face.

"Pup, I seen wounds like this in the war—gonna lose it for sure! Hurts like a red hot poker."

Just then another bullet split the air over head.

"Fools!" he cried. "Why they keep throwin' lead? We ain't even shootin' back!"

The boy took the pistol from his waist band and began waving it in the air. "Ya want I should—shoot back, Jasper?"

"Put that thing away Pup…" Jasper groaned in disgust. "Boy—yer so near sighted yer more likely to shoot yerself—or worse—shoot me! All I want ya to do is—get me out a here!"

"We can't leave—the boss'll have our hides! He gets awful riled when we don't do what he says!"

With his good hand Jasper grabbed Pup by the throat. "Listen here boy! Ya best worry 'bout not getting me riled! I'm here—he ain't!"

Pup pulled free of the older man's grip. "Sure, Jasper, sure. I'll do what ya say!"

⌖

Augusta shot the last bullet from the box, she reloaded both guns, then with her heart pounding, she waited for Timothy to act on his plan. It was a warm day, but chill bumps spread up and down her arms. She couldn't stop thinking of the dream. It always meant heartbreak, and more often than not—death!

Augusta buried her face in her trembling hands. Suddenly, there was a scuffling sound coming from above her, while loose pebbles slid off the boulder she was hiding behind. When she looked up, she saw the silhouette of a man, but the sun blinded her from making out his features. From behind her, she heard Quest scream. Quickly, she spun around—and—everything went black.

⌖

Bending over Jasper, Pup hissed, "Hey, they stopped shooting, but that horse is sure makin' a fuss! Maybe this is our chance to make a run for it!"

Jasper grunted as the boy struggled to help the older man to his feet. He stopped cold when he heard the sound of a rifle being cocked. When Pup looked over his shoulder, his eyes were wide with fear.

"Don't do anything foolish, boy," Timothy commanded. "I'm not sure what your plans were for today, but they've changed!"

Taking another step closer, Timothy added smoothly: "Now, just take your friend's gun belt off and throw it to the side. Then I'll let you help him onto his horse, we'll take him to my brother's ranch, and see to his wounds. Tytus can decide what's to be done."

The boy nodded, and slowly unbuckled Jasper's gun belt, but as he threw it aside he whispered, "The boss'll be back-shoot us if he sees we're headed for the Bar 61!"

Jasper grimaced. "Jes'—do what he says, kid."

Pup couldn't stop shaking. He bent down as if to help Jasper to his feet; but instead, he made a grab for the pistol tucked under his belt. Whirling around, he frantically pulled the trigger.

There was no time to think; Timothy felt the gun buck in his hand, then watched miserably as a red stain spread across the young man's chest—he was dead before he hit the ground.

Instantly, Jasper made a grab for the boy's fallen gun, but another shot came from the bushes behind Timothy. The bullet tore through the man's stomach and slammed his body back against the boulder.

Timothy dove for cover then turned his gun on a rough-looking squint-eyed cowboy walking slowly towards him.

The cowboy quickly lowered his gun, then asked; "You Grainger? Timothy Grainger?"

Timothy eyed the man suspiciously and kept the rifle trained on him as he came closer. "And who would you be?" he asked.

"I'm one of the outrider's fer the Bar 61. Heard all the shootin'—thought I better check it out."

Timothy let out a sigh of relief; he lowered his gun, and walked over to the two bodies. He felt sick—he hadn't wanted to hurt the boy—then he looked down at the older man. He had guessed right: the sharps had nearly taken the man's arm off but the belly wound had killed him. Just then, the wounded man's eyes fluttered opened.

"Wait!" Timothy said, motioning for the ranch hand to come closer. "This one's still alive! Maybe he can tell us what this was about."

Timothy kneeled beside the dying man. Jasper looked up at him then scowled at the cowboy who shot him.

"T—traitor!" he groaned. "Wants yer—wife!"

The man had no more whispered the words when another shot rang out and silenced him for good.

"Augusta—run!" Timothy called his warning as he spun around and pulled the trigger. He knew his shot had gone wild, even as he saw the flames bursting from the barrel of the other man's gun.

<hr />

Augusta felt Quest's breath against her cheek; he was murmuring gently and pushing against her arm. Drawing in a deep breath she looked around—she was confused at first. *Why was she lying on the ground, with her head throbbing?* Gun shots rang out and she managed to pull herself to her feet. Her muddled mind cleared the instant she heard Timothy telling her to run—then two more shots rang out and her heart stopped.

"Timothy!" she cried.

When she heard no answer—she grabbed up her Henry rifle and headed around the boulders. Then—it was as if something touched her, and held her back. She could almost hear Timothy's words: *The best way to take care of our baby—is to keep yourself safe. Get on Quest—and ride for help!*

Her head felt light and her feet felt like lead. Still, she managed to heave her cumbersome body onto Quest's broad back by standing on a large rock. Holding tight to the halter rope, she wove her fingers into Quest's thick mane, and with a slight touch of her heels, they flew from the stone fortress and headed for the center of the twin hogbacks at a dead run!

They'd gone only half a mile when she crested a hill and saw riders coming straight for them. She reined to a stop and fought for her breath. Quest reared and crow-hopped, but she hung on. Suddenly, she had a new fear: what if these riders were partners to the outlaws? How could she know for sure?

But as the men drew close she breathed a sigh of relief. One of the men was dark headed, and his skin a leathery brown, but his face was familiar and dear. "Tytus!" she called with confidence. The man yanked hard on his reins and frowned his confusion.

"Timothy's in trouble! Your brother Timothy is back there—quick—follow me!"

Instantly, Augusta spun Quest around and the three riders followed her at a ground eating pace.

Tytus Grainger didn't like the idea of following a woman into danger—it could be an ambush. But she had recognized him, and said Timothy was in trouble—he had to believe her—for now.

Riding close he yelled above the pounding hooves, "What are we headed into—where's Tim?"

It was nearly impossible to speak, but she managed: "Two men…attacked us…Timothy told me…to run…and…not to come back…without *you!*"

When Tytus nodded, she hunched over Quest's neck, "Ssssst! Quest—" she urged. "Sssst!"

The dark stallion stretched out and Tytus and the men were hard pressed to match his stride as they flew across the prairie.

Before they reached the boulders, Augusta heard Tytus barking out orders: "Hitch, you skirt around from the south, Rusty you come from the north—I'll follow her." Then giving Augusta a wary look he warned his men, "Be careful! This may be a trap, for us!"

They slid off their horses when they got near the wagon, and Tytus looked down at Augusta. "You stay here!" he commanded.

Augusta ignored his order as she pointed with her rifle. "The bandits took cover in those scrub oaks. Timothy skirted around that way to come up behind them. He called for me to run—from there!"

Boldly, she headed in that direction, but Tytus grabbed her by the arm and took the lead. "At least stay back," he growled. "I'll go first!"

Augusta cocked her rifle, noticing the other two ranch hands did the same as they closed in.

At that moment, another cowboy came riding in at a fast gallop then slid to a stop beside Tytus.

"S'everthin' okay boss?" he mumbled. " I heard some shootin'!"

Tytus pulled Augusta down to crouch beside him then hissed: "LeBeau—you fool—what are you thinking? Riding in here like that—get down!"

The cowboy was an older man, unkempt and gruff-looking. He dismounted and dropped his reins. "Let me check it out, boss. Might jes' be them polecats I've been chasin'."

The man stepped confidently around them, but returned a moment later: "They're dead, boss—two of 'em are the rustlers I've been trackin'. But..I'm afraid that third man...he—?"

"No!" Augusta cried, as she pushed her way around the other men, with Tytus right behind her.

"No, no—no!" she screamed. "Timothy!"

Sliding to her knees, she saw his white shirt covered in blood; she tore at the fabric, exposing the wound. "It only just happened—" she hissed, "there has to be something we can do! We just have to stop the bleeding!"

Augusta realized that there was no fresh blood coming from his wound. She felt his throat, and then his wrist—no pulse—and his skin had lost its warmth. It was then that she looked into her husband's wonderful blue eyes—they were gazing off into the distance—they were lifeless eyes. This was the man whose joy of living had been like a burning fire ... he couldn't be dead..it just couldn't be true. But it was—Timothy—*was gone.*

149

PART TWO

Chapter 20

The Bar 61

"For my thoughts are not your thoughts, neither are your ways my ways, declares the Lord. As the heavens are higher than the earth, so are my ways higher than your ways and my thoughts than your thoughts." Isaiah 55:8-9

Early Summer, 1866 – Colorado Territory

Alvaro wiped away tears with the corner of his apron as he stepped from the porch of the hacienda. His view was clouded as he watched the heavy wagon rumbling across the field of waving prairie grass. Rusty had ridden on ahead, telling everyone what had happened, but the old man had held out hope that somehow the tragic news was not true.

A tall black man came from the barn, leaning heavily on his walking stick. Though a free man now, Joseph had once been a slave to the Grainger family. He and his wife Natty May had been there the day the twins were born and had taken it upon themselves to teach the young brothers the truth about Jesus, and about heaven and hell. Joseph knew without a doubt that Timothy was in heaven and that Ty must feel as if he were in hell. His old heart was breaking wide open for his boys, as silent tears made tracks down his ebony face. He made no effort to hide them or to wipe them away, but rested his large hand on Alvaro's shoulder and wept unashamedly.

Alvaro nodded and patted Joseph's hand. "I am so sorry, amigo. We all have broken hearts today."

The two old men watched as the wagon lumbered into the yard. Tytus was driving the team and the look on his face told of a man in unspeakable agony. He hadn't been there in time to save his brother or even to share one word with him before he had lost him forever—to this world, anyway. Although Alvaro and Joseph were strong Christians, even they wanted to ask God—why had such a tragic thing happened?

Finally, Joseph spoke, his deep voice sounding all the deeper for his grief. "Lord—don't understand this—no, Sa'! I don't! But, Lord, your gonna see us through! You always has."

They turned their gazes from Tytus to the haggard young woman sitting beside him. Alvaro took in her beleaguered appearance and leaned close to Joseph. "Oh—I did not think she would be so young! Amigo—I think we shall have a season—best spent on our knees. We two must pray very hard. We must pray—for them both."

As Ty reined the team to a stop, the girl moved quickly to climb down from the wagon seat. Alvaro glanced towards Tytus, assuming he would feel responsible for his brother's widow, but when the big man simply sat there in a daze, Alvaro hurried to help her. As he looked at her more closely, his concern doubled when he realized the young widow would soon bear a child.

"Señora," he greeted tenderly, "I am Alvaro. You have all of our deepest sympathy, my dear. Please allow me to help you into the hacienda."

The man's accent was not familiar to Augusta, but his words rolled over his tongue with such warmth that she was instantly comforted by his presence. His face was tan and leathery; his thick hair and waxed mustache were a snowy white. And yet—it was his eyes that caught her attention: they were as black as a moonless night, but the expression he wore was that of kindness itself.

Taking her arm Alvaro saw that Augusta was covered in dried blood on her forehead, her blouse, and her hands. She looked so confused and lost. He didn't know if it was her blood, or her husband's or both.

"Come now, little one," he beckoned gently. "You have been through so much. Let me tend to you."

Alvaro's words seemed to her like cool water on a hot day—but Tytus had already made it clear—she was anything but welcome.

Cautiously, she glanced at Timothy's dark brother. When Ty stared back at her with a look of contempt, Augusta instinctively straightened and willed herself to stay strong.

All the way to the ranch, she and Ty had been lost in their own grief, neither speaking a word. Finally, just before they pulled into the ranch yard, Tytus asked the question that still haunted her. "How is it you were with my brother?" he demanded to know.

Augusta turned to him. "Timothy wrote you…I'm…Augusta…his wife."

153

Grainger narrowed his eyes, his lips curling as he looked her over, from her dark hair hanging in clumps around her shoulders to the lavender circles under her eyes. Her face and hands were swollen, not to mention her expanding waistline. Augusta's face turned crimson at the man's rude appraisal.

"The only letters I've ever gotten from my brother assured me he had no intentions of marrying."

Ty's face grew dark as he looked at her in disgust, then spoke through gritted teeth. "And if he had, I know the kind of woman Timothy would choose, and it would never have been you!"

Augusta was too overwhelmed to fully take in her brother-in-law's cruel words, and too stunned to respond. From that point on they rode in silence until they came to a stop in front of the hacienda.

Alvaro was speaking to her but there was a loud commotion coming from the back of the wagon.

"Oh dear..." she groaned. "Quest!"

As quickly as her body would allow, she made her way to the rear of the wagon. Augusta was just in time to see her stallion lunge at one of the ranch hands.

"Easy, Quest, easy-easy, boy." she soothed as she laid her small hand on the stallion's powerful neck. He straightened at her touch, but his nostrils flared, and he side-stepped and blew nervously.

"It's all right, boy," she said calmly.

"All right, you say?" roared one of the ranch hands.

Augusta recognized the grizzled-looking cowboy; he was the one who announced that Timothy was dead. In a fury, the man pointed to Quest and began cursing.

Just then, the tall blonde man whom Ty had called Hitch stepped forward. "DEWEY! Watch your mouth!" he ordered.

The cowboy scowled and shook his fist. "Watch nothin'! That devil jes' 'bout took a hunk out a me!"

Augusta stared at the man's contorted face; even in her befuddled state, she couldn't help but take note when Quest instantly disliked someone.

"I'm...sorry!" she said softly. "He'll behave now."

The ranch hands were wary when they saw the young woman untying the ill-tempered stud. However, the moment she had him untied, she quickly pulled a loop from the lead rope through the halter and slipped it over the stallion's muzzle. It was a wise precaution to take, and the men at least acknowledged that the girl knew enough to take it. Nervous around so many strangers, Quest tried to pull away from her. Augusta responded by giving the lead rope one hard downward yank, and in a stern no-nonsense voice, she said simply: "Quest!"

The stallion gave a little squeal, tossed his head in protest, then yielded to his mistress.

Augusta glanced back to see Timothy's brother clinging to the side of the wagon. She could see the muscle in his jaw pulsing as he fought for control. In spite of the man's cutting remarks, her heart went out to the brother Timothy had loved so much.

Ty looked around, suddenly aware that he was being watched, he straightened and bellowed loudly: "You men—get to work. Hitch, put that stud in the barn! Dewey, Rusty, take care of the team."

His voice softened as he gazed over at the tall black man; his voice cracked when he said, "Joseph, I—I—need you—stay with me."

The ranch foremen immediately took over—giving additional orders regarding her trunks and the wagon, then he stepped closer to Augusta and took the hat from his head. "Missus Grainger," he said gently, "my name is Hitch—I'm the foreman...here at the Bar 61. Why don't you let Alvaro see you...into the hacienda? I'll tend...to yer stud."

Augusta shook her head, "That's kind of you, sir," she said dully. "But I know my horse. I'm afraid he will cause you nothing but trouble if I don't see to him. Please—just show me the way."

Hitch studied her for a moment, then, he seemed to realize that she was putting one foot in front of the other by shear will. Nodding his understanding he led the way to the barn. The sooner she got that stud settled down, the sooner Alvaro could see to the her needs.

The other ranch hands trailed behind the young widow, as she led her high-strung stallion towards the barn. Her poise at such a time touched the men. The pitiful little thing looked like the walking dead; her face had no color at all, but for the dried blood and dirt. Her eyes were swollen and red rimmed, and she had a bloody knot on her forehead. They had heard the couple had been attacked, and her husband killed, and yet here she was, making sure her horse was tended to—something any respectable cowhand could understand and appreciate.

Augusta moved as if in a trance. Once she had Quest safely inside the stall, she leaned her forehead on the stallion's long neck. The men couldn't hear her softly spoken words, but there was a sweet gentleness in them as she quieted the beast. When she looked around and saw them all standing there, she explained: "Quest is a good horse. But I don't want him hurting anyone—and he might! So, please—wait for me—to tend to him."

The men were filled with compassion—each nodded their understanding as Augusta closed and latched the stall door. But it was Hitch who watched with concern, as the young woman's eyes seemed to glaze over. Augusta made no move to leave—nor to speak.

"Ma'am?" Hitch asked. "Missus Grainger?"

Augusta wasn't even aware when the foreman gently picked her up and carried her to the hacienda. As he settled her in a large kitchen chair, he whispered gently, "Sorry...fer yer loss, ma'am."

His softly spoken words brought the anguish of losing Timothy crashing over her again, and a fresh wave of tears rolled down her dusty cheeks. Through her weeping, Augusta was only slightly aware that soothing words were being spoken to her while the kind, white haired man was washing her face. Ever so gently, he lifted her hands from her lap and washed them as well.

"Trouble rides a fast horse." she whispered in a bewildered tone.

"Pardon señora?" Alvaro asked.

"My papa used to say that. It's true—everything happened so fast! We were laughing and happy...and then...no—" she moaned. "It should be Timothy sitting here—not me! If one of us had to die..."

"Hush now—do not say such a thing." the old man insisted.

Augusta fought to hold back her tears. She needed this stranger to somehow understand what kind of man had been lost!

"You never met Timothy. He was the kind of man that should live forever—he loved life! And coming here was his fondest dream—to be with the brother he loved! But now—I'm here—alone! My being here—instead of him—it's a mistake—another mistake! Oh, Timothy why didn't you listen to me?"

Augusta covered her face with her hands and wept.

"No, señora! It is not for us to know His ways—but God—He make no mistakes!"

Augusta raised her head to look into Alvaro's dark eyes. "Timothy would have said that. I know he's with God. I saw it in his face, when I tried to hold him."

Augusta looked forlornly down at her hands, only then understanding why Alvaro had washed them.

Suddenly, she swallowed and pushed up from the table. "Where is he? I should go and tend to Timothy. Isn't that right? Isn't that what a wife should do?"

Alvaro shook his head then gently pushed her back into the chair. "No, you must rest—allow El Jefe, the boss, this time with his brother. And Joseph—he also needs this time."

When Augusta looked up in confusion, the old Spaniard tapped his chest and said softly, "I am your amigo, your friend, little one. Allow me to guide you! If your husband could speak to you from heaven, would he not say: 'Be strong my wife, and take care of our child!' Is this not so?"

As if in answer, the baby gave Augusta an insistent kick! In the past few hours she had nearly forgotten the baby, as if everything good that was to be had ended with Timothy's life. But when she felt that tenacious little kick, it reminded her that life goes stubbornly on. She hadn't lost *everything—not yet*.

Chapter 21

Another Grave

"For the Lord himself shall descend from heaven with a shout, with the voice of the archangel, and with the trump of God: and the dead in Christ shall rise first: Then we which are alive and remain shall be caught up together with them in the clouds, to meet the Lord in the air: and so shall we ever be with the Lord." I Thessalonians 4:16-17

Augusta awoke to find the place beside her as empty as her heart. Before opening her eyes, she had prayed that God would allow Timothy's death to be just another one of her many nightmares. But the new day had dawned just where the previous day's misery had left off—Timothy—was gone.

Alvaro had laid out the black dress that Mrs. Drew had sewn for her. Wisely, the older woman had made it a little fuller, for that special time, she had explained. Augusta slipped it on, but when she glanced into the mirror, she was shocked by her own careworn reflection.

She didn't care what she looked like—hadn't even thought to comb her hair. But just then she remembered Ty's dark look of disgust and his biting words: "Timothy would not have chosen you!"

She didn't know if Timothy could see her from heaven or not, but it was comforting to think that he could—and if he could she didn't want to shame him. Sighing, she went to the basin, washed her face, then combed her long hair, and pinned it into a tight bun at the nap of her neck.

Just as she draped the matching black shawl around her shoulders, there was a knock at her door.

"Pardon, señora." Alvaro's warmly accented voice called to her softly from the hallway. "It is time, little one."

The simple words caused Augusta's heart to pound in her chest—she wasn't ready—she would never be ready. He called to her three more times before she could make herself open the door. At first she didn't recognize the man. Gone were the apron and work clothes. Alvaro looked every inch the elegant caballero rather than a humble cook. His suit was jet black; the jacket was cut short at the waist, and underneath he wore a crisp white shirt with a black silk cravat tied at his neck. The stark contrast between the man's black suit and his snow-white hair was like a full moon against a midnight sky.

"Señora," he said gently, "everyone awaits you, my dear."

Augusta nodded in understanding, and yet her legs refused to move.

"I know your pain—señora." Alvaro said gently, "but we must lay your husband to rest."

Alvaro offered her his arm, but the torment he saw in the young woman's eyes nearly undid him. He was about to say perhaps she was too ill to attend, when suddenly Augusta closed her eyes, took in a deep breath, squared her small shoulders, then placed her hand lightly on the old man's arm.

"I am sorry—I—shouldn't be making everyone wait. I'm... ready now."

Alvaro barely knew this girl but he was proud of her. And though her words were brave, he could feel her trembling. Quickly, he placed his free hand over hers and gave it a reassuring squeeze. As he led her from the hacienda, he spoke softly: "When we are weak, little one, God gives us strength. Trust Him now—He will help you."

Augusta thanked God for Alvaro; his kindness meant more than he knew. Still, she felt numb as he led her down a path to a beautiful little opening within a circle of pine trees. Augusta was surprised that there was a proper fenced-in cemetery, and inside, one headstone. Somehow it consoled her to know that Timothy's would not be the first or only grave in this wilderness cemetery. She stopped and read the carefully chiseled granite:

Beloved Wife, Natty May Grainger, Born a Slave 1812—Died a Free Woman—Dec 12, 1861

This was Joseph's wife; Timothy had told her of how they all loved Natty May. Augusta's gaze went immediately to the tall black man, their eyes met, and she knew that of everyone there, he understood.

Finally, Augusta forced herself to look down at the simple pine box, knowing that it held the man she'd known less than a year. And yet in that time he'd given her so much—he'd shown her the way to God. She longed to see Timothy's face once more, not in death but full of life. Glancing at his twin brother, she tried to imagine the two men standing side by side. Both men were of the same mettle. That rare breed of man whose masculine qualities spoke eloquently of their strength, depth of character, and honor. She recognized these traits in Ty's strong face, and the firm set of his jaw. But then, he looked directly at her, and his dark eyes were filled with anger and accusation.

Tytus scowled at Augusta, then quickly looked away; he resented her presence, but then he resented everything about this day. He couldn't measure his pain—nothing had ever hurt like this. Finally, he gave Joseph a nod to begin.

The old man stepped forward. His voice, a deep bass, was like a rumbling thunder that filled the valley.

"Natty May and I was there the day the brothers was born," he began. "Doctor looked at young Tim, and says, that chile won't live out the week. But God had a plan for the lad and he grew to be a fine man, who honored God. Joseph gazed tenderly at Augusta. "God gave him the joy of a good wife and the hope of a chile. Evil men done took his life and that's who's to blame!"

Joseph slanted a quick glance at Tytus but said no more about Timothy's death. Instead, he spoke on about the boy he had known. About what a special person he was and that despite his hardships, he had possessed a wonderful sense of humor and a powerful faith in God. Then Joseph gazed at Ty and spoke of the special bond shared by the twin brothers. Like warm molasses the old man's voice was soothing and deep. Finally, he bowed his head in prayer. "Lord, our Tim ain't in this here pine box." He said firmly, "His soul's up there with You—and with my darlin', Natty M-May!"

When the old man's voice broke, a few of the ranch hands shuffled their feet or coughed self-consciously, for everyone who'd known the old woman had loved her and were sensitive to Joseph's pain.

The old man sucked in a shaking breath, gathered his strength, then continued: "Lord, there ain't nothin' new 'bout sufferin' and it's hard to understand. But we thank you for the good times and we trust you in the bad. We ask you to heal the wound in Mister Ty's heart as he grieves over the loss of his brother, and Lord, we ask your tender mercies and care over his good wife and the lil'n to come."

Augusta's heart quickened; she didn't dare look at Tytus for she could feel his resentment when Joseph included her in his prayer. She stepped closer to Alvaro, who patted her arm, and willed her his strength.

Please, do not hold this sin against Señor Ty, Alvaro prayed inwardly. *He is a good man. Someday, he will feel shame for the way he has treated her. Until then, Lord— please, hold us all in the palm of Your hand!*

As the simple service ended, Joseph nodded to the tall ranch foreman. Hitch picked up his guitar and began strumming. A moment later he blended his tenor to Joseph's low bass as they sang,

"Amazing grace, how sweet the sound, that saved a wretch like me."

A light breeze came drifting through the pine trees, lending harmony to their melody. A warmth stole through Augusta, knowing that Timothy would approve. The music filled all the valley then seemed to float away to the distant hills. The men sang all the verses of the old hymn; but it was the third verse that wrapped itself around Augusta's troubled heart.

Thro' many dangers, toils, and snares, I have already come;
Tis grace hath bro't me safe thus far, And grace will lead me home.

Augusta was lost in the words of the song as it ended. Alvaro solemnly took her by the arm and guided her to a spot closer to the grave. Awkwardly, she bent over and grasped a handful of dirt. She held it out then slowly allowed it to slip from her fingers and fall onto the pine box.

In words only Alvaro could hear, she whispered, "Thank you Timothy— you were my friend—my love."

She hated the sound the dry earth made as it fell onto the wooden planks. Silent tears slid down her face as Alvaro placed a protective arm around her shoulders then led her back to her place among the men.

Tytus was next—his eyes were glazed as he knelt on one knee and grasped a handful of soil. Swallowing hard, he fought down his emotions; opened his hand and stared at the dark, rich dirt. **This** had been *their boyhood dream,* to share this *land* one day. He closed his hand around the dirt, making a fist so tight that it shook. He had loved this place, but not today—today he hated it, every acre—every handful of dirt. Finally, he tossed his token *dust to dust* onto the pine box. In a hoarse voice he whispered muffled words of good-bye to his brother. Everyone waited for Tytus to stand and move away, but the big man stayed, still leaning on one knee as he bent over his brother's grave. Suddenly, his broad shoulders began to shake violently, as an unearthly keening seemed to rise up from someplace deep within him, even as great sobs racked his body. The others watched helplessly, having never seen anyone is such agony of spirit. Joseph went to him, but abruptly Tytus staggered to his feet, and with long strides he made it to the edge of the cemetery where his horse was waiting. Grabbing the horn, he swung into the saddle, and in an instant the horse was off at a run.

No one moved or said a word as they watched him ride away. Finally, Augusta turned to glance once more at the grave. Alvaro gently put his arm around her shoulder. "Allow me to escort you back to the hacienda, my dear,." he said gently.

But Augusta couldn't move. She felt as if she were made of stone. She looked towards the hacienda but it seemed to be pulling away from her. Confused, she looked to Alvaro and then to Hitch,

"I'm sorry. I—don't think I can—"

Suddenly, it was as if a veil fell over her eyes, and she imagined herself to be part of the music that had simply floated away to the distant hills.

※

For nearly a week, everyone feared for the young mother and for her child. Alvaro believed her collapse was brought on by the wound to her head and the combination of exhaustion and grief. The old man feared the worst when she became feverish. Refusing to leave her side, Alvaro bathed her brow and attempted to spoon broth into her mouth.

In her confused state, Augusta would by turn call out for her Papa or Timothy, then her memory would come back to her and she would weep inconsolably. As far as Alvaro and Joseph were concerned, the young woman was completely sincere. But nothing could convince Tytus. He believed that if indeed Timothy had married her at all, she had somehow tricked him into it. In his darkest thoughts, he even considered the possibility that Augusta was an imposture—and that she had shot Timothy herself—before riding to him for help.

Ty had returned to the ranch late the night of the funeral, but when he realized his household was in chaos over *that woman*—he changed horses and told his men he would be back in time for the drive to Kansas. The army had a contract with the Bar 61 for one hundred cavalry mounts to be delivered to Fort Leavenworth. These horses would be assigned to the newly enlisted Buffalo Soldiers, a band of recently freed slaves who were being trained to fight Indians out west.

Tytus told his men that he would return to the ranch—when he had to—and not before.

※

Augusta's eyes fluttered open to a flaming red sunrise, tinting her room in shades of mauve. For days, it seemed as if she'd been trapped in a fog. But now, suddenly, her mind was clear, her stomach was growling, and the baby was vigorously reminding her that though the world might seem empty without Timothy, his child was eager to embrace it!

Augusta laid her hand gently over her expanding belly and whispered, "Hey, little one—I'm so glad you're still here! You can play all you like—I don't mind!"

Outside her window, she could hear the muffled sounds of ranch life, animals calling and the men doing their chores.

Augusta sat up and ran her fingers through her long hair. She knew days had passed, but her last clear memory was standing beside Timothy's grave; beyond that—it all seemed like a dream.

Suddenly she remembered her promise to tend to Quest. "Goodness— I've got to get up from here!"

Feeling as wobbly as a new colt, Augusta finally managed to wash, dress, and run a brush through her hair. She was exhausted by the time she reached the barn; still, she was just in time to hear Quest's familiar squeal and the sound of his teeth snapping shut. Thankfully, she heard only a few mild curses, and no outcries of pain. Stepping into the barn, she ordered, "Quest! Stop that!"

All eyes turned to Augusta and then back to the beast! The men watched in surprise as the animal's demeanor changed from vicious to that of a tattling child. The stallion shook his head, and began murmuring to her in low tones, as if listing his many complaints.

Augusta hurried to his stall. "I know, boy—" she soothed, her voice soft and even, "Sorry, Q."

The ranch foreman and six of the other hands had been taking turns trying to pacify the brute for days. Hitch quickly came to Augusta's side. "Ma'am, ya...shouldn't be out here...ya haven't been well."

Though the foreman wasn't as tall as Ty, Augusta still had to step back, just to look the man in the eye.

"I'm feeling much better, thank you." Augusta glanced around to include all the men. "But I hope you all will forgive me? I promised I'd tend to Quest and then—I don't even know how many days ago that was? I'm so sorry! Please tell me: did he hurt any of you?"

Her sweetly spoken apology as well as her concern, took the men by surprise.

"Got nothing...to be sorry for," Hitch said gently. "Yer stud...hasn't... hurt anybody."

Augusta sighed, then before the men could stop her, she quickly opened the stallion's stall door and stepped inside. The men were amazed at the sudden change in the animal. Yet they noted that even as Augusta stroked her stallion's sleek neck, she wisely kept a careful eye on him.

"Quest is usually well behaved, for a stallion," She said, without turning around. But—he can be as ornery as a badger, when he likes."

"Well...I'll be?" Hitch muttered while the other men chuckled awkwardly.

Just then, a red-headed boy, swung down from the loft. "Would ya look at that, boys?" he mocked. "Why—she's got him purrin' like Aunt Tilly's cat."

While the men shook their heads in disbelief, Augusta could easily imagine what Quest had put them through.

Though the stallion's attitude was greatly improved, he was still full of vinegar from that morning's skirmish. He was also put out that his mistress had ignored him for so many days. So, when Hitch handed Augusta a bucket of grain, it came as no surprise when the stallion tried to nip her! But before Hitch could respond, Augusta doubled her fist and bumped Quest's nose with her knuckles. The stallion squealed and snorted his displeasure.

When the men voiced their concerns, she held up her hand but never took her eyes off her stallion.

"It's all right. I was expecting it. He thinks I forgot about him. Quest has to test me every so often." Glancing at the red-headed boy she added, "He is a stallion and most definitely not Aunt Tilly's cat!"

The men laughed, but they watched closely as Quest approached his mistress, and once again he tried to take another little nip. He didn't lunge with teeth bared like he had with the cowboys. No, like she'd explained, his behavior was that of a naughty child testing his boundaries. For a second time, Augusta was quick with her small fist; just a slight disciplinary measure was called for and that's what she gave him. Quest, however, squealed in loud protest, and pranced around the stall. Augusta piqued the men's curiosity further when she backed out of the stall and latched it, taking the full bucket of oats with her.

Turning to the boy, she asked, "Have you fed the other horses yet?"

"Oh sure," he was quick to answer, "we feed El Loco last cause he's such a sorry...I mean...ah!"

The boy's hand flew to his mouth—but it was a wasted effort—his foot was already there.

Hitch immediately stepped forward. "My apologies, ma'am. We...find it easier to...feed yer stud...last."

Augusta winced and blushed with embarrassment. "I'm afraid—I've caused this—you see, I've always fed Quest first! He—expects it!"

Hitch's eyebrows went up and he wished he hadn't done that. Because Augusta grimaced, then said, "I know—I was foolish to spoil him like that."

Hitch looked down at the self-effacing young widow and felt a sudden protectiveness towards her.

"Ma'am," he said kindly, "why don't you let us men...deal with yer stud... at least another day...you still look awful pale."

Augusta looked up at Hitch, her eyes imploring, "Thank you, but...I need this...I need to do...something—that's familiar."

Hitch tipped his hat and smiled gently. "I can understand that. Just tell us how we can help."

Augusta was drawn to the boy who had spoken up earlier. He looked to be about fourteen years old and could easily pass as Emily's little brother. He had curly red hair and a cheerful face full of freckles.

Turning to the boy, she asked, "And what's your name?"

His blue eyes lit up and his voiced squeaked out his answer. "Who? Me, ma'am? I'm Shep!"

"Nice to meet you, Shep. Will you help me teach El Loco a lesson?" she asked, feeling terribly weary.

The boy responded with a wide grin, "Why sure thing ma'am! Whatta we do?"

Taking the boy's arm, Augusta leaned a bit and sighed. Only Shep could hear and then he felt her tremble. His tender heart quickly recognized her unspoken request for help, and suddenly he seemed to stand a bit taller, proud that she had called on him to help her, instead of one of the older men.

Augusta took a deep breath then asked, "Why don't you introduce me to these other horses?"

She peeked into the stall directly across from Quest.

"What a handsome paint—what's his name?" she asked, as she offered a handful of grain to the tall black and white gelding. The horse gently nibbled the grain she offered, while Hitch stepped forward. "He's my horse, ma'am. His name is Doc," He added proudly. "Best cow pony in the territory!"

Augusta gave the horse another handful of grain. Her actions were not lost on Quest, for he nickered indignantly and tossed his head.

Augusta glanced at Shep. "He won't stand for much more of this!" she whispered.

All the ranch hands smiled and followed along to the next stall. Augusta was surprised to see a fine boned, chestnut mule staring back at her.

"I've never seen a nicer looking mule. Who does she belong to?"

For some reason a round of chuckles came from the cowhands as the boy answered, "This here is Ezmerelda." He grinned and pointed to the foreman. "She belongs to Hitch too! Why—she'd sit up and speak if he asked her to. Ya see, Ezzy's in love with Hitch—she thinks he hung the moon and the stars ta-boot!"

Hitch shook his head good-naturedly, and though he didn't seem shy, his words came out slow and measured. "Don't let...these yahoo's...fool ya. They're...all...right fond...of Ezzy."

Augusta held out a handful of grain but the mule wouldn't take it. She studied the animal for a moment then slowly began scratching one of her extra-long ears. Ezzy enjoyed it so much she turned her head nearly horizontal so Augusta could reach every inch, then turned her head for the other ear to receive the same treatment. The next time Augusta offered the handful of grain, Ezzy happily took it. Hitch glanced around at the other ranch hands, and they all nodded their surprise and approval.

"Got a...nice way about ya, ma'am," Hitch said softly. "Ezzy's...slow to make friends."

Finally, Quest let out an ear-shattering whinny and pawed the ground. Augusta turned to her horse. "Well, Q, are you ready to be a gentleman?"

The dark stallion nickered and tossed his head. The men watched with surprise as the big horse leaned his head over the stall door, and stretched his muzzle as far out as he could, allowing Augusta to place a light kiss on his muzzle.

"That's my boy!" she praised, then turning to the hands she said, "All right—he'll behave now."

The big animal shocked the men further as he stood with perfect manners, while Augusta held the stall door open and the men carried in hay and oats, and two large buckets of water. While Quest calmly munched away on his feed, Augusta turned her solemn gaze to the ranch hands.

"Please know that I appreciate your patience with him."

To varying degrees each man nodded and suddenly found the barn's dirt floor of great interest.

Augusta smiled with understanding then realized that she was beyond weary. She glanced towards the barn door and was greatly relieved to see the old Spaniard, Alvaro, coming towards her.

"Ah, señora, I knew I would find you hear, seeing to your horse. But, now you must rest. Come my dear."

The men watched as Augusta took the old man's arm and the two walked slowly towards the hacienda. When the men were sure the woman was out of earshot, they began to mumble.

"Thought I heard the boss say she was some kind of fortune hunter? Don't seem the type to me!"

"Nope, I heard he thinks maybe she tricked his brother into marrying. And the baby ain't even his?"

Rusty scratched his beard. "Nah, she's a sweet little gal—she wouldn't do such as that."

Hitch, as ranch foreman, felt it was his responsibility to put a stop to any gossip—if he could.

"Men, listen to me," he said sternly. "The boss...got his heart ripped out...when he lost his brother. He's not himself...right now. There'll be...no more gossip." Staring at the hacienda, he added;

"She's been through a lot...and more's coming. We need to help her... all we can."

Chapter 22

Stranger in a Strange Land

"The Lord is close to those whose heart is breaking." Psalm 34:18

Augusta's face was pale and drawn as Alvaro set her down at the kitchen table.

"I fear you have already done too much for your first day up, my dear!"

The old man quickly poured a glass of milk and a cup of steaming hot coffee. He carried them to the table then sat himself down beside her.

"Alvaro, please don't be upset with me," she begged. "You've been so kind and I feel much better! But, I promised to tend to Quest and then I didn't." Her voice trailed off sadly. "Since the day we arrived, Quest and I have been nothing but a burden—and a nuisance."

"It is not true, señora, you are not a…ah…ah—nuisance. This is your home now."

Augusta shook her head. Nothing was as it should be. She felt confused about everything.

"Timothy talked so much of this place," she said sadly. "I had come to think of it as home. But now? Ty sees me as an enemy. For this to be my home, I'd have to earn his respect. If that's even possible."

Absent-mindedly, Augusta touched the tender spot on the side of her head. "I don't even know—how I got this? I have so many questions and no answers. Like how did a careful man like Timothy get shot? Something about the way he was lying there—it didn't make any sense."

Augusta closed her eyes, drawing in a deep breath. Suddenly, the rich aroma of the coffee beckoned to her; without thinking she grabbed the cup and drank. It was like swallowing liquid fire! Instantly, she slammed the cup down on the table, gasping as it scorched a trail across her tongue and down her throat!

Alvaro hadn't meant for her to drink the boiling coffee. Quickly, he shoved the glass of milk into her hand.

"Drink! Señora, drink!" he commanded.

Gratefully, Augusta took the milk and gulped it down.

"Oh, my dear—I am so sorry!" the old man apologized. "The coffee—it was for me, I like it *mucho caliente*—*very* hot! I fear I am kin to the dragon, for I drink fire—no?"

The old man fussed and patted Augusta's shoulder while he refilled her glass. "La leche—it is the best for you, and for the little one as well, hey?"

Augusta blushed as she sipped the milk, holding it in her mouth as it soothed her blistered tongue.

Suddenly, Alvaro's dark eyes became bright as he tapped his temple with one finger. "Ah, señora, God has whispered something in my ear, I think!" He hesitated only a moment then explained: "The men sometimes call me the dragon but the name describes Señor Ty—much better!"

When Augusta gave Alvaro a curious look, he proclaimed: "Little one, you shall be the cooling balm that will take the fire from the dragon."

Augusta swallowed the milk she was holding in her mouth then choked out, "I don't understand?"

"Ah, then—I shall explain. Señor Ty—he is a fair man, and truly, deep inside, he is a kind man!"

"His kindness?" Augusta questioned. "It is far too deep for me to reach I'm afraid."

"No—this is not so!" Alvaro was suddenly filled with hope. "Sí, Señor Ty mistrusts women—and for good reason! And now with the loss of his brother, he believes his dreams are gone as well. Part of his soul—it died with his brother—you saw this too. Did you not, señora?"

Augusta nodded sadly. "Yes," she admitted. "I saw."

"El Jefe—he is a man of passion, who suffers from a pain most terrible! And with this pain comes another woman—someone to blame for his broken heart."

Tears filled Augusta's eyes. "He's not the only one with a broken heart. Perhaps, I should just leave."

"No-no, señora, this you must *not* do! I know this dragon well. His fire will burn us all for a time. And we must all stand our ground, but you, señora, you most of all!"

Augusta's eyes grew wide. "With most of his anger directed at me—I am to tame this dragon?"

"Sí! Bueno! You understand—tame is what you must do!"

Augusta grimaced. "No sir—I don't understand at all and even if I did...
I...I couldn't do it!"

"But, señora, you have mastered this already. I have seen you with your
mighty stallion! You are clever, kind, but also firm. Señor Ty is like a mighty
stallion, only he has been wounded. And the wounded beast is the most dangerous—is it not so?"

Augusta toyed with her wedding band as a tear slid down her cheek.

"Yes...it is so! I know because that's exactly how I was with Timothy
when we first married. I was wounded and hateful. I was the dragon—spitting
fire! But Timothy never gave up on me. Finally, he put out the fire inside me.
His kindness was like a—soothing gentle rain."

"Ah, señora. I have not forgotten that you too have a great wound in your
heart. But you can repay your husband's kindness, by helping his brother. In
your fever you spoke of your many sorrows. Ah, little one, you have known
grief many times for one so young."

"Lots of people—know grief, Alvaro. I know I'm not alone in that," she
whispered.

"Sí, but you, my dear, have walked through grief—and come safely to the
other side, by giving it to God. Señor Ty has known grief, but he declares war
against it—and against God. It is a war that cannot be won! But señora, with
God's help and yours—he too can come safely to the other side—and trust in
God again!"

Augusta was pondering Alvaro's words when they heard the sound of
boots scraping across the stony path leading to the kitchen.

Augusta braced herself when suddenly the dragon himself was filling the
doorway. Her heartbeat quickened; she felt both terrified and intrigued by the
sight of him. He looked angry and dangerous, yet she couldn't take her eyes
from him. Couldn't deny herself the bitter-sweet agony of chancing a glimpse
of Timothy reflected in his brother's face. They both had that same square jaw,
she liked to trace with her fingertips, the deep set eyes, the perfectly straight
nose, those high proud cheek bones she had to rise up on tip-toe to kiss. Sadly,
she looked away. Yes, their features were nearly identical but she saw nothing
of her Timothy. Ty's face held no kindness or humor. How could two men be so
much the same—and yet so different?

Warily, she watched Tytus as he hung his hat on a peg; his thick brown
hair was wavy and in need of a cut. Both brothers were over six feet tall, but

while Timothy had been long and lean, Tytus was built like a warrior. He was all muscle and sinew, broad shoulders, a narrow waist—his powerful arms made strong from heavy lifting and hard work. He seemed to fill the whole room with his presence, as he made his way towards the table. Slowly, he sat down—watching her as suspiciously as she watched him.

Augusta couldn't stop her fear of him any more than she could stop her empathy. It was easy to see this man as a wild stallion, or even more so, a fire-breathing dragon. But even with him glaring at her, Augusta could see that Tytus Grainger was also, just a man, a vulnerable one at that. He looked gaunt, and bone weary, his powerful shoulders bowed as if burdened by an impossible weight. Augusta found herself wishing she could free him of the crushing pain she saw in his eyes. He was a leviathan to be sure, on the outside, but soul-sick to the core.

Tytus stiffened under Augusta's sympathetic gaze; her strange gold-brown eyes were sad and older than her years. Still, he resented the pity he saw in those eyes! How dare this bedraggled young woman look at him as if she understood *his pain* or shared *his grief*. Like salt in an open wound, she would always be a reminder of his lost dreams. He had to get rid of her and soon!

Ty's dark eyes turned to Alvaro. "Coffee!" he growled.

"Sí, Jefe, sí."

The old man had forgotten that he'd set the coffee back to boil, as he filled the boss's mug.

Still glaring at Augusta, Tytus took the cup from Alvaro's hand and without thinking he filled his mouth. Instantly, his face contorted—in a panic he couldn't decide if he should swallow or spit. When he saw Augusta's eye's grow wide, his pride won out. He swallowed it down with one eye noticeably twitching.

Augusta looked away, sensing his embarrassment while Alvaro quickly handed Ty a glass of milk. Then her mouth dropped open as she watched him down the contents of the huge glass in one long gulp.

When Ty observed Augusta's startled expression, he gave her a contemptuous sneer. "A proper 'lady' would know not to stare and—you can close your mouth now!"

Augusta snapped her mouth shut, then squirmed under his hateful perusal.

"Your story doesn't add up," he hissed. "I don't believe you were Tim's wife. And if he didn't marry you that child you carry—is definitely not his!"

"What are you saying?" Augusta gasped.

Alvaro hurried to her side. "Señor Ty, you must not speak to your sister-in-law this way!"

Ty glared at the old man. "Don't call her that!" he growled. "And this is none of your business!"

Alvaro stiffened, he dark eyes flashing. "Did we not come to this land together?" he asked. "From the first—were we not *amigos*? Both sons of privilege—you kept your inheritance while mine was taken. Yet side by side we laid the stones at our feet. I cook—for that is my pleasure. So—now, Tytus Grainger! Has your grief made me your servant?"

Ty's expression was suddenly filled with contrition. "Of course *not*!" he groaned. "This ranch wouldn't be what it is today, but for you, my friend. But... this...this mess is between me—me and *that woman*!"

Augusta gently placed her hand on the old man's arm. "It's all right Alvaro—Tytus is right. This must be worked out between the two of us."

Turning her attention to Ty, she began to speak, "I—understand that..."

Ty held up his hand and interrupted. "Woman, let me remind you, that you are sitting in *my home*! We just buried *my—brother*. You will listen—and then IF you have anything worth saying—then you can speak."

Augusta bristled at his words, but Alvaro had warned her that the dragon would be quick to attack. Though she managed to hold her tongue, she couldn't stop her eyes from shooting daggers.

Ty was surprised by Augusta's defiant stare. *So, the dowdy little mouse has a temper. Maybe if I get her mad enough, I'll get her to tell the truth.*

"I knew Timothy better than anyone!" he began. "I knew his dreams and he knew mine!"

Augusta nodded as she remembered Timothy's love for his twin brother. "He loved you very much," she whispered softly.

Tytus frowned. "I talk—you listen—remember?" He sucked in a breath to calm himself. "Listen—I can understand—women have so few choices. Maybe you met my brother along the way and he said he would help you—I would do no less. Like I said, no one knew Tim better than me. And I can see through all of this. All I'm asking is for us both to talk straight, and tell the truth. I won't be angry with you and I won't toss you out on your ear—if you will just tell me the honest truth!"

Augusta shook her head and almost smiled. How ironic—his words were almost the exact same ones she had spoken to Timothy a year earlier. *'Let's both tell the truth!'* she had taunted.

Augusta's reaction angered Tytus. He slammed his fist down on the table. "Madame!" he demanded. "I have got to know what you were to my brother—if anything!"

Augusta forced herself to look across the table at the dragon who would burn her to ashes, if he could.

"I take it...now...I have your permission to speak?" she asked softly.

"Be my *guest*..." he scoffed, with a sarcastic wave of his arm.

Augusta wanted to cry out for Timothy to come and help her with this impossible situation. Then her thoughts grew tender as she spoke. "But that's our problem—isn't it—Tytus? I am not your guest—I'm family!"

Ty glared and opened his mouth to protest, but she held up her hand. "Wait—it's my turn!" Augusta clasped her hands tightly together then said, "Timothy tried to warn me about you. He said you were hurt badly by your mother and then by your fiancé—and that you viewed all woman through a magnifying glass of suspicion and hurt. Timothy said that even with him here to speak for me—I would still have to work at earning your trust."

Tytus wasn't sure what he expected her to say, but this wasn't it. He ran his large hand slowly over the smooth table, as he muttered. "I know what I know about women—and I know what I know about my brother! Tim *always* told me what was on his mind. He never mentioned *marriage*, and he *never* mentioned *you!*"

Frowning, Augusta asked, "But Timothy's last letter to you—he said he told you about our wedding!"

"I haven't received a letter in quite a while, but the ones I have never talked of marriage!"

"Señor Ty!" Alvaro broke in. "Perhaps the letter was in the freight wagons that were robbed!"

Ty shook his head. "That might explain one missing letter. But Tim would have written a dozen letters over a period of time before he decided to get married! And he would have waited for my answer! No—Tim wouldn't do this!" He turned to Augusta and hissed, "But it works out nicely for you—doesn't it?

With Timothy dead, you don't have to tell me how it was—no, you can tell me how you wanted it to be! You can suddenly make both you and that child of yours my responsibility. There's no proof as to whose child you carry but, on your word, it's now heir to all Grainger assets and holdings?"

Augusta's heart sank like an anchor in the ocean; without Timothy, her claims sounded so self-serving. Suddenly, the baby gave her a sharp kick, reminding her that there was another life to think of just now. She stiffened and raised her chin. "I agree—it sounds too convenient and way too arrogant! But, Tytus, I know what I know too! And my husband, your brother, told me to stand up to you. He said I was as much...your partner as he was. And yes—he did want our child to be raised here, and to be heir to at least his share of this ranch!"

Ty blew out an agitated sigh. "As a lawyer, Tim would have insisted on legal papers." Tytus fixed his dark eyes on Augusta. "I looked through that wagon and his trunks for a wedding certificate. Do *you* have it?"

Augusta was suddenly at a loss, she frowned and tried to think. "No—I—I can't even remember signing any papers," she admitted.

Tytus raised his eyebrows and sneering, he said, "Lady, *if* you married my brother, there'd be papers!"

Augusta bit her lip, "My father was dying. I hardly remember the wedding." Then she simply nodded her head. "But—you're right—there have to be papers! Timothy would have made sure of it."

Ty had expected her to make up excuses; instead, Augusta looked straight into his eyes and said, "I'll find them. But until then, you'll just have to take my word—that I am who I say I am."

Ty's dark eyes flared. "Not a chance, lady. You mean nothing to me and your word means less."

Augusta swallowed back tears, trying not to show how he was hurting her.

"Listen to me," she said firmly. "I can very well imagine your pain, but only because I know what losing you would have meant to Timothy."

"Woman," Ty growled, "you can coat your words with honey—but I don't have to swallow them."

"El Jefe...*por favor!*" Alvaro begged.

Augusta pushed back from the table and stood to her full height. "It's all right, Alvaro," she said softly. Then turning to Ty she added: "Actually, I never

174

understood why Timothy wanted to marry me—but he did! I'll do what I can to earn my keep. And after the baby comes, I'll do a lot more—you'll see! However, I promise that neither the baby nor I will ever be a burden to you."

Tytus narrowed his eyes. "Lady," he grumbled, "*you* already are!"

Suddenly, out of the corner of her eye Augusta realized, that an audience of ranch hands had gathered around the kitchen door. Flushing with embarrassment—her first thought was to turn tail and run to her bedroom. But she couldn't bear the idea of Tytus Grainger thinking her a coward. His opinion of her was poor enough already. Instead, she gathered her courage and walked down the length of the long table until she stood beside her brother-in-law, and speaking so only he could hear her, she whispered:

"Tytus Grainger, I am sorry...for your loss...and for mine. But know this—I am not now, nor will I ever be—afraid of you!" Then she spoke very slowly so he wouldn't miss a single word: "I am your brother's widow, I am your sister-in-law, and I am the mother of *your* niece or nephew. My name is Missus Timothy Grainger. You wanted the honest truth? Well—there it is!

Chapter 23

Trouble

"Though I walk in the midst of trouble, you preserve my life; you stretch out your hand against the anger of my foes, with your right hand you save me." Psalm 138:7

Augusta's eyes flew open when the baby landed a hard kick to her ribs. As she did every morning her hand immediately reached out, but the place beside her was empty. Timothy wasn't there. Sometimes it felt like his death had been a bad dream and that surely she would wake up, and find him smiling down at her. While at other times she felt as if her marriage to Mr. Timothy Grainger and everything that happened since had been the dream. After all, their time together had been so brief—it was almost as if she had only imagined the happy, long-limbed man with the sky-blue eyes. Nights and early mornings were the most difficult, and she struggled against her tears. Alvaro had warned her not to give into her grief. He feared that if she yielded to strong emotions, her labor could start before the baby was ready! His gentle warning was enough for Augusta. She wanted Timothy's child now, more than anything in the world!

The best diversion from her grief was spending time with Quest. She would lead him out under a stand of tall shade trees, and tell him about all her fears and worries while she brushed his coat until it shone like fine ebony. The ranch hands marveled at how gentle the stallion was with his mistress.

Quest bent his head and nibbled at Augusta's apron pocket as she brushed his back.

"All right, boy, you knew I had carrots, didn't you?"

She fed him small bites, as Hitch came up behind her.

"Hey now...we cowboys like those...in our stew, you know!"

Augusta was startled. "Oh, I'm sorry—I only took the soft ones!"

"S'all right, ma'am," he added sheepishly. "Only teasin'. I... just got back...from...the Triple R."

As he held his hat in both hands, Augusta thought she noticed a hint of a smile.

"And what's at the Triple R? Someone special?" she ventured to ask.

"Reckon—you'd think so! They got women at the Rosenquist Ranch—Granny Rose is a mid-wife!"

Augusta watched as the man's face turned to crimson then added quietly, "I asked her...if she'd come and...help ya."

"She'll come here? She'll deliver my baby?"

By the shocked look on Hitch's face, Augusta realized that the man was hoping to be less descriptive.

"Yep—" the foreman muttered, keeping his head down, he added in his painfully slow way: "Granny'll come...in about...a week...she'll stay...till ya...send her home."

Augusta felt like the heaviest burden in the world had just been lifted from her shoulders. "Oh Hitch, you'll never know—not in a millions years—what a gift this is! I've been so...I...just—"

Realizing that she was babbling like a ninny, she smiled at the man and said sincerely, "Thank you!"

In her relief Augusta nearly threw her arms around the man. But, realizing that would be improper, she impulsively hugged Quest's neck instead.

Hitch hid his grin behind a calloused hand. This little woman was about the sweetest thing he'd ever known, and not for the first time he felt a bit envious of that cantankerous *El Loco!*

When Augusta turned her grateful smile back to Hitch, the man tipped his hat and said simply, "Ma'am."

But as the foreman of the Bar 61 walked away, he felt enormously pleased with himself. It had been a long ride to the Triple R but worth every mile to see the look of relief in those golden eyes. He'd even seen her smile—and now that he'd seen it, he was determined to see it again!

⚜

The following morning, Augusta felt sure the baby must be bull dogging steers when she awoke.

"My goodness, but you're busy today!" Augusta spoke softly to her baby as she rose from her bed and dressed for the day. "God is taking care of us little one! We have a roof over our heads, a mid-wife is coming, and even Quest is settling in. And best of all," she added dryly, "your Uncle Dragon is leaving tomorrow!" Smiling at her new name for Ty, she sighed, "And we won't have to deal with him—not for weeks and weeks!"

For the first time since Timothy's death she began her day with a glimmer of hope. And so, as soon as she entered the kitchen, Augusta lifted her chin and commenced with her rehearsed speech. "Alvaro, the men won't let me clean barns, but I insist you let me help—I can cook—and do laundry."

Alvaro put his hands on his hips, purposely ignoring her words. "Buenos días, señora! Sit down, my dear, I will bring your milk."

"No!" Augusta grimaced at her sharp tone. "Thank you—but—no! Please—Alvaro, you must stop pampering me. I have to earn my keep! I beg you: give me something to do."

The old man understood only too well, he rubbed his chin, then said, "I suppose you could make the tortillas."

Augusta stared at him a moment; she could make excellent biscuits and rolls and flapjacks. But the men were all used to Alvaro's Mexican cooking. It would be rude and probably arrogant to suggest the menu change just to accommodate her abilities. No, she told herself, it's best if I just fit in. Rubbing the palms of her hands against her apron she smiled at the older man and tried to look confident.

"Certainly, I—could help with—those. If you wouldn't mind teaching me?" she added sheepishly.

Alvaro chuckled. "Ahh, bueno! You watch me, hey?"

He pointed to a bowl filled with dozens of dough balls; he took one and handed another to Augusta.

"This way!" he said. He quickly flattened the ball with his fingers and thumbs, then began slapping the flattened dough back and forth from palm to palm, and in no time at all, he had a perfectly rounded circle of thin dough. With a small brush he painted a bit of melted lard onto the flat surface of the big iron stove. Then like a card dealer he slid his tortilla, and ten more just like it, onto the heated surface. As a delicious aroma filled the kitchen, he used his fingers to turn them over, and when they were done, he flipped them onto a platter already stacked high with tortillas. Augusta knew the men would soon be filling them with spoonfuls of fried potatoes, onions, sausage, peppers, and eggs. Or sometimes the men would simply slather them with butter, drizzle them with wild honey and enjoy them as a sweet.

Augusta thought she was doing exactly as Alvaro did, but her tortilla was neither flat nor round, and when she tried to slap it from hand to hand—it wound up on the floor.

Knowing it was difficult for Augusta to bend, Alvaro quickly scooped it up.

"Do not worry, señora.," he said soothingly as he tossed her efforts into the slop bucket. "The pigs will not mind a little dirt," he assured her. "Perhaps, it would be best for me to make them and you to cook them—no?"

Augusta happily took Alvaro's place at the stove, but her efforts were even less successful. She either burned her fingers or the tortillas. She was getting more and more flustered, and even Alvaro's endless patience was wearing thin. It seemed she'd always had this problem: the harder she tried to do something, the bigger the mess she made. It was irritating, for she had prepared all sorts of dishes at the Dutch Oven and done them well! But then, she recalled that first calamitous meal she'd made for Timothy and decided to give up.

"Alvaro—" she groaned. "When I'm like this, I can't do anything right. I think I'll just pour the coffee."

"Bueno, señora. I think that is best!"

Alvaro rolled his eyes and shook his head when she turned away. He understood her need to be useful, but he'd never liked having anyone in *his* kitchen. A few minutes later a dozen hungry cowboys swarmed in for breakfast. They were full of energy and excitement as they chattered about the upcoming drive. Augusta was caught up in the current of masculine exuberance and anticipation. The men had worked hard at training the horses they were driving to Fort Leavenworth. A great adventure awaited them! Half of the ranch hands would be going on this drive. The rest would stay behind, watching over pregnant mares and cows as they gave birth. Augusta chaffed at the realization that she and the only other *females* on the ranch had so much in common.

The next big event for the ranch hands would come in late summer and early fall with a big cattle round-up. The new calves would be branded, dehorned, and castrated. Then two-year-old steers, fattened on mountain pastures, would be driven, nearly seven hundred miles, to Sedalia, Missouri, where they would be sold and loaded onto cattle cars—eventually gracing the tables of the East with succulent Western beef.

Augusta helped Alvaro set the rest of the food on the table, when every man had hung his hat on the back of his chair and lowered his head. Alvaro thanked God, then asked for His protection and blessings over them all.

Augusta wondered what these men believed but each man said a hardy "amen" before picking up his fork. Ty was the first to snatch the top five tortillas off the platter nearest him, Hitch snagging the next five, and so it went, as platters—mounded high with food—ricocheted around the table. As they filled their plates, the men joked good-naturedly bragging about who was the best bronc rider, best roper, and best wrangler. Hitch apparently was the one they all hoped to beat one day. Challenges and bets flew from man to man, until suddenly, Ty bellowed: "Alvaro? What happened here?" He held up a few burnt tortillas. "These aren't fit for the table!"

Ty glanced around at the men. "Am I the only one who got his breakfast burnt this morning?"

Alvaro turned in confusion to see the blackened circles Ty was holding up with a scowl.

"Ah, Jefe, I did not see those. Do not worry—there are plenty more."

Ty's eyebrows went up as he spread the others out like a hand of blackened poker cards. "All of mine are burnt on one side!"

Alvaro hurriedly swiped them out of Ty's hand and put a stack of fresh tortillas on his plate. "My apologies, Jefe!"

When Alvaro turned back to the stove, Ty took a swig of coffee then spewed it back into his cup. Grimacing, he hurried to the sink, pumped water directly into his mouth, then spit out the rest of the coffee grounds.

"Hey, *amigo*—you mad at me? Giving me burnt tortillas and a mug full of coffee grounds?"

The rest of the men eyed the mugs cautiously, then each man stood in line to pour out the grainy brew.

Augusta put her hands to her flaming cheeks; she couldn't allow Alvaro to take the blame.

"Oh, dear!" she exclaimed. "It's my fault! I was just trying to help. I guess I should have…"

"ENOUGH!" Ty bellowed, holding up his hand to stop whatever she was about to say.

"You foolish woman! Why pick today of all days to help? We're gearing up for our big drive—we have a lot of work to do around here—lady. And if you don't know your way around a kitchen—then stay out of it! If you want to help—wash something—better yet, wait until after we've gone!"

Augusta was mortified, "I am sorry..I…"

Feeling tears threaten in the back of her throat, she stiffened, knowing every eye in the room was watching her. Finally, she managed to gather enough composure to walk quietly to Alvaro and whisper, "I'll be back to do the dishes."

Stepping outside, she rushed to the spring feed creek that wound through the trees behind the hacienda. Her knees were shaking so hard she barely made it to the little bench that sat in the shade of an elm tree.

"Lord!" she groaned, "Timothy told me you never give us more than we can handle."

Augusta looked up through the canopy of leaves, and allowed her tears to fall. "It sure feels like more. Feels like a whole lot more than I can handle!"

Closing her eyes, she imagined Timothy's voice in the wind as it whispered threw the leaves.

'Hey my darling,' he would say, *'don't mind Ty, you can win him over—if anyone can—it's you.'*

Augusta sighed in defeat. "Well, I've certainly won your brother over today!" she mocked. Still, she couldn't bear the thought of letting Timothy down. He had counted on her to be the one to help Ty, and Alvaro had said the same thing. Straightening, she glanced back at the hacienda and spotted a large wash pot boiling over an open fire, and beside it, sat a table piled high with dirty long johns.

"Well now," she mused. "Even a *'foolish woman'* can wash—*unmentionables!*"

Besides, Augusta wanted to do something to repay Alvaro for all his kindness. After all, he would be driving the chuck wagon and preparing the meals all the way to the fort. She knew it would take him all day and half the night to finish what he still had to do to get ready.

Augusta smiled to herself and began rolling up her sleeves. "This is the least I can do."

It seemed Alvaro had finished most of it; only this stack of undergarments were laid out to wash. Feeling a surge of confidence, she quickly shaved some soap into the water, then one by one she dropped each Union Suit into the boiling pot. Using a large wooden paddle, she stirred them and poked them, then lifted the steaming garments onto a scrubbing table. After they cooled a bit, she scrubbed each one against the washboard. Finally, she rinsed them twice, wrung them out, and hung them to dry in the sweet breeze that rolled down from the mountains.

When she was finished, her back was sore and her hands felt like dry pine cones—but she didn't care—it felt so good to finally do something helpful! Not wanting to leave any of this for Alvaro to do, she ladled water from the pot to put the fire out. Then, Augusta pushed a damp curl from her eyes as she gazed into the pot, and realized there was still one more garment left.

"Oh bother," she grumbled, "how could I have missed that?"

Using the paddle, she fished something pink from the water. That didn't surprise her—few of these garments were still red—they were mostly faded to various shades of pink. Still, this last garment was different somehow. As she raised it high to get a better look, she discovered that it wasn't a pair of long johns at all.

*Hmmm—it's a shirt. A fancy dress shirt—a BIG man's—fancy dress shirt— and—it's—**pink**!*

Feeling that she might just be sick, she fingered the material carefully. Augusta knew the feel of expensive fabric and the look of expert stitching! The shirt couldn't belong to anyone but—Tytus!

"Oh no! I can't believe I just did this." she moaned. "Oh, Lord…help! I'll have to tell him—I—."

Suddenly, from behind her there came a roar and she knew the dragon had already seen for himself.

"Why you little—that was my best shirt!" he hissed. "I was planning to wear it for an important meeting with General Mitchell! Wasn't it enough for you to burn my breakfast and give me mud to drink?" He fumed. "What kind of games are you playing?"

Augusta was shaking her head. "I didn't mean—to do it! I can't tell you how sorry I am—I—"

"STOP!" Ty demanded. "I can't tell you—how glad I am to be LEAV- ING!"

Augusta stepped back in alarm as Ty stormed towards her, grabbed the shirt from her hands, then shook it in her face, as he growled. "This—was my *favorite* shirt!"

Disgusted he threw the thing to the ground and walked away.

Augusta called after him, "I truly only meant to help…" but the dragon merely waved her off and kept walking.

⌦⌤

Tytus and Hitch rode in silence, checking on the brood mares and cattle.

"Hitch," Ty groaned, "you're just like my father! That man could give me a thorough dressing down and never utter a word."

The foreman only pursed his lips while Ty shook his head. "Okay—I know—I've been too hard on her. And yeah, especially considering her con—di—tion!" He drug out each syllable with disgust. "I'm grateful this drive will take me away for a while. I feel nothing but anger when I'm around—*that woman*." Rubbing the back of his neck he grumbled, "But when it comes to her there seem only to be questions and no answers like—who was she to Timothy? And who killed him?"

"Well, boss," Hitch drawled, "*that woman*—didn't do it!"

"Sounds like she's got you right where she wants you."

Hitch gave Ty a side-long glace and said in his slow way: "Boss…she's…a sweet little thing!"

Ty surrendered. "All right—maybe she didn't pull the trigger, but somebody did! There were two other dead men there and neither one of them shot Timothy."

Hitch's eyebrows rose as he tilted his head.

Ty knew the gesture all too well. "I know—I'll feel bad if I learn that she was Tim's wife and he really loved her. But, I—just don't know?"

Their conversations were always like this: Hitch would gesture and Tytus would talk.

"Hitch, you didn't know my brother!" Ty added angrily, "I tell you if Tim took a wife, she'd be something very special! She'd be poised and accomplished. He wasn't a snob but he wouldn't have some dowdy little thing like her, waddling around, burning his breakfast and turning his clothes pink! I know from his letters the kind of woman that impressed him!"

Hitch frowned; he'd always been a man of few words, but just now he had a lot that needed saying.

"She's pregnant, and grieving—and the poor thing is surrounded—by a bunch of strange men."

Ty stared at Hitch, surprised he was having so much to say on this subject.

"And she ain't dowdy," the foreman added. "When that—baby comes! Your sister-in-law'll be—a real looker!"

"She is not my sister-in-law!" Ty snapped.

"Maybe she ain't!" Hitch snapped back, "Just sayin', after the baby comes—she'll—turn a man's head."

Ty groaned. "That's all we need! Some conniving little trollop trying to turn all the men's heads."

Hitch muttered under his breath as he stopped his horse and dismounted. Then, grabbing the horn he shook the saddle side to side, tightened his cinch, then remounting, he added: "I believe her! And…I think…your brother chose well."

Tytus frowned at his friend and foreman, and Hitch figured he'd said more than enough.

They rode for a while in silence, then Ty spoke up, a bit of sarcasm tingeing his words. "So, you're so sure—how about a little wager? I'll bet she'll be twice as haggard and three times the nuisance after that baby comes."

A broad grin spread across the foreman's face. "What'll I win?"

Ty thought for a moment then boasted, "When I win! I want that nice Mexican saddle you won with a royal flush last year. "If you win I'll sell you that parcel of land—you've been wanting."

There was silence. Then Ty added sarcastically, "But I wouldn't go organizing a house raising if I were you. *That woman is not gonna win you that bet!*"

Chapter 24
The First Ride
Earning the Privilege

"Do what is right; then if men speak against you, calling you evil names, they will become ashamed of themselves for falsely accusing you when you have only done what is good." I Peter 3:16

Hitch let out a low whistle and sighed. "That sure is...a...mighty fine sight!"

The men looked down on the valley where a dozen ranch hands were rounding up one hundred high-spirited horses, and heading them east towards Kansas.

Ty crossed his hands over the saddle horn, and nodded his agreement. And yet, after Timothy's death, even this was bitter-sweet. Sights like this used to stir his blood and fill him with pride. He would keep a journal of each horse and cattle drive and when it was over, he'd send it to his brother. Often writing on the last page: "Next year brother, we'll make this ride together!"

A cloud of pain floated across Ty's face. Where he once saw his future, now it just seemed so pointless. He had felt like that when his fiancé had left him, but then there was always the hope that Timothy would join him and they would run the ranch together! But now—who was he doing all this for?

Ty sighed and checked the count once again. "One hundred head, and everyone is just what the cavalry Quarter Master is looking for—long legged, deep chested and, easy to handle."

"Don't know...about—easy...boss. Hitch muttered, "Some still have a few rough corners but the men'll change mounts often. They'll ride the hound out of 'em all along the way. That's all they need."

Ty nodded but his mind was already on a bigger problem. He shook his head in frustration. "You know El Loco will probably have our barn kicked down by the time we get back? I should have just saddled that stud up this morning and left her a note."

Hitch shrugged and blew out a breath, "He's her...best friend boss."

"He was probably my brother's horse—which makes him mine anyway!"

"That's kinda convenient—ain't it?" Hitch mumbled the words while he shook his head.

"Well now, Hitch!" Ty growled, shooting him a look that would have cowed most men. "You've gotten downright chatty since she's come. So, if you got something to say—say it plain!"

Hitch straightened. "All right...I will! The man comes with a stallion and a pregnant wife. You like the stud so you figure he belonged to your brother. You don't like the woman so...you figure she didn't belong to your brother! I think yer figurin'—is a might convenient—that's all! And...if ya...don't like my words...maybe ya need...another foreman!"

Ty snatched his hat off and slapped it against his side, "Dog-gone-it, Hitch! You know I don't want another foreman!"

Ty closed his eyes and groaned; he allowed them both to cool down before he spoke again. "Could be you're right—about the horse anyway." Ty blew out a breath. "I don't know anything anymore. And until I know what happened to Timothy—I'm not gonna be fit company for man or beast."

Hitch softened; he had always believed Tytus Grainger to be a fair man and a good one. "S'alright, boss," he said sincerely. "Probably feel the same...if it was me. But she's got good sense. Ride back...talk to her. We'll move these ponies along slow...when we get to the crik...we'll give 'em plenty of time to fill their bellies with water. You'll be able to catch up!"

⚜

Augusta was already missing Alvaro, even though he'd only been gone a few hours. And yet, this cloud had a wonderful silver lining. She would not have to see or deal with the dragon of the Bar 61 for at least six weeks! She was also thankful that she had awoken that morning feeling so much stronger. The baby had even gifted her with a full night of sleep for a change. And it seemed to have changed positions and finally, gotten comfortable. Hopefully, not too comfortable, she thought ruefully. Augusta laid her hand on her stomach. "I'm looking forward to meeting you and playing with you and even sometimes—putting you down!" she groaned. "For baby—you sure are getting heavy!"

The baby replied with a few faint kicks.

"You want out?" she whispered. "Well, just wait a few more days and Granny Rose will be here. We will welcome you with open arms!"

The thought of giving birth still frightened her, but now that she knew someone was coming to help, she was just looking forward to getting the job done. And yet, before she could do that—she needed to clean!

Alvaro was a wonderful cook and he kept the hacienda tidy. But, his definition of clean and Augusta's were miles apart. So, the moment Ty and the men left out early that morning, she attacked the hacienda with a scrub brush and pail! Augusta felt like a whirlwind; as she swept the log walls, then gave the stone floors a cleaning they would never forget! By the time the sun was spilling its buttery rays across her freshly polished floors her back was aching something fierce.

Still, Augusta was pleased with her accomplishment, sighing contentedly she poured herself a cup of coffee, and with her hand on her back, she wandered out the kitchen door. The barnyard seemed so quiet with so many of the ranch hands gone. Reaching for the small carrots in her apron pocket, she headed to the barn, looking forward to giving Quest a treat. She was just opening the gate when she looked up and saw Tytus canter into the yard.

When he headed straight for Augusta, she stiffened but tried not to frown. "Thought you'd be miles from here by now—has something gone wrong?" she asked.

Ty shook his head, he lifted his hat, wiped his brow on his sleeve, then settled it firmly back into place. It bothered Tytus to have to *ask* the woman for anything. After all she treated his home as if it were her's, so why shouldn't he treat her stallion as if it were his?

Augusta shaded her eyes from the sun, and wondered why he had come back. Suddenly, she braced herself—she wasn't going to like whatever it was he was about to say.

Ty's mouth was a grim line as he stared around the barnyard. He seemed to be looking for someone.

"If you're looking for Shep," she volunteered, "he went to help Rusty pull a calf and Joseph said he wasn't coming back until he caught enough fish for dinner. The other hands are riding circuit."

Ty nodded. "Wasn't looking for them." In a surprisingly congenial way he added, "Actually, I came back because I wanted to speak to you about something."

Augusta was instantly on her guard. Her wary look irritated Tytus and he began to stammer. "Y-you see it's—well, I've been thinking. There's something I should do but—it will probably make you mad!"

Augusta was confused as she looked up at the big man. "Maybe not," she said cautiously. "What is it?"

Tytus blew out a breath. "Well, it's about that stud of yours."

When Augusta frowned he held up his hand, then went on: "Now just let me get this out before you say anything. He hasn't gotten much exercise since he's been here. He's edgy and ornery with everybody but you and Hitch—and me! It's just because he needs to be ridden, and it's gonna get worse cause— you're ... well, you're...?"

"Because I'm what?" Augusta asked drolly, enjoying his discomfort.

Ty ignored her, but felt his face grow warm. "I want to take him on the drive! I think it would be good for him. And..." Ty rubbed a gloved hand over his chin. "Now, I know how you feel about him but if you really cared..."

Augusta held up her hand. "Stop—you don't have to convince me. You're right!" she shrugged.

"I am?" Ty asked in surprise.

"Absolutely! I was worried how I'd keep him from kicking the barn down while you all were gone. It's a perfect solution." Staring up at him she added, "Thank you!"

Ty was stunned, "So, you don't mind?"

"Not as long as you don't sell him to the Army!" Then, she said slowly, "Timothy told me you were the best horseman he ever knew and Alvaro said the same! I trust you, and—I will trust Hitch—but only you two! I don't want anyone else riding him. All right? Absolutely, no one else!" She added firmly, "I don't want him coming back with a hard mouth and bad manners!"

"Heaven forbid!" Ty grunted, shaking his head at how easily this was going.

"I know you're in a hurry to catch up to the others so let's get him saddled up—then I need to walk you through how to mount him, and..."

"Hey, you just said you trusted me!" Ty grumbled as he swung from the saddle and followed Augusta into the barn. "Believe me—I don't need some little girl telling me how to ride a horse!"

Augusta spun around to face him, then had to take a step back so she could stare up at him. "No—you don't," she agreed through gritted teeth, "but you do need to listen to this little girl—if you want to mount Quest for the first time—without him breaking his neck—or yours!"

Tytus seemed to grow taller as he glared down at Augusta; his look was intimidating and meant to be so, but Augusta's gold-brown eyes met his without flinching as she took a step towards him. "Do you want to take him with you or not?"

"Yes!" Ty flinched. "I want to take him! So, what is this all about?"

Augusta's face took on a tender smile as she explained, "My father was an excellent horseman. And yet, when he broke Quest to the saddle, the stubborn animal just would not stand still for mounting. Every time Papa tried to get Quest to be still, he would rear up and throw himself backwards. Finally, Papa decided that Quest was too valuable to risk getting hurt or even killed. He always said Quest was a privilege to ride and that he was worth the trouble. In a week or two *if* you've earned his respect, he'll stand still for you. But I promise you that if you don't do as I say, he could *cripple himself* or *you!*"

When Ty looked bemused Augusta suddenly smiled with pride. "I know it sounds strange but I promise you—once you've ridden him, you'll understand why he deserves this measure of respect."

Ty was both irritated and intrigued. Begrudgingly, he nodded his agreement. "All right, let's get this over with," he moaned. "We're burning day light."

Quest was quickly brushed, saddled, and bridled. As Tytus led the horse around the corral he muttered, "You know—he's probably outgrown all this nonsense."

As his gaze fell on Augusta he thought she looked a little green as she leaned against the corral fence.

"Hey, you're not one of those silly females that get the 'vapors' are you? If all this is upsetting you, why don't you just go on into the hacienda? I'll introduce myself to your stallion, then we can be on our way."

When Ty gestured as if to shoo her away, Augusta stepped towards him, eyes flashing.

"I am not silly nor am I upset! And I have never and will never get 'the vapors'! But I've lost just about everyone dear to me in this world and if you do anything foolish to hurt Quest...I'll..."

"Whoa there, mama bear!" Ty put his hands up in surrender. "Pull those claws in. I'm not going to do anything to hurt this big baby of yours."

He took Augusta by the arm, and speaking as if to a dull-witted child, he said calmly: "Just stand over here, out of the way, while I walk the hump out of him and then I'll get mounted up." Quest, like many horses, held his breath and bowed his back when the cinch was pulled tight. As he walked him, the stallion relaxed and Tytus stopped to tighten the cinch.

Augusta's eyes were suddenly drawn to a falcon spreading his wings to catch a high current. It soared and dipped, then sailed over the spruce and pine-studded mountains. While the woman's attention was elsewhere, Ty quickly slipped the reins around Quest's neck and grabbed the horn. But when he started to swing up into the saddle, the stallion's eyes grew wild. Immediately, he reared and stood straight up on his hind legs, and walking backwards, he leaned farther and farther back.

"Turn him loose!" Augusta screamed. "Let go!"

As soon as Ty released him and stepped away, Quest came down hard on his front legs, and began blowing and snorting. When Tytus tried to approach him, the stallion side-stepped; as he watched the man warily, with the whites of his eyes showing and his nostrils flaring.

Augusta hurried to Quest's side, her voice soothing and low. "Eee—zy, boy. Easy, eee—zy now."

She gave Tytus a look that could melt steel while she continued to speak calmly to her horse. "I'm so sorry, Q. I should have known better than to trust you to an arrogant, pig headed, stubborn, fool hardy, un-trustworthy—!"

"All right!" Tytus grimaced and rolled his eyes. "I think you've made your point! I am sorry. I guess I deserve that. Some of it, anyway. But I'm pretty fast and I...figured—"

"And you figured that even though I've grown up with this horse—you knew him better! Right?"

She had him there. "I apologized, didn't I? It *was* a fool thing to try! And— I won't do it again and I won't let Hitch try it either."

Quickly, Augusta turned her back, not because she was angry, though she still was! But to hide a sudden pain that seemed to hold her in a vice-like grip. She wasn't about to let Tytus know, certain that he would only think her a weak, silly female. Thankfully, her distress seemed to ease almost as quickly as it came and she rested her cheek against her stallion's smooth neck while she regained her composure. Quest, however, seemed to sense something was amiss; he pricked his ears forward, and murmuring, he gently nudged Augusta's side.

Tytus didn't like this woman but he couldn't deny a begrudging respect for the rapport she had with her stallion. Suddenly, anxious to go, Ty raked his fingers through his hair, then put his hat back into place.

"Listen," he said, "let's start over. This time—I'll do exactly what you tell me—I promise."

Augusta nodded her agreement then said, "Quest will make three circles to the left, first gather your reins, and cheek him—that's when you..."

"Woman," Ty said through clenched teeth, "I know what it means to cheek a horse."

"Sorry!" she muttered. "That's when he'll make his first turn. As he begins the second circle put your foot in the stirrup—on the third circle grab the horn and swing up. You *must* be seated square in the middle of the saddle when he finishes that third circle."

Squinting one eye and trying to sound only mildly curious, Tytus asked, "Exactly what happens if I'm not *square* in the middle of the saddle, when he makes that third circle?"

When Augusta seemed distracted, Ty asked again, "What does he do if my timing's off?"

Augusta expelled a long slow breath, before she answered, "Well...he will do one of two things: he'll rear straight up and throw himself backwards, or he'll buck like the worse bronc you've ever seen—then he'll aim you like a bullet at that barn wall."

Ty raised his eyebrows, he gave Quest a long hard look, then he shrugged and gathered his reins.

Augusta watched like a worried mama, as Ty grabbed the cheek of the bridle, and the big stallion began the first of three circles. Carefully, Ty placed his boot into the stirrup and grabbed the horn as the stallion finished his second circle. Before the third circle was finished, Ty was seated firmly in the middle of the saddle. The high-strung stallion seemed almost disappointed that the big man had made it on his first try. He arched his graceful head then filled his lungs and nickered loudly as he side-stepped and danced around the corral.

A spark of pleasure came into Ty's eyes. Quest's coat glistened like midnight gold—it was like sitting atop a charging locomotive. The stallion's every muscle was coiled and ready for release, his ears pricked forward, his large eyes taking in everything around him.

Tytus couldn't stop from grinning, the first in a long time, then he said: "He senses an adventure and he's more than ready! This is just what the old boy needed!"

Smiling sadly, Augusta swallowed back her misgivings as she opened the gate.

Tytus was anxious to be on his way, but then suddenly he turned around. "Don't worry—" he said, "we'll treat him right."

Chapter 25
A New Filly

"For I am the Lord your God who takes hold of your right hand and says to you, do not fear; I will help you." Isaiah 41:13

Augusta watched until Ty and Quest had ridden out of sight while she clung to a fence post. She couldn't have moved anyway; she was riding out another sharp pain. This one just about took her breath away as it spread from her backbone around to her stomach. She wondered if she shouldn't have mentioned it to Tytus—but now it was too late. Anyway, Ty had been in such a hurry to catch up with his men, and if she'd told him, he probably would have accused her of being weak or silly or getting the vapors again. They would have both ended up snapping at each other. Anyway, Aunt Sis had warned her that she might have sporadic pains for weeks before the baby came. And that's what this was—surely.

This isn't anything to be frightened of—it might not be the baby at all! Could be too much of Alvaro's spicy cooking. Or maybe I shouldn't have cleaned quite so vigorously this morning.

Suddenly, a powerful cramp took hold of her body and she squeezed her eyes shut. She didn't even realize she was crying until she felt tears seeping out from under her eyelashes and wetting her cheeks.

Slowly she managed to make her way across the yard towards the hacienda.

It's all right! It's far too early for labor! Granny's coming to help me next week!

Despite all her hopes—the moment she stepped onto the porch—a gush of water fell from her body.

"NO!" she groaned. "No—this can't happen, it's way too soon!"

But Aunt Sis had warned her: "There's no stopping it—when your waters come."

Then Augusta remembered Rachel's long labor and Aunt Sis saying that first babies *always* come slow!

"There's plenty of time!" she said out loud. "Joseph will be back before noon. He'll send a fast rider to fetch Granny Rose. Until then I'll just get busy doing all the things Aunt Sis told me. There is nothing to worry about!"

But Augusta was more than worried—she was terrified! And she was also suddenly filled with an all-consuming fury for being stuck in this predicament.

"Bull O'Brien—Timothy Grainger!" She fumed." I hope you two can hear me? Just look what you've done!"

Her stern voice seemed to echo and fill the empty hacienda.

"Look down from heaven and see just where all your scheming has left me. Both of you were so worried about my being *alone*. Well, just look at me...I am completely alone! When no woman should ever be *alone*!"

She was about to give into her panic, when she realized she was only making things worse.

"Stop it!" she cried. "Being angry isn't helping."

She drew in a breath as she recalled telling Aunt Sis that she didn't think she could do this without her. The old woman's last words were: "Ya can and ya will!"

"All right, Aunt Sis! I best just get busy. I can do this—because—I have to."

Fighting down her terror, Augusta closed her eyes. "Lord, I'm sorry for being angry at Papa and Timothy. Neither of them would have wanted this to happen. Not like this! I forgive them—but I'm in a bad way here. Please—help me!"

Augusta would never be able to describe it, but the sharp terror she'd experienced earlier seemed to fall away while a peace settled around her. She was still afraid but she didn't feel alone anymore. There was a presence with her and for a moment the pain eased.

She breathed her gratitude as she hurried towards the kitchen. Quickly, she filled two pots of hot water from the reservoir in the back of the iron stove, and between pains, she carried them to the bathing room. By the time she made her way to her bedroom, she felt like a vise was clamped tightly around her middle. Falling to her knees, she opened her trunk and withdrew Aunt Sis's birthing bundle. Clutching it in her arms, she rode out another contraction, calling to the old mid-wife as if she were there with her.

"Aunt Sis—this isn't happening at all—like you said it would. The pains should be hours apart at first. But...these started...minutes apart and now...it just hurts all the time!"

Finally, Augusta filled her lungs, then scooped up the bundle and staggered down the hall to the bathing room. Biting her lip from the pain she untied the bundle and spread it across the stone floor.

She hadn't looked at the birthing bundle before. It consisted of three layers: a sheet of canvas, a soft blanket, and a clean white sheet on top. The layers were held neatly together, in the fashion of a tie quilt with small lengths of yarn threaded throughout all three layers and tied in knots. As she rolled out the bundle, she found a small pouch made from an old flour sack. Quickly, she opened it and found Timothy's pen knife, (the one he'd used to cut the apple the day he met Quest). Along with the knife was a length of string—to tie around the cord—and a note. Augusta's hands were shaking so hard she could hardly hold onto the bit of paper while she read.

"You can do this, honey! Remember your verse: 'I can do all things with Christ who strengthens me.'"

Augusta sighed through her tears, imagining Aunt Sis preparing the bundle and penning the words.

"Oh, Lord," she prayed, "I know you're here—but I'm still awfully scared! It's too late for Granny. And—I don't want Joseph or Shep. It's got to be you and me Lord. Please—help me deliver this baby!"

Augusta spotted Ty's shaving mirror hanging over the wash basin. With trembling hands she quickly took it off its hook and stood it up at the foot of her pallet.

Suddenly, a chain of sharp pains followed one after another, enveloping her body. The pain never seemed to leave her, but grew in intensity. Her legs were now shaking so hard she didn't dare try to walk again.

Aunt Sis believed it was easier for a woman to sit up for the delivery, so she braced her back against the cool metal tub.

"Lord," she whimpered, "I'm already so tired—I can't bear much more of this. Help me..."

Augusta clutched Aunt Sis's note in her fisted hand and repeated the verse.

"I can do all things...with Christ....who...strengthens me."

Over and over, she whispered the words, she cried them, and she shouted them. Augusta felt like a huge fist had caught her around the waist and was squeezing her in half. She pulled her knees up, fighting the urge to push. Aunt Sis had warned her not to give into the desire until she could see the baby's head. It seemed forever but finally she looked into the mirror at her feet. And through her tears she could see the top of the baby's head.

"Oh—Lord! Help me! Help me!" she wept.

Augusta felt so exhausted, she feared she hadn't the strength to finish her work.

Suddenly, a shattering scream rose from her throat, and she bore down, while pulling her knees to her chest.

"Lord—Lord—Lord!" she chanted and screamed and cried while she pushed with all her might. Finally, feeling spent and exhausted, there was a sudden whoosh as the slippery baby slid from her body.

"Awww, thank you!" she whispered so weakly she could barely hear her own voice. Then she froze—the baby's backside was facing her. She couldn't remember what she was supposed to do next. Then with fumbling, shaking hands, she awkwardly took a towel from the shelf beside her and laid it over the tiny infant then gently turned the little body over.

"Oh—my sweet little girl!" She cooed as she cleaned her mouth and wiped her face.

Carefully, Augusta lifted the baby and laid her over her stomach. But her tiny lips were blue and she wasn't making a sound.

Why isn't she crying? She should be crying—shouldn't she?

Still trembling so hard, Augusta didn't dare pick her up by the heels as Aunt Sis had instructed Timothy to do. Gently, Augusta gave the baby a little swat on her backside—the baby didn't react. Suddenly, this moment was more frightening to Augusta than any terror she'd ever known. Gathering all her strength she lifted her arm again and the tiny bottom received another slap. This time the baby let out a tiny whimper, followed by two little coughs. Still, the baby didn't cry, and the weary young mother didn't know if this was enough to get the baby's lungs working as they should.

"Lord, please…" Augusta begged. "Help!" Lifting her arm she gave the tiny backside another good 'thwack'. Immediately, the little face puckered and turned red, then a lusty cry filled the air.

"That's my girl!" Augusta cried in relief. "Oh, thank You, Lord!"

The baby hushed the moment she heard her mother's voice, turning her little face towards the sound. Just then, mother and child regarded each other, and Augusta's heart filled with love, the likes of which, she'd never known.

Suddenly, there was another sharp pain and the after birth was expelled from her body. Augusta felt a few more pains but knew that there was still work to be done. Carefully, she laid the infant down and took the bit of string from the pouch and tied off the cord, just as Aunt Sis had taught her, then she cut it with the knife. Augusta spoke tenderly to her daughter while she carefully washed and swaddled her tightly in a clean towel.

Holding the baby close she kissed her forehead. "Hello, my love!" she said softly. "I'm Mama and you are Miss Tessie May Grainger."

As Augusta gently dried the baby's hair, she was pleased to see it was thick and blonde and curly. And for now at least, her eyes were as blue as … .

"Oh, Timothy—" Augusta whispered, "you have a daughter, and—she looks just like you."

The baby seemed content to listen to her mother's softly spoken words, while Augusta managed to wash and put on a clean nightgown. Before long, the two were settled deep into the down-filled mattress, and while the baby nursed, her mother repeated the words: "Thank you, Lord! Oh, thank You!"

Augusta thought she was awaking to a new day when the sound of a deep crackling voice penetrated her dreams. It was like a rolling thunder coming down from the mountains.

"Why, you po' lil' thing! Is you all right?"

The young mother's eyes fluttered open, finally focusing on old Joseph's dark and familiar face.

As promised he had caught a stringer of fish for the noon-day meal. But when Augusta didn't answer his calls, he hurried down the hall. Then when he saw the state of the bathing room, he feared the worst! Even more so, when she didn't respond to his knock on her door. It wasn't proper but he had to see if she was all right. Joseph stepped inside her room and the old man's tender heart nearly stopped when he saw how pale she was. He just knew she'd lost the baby.

"You po' chile. Old Joseph never should-a left you this mornin'," he groaned.

But Augusta just blinked up at him and gave him a radiant smile. "It's all right, Joseph. I'm pretty tired—but we're both just fine!"

Yawning, she lifted the coverlet, proudly revealing a very new, newborn baby! The baby was a rosy pink, round faced with a button nose, and sucking away on a tiny fist.

The old man put his hand to his fluttering heart. "Thank you, Jesus!" He grinned, then asked: "You sho you's both—all right?"

Augusta's eyes grew misty. "Oh, yes—Joseph! I felt the Lord right here with me." Then she sighed loudly, "It took forever but we made it!"

Augusta fingered the baby's soft curls then she smiled sweetly at the old man and said, "Joseph, I'd like to introduce you to Miss Tessie *May* Grainger!" Adding reverently, "Timothy and I had decided if it was a girl, her name would be Tessie after my grandmother, and May—for Natty May—*and for you!*"

The old man nodded as his eyes filled with tears, then a huge smile covered his face.

"My Natty May be plum tickled to know that. Thank you, missus!"

Joseph reached down to touch the tiny fist, saying in wonder, "This young-un sho got in some kind-a hurry! I just left you a few hours ago—had me no idea somethin' like this was a-goin on."

Augusta blinked up at the old man, "But...Joseph, what time is it? What—day is it?"

Joseph's eyes filled with concern as he frowned down at the weary young woman. "Why, it's just now comin' noon! It were jes' a lil' while ago...I says I'm agonna catch us a mess a fish for the noon-day meal? And you says right back at me, 'You catch 'em Joseph—I'll fry em up!'"

Augusta closed her eyes and put her hand to her forehead. "My goodness, that means I was only in labor for about—two hours!"

"Like I says—that lil' gal sho nuff was in a hurry! Took no time a'tall!"

Augusta looked a bit indignant when she muttered, "Well—maybe not— but I can tell you—those were the longest two hours I ever spent!"

Joseph couldn't help himself; his deep bass cracked like ice on river, as he leaned back and shouted with laughter. The joyful sound made a wave of sweet comfort wash over the young mother. Timothy wasn't here to share this moment, and yet she was filled with gratitude and relief! Her baby was here now, safe and sound. Something she had feared terribly was now behind her.

Augusta bent to kiss Tessie's soft curly head. "The hard work is behind us now, sweet girl," she sighed. "Only good days ahead for you and me!"

Chapter 26
Burdens Turned to Blessings

"The heartfelt counsel of a friend is as sweet as perfume and incense." Proverbs 27:9

Augusta had never been more miserable. Tessie's cries were like tiny sand burrs in the air and they set her mama's teeth on edge. The young mother stared down at the reddening face of her little daughter, and had no earthly idea how to calm her child.

Actually, Augusta didn't want to admit it, but it was her fault. She'd been crying all morning and her three-week-old daughter had decided to share in her mama's misery. Physically, Augusta grew stronger every day, but her emotions had gone awry. The tears that she had not allowed before the child came now refused to stop. Every time she looked at her beautiful daughter she expected to turn around and find Timothy smiling at them, and sharing the moment. So, Augusta carried her squalling baby from room to room, frustrated by Tessie's tears and thoroughly disgusted by her own.

Lord, what's the matter with me? Timothy would be so disappointed if he saw me wallowing in self-pity like this. But I've lost my father, my home, my friends and now Timothy. I love Tessie, but I'm scared that I could lose her too. And what am I to do about Tytus? He'll be coming home in a few weeks, and the baby and I are about as welcome here as—General Grant at a Lee family reunion.

Augusta went back and forth as to what to do; Mrs. Drew, she knew, would welcome her, take her in without question. And Tytus would be thrilled to see them go! But New York meant tea parties and riding side-saddle and being—oh, so proper! Augusta grimaced at the very idea. Timothy and Papa had been right about her and the ranch—it suited her right down to the ground. Even in her grief, it felt right being here. She loved everything about the Bar 61: the land, the unending mountain ranges, the stock, the beautiful hacienda. Shep and Alvaro and Joseph already seemed like family. She got along with everyone—everyone but Ty, that is. As the days went by, she dreaded and even feared—the return of the Dragon! And so while Augusta sobbed out her misery, the baby scrunched up her tiny face and added her own harmony to her mother's sad song.

Augusta glanced out the window, disturbed when she saw Shep riding away. The freckle-faced lad with his silly antics had become like a brother. His and Joseph's presence eased the void in her life.

Augusta quickly hurried from window to window, searching for a glimpse of Joseph puttering about. When she failed to see the old man, she wrapped her crying baby in a blanket and hurried to the barn.

It was cool and dark when she stepped inside. "Joseph, Joseph, are you here?" she called.

When there was no answer, a fear so strong closed in around her and a shudder passed down her spine. A new rush of tears began clouding her vision and closing her throat. Her skirts billowed about her as she sank to the floor. A moment before her knees touched the ground, she felt a large hand taking hold of her elbow, while the other came up to support the bundle in her arms. Through the haze came the rumble of Joseph's cavernous voice. "Hey now, what's troublin' you, missus?"

Augusta looked up with relief, as old Joseph gently guided her towards a wooden trunk to rest upon. Breathing in the familiar scents of saddle leather, hay and horse, calmed her as they always had.

Taking the baby into his own arms Joseph crooned, "Let me hold that precious chile. Don't think she'll stop cryin'—'til her mama does."

The old man's voice was as rich as molasses and his eyes held such a tender understanding that Augusta was content to watch as he cuddled her baby close. At once he began humming a deep melody that was so low and sweet it quieted not only the babe in his arms but her young mother as well.

"Th-thank you, J-Joseph," she stammered while she dabbed at her cheeks with a soggy handkerchief. "I warned T-Timothy, told him I wouldn't be a very good m-mother."

"Now, now missus," the old man interrupted. "You's a good mama—and there ain't no shame in tears—no how! Only-iest thin' I can tell you is—give your troubles to the Lord! He'll help you!"

Augusta turned to the old man, her eyes pleading with him to have the answers she needed.

"Oh, Joseph, God seemed so close when the baby came—but now? I feel like He's left me! Like Mama and Papa and Timothy. Why doesn't He always answer prayers? I know He did with Tessie but when I prayed for Papa and then Timothy—He took them both away. Today, I prayed for His help, and I haven't been able to stop either of us from crying."

"Oh, missus," Joseph groaned. "Folks always gets confused 'bout prayer— but God ain't no puppy! That we ask him to sit so—He sits! God always answers prayer but sometimes He says NO! Prayin' is for praisin' and—for askin' but if you is a Christian, your gonna trust God to do what's best. Truth is, life's plum full a hard times—that's a fact. But the Lord loves you chile—He'll turn your burdens into blessings—if you let him!"

"I don't feel loved, Joseph. I believe in God but—He keeps deserting me."

Joseph swayed gently with the baby in his arms and asked softly, "Tell me somethin'—missus. How long twas it that you was alone after your papa died? Before you married up, with Timothy I mean?"

Augusta frowned, "I—I never was *alone*. I met Timothy the night Papa had his heart attack—he wouldn't rest until I agreed to marry Timothy. Our wedding was the next day—Papa died the day after."

Joseph stared into Augusta's golden eyes. "Sounds like the Lord may not a answered the way you wanted, but provided for you, jes' the same."

Augusta frowned skeptically. "But I prayed for Papa to live and—then he died!"

Joseph inclined his head and gave Augusta one of his knowing looks. "There's a time to be born and a time to die. Twas your papa's time, chile. Still and all, the Lord waited to take him—waited 'til you had a husband to stand by you!"

Joseph stared wistfully down at the tiny baby as she contentedly sucked her thumb and said, "I know'd Tim back when he was jes' this size! Never was there such a chile! S'only 'bout five years old, when he took my hand and says to me: 'Joseph, Natty May, and me—we'll be in heaven before you. She'll go first, then me—but don't worry, we'll both be waiting for you in heaven when it's your time.'"

Joseph shook his head, remembering the day so clearly. "I'll tell you— that lil' speech shook me up good. And I says, 'Now, boy, I's the oldest. I'll be goin' first, I reckon, then Natty May. But it'll be a long time afore you and your brother make that trip.'"

Something within Augusta's heart quickened as Joseph shook his head and continued to speak: "But that boy just cut them sky-blue eyes up at me.

'No, Joseph,' he says, 'Jesus told me how it's gonna be—jes'—don't want you to worry!'"

A shiver ran through Augusta. "I've wondered if Timothy didn't have a feeling that day. The way he looked at me that last time...I—"

Her words trailed off then she added sadly, "And God had warned me in a dream that something bad was about to happen. He's done that before."

A gentle smile crossed Joseph's face. "God promises to never leave or forsake his chil'ren missus. And He's been working in your life—you just have to open your eyes to see it! When your papa died, He gave you a husband, when Tim died He gave you—all of us here, even Mister Ty!"

When Augusta rolled her eyes at that, Joseph chuckled. "Now, now—me and Natty May would've died in slavery and many others too—if it weren't for that man. He is a good'un! Just lost his way for a spell—is all!"

Just then Tessie yawned, her Cupid's bow mouth forming a perfect "O".

A low rumbling chuckle came from Joseph's chest as he looked down at the beautiful baby. "The good Lord's got plans for you too, lil' miss. I reckon it'll take both a you gals to show ol' Mister Ty the way back!"

Augusta slowly walked down the hallway and shook her head at Joseph's comment. "You sound like Alvaro—and Timothy too! They both told me the same thing."

Deep in thought, she was surprised when she felt a warm breath brush against her cheek. Turning quickly Augusta was instantly charmed by the beautiful mare that was staring back at her. Gracefully, the horse arched her long neck over the stall door, then playfully tried to get Augusta's attention.

"Oh my—Arabian, isn't she? She's—magnificent! Why on earth haven't I seen her before now?"

"Why, Tanner McGee jes' brought her back this mornin'! She had a cut on her neck but McGee—he knows healin'—real good. Go ahead on and take a good look at her!"

Augusta stepped into the stall for a closer look at the mare. Her coat was a burst of gun-metal gray dapples, draped like a lacey veil over her shining silver coat. There wasn't even a scar on the mare's neck; in fact, the horse seemed flawless and delicate in every detail. It was if she might be made of glass.

Joseph smiled as he watched these two fine ladies appraise one another. It was plain to see something special was taking place between them. Augusta smiled when the mare murmured gently and pushed her dainty muzzle into the palm of her hand. She stared into the mare's dark eyes. They were large, bright, intelligent, heavily lashed, and set wide above the classic dish face of a pure-bred Arabian!

Augusta leaned her forehead against the mare's cheek; not since her beloved Quest had she felt such a strong connection with a horse!

Joseph grinned with pride. "My Natty May would a looked at you two an' called ya—kindred spirits."

Augusta smiled at the implied compliment. "What's her name, Joseph?"

"Her proper name's Sahara Storm! We been callin' her Stormy. She come a long way to make her home here. She's been a lil' sad an' lonely—jes' like you."

"Well!" Augusta breathed. "I've never seen a horse with finer lines. She looks like a figurine—come to life!"

Joseph grinned with satisfaction. "Yes, ma'am!"

The old man watched both Augusta and the mare with keen eyes; these two had taken to each other, just as he hoped they would!

Augusta sighed as she walked back to him and ran her hand gently over Tessie's curly head. "Thank you, Joseph. I don't know what we'd have done without you today. And you've reminded me of a promise Timothy and I made to each other. That we wouldn't mourn over yesterday's tears, and find that we'd missed today's blessings! I have a beautiful child, a safe place to live and …." She glanced up into the old man's face. "And—a good friend, I hope?"

"Why, sho, missus." The old man's words became a pledge. "Ol' Joseph's your—good friend!"

Carefully, Augusta took her now sleeping baby from Joseph's arms, then she looked up at him. "Joseph," she began softly, "Timothy got me into the habit of reading a chapter of the Bible every day. He used to answer all my questions, but now? If I don't understand something—could I come to you?"

The old man's smile was as radiant as the rising sun. "Aww, missus, nothin'd please me more! Young Shep gave his heart to Jesus jes' before you come. Why don't we all read a bit, of a mornin' after breakfast—how'd that be?"

Augusta smiled. "That would be wonderful! Thank you Joseph."

Chapter 27
Return of the Dragon

**"God has caused me to be fruitful in the land of my affliction."
Genesis 41:52**

'Welcome back!" Shep yelled as he ran down the lane to greet Ty and the men.

The ranch hands looked like a gang of raunchy bandits with their heavy beards and dirty clothes.

"'Bout time y'all came back! Seems like ya been gone forever! Ya run into trouble?"

Shep's eager questions ran into each other, not giving the men a chance to reply to any of them.

Finally, Hitch let out a loop and tossed it over the boy as he jogged beside them.

"Hey! What's the idea?" the boy groused as he tried to wriggle free.

Hitch tightened the rope and dallied it over his saddle horn. "Figured, it's just 'bout time…to rope…n'…brand all the ornery calves…reckon I'd…start…on you!"

Hitch pulled the rope, bringing Shep up close; then he leaned over and grabbed Shep by the shoulder and gave it a squeeze.

"Hey, boy!" he said grinning as he pulled the rope free. "Been bored? How about next time—you come along with us?"

Shep grinned from ear to ear. "Ya mean it?"

The ranch foreman laughed. "Sure! You've grown so—I thought—we had a new man on the place. And, uh—tell me—did Missus Grainger's baby get here with—without any trouble?"

Shep grinned and blushed at the same time, then something sparkled in his blue eyes. "Yep, that baby got here—easy as pie and—a long time ago! And I ain't been bored!"

The boy's cheeky grin left Hitch wondering what he might have missed.

Just then Joseph's deep voice thundered as he wandered out of the tack room.

"Sho nuff is good to see you boys!" he said chuckling. But, you's gone s'long, we reckoned you got lost."

A dozen weary men greeted Joseph and teased Shep as they trotted towards the corral. They were all exhausted but happy to be home. Tytus looked especially drained as he scratched at his thick growth of beard. Quest was the only one who seemed to have energy to spare as he cantered into the yard with his neck arched and head high. As the dark stallion pranced towards the barn, he nickered loudly as if to tell all the mares that he was back! Ty and Hitch shared a knowing look, then shook their heads.

Joseph grinned, too, impressed by the stallion's antics. "Trip didn't hurt him none—did it?"

Then he turned towards Ty and asked, "Still, we was gettin' a mite worried—was there trouble?"

Tytus groaned as he swung down from Quest, then immediately began tugging at the cinch.

"Not really," Ty said with a sigh. "But it's been a wet year—nearly every creek or river we crossed was running high. Other than that, things went well enough."

He turned the stallion loose in the corral and watched as Quest immediately dropped to roll in the sand.

Side by side Joseph and Ty watched the big stud, then as if confiding a secret, Ty muttered, "That stud's as game as Echo ever was! In fact he reminds me of Echo. Remember the way he used to lower his head and accept the bit? And even his gaits are similar—smooth as glass—he's quite a horse!"

Ty slapped his gloves against his chaps, raising a cloud of dust—while he hesitantly glanced towards the hacienda. He had looked forward to the end of the ride but now it felt uncomfortable to be home. Finally, Ty squeezed Joseph's broad shoulder and said apologetically, "I'm sorry I left you saddled with a pregnant woman! Shep said the baby got here. Bet the both of them have been running you ragged. But we'll get things back to normal soon. My hope is to ship her off to Denver as soon as possible. Anyway, I figure you've got a lot to complain about, so go ahead and tell me about—*that woman!*"

Joseph's happy face had turned sad as he listened to Ty, then he shook his head, and spoke softly: "I'll sho nuff be happy to tell you, 'bout *that woman!* Bet you didn't know she's only seventeen—jes' a chile herself. She was a-goin' into labor while you was ridin' out that first day. She told me she wasn't sho an' didn't want to both'r you none. All of us men was out and doin' that mornin'. While we was all away, her time come—it come fast'n hard! That po' lil' thing—she done it all by herself! When I got back from fishin' she had herself and her lil' babe all clean—'n—sweet—'n tucked into bed. But I ain't hardly been able to keep her there—no how!"

As Ty listened to Joseph's story, he felt like he had just been kicked by a mule. There was no excuse as to why he hadn't done more for her. He knew women suffered greatly in childbirth, and was she really only seventeen? Lord! How frightened she must have been! Suddenly, Ty was reliving all the fights he'd had with his father before he died. Ty wanted the slaves freed, and when he realized that would never happen while his father lived, he begged the man for humane care for the plantation slaves. Ty hadn't even done as well for the woman who might be his brother's wife as his insensitive father had done for his pregnant slaves. Ty felt sickened by his own neglect, but then he stiffened and said with a frown, "This just proves what I've always said, women don't belong on the Bar 61." Still hiding behind a wall of indifference, he muttered, "What I want to know—is—are they well enough to travel?"

Joseph, seeing through Ty's words, simply shook his head, then, his deep bass rumbled: "Why—Mister Ty, they's both fit as a fiddle. But Tim would want 'em here—you—know he would."

Ty was too tired and ashamed to argue. Sullenly, he headed into the barn asking: "Did Tanner bring Stormy back? Did her wound heal?"

It was old Joseph's turn to grimace, knowing that he had to explain what he'd done in just the right way.

"McGee fixed her up good—ain't even a scar! But—Mister Ty—Stormy, ain't in there. Now—nothin's happened to her—she's just fine but—"

Ty folded his big arms over his chest. "I'm not going to like what I'm about to hear—am I?"

Joseph faced Ty with his own jaw set squarely. "Don't reckon—you will—but the mare was unhappy and so was that sweet lil' gal—why, she's had nothin' but heartache. And, when I put them two together—somethin' real fine happened. They's out for a ride—right now!"

Ty threw his hat to the ground. "Joseph, has she made you soft in the head?" he bellowed. "I paid a fortune for Sahara Storm and you knew I was bringing her along slow!"

"Yes, sa'—Mister Ty!" Joseph said, his voice sounding even deeper than usual. "And—as I recall—it were me that taught you—how to bring a horse—along slow. That gal's got a light hand—rides like she's born to the saddle. They goes out ever'day while me and Shep watch the lil'n."

Ty respected Joseph too much to press him, but the old man had taken her side, and he didn't like it.

"You say they're out now?" Ty asked. "So—who's watching the kid if you and Shep are out here?"

Joseph's expression softened. "Why, she's a-sleepin' in her cradle right inside the tack room." Grinning he waved his hand. "Come on back and take a look—why she's the prettiest lil' thing you ever seen."

Something twisted inside Ty's heart; he wasn't ready to see that baby. What if she didn't look anything like Timothy—what if she did? He knew he shouldn't feel angry but the feeling was there just the same.

"No, I'm not in the mood!" he groaned. "And what kind of mother leaves her baby in the barn?"

Now—Joseph owed Ty for his freedom, as well as his home, but he knew the man was just being contrary.

"Mister Ty," he said sternly, "I keep my tack room pert'near as clean as your parlor! And there ain't nothin' wrong with bringin' up a chile to the scent of horses an' saddle leath'r. That's how you was raised!"

"All right, Joseph, all right," Ty mumbled.

There was an awkward moment, then Joseph clamped his huge hand on Ty's shoulder. "Listen here, why don't you—take a lil' ride to the top a that hill yonder? See for yourself, just how Stormy's comin' along."

Tytus picked his hat up off the ground, slapped the dust off it, then put it back on his head. "Hitch!" he called. "Feel like taking a ride?"

"Sure...boss!" the foreman said with a slow grin. "We'll—settle that bet!"

Quest was covered in dust; so Ty caught up another horse from the corral and swung up bareback.

Before he rode away, Ty remembered something he needed to tell Joseph and Shep: "Almost forgot—Alvaro drove the chuck wagon onto the trading post for supplies; won't be back until noon tomorrow. I figure you're both sick of cooking but I'll need you to rustle up dinner for all of us all tonight and make breakfast in the morning. Once Alvaro's back, then things can get back to normal."

"No need, Mister Ty" Joseph interrupted. "The missus will…"

Ty held his hand up. "I've heard enough about *that woman*—and I'm not about to eat her cooking."

Before Joseph could explain about Augusta's cooking, the two men were already riding away.

"Now," Ty reminded Hitch as they headed to the top of the hill, "it isn't whether or not the shrew can ride. It's about her being as unappealing as she was before we left! So, wipe that smile off your face, your saddle isn't safe yet."

"Not worried," Hitch laughed, "But, I reckon yer in fer a surprise!"

"Not likely!" Ty hissed.

Actually, neither man was prepared for the sight that met them when they looked down into the valley.

Hitch let out a long low whistle, while Ty watched in silence as horse and rider seemed to dance across the valley in a series of figure eights.

"Joseph was right!" Hitch remarked. "She was…born to the saddle."

Ty squinted his eyes but made no reply as Augusta lined the mare out to canter straight across the meadow. Every sixth stride Augusta would cue the mare to make a flying change of lead and canter for another six strides then change again. They rode across the meadow with the mare changing leads from left to right, every six to seven strides.

Hitch whistled through his teeth. "Admit it—when—have you seen anything as fine as that?"

Ty's eyes narrowed but still he said nothing.

Finally, Hitch slapped him on the back. "Better—loosen yer jaw, boss—she's comin' this way."

Augusta galloped Stormy towards them, and with only a word, she brought the mare to a sliding stop.

Ty was shaken—his reaction to the woman was irritating. How had that dowdy little creature suddenly become such a beauty? Even simply dressed in a black riding skirt, with matching vest over a soft gray blouse, she managed to look elegant! Ty's eyes dropped to the wide waist band showing off an incredibly small waist for a woman who had just had a child. Her thick hair was held back in a black lace snood, and to protect her porcelain skin, she wore a black carriage hat with a black ribbon trailing down her back. Augusta brushed at the thin wisps of curls that had worked free and blew across her flushed face. Sitting straight and tall in her saddle, she gave both men a faltering smile.

"Welcome home," she said shyly. "Did the drive go well?"

A tender smile crossed her face as she gazed down at the corrals and saw Quest kicking up his heels!

"Oh, he looks good! But, I sure have missed him." Her eyes were shining when she looked back at the men. "How did he do? Joseph thought you'd be back sooner—we were beginning to worry."

Tytus couldn't seem to take his eyes from her and couldn't think of anything to say. There was a sweetness about her that he hadn't seen before. Maybe he hadn't wanted to see it. Feeling suddenly embarrassed and confused, he pulled at his collar, reminding himself that he did not trust this woman. Manufacturing a frown, he decided it was arrogantly presumptuous of her to welcome *him* home? She had no right—this was his home—not hers!

Seeing the play of emotions cross Ty's face, then end in a scowl, Hitch decided he better speak up. "Ma'am!" he drawled, tipping his hat, "the drive... was fine...but...the rains...slowed us down."

Then the foreman nodded towards Stormy and asked, "What do you think of her?"

Augusta smiled as she reached down and patted the mare's silvery neck.

"I've never seen a horse so finely boned; she's quick to learn—eager to please! My father told me once that, Arabians were called 'children of the wind'. That's what riding her feels like!"

Glancing towards Quest, Augusta lifted her chin. "And...what did you men think of...my pride and joy?"

Ty lowered his head, pursed his lips for a moment, then begrudgingly said: "Your father was right—that horse—is a privilege to ride."

Making the small confession stuck in Ty's craw. He didn't want to concede that Augusta was right about anything, or worse, that he might be wrong about her.

Augusta felt confused; Ty's words didn't match his fierce expression. Quickly, she changed the subject. "Have you two—seen the baby yet?"

When Hitch shook his head and Ty said nothing, she smiled and said shyly: "Well, I don't like to be away too long. Come and I'll introduce you."

The men held their horses a moment and watched Augusta ride away. Then Hitch turned to Ty with a lazy grin. "Reckon...ya kin...draw up that... land deed tomorrow?"

Tytus narrowed his eyes and gave his foreman a contemptuous look.

"Boss!" Hitch chided, "She took our breath away...even...left *you*... tongue-tied!"

Ty grimaced; he was disgusted by his reaction to *that woman*. Lowering his head he mumbled, "All right, you win, but there'll be no more talk about it. And her being pretty doesn't mean I trust her."

They quickly caught up with Augusta, and as they reached the corral, Hitch gallantly swung down and took Stormy's reins while Augusta thanked him, then ran to greet her stallion. Quest nickered and trotted towards her, seeming just as pleased to see his mistress.

After properly welcoming her stallion home, Augusta stripped off her gloves and hurried into the tack room. A moment later she returned with a proud smile and her two-month-old baby in her arms.

"Gentlemen..." she called shyly as the cowhands all gathered around, "I'm afraid I have to warn you—there is now another *worrisome female* residing on the Bar 61!"

Carefully, she lifted her bundle towards the men and said, "This is Miss Tessie May Grainger!"

Ty stood back a-ways and scowled when Augusta mentioned the baby's last name, while all the other men gathered closer for a better look.

Hitch's heart went out to Augusta, as her happy expression fell when Ty blatantly ignored the baby then turned towards the circle of pine trees, no doubt to visit Timothy's grave.

Trying to bring her smile back, Hitch said happily, "Ya shor got a...purty baby there, ma'am."

When the baby grinned up at him, his eyes grew wide. "Hey—she's even got the—Grainger—dim..."

"Shhhh!" Augusta hissed softly, then including the other men standing about, she explained: "Tess is the image of her father, but Tytus has to see it for himself. I'd rather not have anyone mention it."

When the men all nodded in agreement, she thanked them, but before she went into the house she added, "I'll have supper ready at the usual time, but if you're all starving, I could hurry it up a bit!"

"No need to bother," Hitch assured her. "Ty asked Joseph and Shep to round up the vittles tonight."

Augusta rolled her eyes. "Those two know I have supper well on its way, by this time of day."

Shaking her head she carried Tessie towards the hacienda; then turning back to the men she added: "You all can thank Shep for our dinner—he shot a deer yesterday! We'll have venison stew tonight."

She waited, allowing the men time to praise the boy and slap him soundly on the back.

Then she added with a grimace: "I'm afraid, I still haven't learned how to make a decent tortilla. So, I hope you all won't mind having hot rolls instead."

When Augusta quickly disappeared inside the hacienda. The men stared after her then looked at each other, and asked: "Did she say—*hot rolls?*"

Chapter 28

A Woman's Touch

"She sets about her work vigorously; her arms are strong for her task." Proverbs 31:17

Anxious for another look at the pretty young widow, and the new baby, not to mention the promise of hot rolls—something they had all dreamt of—the men finished their chores in record time. Soon they were bursting into the kitchen with hair slicked back and shirt collars wet from washing. With what could only be described as a shy reverence, the men gathered around the cradle, chuckling as Tessie entertained them with waiving fists and squeals of delight. Many of them hadn't seen a baby since they were children themselves, and the sight of the delicate little thing was as much of a marvel to them as was the reality of a pretty young woman bustling about the kitchen, preparing their evening meal.

It was touching for Augusta to see these saddle-weary men gaze in wonder at her little girl. Only the older wrangler, Dewey LeBeau, seemed to take no interests in the child, which suited Augusta just fine; she hadn't trusted him since the day Quest had shown how much he disliked the man.

When Tessie began to fuss, Hitch asked to pick her up. The men all laughed when Shep insisted he show the man how to hold her just right! The mood was that of a jolly homecoming until Tytus strolled in and took his place at the head of the table. But even he couldn't dampen the men's delight with their meal; the venison stew, though not as spicy as Alvaro's was delicious, never the less. But the real welcome home to the men—were the hot flaky rolls! They acted as if they'd discovered gold!

Augusta was pleased, then embarrassed by the men's exuberant joy over something so simple. But to the men, these light—as-air golden creations, were a reminder of hearth and home. Alvaro made delicious tortillas by the dozens but he never baked bread, and these men hadn't realized how much they'd missed it. Their praises made Augusta uncomfortable, and Tytus angry. His men were making fools of themselves over *that woman*, her baby, and her cooking!

Sensing Ty's mood; Augusta quickly looked to Joseph to change the subject but then grimaced when Shep jumped in and told them all how she had delivered her own child, and all alone, while he and Joseph had both been away.

Ty frowned as he listened again to the story; he knew he should apologize, but he wasn't going to! He was noticeably relieved, however, when Augusta with overly pink cheeks interrupted by asking, "Who would like more coffee?"

Tytus took that moment to stand. He cleared his throat self-consciously, then said, "Men, I want to thank you for your hard work. The drive went well and it was plain to see as we rode in today that those of you who stayed took good care of the ranch!"

Reaching into his vest pocket he pulled out a number of small envelopes. "So, all of you have earned a little extra in this month's pay."

On another occasion the men might have cheered their appreciation but Tessie was asleep in Shep's arms—and of course there was still a spirit of mourning that hung heavy over both Tytus and Augusta. Respectful of this, each man took his envelope and quietly thanked Ty with a hand shake and a nod.

Finally, Ty added in a weary voice, "Well—men, all I want to do right now is throw a loop around a pillow. I suggest you all do the same."

Taking their cue, the men headed for the door, thanking Augusta for the fine meal.

Ty frowned at her instead. "Joseph and Shep were to fix dinner tonight and breakfast in the morning."

Augusta shrugged as she carried dirty dishes to the sink. "There wasn't any need—it was already done."

Ty was suddenly battling his conscience. He felt terrible about her having the baby without anyone to help. He was trying to think what to say when the completely wrong words sprang from his mouth.

"Augusta—I—well—did you—find that marriage certificate yet?"

Ty scowled—*why had he said that?* He didn't know why he became such an unfeeling brute when he was around this woman but that's how it was. He felt even worse when her golden eyes clouded with tears and she shook her head. Not knowing what else to do; Tytus simply nodded and went to his room.

Augusta watched Tytus walk away. His words had wounded her and she was surprised that she didn't hate the man. But—she understood him—too well. When he looked at her, he longed to see Timothy, just as when she looked at him and longed for the same.

Augusta had been a bundle of nerves, as she waited for Ty and the other men to return! She was exhausted and desperately wanted to head for her own bed. But then, she remembered Ty telling Joseph and Shep to cook breakfast the next day.

"Not a chance!" she hissed. "Tytus Grainger, you are going to have a breakfast you will never forget!"

☙❧

Tytus awoke just before dawn. He had dreamt of Natty May. She'd come down from heaven looking as she had in his youth, her ebony skin and pearly teeth shining as she served him his favorite breakfast: steak and eggs and—*cinnamon rolls*! The dream had been so real he'd awoken to the sound of his stomach growling, and even the scent of cinnamon seemed to be heavy in the air!

Still in a sleepy haze, Ty stretched his long limbs, breathing deeply, his eyes suddenly flew open. "That is cinnamon!"

He sniffed the air again, filling his nostrils with the heavenly aromas of fresh coffee, bacon and—venison!

Confused, Ty sat up and ran his hands through his hair. *Alvaro's at the trading post. Joseph's culinary skills consist of porridge and burnt bacon. There's that woman. She did all right last night but—no—she's no doubt still in bed!*

He didn't know who was cooking but the savory scents of venison and cinnamon were undeniable. Suddenly, Ty figured it out. With a growl, he sat down and shoved both legs into his pants at the same time then threw on a shirt as he stormed down the hall. It had to be Alvaro in the kitchen; it would be just like the soft-hearted Spaniard to worry about—*that woman*! So much so, that he would risk driving a team and wagon-load of supplies in the dark. The old man was bound and determined to protect la señora from El Jefe's anger! And the more Ty thought of *that woman* and the foolish way the usually sensible Joseph and Alvaro were becoming—the more his anger grew!

Suddenly, as he reached the kitchen, his feet skidded to a stop. He blinked then looked again; he was no longer sure if he were awake or perhaps still dreaming?

For the sight before him *was* from a dream! All the while he was building his hacienda; a cherished picture had been painted in Ty's mind and in his heart. It was an image of a dark-haired young woman, preparing a meal in his kitchen. She was standing in profile, looking just like Augusta was now. She was lovely of face and form, with dark curls falling in ringlets to her waist. In his vision the woman would somehow sense his presence—then slowly she'd turn towards him and smile.

Ty had convinced himself that his fiancé, Savannah Summerville, was that woman, even though her hair was golden and she'd never once lifted a finger in any man's kitchen. Still, he clung to that picture until the day Savannah arrived. Within hours, however, the woman had expressed her aversion to everything he had built. All that he was so proud of she had despised. And as Tytus watched Savannah ride out of his life, he declared himself ten times a fool for harboring such lofty notions about women and the West. And yet—there before him—in flesh and blood was that sweet picture of a very private dream.

Augusta was humming softly, stirring a pan of gravy, the steam curling up all around her. Under her white apron, she wore a very proper dark gray dress, and yet it could not hide her feminine curves. She was a treat to the eyes; suddenly, with blushing cheeks she turned shyly and said: "Good morning, Tytus."

Augusta was intrigued by the expression on Ty's face; she'd never seen that look before—it was gentle, almost tender, and his dark brooding eyes seemed bemused. He stood there bare footed, his hair was tousled, with his shirt unbuttoned. Suddenly, Augusta felt terribly self-conscious; she forced herself to turn back to the stove, then keeping her eyes downcast she stuttered, "Th—the m-men are washing up now—you might want to finish dressing before—before breakfast."

Ty couldn't seem to make himself move. Instead, he feasted his hungry eyes on the apparition; it couldn't be real anyway. When he finally realized what he was doing, his face colored, then his discomfort quickly turned to anger and his tender expression became a frown.

Just then, the men came bursting into the kitchen with Ty still standing in the doorway—scowling.

"Come on in," Augusta called, "breakfast it's al—most ready!" She groaned, as she struggled a bit under the heavy weight of the platter she carried to the table.

"I promise the coffee grounds have settled," she said with a roll of her eyes, "so, please pour yourselves a cup, while I finish laying everything out."

The men bumped into each other as they entered the kitchen, spellbound by the feast that greeted them.

Shep peeked around them all and grinned. "See—what'd I tell ya, boys? She's a ring tail wonder in the kitchen!"

For the first time, Ty turned his gaze to the table. There were steaming platters of thick venison steaks, fried potatoes, bacon, and eggs. Then his gaze focused on three trays covered with glazed cinnamon rolls, as big around as his hand. Between the rolls were two baskets filled with fluffy, golden brown biscuits with a pitcher of cream gravy setting beside each basket. The sight and scent of it flooded Ty's mind with memories of happier times, of Natty May and her big white smile, and her lavish meals prepared with loving hands. Ty took it all in as he leaned back, holding onto the door jamb. The men shot amused glances at each other, regarding the boss's expression, not to mention his state of dress.

Suddenly, Tytus grew red in the face and grumbled, "Shep, thought I told you and Joseph to cook breakfast!"

As one—every man turned to Ty with slack jaws and wide eyes. How the boss could be unhappy about a breakfast like this—they could not imagine.

Joseph broke the tension with his deep crack of laughter! "Why, Mister Ty, didn't know you was so fond of my porridge. I'll sure rustle up a big pot of it—iffen you like?"

When the men started to guffaw, Ty shot them all a threatening look and the room grew silent.

"Never mind, " he grumbled as he hurried back to his room. And although his mood was as prickly as an old cactus, the man had his boots under the table by the time Augusta was forking a huge venison steak onto his plate.

Discreetly, she leaned towards him and whispered, "Please, don't be angry at Joseph and Shep. I wasn't about to let them do my work—not while I'm able."

Ty shrugged and made a point of not looking at her, while he placed three perfectly cooked eggs on top of his steak and managed to snag two cinnamon rolls and three biscuits from the basket as it passed by. Still, his curiosity soon got the better of him. Around a mouthful of steak he muttered cynically, "You know, this proves you tried to ruin our breakfast before we left for the drive!"

Augusta swallowed down her hurt. Not a word of thanks or praise for the beautiful breakfast she'd worked nearly all night to prepare, just a hateful question about a mistake she'd made months ago.

"No!" she insisted. "I—I would never do such a mean thing." With a sigh she added, "But—I do tend to mess things up when I get nervous or when I'm *trying* too hard." She looked around at the men, "I did hope a nice welcome-home breakfast might make it up to you all, though!"

Feeling protective of Augusta, and since he knew her better than the rest, Shep was quick to speak up, "The boys'll be happy to forgive ya—if ya promise to make more of these rolls! Right fellas?"

Augusta received her answer when nearly all the men cheered and went on about how this was like their ma's home cookin'.

Ty watched her walk around the table refilling coffee cups and chatting amiably. This woman puzzled him; he knew what to do with someone like Savannah Summerville. He had told her to accept him the way he was or leave and—she left! But what was he to do with this one? She appeared out of nowhere, then led him to his brother's dead body. She looks like an angel, rides like a caballero, smells of cinnamon and lilac, and cooks like Natty May. But was she the good woman she seemed to be or was she even more devious than any woman he'd ever met? By the looks on his men's faces, they all thought she was just about perfect. It seemed every man but him had fallen under the spell of her siren song. Well, he was one man who would not follow her around like some adoring puppy. He would not allow it to happen to him!

Chapter 29

Good News

Whatever is true, whatever is noble, whatever is right, whatever is pure, whatever is lovely, whatever is admirable—if anything is excellent or praiseworthy—think about such things." Philippians 4:8

Spring – 1867

Augusta re-read the wonderful letters Rusty had brought to her yesterday. He'd gone to pick up supplies at the trading post and three letters had been there, waiting for her. She had written her New York friends only twice, and those were just notes, really; the first was a heartbreaking letter, telling of Timothy's tragic death and the second shared the news of Tessie May's arrival.

Her friends' letters to her were filled with words of comfort and their deep concern. But they also included some very happy news that thrilled Augusta! She hugged the pages to her heart then read each one all over again. Then she picked up her Bible. She and Shep were reading the book of Proverbs; they read chapter one on the first day of the month and planned to read one chapter each day until the end of the month. It was April 25th, so she opened her Bible to Proverbs 25. More and more, the Bible was coming alive to her. As Timothy used to say: "God speaks to us through His Word!" It was true! So often the words she read soothed the hurt of that day so well that it was like a caress from the almighty Himself. Whether the message was simple or profound, it reminded her that God was near and that He cared. When she read the 25th verse she laughed. "Like cold water to a weary soul is good news from a distant land."

"Lord, thank You for Your Word and the loving words sent to me from my friends. You know how hard this year has been for me and that I needed to hear from them! But—they sound worried—so now I need to bless them with some good news."

Augusta sat down at the small writing desk, and while Tessie lay sleeping, she began her letter.

To my dear friends: Mrs. Drew, Emily, Wes, and Master Timothy!

I haven't the words to tell you how terribly I miss you all, but never so much as the moment when I received your wonderful letters! Congratulations on the birth of Mr. Timothy Barrett Tylane! Papa and Timothy would be so proud to know that you have honored them both in such a special way. I dream that one day we might all be together, with little Timothy and Tess playing happily together, while we share the news of each other's lives. In the meantime, I hope you will write often and tell me all about your adventures and especially about that handsome young man of the house.

It sounds like you all are settling very well into New York society. Emily, how I would love to see you and Wes in your ballroom finery. I'm sure you're all prettier than a hound dog on hunting day!

Your letters have been such a comfort to me, and although I appreciate your concerns, please—don't worry! You asked me to be honest and tell you truly how Miss Tess and I are doing, and so I will.

As to be expected, my first winter without Timothy has been very difficult. On bad days, I feel as if sorrow is the only companion that will never leave me. And on better days, I think of Timothy, and I am reminded of how that man looked upon his life and the world in general. He accepted hardships and blessings alike, with both wonder and appreciation. I know his attitude pleased God, so I'm trying to be like him. And in so doing, I find many things to be grateful for, such as my new friendships with Alvaro, Joseph, Shep, and many of the other ranch hands.

Yes, this has been a season of pain—but it's also been a season of beauty. I love Colorado; the hacienda is lovely and comfortable. The mountains and lowlands here are glorious! I think of my bedroom window as if it were a magical painting—for the scene before me is constantly changing! Autumn was a kaleidoscope of changing colors from green, to gold, to deep crimson. Then winter came and covered everything with a magnificent coat of glistening white. At sunrise the Rockies are cloaked in muted shades of lilac and rose. By dusk, the mountains become purple silhouettes against a sky painted in colors from lemon yellow to copper, from magenta to a deep cranberry red. Just now heavy flakes of snow are fluttering down like thick white feathers in the moonlight. Emily, it reminds me of your luscious sugar frosting, as it tops the fence posts and pine boughs in shimmering mounds of white. I wish I could describe it all in such a way that you might understand what my life is like now. I don't want you to worry, but to know the wondrous place that is becoming my home.

I've come to look on the beauty and the pain in my life like two sides of a coin— they are reflected in the faces of Tessie and Tytus. Baby Tess, she's so like her father—she is all that is fine and good—she's a little bit of sunshine for all of us, with her ready smile, her inquisitive blue eyes and golden curls. Tytus, on the other hand, is the very picture of pain. He denies us nothing, we are well cared for, but the man moves around us as if we're invisible. I'm praying that God will open his eyes and heart one day soon, that he will look into Tessie's face, and see that his brother lives on—in her! Still, I don't feel that I should press him; his pain is still too raw. And perhaps so is mine! But they say time heals all wounds—and so—I will wait!

I suppose the oddest thing about my life here is that I haven't seen one female since leaving the wagon train. Even so, I feel quite safe here, and most of the time, I truly am content.

And yet for all I've just said, I still miss you all dreadfully! I will never replace you. But I am adding new friends; all the men are kind and Joseph and Alvaro are like two loving uncles; and Shep is like a little brother. Tessie keeps me busy and fills my days. That little charmer has not only her mama but nearly all the men here wrapped around her pudgy little finger.

I hope you will understand why I simply cannot accept your kind offers to join you all in New York. Timothy's greatest desire was for his child to know his brother and be a part of this ranch. Despite all that's happened I feel a kinship to this land and to the Bar 61 itself. You know I am best suited to this life. Can you imagine me riding side-saddle or accommodating the proprieties of society? Yes, Mrs. Drew, you taught me well, but you know my heart. There is little society to worry with here, and time passes with even less fanfare. Poor Tytus—he even tried to banish Christmas this year—but we rebelled against the dragon, and while he was away for a long ride, we celebrated the birth of our Savior anyway!

I believe Timothy would be pleased by my life here. Alvaro and Joseph are continuing where he left off, teaching me daily to put my trust in God! I am able to look at my hardships now—and see God's hand of mercy and provision. God has and is taking care of us! I am determined to trust Him for Tessie's future, and for mine!

Easter has long since passed, and though the men promise me that spring does come to this part of the country, <u>I remain skeptical</u>! Every day I look out from my magic window and the ground, and trees, and mountain-tops are all still wearing their wintry coat of white, while I long for green grass and that first flower of spring!

In fact—when I find that first blossom, I will make it my gift to you all! I will press it, and wrap it carefully, and send it on for little Timothy, as a keep sake from his friends in the wilderness!

As for this letter, I must end it now, for I have urgent baking to do! Four dozen molasses cookies are the going rate for this letter to be delivered to the trading post. You'd be surprised all the things a few cakes and cookies can buy on a ranch full of men!

Again, my dear friends, please put your minds at rest and know that both Tessie and I are well!

Please keep us in your prayers as you all are in mine.

With all my loving regards,

Augusta Colleen O'Brien-Grainger

Chapter 30
Secret Friends

"Children are a heritage from the Lord." Psalm 127:3

Tytus watched from the porch of the hacienda as Augusta rode out on Quest.

"Born to the saddle," he muttered under his breath then grew irritated at his traitorous appraisal.

Now that the snow had finally melted, *that woman* would no doubt resume her daily rides. Though he tried not to, he couldn't help but admire the graceful way she sat a saddle.

Well, it's good not to hear her humming or have her bustling about while I'm trying to work on my books. Surely she knows not to ride too far? Maybe she shouldn't ride alone; maybe I...should?

Ty groaned as he headed for his library; it was irritating how often his thoughts turned to *that woman*. Like her or not she was under his protection; he had failed her when she gave birth to her child. But since then he made sure she always had whatever she needed—at least he thought he had. He wasn't sure about anything anymore. It'd been a long miserable winter, with him acting like a wounded bear. And now that spring was here, he just felt empty. He hadn't only lost his brother; somehow in the past few months he felt as if he had lost himself as well. He'd watched from a distance while Augusta and her baby seemed to fill a void in the lives of his men. They never seemed happier, while Ty on the other hand, had never felt so alone. It was his own fault, of course, for in keeping his distance from *that woman* and her child, he had distanced himself from everyone, including Alvaro and Joseph. He had turned his library and his bedroom into little more than prison cells. And he couldn't even rail against it, for he himself was the jailer. His heart and mind were in turmoil.

I've got to get a handle on things. The men step around me, as if I were a badger. I've got work to do! A ranch to run—can't believe I haven't touched the books since before the drive to Leavenworth.

The thought was like the twist of a knife. If Timothy had lived, he would have taken over the account books. When he reached the threshold of his library, his eyes widened and he came to an abrupt stop.

"Alvaro!" he howled. "What in the *Sam Hill* is this baby doing in here?"

When the older man didn't come running, Ty spun on his heels and stomped towards the kitchen. "I want that barricade and what's behind it out of there—now!" he boomed.

But when Tytus entered the kitchen he found the old man with both hands plunged deep into a bowl of sticky bread dough.

Smiling sheepishly, Alvaro looked up, then raised his gooey hands into the air.

"Ah! Jefe! I practice the making of bread! The little señorita—she needs the morning sun—the library this time of day—is perfect! She's no trouble—do not fear."

At Ty's look of disgust, Alvaro simply smiled and waved him away with dough covered-hands; "Amigo," he added gently, "allow the child to smile on you—you will feel better—I promise!"

Tytus grumbled under his breath as he returned to his library. "*Do not fear,*" he mimicked sarcastically.

Stepping through the doorway, the big man peeked into the room, sulking like a disgruntled schoolboy. At least Alvaro had corralled the child into one corner by laying two heavy chairs on their sides. Then he looked down at her; the morning sun was caressing Tessie's golden curls like a benediction. She wore a blue cotton dress with matching bows in her tiny pigtails. Tytus watched from the doorway; the child seemed mesmerized by the butter-colored sunbeam that slanted through the window. Her perfect pink tongue was set to the corner of her mouth in concentration, while one tiny thumb and fore-finger reached out, trying to pluck the dust fairies from mid-flight as they danced and swirled just beyond her grasp. Hearing voices out the window she crawled to it, and with much effort, she pulled herself up to look out. Pleased with her accomplishment, she gave a little squeal then clapped her hands in delight! Of course that was her undoing, and down she went on her well-padded backside. Ty braced himself for a shriek that would surely follow—but when the little imp lowered her head and giggled instead, he found himself chuckling too.

Hearing the man's laughter, Tessie turned quickly around and tipped her face up to his. Her mouth formed a perfect "O" and her huge blue eyes sparkled with curiosity.

"Woo!" she chirped, then with surprising speed, she rolled to her hands and knees to get a closer look. Ty was somewhat taken aback by how quickly she crawled towards him. When she came to the chairs that blocked her way, she pulled up to a wobbly stance. As she had before, she squealed with pleasure over what Ty assumed was a recently acquired feat.

"All right," he said, stepping hesitantly into his office. "Maybe you *won't* bother me—too much—if you behave yourself."

As if in agreement, she looked way up and nodded her head, her whole body rocking back and forth.

He frowned down at her and was surprised when she—frown right back! Her wide-eyed gazed seemed to scrutinize him from head to toe. Soon, she lost her tentative balance, however, and down she went. And as she had done before, she put her head down—and giggled.

Ty gave a slight chuckle, then looked around to make sure no one heard. Quietly, he closed the door behind him, then crouching down on one knee, he whispered, "Hey—just 'cause you're cute—doesn't mean we're family."

Ty studied her little face. Timothy always said he would never marry. Which made Augusta a liar, and this little girl another man's child. But he had watched the woman all winter; she didn't seem the type: to lie and connive. But if Augusta was telling the truth—that would mean that Ty didn't know his brother as well as he thought. Now he found himself alone with the child and decided it was high time he take a good long look. She certainly didn't favor her mother. The baby's eyes were a cobalt blue; soft wheat-colored curls framed her face—just like—Timothy's, Ty had to admit. But then blonde hair and blue eyes were common enough. Just then Tessie yawned—and her perfectly formed button of a nose crinkled slightly and she rubbed her eyes with her chubby fists. Then, she looked up with twinkling eyes—and grinned.

A hammer blow to the chest—would not have hit the man any harder than did that one smile! The truth was as clear as a mountain stream on a sunlit morning—she looked *exactly* like her father, left dimple and all!

"Ah—Tim," Ty groaned, "she's yours all right!"

Just then Alvaro's words came back to him. "Let the child smile on you—and you will feel better!"

Now that he finally took the time to look at her, it wasn't only that she looked like Timothy but she acted like him too, the way she lowered her head and giggled instead of crying. Tessie May Grainger was his niece. He needed no proof, no wedding certificate. Tessie wasn't just a baby whose mother was down on her luck, as he had wanted to believe. Tessie was a Grainger, and the rightful heir to the Bar 61! Suddenly, there was a lump in Ty's throat as Tessie reached for him. When he took the child into his arms, she gavee a little sigh. It was sweeter than anything he had ever heard in his life, and then she laid her head on his shoulder, as if she'd been longing for him to hold her—just like that!

Ty stood and gently rubbed her back as he pondered this new revelation: Tim was an honorable Christian man, and this baby was his, which meant Augusta *was* indeed Tim's wife! Ty wanted to kick himself for walking around in such a fog all winter. However, trusting *that woman*—it still wasn't going to be easy. Why hadn't Timothy ever mentioned marriage or Augusta by name. The other burr that nettled him, was that he still didn't know who had shot his brother. He knew that neither one of the dead men lying next to Timothy, had shot him. But someone had, and it looked like they had brushed away their footprints. He couldn't imagine Augusta hurting anyone, but as far as he knew, she had been the only other person there that day. He was sure now, that Tessie was family. But where *that woman* was concerned, he still had more questions than answers.

Ty gently cradled Tessie in his arms, until he heard hoof beats in the yard. When he heard the sound of Augusta's feminine voice, he carefully returned his niece to the sunlit corner of his office. Smiling, he ran his large hand over her soft curly head, and whispered. "I'll see you later, Little Bit."

Alvaro grinned as he heard the jangle of Ty's spurs going out the side door of the hacienda. As he scrapped the messy dough into the slop bucket for the pigs, he sent up a prayer of thanksgiving.

"Gracias, my Lord! You have opened his eyes. The journey begins with the first step, and finally, he has taken it!"

Chapter 31
Picnic for the Ladies

"A man that has friends must show himself friendly: and there is a friend that sticks closer than a brother." Proverbs 18:24

Tessie giggled and reached up to Alvaro as the old man scooped her up from the floor where she had been playing with his wooden spoons.

Augusta enjoyed watched this gentle man joyfully play with her daughter while she folded diapers and sheets.

"Alvaro, you spoil her!" she teased. "Tessie thinks your sole purpose in life is to make her smile!"

The old man twirled the little girl once more and laughed at her happy giggles. A moment later, he sat down in one of the big kitchen chairs to catch his breath, still chuckling and cuddling her close.

"Ah, señora, I wish it were so easy to put a smile on your lovely face."

"Nonsense. You spoil me every bit as much as you do Tessie!"

The old man shook his head. "No-no—it is not the same—you smile while you work. It is my wish to see you smile with a joy that comes from inside, like our little Tess. It is time for you to enjoy being young and bea—u—ti—ful! It is time to for you to live again!"

A shadow flickered across Augusta's eyes. "But, I enjoy working—and I need—to stay busy. Besides, I am a mother now—that's enough for me."

Alvaro knew Augusta still grieved though she was careful not to call attention to her sorrow. He had stood beside her door late at night, and prayed while he heard the young woman's softly muffled sobs. Too many times, he had seen the evidences of her tears, when she returned from her daily rides.

"Ah, sí, you are a fine mother, and to be busy—is good," Alvaro agreed. "But it is time to put aside your mourning."

The old man stood with Tessie in his arms and held out his hand to Augusta. "Come, my dear." With his dark eyes sparkling, he added, "Today, we have for you, a surprise! Quickly now, go and fetch your bonnet. For today you will be busy with the...uh..the pic-nic! El Jefe has need of me today, but Señor Hitch will take you and Tess—to a place most beaut—i—ful!"

When Augusta stared at him blankly, he explained, "Señora, have you not longed to see the—wild flowers? Señor Hitch tells me of a lovely meadow where the flowers grow—like the stars in the sky! Today your work—is to enjoy—life—sí? *Bueno!*"

"A picnic?" Tears came to Augusta's eyes, remembering her outings with Timothy. But when she saw the flash of concern in Alvaro's face, she quickly turned her expression into an appreciative smile.

The old man grinned, and before she could think, he had settled her and Tessie into the buggy beside the big foreman. Hitch's face turned crimson when he saw her, then he tipped his hat and grunted, "Mornin'!"

Augusta stuttered, "G-good m-morning!" in reply, then realized that she, too, had nothing else to say.

Hitch, as always, was stingy with his words. He was content to simply drive the buggy. One quick slap of the reins, and they were off, with Augusta suddenly wondering, *what had just happened?* Was it even proper, for a widow, to be on an outing with the ranch foreman? But—there she was—feeling terribly aware of the big man sitting beside her. And the man...looked different somehow. After a second glance she realized he was, what Emily would describe as, *spit and polished!* His square jaw gleamed from a fresh shave, his mustache was trimmed, and he smelled of shaving soap, hay, leather, and—*bay rum!*

Finally, Hitch broke the silence, and as usual his words were slow and measured: "Been a...long winter...it's...good to get out."

For him it was a long sentence that was followed by a soft sigh and a self-conscious smile.

Augusta turned away and bit her lip; the use of so many words seemed almost painful to this gentle man. Soon, however, she settled back to enjoy the ride, finding that she really didn't mind the lack of conversation. Springtime in the foothills of the Rocky Mountains was entertaining enough! The turquoise canopy overhead was adorned with an array of translucent clouds. It was as if God had dipped a dry brush into whitewash, and then He had splattered and dotted and stroked the sky with a playful hand. Her eyes soon wandered to the lush meadows. And in the distance rose the never-ending mountain range that—as always—filled her with wonder!

As the buggy bumped along over an open field, Augusta drank in each and every sight and scent.

Finally, Augusta whispered softly, "Thank you Hitch—this was a—very nice surprise."

Hitch smiled down at her, but she didn't notice for she had closed her eyes and tipped her face up for the sun to kiss. He watched her dreamy expression as she breathed in the crisp mountain air—savoring this sweet pleasure! It pleased him that this woman could be so appreciative of something so simple.

As they rode Augusta contemplated how she might describe all of this to her friends back East. But her thoughts brought on a dreadful homesickness. Oh, how she missed having another woman to talk to.

Augusta suddenly heard herself give voice to her thoughts: "I'm sorry I never got to meet Granny Rose."

Not wanting to sound as if she were complaining she added quickly, "God worked it all out of course. I ended up not needing her, and with their youngest getting sick, it was good that she never left. But—well—do we happen to be close enough to stop by for a visit today?"

Hitch could hear the loneliness in her voice, and for the first time he caught a glimpse of just how hard it must be for a young woman, alone, on a ranch full of men. "I'm sorry, Augusta. " he said, meaning it. "They're in the opposite direction and a day's ride away."

"Oh—that's fine—it was just a thought," Augusta remarked, trying not to show her disappointment.

"Hmm—ya know?" Hitch mused, chewing on the idea. "The boss mentioned...a party once. Maybe...we could...remind him."

Augusta hung on every meandering word from the man's mouth then shook her head. "We couldn't—but you could! The boss might even agree—if you told him—I hated the idea!"

Hitch shook his head and chuckled. "A party'd...be good medicine...especially...for him!"

Augusta's spirits lifted at the very idea of a get-together. "A party would be good medicine for all of us! And the Rosenquists would come—wouldn't they? And all the ranchers and farmers would come and surely there must be others with wives and children!"

It tickled Hitch as he watched Augusta's mind take wing; she was suddenly all a-glow, her golden eyes sparkling, her face flushed and rosy. Augusta wrapped her arms around Tessie and rested her chin atop her curly head, as her mind whirled with a thousand ideas.

"You know, it could become an annual event and then we'd know when there'd be enough children to build a school. And maybe there's already enough of us to build a church! Papa always said folks should be mindful of where they build churches and schools because whole towns spring up around them! It should be planned very carefully. Wouldn't a town be pretty right here with the streets lined up towards the mountains and..."

After a quick glance at Hitch, Augusta clamped her mouth shut. The man was grinning from ear to ear. Embarrassed, she laughed. "I-I'm sorry. I love planning things—I tend to get a little carried away."

Augusta shook her head. "You mention a party and I've built a town and elected myself—mayor!"

"I'd...vote for ya!" Hitch grinned. "Got some...good ideas." Then he leaned close and asked seriously, "But...what I want to know is...where ya... puttin' the courthouse?"

Augusta rolled her eyes at his teasing, then she straightened and answered smugly, "I'll have to think on it and get back to you."

Hitch's grin grew wider, then he slapped the reins and they both settled back to enjoy their ride.

Augusta couldn't help but ponder the man sitting beside her; he had always been as kind as could be. And though she hadn't really paid attention before, he was also a very handsome man, with high cheekbones and a slightly crooked nose. He was a quiet and reliable man with a dry sense of humor. He wasn't arrogant, and yet fully aware of his own abilities and worth.

Just then Doc swished his tail, and for some reason, Tessie thought it was hilarious! She let out a deep belly laugh every time the horse flicked his tail. Her delight proved to be contagious and soon Augusta and Hitch had joined in the merriment. After a while, the swaying of the buggy and the rhythmic sound of the horse's hooves lulled the little cherub to sleep. Augusta turned her around and cradled her in her arms to make her more comfortable. When she looked up at Hitch, she found him staring tenderly at both of them. His expression troubled Augusta. Surely, he didn't have courting on his mind. And yet there he sat, all spit and polished, smiling and laughing—he'd even blushed a time or two.

Before she could think on it further, Hitch guided the buggy through a dense grove of pine trees that opened up to reveal a beautiful hidden meadow.

The knee-high grass swayed and rolled like waves on the sea. But what thrilled her was that everywhere she looked there were splashes of brilliant color. A fairyland of wildflowers, there were clusters of red Indian paint brush, purple lupine, the snowy white blossoms of the prairie primrose, and even the prickly pear, flaunted it's brilliant yellow flower.

"Oh, my!" Augusta exclaimed as she tugged on Hitch's sleeve. "This is it—isn't it?"

Hitch smiled at her excitement. "Yep, this is it!"

Tessie awoke to the sound of her mother's delight! It was all so perfect! There was even a lazy little stream weaving through the meadow. And all around them was the whisper-like melody of the wind gliding through pine boughs.

The moment Doc stopped and began cropping grass, Augusta placed Tessie in Hitch's arms then jumped from the buggy. "Oh, it's all so wonderful here—it doesn't seem real!"

As if the bounty of flowers might disappear if not picked immediately, she hurried to make a bouquet.

"Alvaro would've loved to see this!" Turning towards Hitch she asked, "What did grumpy old Ty need him to do anyway? Bet 'the boss' was just being ornery not to let him come—don't you think?"

Hitch pulled on his collar and shrugged self-consciously. "Yep, I...reckon...ya hungry?"

Augusta stopped and grinned. "Yep!" she mimicked, surprising the man with her youthful antics.

Chuckling he climbed from the buggy, and holding Tessie in one arm, he grabbed the basket with the other.

Augusta picked up her skirts and trotted back to share her treasures. "Look Tessie, pretty flowers!"

Hitch grinned at the delight he saw in Augusta's face, then waved his arm around the meadow; "Ladies choice," he said. "Pick yer spot!"

Augusta spun around considering several locations, and finally settling on what she proclaimed to be the perfect view of both flowering meadow and the majestic mountains.

Hitch spread out a large quilt, and eagerly helped Augusta unpack their feast. There was fried chicken, bread and butter sandwiches, wedges of cheese, carrot salad, and for dessert—Hitch's favorite—molasses cookies. Alvaro had also included a large jug of apple cider to wash it all down.

Something stirred in Hitch as he watched Augusta tear tiny bits of bread and chicken for Tessie, then giggle when the little girl smacked her lips and tried to shove too much food into her mouth.

Full and content, he leaned back on one elbow, thinking he'd never seen a more appealing woman, or one more suited to the West. He had observed this young widow from her first moment of grief, and seen her struggle through a long lonely winter. Now like the wild flowers she had so longed for, she was blossoming before his eyes. Augusta's smile was heady stuff for the big man, as was her laughter. She was sweet and young and pretty, and giving her this day made Hitch feel ten feet tall.

Augusta licked her fingers with a thoughtful look on her sweet face. "Why does everything taste better when you eat it—in a place like this? Is it being outside or is it the view? Is it like this on a round-up?"

"No ma'am," Hitch said with a grimace. "We're too tired...and...eat too much dust to taste the grub!"

With his eyes full of the woman before him he added, "But for me...right now...it's the view!"

Augusta looked to see which view Hitch was referring to, when suddenly she realized he was looking at her! Their eyes met for an instant and once again his tender expression caught her off guard. Quickly, she lowered her gaze but she could feel herself blush as she focused all her attention back on Tessie.

Hitch enjoyed the rosy color that spread across her cheeks, but his goal was not to make her uncomfortable. He reached over and tickled Tessie's bare foot.

"Hey...Miss Tess," he drawled, making her giggle. "How 'bout...lets... walk off our dinner?"

Hitch stood and swung the little girl onto his shoulders, then helped Augusta to her feet.

They strolled along the bubbling creek, in the shower of leaves Tessie pulled from the overhead branches. Smiling patiently, he led the way. Tugging lightly on Augusta's sleeve he asked, "How are things...between you...and the boss? Would ya...care to talk?"

Augusta was tempted to say everything was fine! But she was troubled, and Hitch at the very least, was offering her his friendship and a listening ear.

"Oh, Hitch, they aren't good." she found herself admitting. "We made the poor man so miserable this winter. He avoided me—wouldn't even look at

231

Tessie. I get mad at him for being grumpy. Then I feel guilty because I know that—I'm the cause! I'm doing exactly what Timothy told me to do, but—I hate it. I'm forcing Tytus to accept us as if he has no say in the matter. I know how that feels—and—it's awful!"

Hitch sat down on a rock, swinging Tessie down to sit on one knee. "Ty always said the Bar 61 was…as much…Tim's…as his. He's a fair man…it'll all work out."

Augusta sat down next to him, pondering his words, while a breeze teased a wisp of hair from her bun.

Hitch couldn't stop himself from gently slipping the stray curl back behind Augusta's ear. "I admire you!" he said softly. "You're all alone…with a cantankerous brother-in-law and…a bunch of rowdy cowboys. You…are a… brave woman!"

Augusta gave a rueful smile. "Not a brave woman, just one with few choices. I was scared to death when Timothy warned me how it would be. But you and the men have all been so kind. Timothy told me to treat all the men like brothers. So, that's what I've done. It's worked pretty well—don't you think?"

Hitch raised his eyebrows. "Brothers…huh? Ya do know…they're all smitten?"

Blushing, Augusta frowned and made a slightly indignant snort. "They are not! Every man has been a true gentleman. I—I know, they pay attention to me. But only because—well—I'm a novelty—the only female for miles."

Hitch's hazel eyes were warm as he leaned close, realizing again how very sweet and innocent she was.

"Don't to be too trustin'! Mostly they're all good men, but… they ain't… yer brothers."

"Oh, Hitch," Augusta chided. "I'm just a paint pony in a herd of bays. It doesn't mean anything."

He grinned broadly, then he shocked Augusta by taking her hands in both of his. He looked into her eyes in such a way that she felt it all the way down to her toes and had to fight down the childish desire to make a run for the buggy. Somehow, she managed to sit quietly, and although her heart was pounding, she forced herself to be still and listen to what the man had to say,

"You are…as sweet…as a peach!" he said softly. "I like…yer thinkin' of the men…like brothers."

Then he drew her hand to his lips, and kissed her fingers. His look became intense and direct.

"But, don't...think of me that-a-way!" he said sternly. "Maybe, it's too soon to speak of...but there will come a time...you'll need to choose. And...I want to be the one!"

Chapter 32
Midnight Talk

"You will know the truth, and the truth will set you free." John 8:32

The clock on the parlor mantle chimed twice as Augusta slowly rocked; she hummed a vague tune while Tessie chewed on a rag dipped in water with oil of clover. Though the remedy soothed the pain of teething, it didn't help the child sleep. Of course, it didn't really matter; Augusta couldn't sleep either, but for far different reasons. Pulling Tessie close, her mind began to wander. Life had become decidedly more complicated since the day of the picnic. Hitch's words had been disconcerting, and now she didn't know how to behave around the man. To make things worse and on the same day, Tytus began behaving oddly as well!

When she and Hitch had returned from their picnic, the dragon of the Bar 61 had been waiting for them.

Ty immediately stalked to the buggy, muttering, "Pleasant day, I trust!" Then, with the manner's of a Southern born gentleman, he offered to help her down. Although his words sounded kind she believed he was being condescending when he said, "Alvaro's tired—why don't you go on in and see if you can help?"

Augusta only nodded as she hurried toward the hacienda, fighting down the desire to either burst into tears or put that man in his place! As if she didn't always help Alvaro? And hadn't they returned in plenty of time to do just that?

Then she wondered if she should be ashamed? Had she been unfaithful to Timothy by going off with Hitch. Surely, Alvaro wouldn't have suggested it if it weren't proper! What would Mrs. D think? No—she chided herself, she should be asking God what He thought.

So, while Tessie chewed on her rag, Augusta rocked in the darkness, and prayed: "Lord, I want to do what's right. But You need to help me—I don't always know what right looks like."

She leaned back in the rocker, feeling defeated and confused, while through the open window, she heard the chirping of crickets and the shrill song of a coyote as it floated across the open range. Tess brought her mother back to task as she reached for her cup of milk. After Augusta helped her to a drink, Tessie produced a loud burp—very loud for such a tiny body. Both mother and child turned suddenly when they heard a rumbling chuckle coming from the doorway.

Augusta nearly dropped the cup when she realized it was the dragon himself, standing there. Quickly, she sat the cup down and hurried to vacate Ty's favorite chair.

"Hold on now—don't get up!" he said calmly. "Please, in fact..." he asked amiably, as he stepped into the room. "Would you two mind—if I join you?"

Augusta stared for a moment, then stammered, "Of...of course not!"

Feeling as if she'd been caught in some mischief, she immediately apologized if they woke him. But the words were no more out of her mouth when she became angry at herself for sounding so like a mouse cowering before a hungry cat. She *was not* afraid of Tytus Grainger. Not—really, but then she made it worse by blathering on.

"I really do try to keep from disturbing anyone. But...you see...she's teething and..."

"It's all right, Augusta. You didn't wake me. I went to check on the stock and got hungry."

He held up a glass of milk and a handful of cookies, then took a seat on the settee nearest the rocker.

"I heard your humming...and—I—hoped Little Bit, there, wasn't ill."

Augusta leaned back in the rocker and studied the man. Tytus seemed strangely at ease, even friendly. She wondered how long it would be before he'd ask if she'd found the wedding certificate. Actually, he hadn't asked lately, but for many months, his asking had been almost a daily ritual. She had looked everywhere, but didn't think she could say the words again: "No, I don't know where it is." Augusta waited, but he didn't ask.

Just then, Tessie hiccupped; she looked up at her mama with a mournful face and stuck out her lower lip.

Tytus watched as the young mother tucked her curly-headed daughter under her chin and cooed, "Oh, my poor baby—hiccups hurt, don't they?"

Augusta cuddled her daughter close, then kissed Tessie's forehead. But when she looked up to find Ty staring at her, it seemed as if he were seeing her for the first time. There was a cloud of emotion in his dark gaze—confusion,

235

pain, and sorrow. For a long while they were unable to take their eyes from each other, for it seemed their hearts were speaking in a language their minds refused to translate.

A powerful yearning was cinching through Ty's chest; he had thought he had tamped down his desire for a wife and family. But looking at these two brought on such a wave of longing, he found it hard to breathe. He hadn't been like other men who feared being trapped and hog-tied by a woman. Instead, Ty had embraced the idea of being a husband and father. He had worked hard to build a home to share with a loving wife and had hoped for a home full of noisy, happy children. It was only when Savannah Summerville rejected him that he had abandoned his dreams as a lost cause.

Ty was jolted back from his thoughts when Tessie hiccupped again and began to cry; to Augusta's great surprise Tessie lifted her arms, wanting the big man to hold her.

Ty shrugged, then grinned sheepishly, as he took the child into his arms. "Come here, Little Bit," he soothed.

Augusta couldn't hide her amazement, as the dragon of the Bar 61 paced the floor, humming his own little tune, tenderly soothing his niece just as any loving uncle might.

Feeling uncomfortable under the woman's stunned gaze, he smiled at her and explained, "There's no accounting for it—children…just seem…to like me!"

It wasn't long before he whispered, "She's asleep. I'll carry her back to your room."

Mutely, Augusta followed the man down the hallway and watched him as he ever so gently tucked Tessie into her bed. He lingered a moment, touching the child's golden curls as he spoke, "Tim would be strutting around like a peacock over this little girl! She looks just like him."

Augusta was completely taken off guard. She blinked up at him with wide dark eyes as he walked from the room. Then he turned before he got to the door, adding sadly,

"It's not that I want to hurt you. I've known for a while who *she* is. It's just that—I'm still confused—*about—who you are.*"

Chapter 33
Besting the Dragon

"Be kind one to another, tenderhearted, forgiving one another, even as God for Christ's sake has forgiven you." Ephesians 4:32

The men cheered as Tessie May tottered from man to man around the kitchen table. Augusta joined in their laughter while she dried the supper dishes.

"As well as she's walking, she'll be running by her birthday. It doesn't seem possible that my little girl will be a year old soon!"

Alvaro scooped her into his arms, "We must have a *fiesta!*"

"What's a *fiesta?*" she asked.

"He means a party!" Shep explained with a grin.

Augusta exchanged looks with Hitch. "A party?" she questioned.

The foreman gave an imperceptible wink. "Sure...we should...and invite the neighbors."

Shep was quick to pick up on the idea. "Ya mean: all the ranchers and their hands?"

"And surely some of them have wives and children—they would come too!" Augusta flushed, then quickly turned and busied herself at the sink.

Tytus wasn't fooled; there was a trap being laid—and if he wasn't careful—he'd fall right in.

Hitch leaned lazily back in his chair. "Ya mentioned ... a party...last year...remember, boss?"

Tytus scowled as he bent over the table, dropping a few drops of oil on a whetstone. "Can't say that I do," he muttered. "Sounds like more trouble than it's worth."

Holding the blade of his skinning knife at the perfect angle, Tytus made a series of even circles, slowly dancing the blade down the stone, as he put a razor-sharp edge on his knife. He tested the edge of the blade by drawing it down a length of paper, slicing through it as if it were air; then without ever looking up, he muttered: "There's no time to spare for such nonsense."

Augusta felt her hopes were being shredded, just like that piece of paper. She knew she should keep quiet and let the men talk Tytus into it. But, suddenly, she heard herself say, "What if I do all the work? Or, most of it anyway—and ALL the organizing?"

Tytus squinted up at her; Augusta had proved to be a hard worker. All through the winter she'd given him a wide berth, even though she said, she wasn't afraid of him. But now—he liked the way she was speaking up!

"I can do it!" she declared, her face aglow with excitement. "Well, of course I couldn't build tables and benches but I can do all the planning and all the cooking!"

Alvaro gave Ty a wide grin. "And I would be most happy to help, Jefe!"

The rest of the hands were quick to catch Augusta's excitement. They had never seen her look so happy. Their eyes followed her as she paced about the table, leaving in her wake the scent of lilac and cinnamon. Her long skirt swished as she did the mental calculations; her golden eyes sparkled with ideas. The men watched Augusta as if she were the dawn of spring after a winter storm. Her long chocolate-colored hair shone in the lantern light, and fell in a spiraling cascade down her back where the wide bow of her apron accentuated a healthy, hour-glass figure.

"Hitch," she asked, touching the foreman lightly on his shoulder as she passed. "Would one steer be enough? Or would we need two?"

Ty scowled as his foreman drew in his breath at her touch, and all four legs of Hitch's chair hit the floor. "T-two b-be best," he stammered.

Suddenly, Augusta turned to Ty, "I suppose we'll have to cook them on a s—spit? Is that ...."

She didn't finish her question, for when she saw the harsh look on Ty's face, her words stopped.

When Tytus realized he had caused her face to pale and her eyes to grow wide with apprehension, he immediately softened his expression. He didn't know what to do with this woman but he didn't want her fearing him. Slowly, he gave her a half smile and saw her relax.

Augusta couldn't believe how bold she suddenly felt, but after the other evening when Tytus had acknowledged Tessie, she decided it was high-time she spoke up for the women of the house.

"Tytus…" she began softly, "wouldn't a party be good—for everyone? And—if I promise to do all the planning and most of the work, and only bother the men for a little help, here and there?"

Ty chewed on his lip; honestly, he didn't know what would be "good" anymore. His being stern had become a habit, and even though he didn't feel like being stern now—he didn't know any other way to behave.

"No!" he heard himself growl. "Besides," he added with a frown in Augusta's direction, "you're awful free with my beef! If we don't have a party we won't need any steers at all!"

Augusta was suddenly fearless—dragon or no. She lifted her chin, then was stunned by her own words: "I hadn't any intention of using your beef at all! Be it one or two or three, if that is what's necessary."

Ty leaned back in his chair. "That's sure interesting—tell me now— whose beef do you intend to use?"

Augusta took a quick look at Alvaro for support then looked directly into Ty's dark eyes. "I intend for the men to butcher only steers that belong to—Tessie—and me!"

Though her words were boldly spoken, Ty noticed she wrung her hands nervously, a telling sign.

"Only the steers that belong to Tessie—and you?" Tytus asked with frightful calm. "Did I hear that right?"

Ty realized he was proud of the way she was standing up to him. He liked her this way! Obviously, the party was important to her, but he was curious just how far she would go—to get it? He felt something cold inside him, thawing, just a bit. He was enjoying this little tussle and didn't want it to end too soon.

"That's right," she said, managing to just barely hold his gaze.

"Well, since your cows and mine all wear the same brand, how do we tell them apart?"

One side of Ty's mouth lifted only slightly but his dark gaze captured Augusta's, and silence fell across the room. The man all but admitted that they were partners. He could have said that none of the steers were hers; instead, he asked how would she know which ones were hers. His subtle remark was lost on no one in the room.

Feeling emboldened by his comment, she stated matter-of-factly, "I'll simply use numbers and percentages."

239

Shep scratched his head, being the youngest and not knowing this might be very shaky ground, he asked, "Ma'am, would you mind explainin' how that works?"

Making a point of not looking at Tytus, she smiled at the young redhead and said: "Well, Shep, it's simple really. First, we'll cut out four steers from the herd. Tessie and I h-have uh—fifty percent—more or less..." she stammered.

Chancing a glance in Ty's direction, she was pleased to see he looked only arrogantly amused. And it bode well that he wasn't slamming his fist on the table or spitting fire. And since that was a definite improvement over many of their previous conversations, she continued. "The steers will be equal in age, height, and weight. And...well...the...two...on the LEFT—are mine!"

Everyone, except possibly Shep, knew she'd made the whole equation up on the spur of the moment. Some of the men hid their smiles, while others stared at the boss and waited for lightning to strike.

Tytus only turned away, mumbling to himself, "The two on the left?" Then more loudly he added, "I still think a party is way too much trouble!"

Augusta bit her lip in frustration; until that moment she hadn't realized just how desperately she wanted, even needed, this party! Just then an outlandish idea popped into her head, and she began rolling up her sleeves, as she defiantly turned to face the dragon of the Bar 61.

"All right—Tytus Grainger!" she challenged. " I've watched how you and the men settle your disputes. What if I wrestle you for it? If I win we have a party and the men help. If you win I won't say another word about it. What do you think of that?"

At first the men all laughed, then they began taunting Tytus to accept her challenge.

Ty simply folded his powerful arms across his chest, and let out a loud sigh.

"Lady, I don't think your thinking!" Then he added, "No one—has ever beat me at arm wrestling! I assume that is the kind you had in mind," he said with a grin. "Or was it two out of three falls?"

Augusta pursed her lips and narrowed her eyes. "You are very amusing, Mister Grainger, but I meant arm wrestling."

Just saying the words caused Augusta's face to redden—she'd never done anything so un-ladylike. And if Mrs. Drew ever found out, she *would* have the vapors! And yet it was Mrs. D. who taught her that a woman must be clever to live in a man's world. Besides, Tytus had maintained his low opinion of her for nearly a year now—she had nothing to lose!

Looking around the room she said sweetly, "Gentlemen, isn't this when you usually—place your bets?"

All the men smiled, for her gently spoken words did not match her actions. She had watched this manly ritual a dozen times. Mimicking their behavior she paced around the room, opening and closing her small fists and swinging her arms back and forth. Tytus watched her, finding it necessary to rub his hand over his face, to hide his amusement. He couldn't imagine what she was thinking—and yet, she was—awfully cute like this.

Finally, Ty turned away, making a show of rolling his eyes, and glancing around the room.

A moment later, Augusta turned to him, and with her sweetest smile she asked: "Of course I'll understand if you'd rather not tire your roping arm. You—could just say—yes!"

The big man stared into her golden eyes, then arrogantly he rested his elbow on the table with his right hand up in the air, he growled, "But—I still say—NO! All right lady—I'll accept your challenge!"

Augusta blew out a breath, while pulling out the chair next to Ty, but before sitting down she said: "Now—I really wouldn't want to rush you—so—you just tell me—whenever you think you're ready."

The men were all spellbound by this different side of Augusta. They had all just about forgotten that she was only eighteen years old—just a girl really. But now she didn't act or look like a widow and a mother. She was just a delightful young girl, full of life! A girl, who wanted a party!

"I'm ready!" Tytus groaned, wincing slightly as he read the pensive looks on the faces of his men. Each man was sending him an unspoken message.

Come on, boss—she's just a girl—go easy on her!

Meanwhile, Augusta still had not sat down; she circled the large kitchen table and then questioned once again, "Now, are you absolutely *sure* that you're ready? And you haven't changed your mind?"

"I have not!" Ty growled, however, his eyes sparkled when he said it. "But now, if are you getting cold feeeee—"

Before Tytus could finish his taunt, Augusta catapulted herself across the table. She clamped onto Ty's right hand with both of hers, and while her body came down, her feet flew up into the air. The next sound was that of Ty's knuckles crashing down onto the table with a resounding—crack!

Shep, being the closest, shouted with laughter as he reached down and helped her back onto her feet.

A cheer went up all around the kitchen—and mayhem broke loose—the men laughed until they cried. Young Shep finally had to sit down on the floor while Alvaro wiped the tears away with his apron.

When the chaos subsided Augusta looked around the room; her face was glowing as if she'd swallowed sunshine. However, as the laughter began to subside, Augusta forced herself to face Ty. Cautiously, she asked,

"I won—so—we are—going to have a party?! Right?"

"YOU CHEATED!" Ty's voice rumbled, but he couldn't quite manage to hold his frown. Her sweet joy was too contagious. Amusement sparkled in his eyes, and though he didn't really smile, his lips drew in and that dimple in his right cheek was obvious.

When Ty narrowed his eyes, Augusta tried to mimic his fierce expression but a giggle betrayed her.

"That WAS NOT FAIR! Lady, you cheated!" he protested, his deep voice sounding like thunder.

But Augusta was not intimidated; she put her hands on her hips as laughter bubbled up between her words: "Well—of course *I cheated!* If I'd wrestled *you,* would that be fair? Your right arm is like a side of beef and your hands are the size of—my flapjack griddle!" The men laughed as she added, "Whoever won—would be a cheater!"

Then a proud grin covered Augusta's glowing face. "But—I cheated first!" she boasted. "So I won!"

Augusta glanced around the room, asking, "Isn't that right, men?"

Every man but Ty whooped and applauded, proclaiming Augusta the winner!

Finally, the moment came when the room fell silent and everyone waited for the boss to speak. Would he agree or not? After a dramatic pause, Tytus stood, and as he walked past Shep, he squeezed the boy's shoulder.

"Hey, boy?" he asked. "I bet you have never been to a dance—have you?"

"No sir," Shep replied his eyes wide. "I never have."

"Dance?" Augusta asked, as her eyes became even wider than Shep's. "Y-you want a d-dancing party? I've never been to a dance either!"

Tytus gave her a long appraising look. "If the Bar 61 is going to host a party—we'll do it right! We'll start the day with a short preaching service, have games, food all day, and when the sun goes down—there will be music and—dancing!"

⚜

"BLAST THESE SORRY NUMBERS!" Ty bellowed as he flung the ledger out the library door.

But when he saw Augusta jump out of the way and yelp in surprise, Ty bounded after her. "Augusta—I'm sorry!"

She put her hands on her hips. "Sorry you threw that ledger—or sorry you missed?"

"Sorry I threw it..." he groaned, as he raked his hand through his hair.

Augusta picked up the ledger, but she didn't give it back to Ty, instead she held it to her chest.

"You know," she began softly, "bookkeeping is one of those things—you either love or you hate! I love it—used to do all my father's paperwork."

Ty frowned, and rubbed his jaw—he hated asking for help—and, worse, he hated admitting that he needed it.

Augusta hid her smile; something was happening lately that she couldn't quite put her finger on but Tytus was—*different*, or maybe she was! At any rate, *something* was *different*. Alvaro and Joseph had encouraged her to spend more time praying for Ty and less time thinking up ways to prove herself. And now here he was, the dragon of the Bar 61, standing over her, looking very handsome and quite vulnerable all the sudden. At the moment he was clean shaven, but still the dark shadow of his beard lingered under his skin. He smelled of shaving soap, leather, pine trees, and sage. His loose fitting white shirt was tucked neatly into a pair of gray trousers, and cinched tight with a wide black belt. Augusta blushed when she looked down and saw that the man was barefooted. He usually wore knee high boots. But he'd wandered to his desk early that morning and had been wrestling with his account books ever since. Seeing Ty in his bare feet made him seem less formidable, less like the dragon!

Ty shook his head. "You actually *like* bookkeeping?" he said grimacing. "I hate it! *Really* hate it!"

Augusta smiled, noticing the ink stains on his fingers and that his dark wavy hair was all tousled. He had the habit of dragging his hands through his hair whenever he was aggravated.

Suddenly, she was unsure of herself. "I don't want to mislead you—I have no formal education. My father was my teacher. I think I took to doing sums, partly just to please him—he hated paperwork too."

Augusta gave Ty a hesitant smile, as she walked past him and into the library. "Actually, you'd be doing me a favor. Papa always said if you don't use a skill, you'll likely lose it!"

Ty held his desk chair for Augusta to sit. "Please," he said with a gallant gesture. When Augusta gracefully sat down, he added, "Far be it from me to cause you to lose one of your skills."

Ty waved his hand over the pile of receipts and slips of paper, adding in disgust, "Me, on the other hand, I'd rather skin a skunk than do this—only part of running a ranch I don't like."

Augusta smiled to herself; Tytus was a complex man. She'd mostly seen the rough ranch boss but down deep he was also the refined southern gentlemen.

Ty leaned over Augusta while he opened the ledger; he couldn't help but breathe in the soft scent of lilac. When she looked up at him, he noticed her eyes were dark-rimmed circles of pure gold.

"I, uh—I've...deducted our losses from the estimated number of cattle that have been rustled and the freight supplies that have been stolen this year." He shook his head then pointed to one column. "I think I've listed everything but still...I've added these blasted numbers three times and I..."

Augusta nodded her understanding. "And you keep getting a different answer? I've had days like that too!" she said sympathetically. "Why don't I start with this 'blasted column', while you stretch your legs. And—should you pass the kitchen, you might find that a piece of cherry pie and a glass of milk could put you in a much better mood!"

Ty's eyebrows rose. "Cherry pie? I haven't had cherry pie since—?" He stiffened then grunted, "Even so, it'd have to be awfully good pie to put me in a better mood."

Augusta had already begun her calculations when without looking up she muttered, "I'd thank you not to underestimate—*my* cherry pie!"

Much later, Ty propped his feet up on the desk while he finished off his third piece of pie. Reverently, he slid the last bite into his mouth, savoring the warm buttery taste, the flaky crust, and the perfect not too sweet, not too tart, crimson filling. His eyes closed blissfully, as he washed down the last crumb with cold milk and sighed with satisfaction. "I will deny it if you tell Joseph, but not even Natty May could bake a pie any better than that!"

Other than blushing at his compliment, Augusta paid him no mind except to ask an occasional question. He'd answer, she'd nod in understanding, then dip her quill into the ink well and continue her work.

In a much improved mood, Tytus stretched his long legs out, folded his arms over his chest, and flagrantly scrutinized the woman who had invaded yet another area of his life. He could no longer deny his attraction to her, and so too, he had to admit that she could have easily altered Timothy's commitment to stay unmarried.

Augusta had told Alvaro that her father had raised her. Tytus found that hard to believe, for she was such a feminine creature, so poised and graceful. Just now she was stunning in a copper-colored gown, trimmed in white. Her dark hair had a luster as it fell over her shoulders and framed her face in soft curls. Her skin had the look of fresh cream, and he had to stop himself from reaching out and touching her cheek to see if it was as velvety soft as it looked. And it wasn't just the way she looked. There was a serenity about this woman. It made being near her—soothing. Even her frowns made him smile. Ty was thankful she was so intent upon her work, or she would see far too much in the way he was watching her.

While Augusta studied each receipt, she absent-mindedly brushed the feather tip of the quill across her soft lips.

Ty drew in a breath; he had done the same thing with that quill. He felt heat creeping up his neck. It was ridiculous—a school boy's fancy, really—but he couldn't help but feel as if he had just stolen a kiss.

Augusta had changed the mood of the Bar 61. He hadn't wanted to admit it, but except for Timothy's untimely death, Augusta's presence had made everything better. There truly was something about a woman's touch. Her gentle spirit made all the men want to be better men. Daily, she was living out her Christian faith before them. Though surrounded by men, starved for the sight of a woman, she had remained ladylike and proper. Ty had feared the havoc one woman might wreak on a ranch full of single men; but somehow she had managed to treat every man like a treasured brother. And to Ty's amazement, the men seemed to treat her with an almost reverent esteem.

Ty recalled the day he had opened his chiffarobe and found a new white shirt, exact in every detail to the one she had turned pink. He knew she'd worked hard on it but she never mentioned it; and to his shame, neither did he. Every day Augusta rose early, took care of her baby, and worked hard. In her own quiet way she was turning his hacienda into a home. There were curtains at the windows and cushions on the chairs. Ty couldn't bring himself to thank her or even acknowledge any of her changes, but he liked them just the same. His home was becoming as he'd dreamt it would be—at least while his dreams for a wife and family still lived. And now *that woman* was helping him with his hated paperwork? Ty felt the walls he'd built around himself crumbling. He was trusting this woman with all that he had. Tessie was becoming his joy and delight. He'd never been wise when it came to women. So, was it wise for him to trust Augusta? He still didn't know.

Chapter 34
Treachery

"The Lord gave me into the hands of those whom I cannot withstand." Lamentations 1:14

Augusta reined the bay mare into another figure eight. The horse was quick and responsive, and she couldn't understand why Dewey thought his mare needed more training.

She'd been surprised that morning to have Dewey LeBeau, of all people, ask her if she would work with his mare. The man had never said more than two words to her since she'd arrived nearly a year ago. Later, the scruffy man had even led his horse up to the door of the hacienda and gave her a warm greeting.

"Sure obliged, ma'am!" he muttered. "Since the boss and Hitch are ridin' Quest and Stormy this mornin', I reckoned m' mare'd give ya a nice ride. And she could sure stand with the kind of polish you put on a horse!"

Augusta had never liked this man; then suddenly she felt a pang of guilt—maybe she'd misjudged him.

Dewey gave Augusta a sheepish look. "Went ahead 'n put yer saddle on her—know'd ya don't fancy being away fer too long."

Augusta smiled. "Thank you—I'll be just a minute."

The man grunted while Augusta stepped back into the kitchen. Finding Alvaro sitting on the floor playing with Tessie, she said, "I'm taking Dewey's mare out this morning and—don't worry I'm remembering my protector!"

She'd forgotten to take her gun one day and Alvaro had chastised her. Augusta blew them a kiss, then she took her hat from its peg, tied it securely, then carefully took her derringer from the shelf. After checking it to make sure it was loaded she slipped it into her skirt pocket.

After Augusta mounted the mare, she straightened in the saddle and asked, "What's her name?"

The grizzled man shrugged and headed for the barn.

"Dewey," she asked again, "what do you call her?"

LeBeau turned and frowned. "I call her—m' bay mare."

Augusta hid her smile as she guessed what Dewey's name for his bay gelding must be.

Though her name was unimpressive, the bay mare *was!* She was giving Augusta far more than a nice ride—it was too nice! The mare was as well-trained as any horse she'd ever ridden. What kind of polish she was to put on the mare—Augusta couldn't guess. The mare responded instantly to every command, as if she were terrified to do otherwise. Following a hunch, Augusta dismounted, then checked her sides—*just as she thought*—the mare had scabbed over gouge wounds from long roweled spurs used liberally during training. Augusta's first opinion of Dewey LeBeau had been right after all—he was an unkempt scoundrel. Quest had never trusted him and neither would she.

Remounting the mare, she patted the horse's shining mahogany coat. "Well, girl, you don't need polish but I can give you a little kindness—like extra oats when we get back."

Cantering the mare across the field, she couldn't help but wonder what Dewey was up to. The man had always avoided her before and his horse certainly hadn't needed to be ridden. As it happened, Augusta didn't have long to reason it out, because at that moment she saw LeBeau riding towards her on his bay gelding. An uneasy shudder ran through her when she suddenly recalled the few times she'd caught Dewey staring at her. He raised his hat in greeting, and her heart started hammering inside her chest. Instantly, she reined the mare back towards the ranch. As she reached Dewey, his grin showed a mouth full of brown teeth.

Augusta bit down her disgust and carefully schooled her features. "I've had a nice ride, thank you! You've done a fine job training her. But it's time I get back!"

Dewey rested his hand on the handle of his gun and kicked his gelding up to block her way. "Don't hurry off. Hitch showed ya the wildflowers—thought I'd show ya the Kettle Creek country."

Though his words were pleasant, the look he gave Augusta wasn't. Swiftly, she reined the mare away, not wanting him to see how the man unnerved her.

"Perhaps another time," she said softly. "Alvaro's expecting me back now."

Augusta forced a smile then clucked her tongue, relieved when the mare fell right into a nice cantor. They traveled only a dozen yards when she heard Dewey's gravelly voice call out: "Whoa, mare!"

Augusta nearly flew over the horses' neck, when without warning, her mount came to a sliding stop!

She turned back and stared at Dewey. "Clever! But I don't have time to see more of her tricks. I must get back—don't want Alvaro to worry."

This time Augusta dug her heels into the mare's sides, but the horse stood like a statue. With a quick glance, she saw Dewey's gelding moving fast towards her. Terrified, Augusta fumbled in her skirt pocket for the derringer: she had just managed to pull it free when Dewey whipped his hat off and slapped the gun from her hand.

Augusta jumped from the saddle and made a desperate run for the ranch. She screamed for help as she ran, all the while hearing the rumble of hoof beats right behind her. She hadn't gotten far, when she felt Dewey's grimy arm curling around her waist then lifting her into the air. An instant later he threw her roughly back onto the mare's back. She fought him, screaming and thrashing until he back-handed her hard across the face, then ordered. "Ya hush that, cat-erwauling gal—and do what I say!"

Reeling from the blow, Augusta went still. Forcing her voice to sound calm, she said, "Please, Dewey, Tessie needs me—I have to get back to her!"

"You listen up," he hissed. "I been offered good money fer ya. Ain't had no offers fer yer kid, but I know a Mescalaro that'll trade me a fine horse fer a purty fair-haired child!"

Augusta's stomach clenched at the thought of anything happening to her daughter.

Dewey sneered, "You decide, ya gonna go easy? Or do I tie ya up, 'n fetch the kid?"

"No!" Augusta was quick to say, "I'll go easy, but this doesn't make sense—who—would offer money for me?"

"None a yer business, gal." He grunted as he spurred the gelding, and the mare instantly followed.

When Dewey heard Augusta's weeping he back-handed her again.

"Won't have no crying nor complainin'! Ya hear me now? Best ya get used to my company, fer it'll be jes' the two of us fer quite a spell."

Ty and Hitch road into the ranch yard at a hard trot. They were to have been gone all day but a suspicious black cloud looming over the distant peak had warned of a bad storm heading their way. Still, it seemed that not even a tempest could keep Ty's thoughts from wandering back to arm wrestling with Augusta or to the day he spent with her, over cherry pie and ledgers. He had always despised paperwork, and yet sitting across the desk from her had made for—a very enjoyable day.

Tytus flipped Quest's reins over the hitching rail then jumped onto the porch while Hitch headed to the barn. Just then Ty heard Tessie's loud heart-breaking cry.

Turning towards Hitch he yelled, "Something's wrong—I've never heard her cry like that! Find Joseph!"

Ty ran along the porch then charged through the door shouting, "Augusta! Alvaro!"

No one answered but he found Tessie sitting on the floor of her room. When she saw Ty she shrieked and raised her tiny hands to him. In one motion Ty crossed the room and scooped her into his arms.

"Hey, Little Bit—hey now, it's all right," he crooned, holding her close but not believing his own words.

Something was terribly wrong—one look at the child's tear-stained cheeks and the sound of her broken sobs told him she must have been crying like this for some time.

A sickening fear gripped him as he hurried towards the kitchen. His heart nearly stopped when he found Alvaro—on the floor, tied and gagged, with a large bump on the back of his head.

Still holding Tessie, he freed the old man and helped him into a chair. A few moments later, Hitch came in with Joseph; he too had been knocked unconscious and tied.

Alvaro shuddered then he looked up at Ty and spoke with tears in his eyes. "I am an old fool, Jefe! El diablo has taken our sweet señora!"

"The devil?" Ty asked. "What do you mean, amigo?"

"He chose the perfect day—you and Hitch were to be at McGee's. All the men were to be away. Dewey was to have returned to his line shack at first light. I wondered why the man was still here but—I did not think! Oh, Señor Ty, I just did not think!"

"You sure…it was Dewey…that took her?" It was Hitch that voiced the question.

250

Alvaro's hand trembled as he rubbed his face. "She told me she was going to take Dewey's mare out. I should have remembered that the man never lets anyone ride his horses. It was for me to protect our señora!"

Ty squeezed the old man's shoulder. "It's not your fault. You couldn't have known he'd do this!" Turning to his foreman he said, "Hitch, our fastest horses are Stormy and Quest. They're already saddled and have the stamina to last for days. Go pack some grain and our bedrolls. I'll get my Sharps and plenty of ammunition."

Ty gently laid the now sleeping child down in the little bed that Augusta kept in the kitchen. Kneeling beside her, he fingered one blonde curl as he whispered: "I promise Little Bit—I'll bring your mama back!"

When he turned to ask Alvaro to pack some supplies, he saw the man was already filling saddle bags with tortillas, jerked beef, and coffee. Ty nodded then headed for his gun cabinet.

When he returned to the kitchen, he found only Joseph, quietly sitting beside Tessie, her small fingers wrapped tightly around his thumb. The old man looked up at Ty then back to the little girl, "Near broke m' heart to hear her cries. You bring that good woman home where she belong—Mister Ty! We all needs her!"

For a moment Ty stared down at his niece; he felt a fierce protectiveness towards her. But he felt the same for her mother as well. Joseph was right—they all needed Augusta—and just then he realized, he might need her most of all! He swallowed back the lump in his throat as he slipped the Sharps into its scabbard. With quick long strides he went to the shelf that held ammunition.

"Joseph," he said, keeping his voice low, "pray for God to lead us to her—pray like only you can!"

Ty quickly slipped the boxes into his saddlebag, then ran a shaky hand through his dark hair.

"I'm ashamed of how I've treated her, and now just the thought of how Dewey might treat her, I—"

Joseph nodded solemnly. "Started prayin' the minute I come to, Mister Ty—you know that! But I can recall when you was a praying man too! But prayin' ain't gonna do you no good 'til you humble yourself before the Lord! Cause if things ain't straight between you and God, why, then everthin' else is crooked!"

The old man's words felt like a blow to Ty; he frowned but couldn't deny the truth of what Joseph said.

251

"Maybe it's too late to straighten things out. I used to be close to God, but that was a long time ago."

A hopeful light came into the old man's eyes. "All time belongs to God, boy, and so do you! I 'member the day you gave your heart to Jesus. And He don't turn you lose once your His! You may have forgotten who you belong to for a spell, but God never did. And it's *time* you start talkin' to the Lord again! And livin' for Him too!"

❧

Ty and Hitch followed the tracks of two riders heading straight for Denver; but the trail seemed too obvious and they soon grew suspicious. Sure enough they rode another mile and the trail went cold.

"They've backtracked Ty," Hitch groaned.

Ty took his hat off his head and slapped it hard against his leg, raising a cloud of dust.

"Just look at that, will you?" He swung his arm, indicating the massive mountain range. "We're gonna need a miracle to find them before dark! And—before that storm hits! Dewey knows this country—knows the foothills, every mountain pass, and every Indian trail. And worse, he knows every cave and water hole on both sides of these mountains."

Ty settled his hat back on his head with a firm hand and a look of disgust.

"We're not quittin'!" Hitch growled.

Surprised, Ty frowned up at his foreman. "Of course—we're not quitting! What's the matter with you?"

"Not...a...thing!" Hitch drawled defensively. He took in a deep breath and made himself admit the truth: "I reckon...yer right...except for an Indian...Dewey knows this country...better than anyone."

Hitch scanned in every direction, hoping to see a wisp of dust in the air. "He's a...cagey old fox! Could be...he's only lettin' us see...what he wants us to."

"Then we outfox him!" Ty hissed. "He's all but pointing the way to Denver—but I think it's a trick."

"Trick or no...I'm not stopping...not 'til I find her!" Hitch declared.

Ty frowned at his foreman again, then nudged Quest forward. "Have I said anything about stopping? I want her back as much as you do Hitch—maybe more!"

"I...doubt that," Hitch grumbled. "It's best you know...I'm gonna marry her."

Stunned, Ty sat back in his saddle. "You've asked her?"

"No...it's too soon just yet," Hitch muttered. "But I let her know...when she's ready...I'm the man!"

Hitch frowned when Ty looked at him as if he were crazy. Without another word he quickly turned his attention back to quartering the area, trying to cut Dewey's trail. But then the foreman added with his voice low, "The rich don't always...get the best o' things. It's good...that ya stopped being mad at her...but...she's gonna be mine!"

Suddenly, both men squared off at each other. They stared until, finally, Ty blew out a frustrated breath.

"We're wasting time!" he spat out. "So—go ahead and marry her—but we've got to find her first!"

Unexpectedly, Quest and Stormy nickered at a horse and rider thundering down the hill at a neck-breaking pace. It was Shep, and he was covered in dust and his mount was lathered and winded.

"Whoa—son!" Ty yelled. "What's happened? Looks like you just about rode that horse to death!"

"Had to—got—ta—tell ya!" Shep fought to breathe and talk at the same time. "Heard—'bout—Augusta!"

"I know you're fond of her," Ty said kindly, "but do you know something or did you just come to help?"

"No—I mean—yes. I know something 'bout—D-Dewey," he choked out.

Hitch handed the boy his canteen, and after Shep had taken a few swallows, he looked straight at Ty. "Boss—I know where he might take her! Or at least where they could hide out for a while—anyway!"

"Where?" Both Ty and Hitch bellowed.

"Dewey threatened to cut my tongue out if I told—but I ain't gonna let him hurt Augusta!"

Shep took another sip of water and wiped his mouth on his sleeve. "He's got a cave just beyond the south bend of Kettle Creek. We were out huntin', winter before last, and run out of food and ammunition. The snow was awful deep, and we was having a heck of time getting back to the ranch. Dewey had me wait at the top of the ridge and hold the horses. The next thing I knew he

253

had a saddlebag full of jerked beef, shotgun shells, coffee, and a jug a rotgut. But when we finally got back to the bunkhouse, he turned real mean. Said he'd skin me alive if I talked. I was already running a fever, so I just played it up a little! I talked kinda crazy and told him I didn't remember what he was tellin' me to forget!"

"You did just right, Shep! Then and now too!" Ty praised.

The boy suddenly seemed to stand a bit taller; he was flustered for a moment then went on, "I, uh…well, when Alvaro told me what happened I followed ya. When I saw all the tracks headed north, it come to me that Dewey might be faking a trail north just to throw ya off. The place where we stopped was south of the ranch. I reckon he's got him a cave full of supplies—'cause Alvaro said he didn't take any!"

"Shep," Ty asked, "do ya think you can find that spot—at least where you held the horses?"

"I know I can. It was just above an arroyo that cuts deep and leads down to the creek bed. There's a tree at the top—it got struck by lightning—split that big old tree right down the middle!"

A glimmer of hope passed through the men.

Ty gripped the boy's shoulder. "Thanks, son, you've brought the best news we've had all day!"

Chapter 35

Facing the Giant

"The Lord is my light and my salvation, whom shall I fear? The Lord is the stronghold of my life, of whom shall I be afraid?" Psalm 27:1

Dewey slowly picked his way through the dense timber of the Black Forest. Augusta trailed behind, thanking God that the trees here grew as thick as porcupine quills and were doing a good job of slowing them down. Still, she couldn't quite believe this was really happening to her. She strained her ears for the sound of riders coming to rescue her, but there was only the crunch of hooves stepping on dry pine needles, and the creak of saddle leather. And all around her was the ghostly forest song—a simple breeze gliding over pine boughs. Timothy had called it God's violin, a melody as old as time. Always before she'd thought the sound soothing, but now it seemed to whisper a warning.

When they were finally clear of the forest, Augusta slid from her saddle before Dewey could protest.

"My leg—the muscle's cramping!" she explained. "I have to walk it off!"

"Get back on that horse," Dewey growled.

Wincing with each step Augusta ignored him. "Please!" she moaned. "I'll be fine—in a minute."

Dewey stood up in his stirrups and checked their back trail. "A minute and no more!" he barked,

Augusta hated to lie, even to a man like Dewey LeBeau.

Forgive me Lord, she prayed, *you say when I am afraid I can trust in you. Well, I'm afraid Lord!*

"Hurry it up!" Dewey growled.

Augusta straightened; she would not give this man the satisfaction of seeing her fear.

"You know," she said trying to sound calm, "the men will come—you'll never get away with this!"

"Hah! Ya have no idea how much I've gotten away with already," Dewey bragged. "Besides, when Grainger finds out yer gone, he'll be the happiest man alive! He's been wantin' ta get rid of ya!"

To prove his confidence, he curled one leg around the saddle horn and began rolling himself a smoke.

Augusta couldn't help but wonder how Ty would feel when he realized she was gone. Things between them seemed so much better, but would he secretly be relieved? He'd told her he knew who Tessie was but still wasn't sure about her. Was that still how he felt? Slowly, she reached for her canteen, lifting it to her lips as she scanned the horizon. It all seemed strangely familiar, even though she knew she'd never ridden this far from the ranch.

Just then, she felt the goose flesh spreading down her arms. From the edge of the forest where she stood, a wide meadow—dressed in wild flowers— rolled out before her. Along the foothills strange jagged spires rose from the earth. They stood like dull red statues, carved by the hand of God. And looming behind these odd formations, stood a vast mountain range with an imposing peak in the center. Suddenly, she knew why it was all so familiar. She *had* been here before—in that one dream that had always become—a *nightmare*!

"Mount up!" Dewey growled. "You've rested long enough!"

Nodding mutely, Augusta stepped back into saddle. She was in the exact place where the nightmare always began. The beautiful valley with the giant peak in the distance!

"This can't be?" she mused, "—but it was!"

Dewey kicked up his mount and soon both horses were moving out at a ground-eating gallop. As in all her dreams, she was riding fast across the valley blanketed in a rainbow of flowers, and she was heading straight for the giant. The majestic mountain *did seem like a guardian of the Rockies*. She had thought it a dream's fancy to compare a mountain to a giant protector. And yet the likeness was there to be seen; the highest peak soared above timberline with a ridge that ran down the middle, like a patrician nose on a large and craggy face; the lower peaks and ridges rolled away like muscular shoulders and arms. She'd seen it—so many times before—and now, she was living her nightmare within a nightmare.

"Lord," she prayed, "I'm in terrible trouble! Please—help me!"

Just then an icy wind hit her full in the face; she looked up and saw a wall of black churning clouds breaking over the mountain like a tidal wave, as both horses crow-hopped and blew nervously.

"Don't get any ideas," Dewey roared. "—you best stay close to me!"

⸙

The three riders kept to the cover of the forest for as long as they dared, hoping to find but not overtake LeBeau and Augusta. They breathed a sigh of relief when they reached the edge of the forest and spotted the two bays racing across the meadow below.

"We've got to stop Dewey before he gets to that cave!" Ty hissed. "If we can at least wound him…"

Hitch nodded. "That's my thinkin'…he's not as likely…to hurt her…if he's in pain himself!"

Dismounting quickly, Ty handed his .50 caliber Sharps to Hitch, for he was the better shot.

Hitch took the rifle, taking note that the wind was growing more fierce every second. He rested the heavy gun on Ty's left shoulder and sighted down its length.

"Augusta," he mumbled through gritted teeth, "give me a little help, gal—pull away."

Finally, he triggered the gun, just as a blinding rain fell from the sky!

"You winged him—let's go!" Ty bellowed over the storm's sudden fury.

The men remounted their skittish horses, then Ty reached over and grabbed Shep by the arm. "Listen," he roared, trying to make himself heard above the buffeting wind. "Hustle back to the ranch—bring a dozen men to the lightning tree. Then search for the cave!"

Shep didn't waste any time; he simply nodded, and then disappeared behind a veil of silvery rain.

⸙

At first, Dewey didn't know if he'd been shot or struck by lightning. But he howled and cursed at the red-hot agony that burned through his right arm. The impact of the bullet nearly knocked him out of the saddle. But no matter what—he would never let the girl get away! Before Augusta could make any attempt to escape, he shoved his reins between his teeth, then reached down and took hold of her right rein in his left hand.

The horses ran on in terror as the lightning flashed and the icy rain stung them like shards of glass. In seconds they had reached the ledge at the top of the hill; quickly, Dewey pulled the horses up. They had stopped on the edge of a cliff overlooking a deep ravine. It was a sheer drop of more than twenty feet. Dewey seemed desperate as he dug his spurs into the gelding's side. They raced frantically along the ledge, the wind and rain pummeled them, while he searched for a pathway leading to the creek below.

As a wild bolt of lightning exploded right beside them—both horses reared up in terror. A tug of war ensued over control of the bay mare, with both Dewey and Augusta pulling in opposite directions. Confused and terrified, the mare reared up and twisted on her hind legs—but when she came down, her front hooves landed hard on the slippery edge of the cliff. Augusta felt the soil beneath them give way, and before she could jump free, she and the mare were tumbling over the precipice.

⚏

Ty yelled as loud as he could over the horrendous mayhem of lightning, wind, and rain.

"Hitch," he called. "We're going to lose them in this storm. Head south along the ravine—see if you can get a drop on them before they get to the cave. I'll follow from here—Augusta will try to get away in the confusion—I'm sure of it! If she does, she'll need help!"

Hitched nodded and reined Stormy south, while Tytus followed Augusta and Dewey up the hill.

Once on the ridge he saw Augusta struggling to get free. The sight unleashed a roaring fury within him, but suddenly the hairs on the back of Ty's neck rose, and the sound was so horrendous and the light so fierce, it seemed to shatter and break all around him.

Hours later, while the storm played itself out, Ty awoke, lying in the mud. He knew—that he hurt—but didn't know why. He forced his eyes to open, only to realize that Quest's still form was pinning his left leg to the ground. His first thought was that—he had failed Augusta! He hadn't any idea where Dewey had taken her. And quite possibly he'd ridden her beloved stallion to his death.

"Quest—" Ty groaned, struggling to sit up. "Hey, ol' man, Augusta needs us! We can't quit now!"

Ty fell back in the mud; his ineffective efforts had only produced a throbbing in his head.

"Please, God!"

The words caught in Ty's throat as a wave of regret and shame overwhelmed him.

"I've brought this about—haven't I, Lord?" he stammered. "If ever a child of God deserved Your chastisement—it's me!" Ty blinked up into the crying sky as he confessed: "My whole life I've nurtured hatred in my heart. And when Savannah added her rejection to my mother's—I wallowed in it like a pig in the mud. I'm ten times worse than either of those women. Because, knowing the pain of it—what did I do?—but reject Augusta and even little Tess! Oh, I saw my mother's and Savannah's arrogance and judgmental ways, but was blind to my own!" Ty felt the weight of his own sins bearing down on him as he cried out: "Lord, I forgive mother and Savannah! You've been so patient with me, while I've acted like a spoiled child. Savannah left because we were wrong for each other. And then You let me see what a good woman looks like—and like a fool—I treated her shamefully! I gave my heart to You, a long time ago, Lord, but I've failed You! I should have clung to You in my grief—instead I turned away. I've failed the men I should have had a witness before, and in my self-pity and arrogance, I've failed my brother and Augusta and Tessie!"

Ty buried his face in his hands. "Dear God, I can't bear it. I'm so sorry... please, forgive me! Lord, I'd gladly trade my life—for Augusta's!"

Ty didn't know how long he lay in the mud, confessing his sins and beseeching God for Augusta's life. But imperceptibly, like the rising of the morning sun, a warmth made its way into Ty's soul. He felt a peace he hadn't known for so long that he almost laughed out loud with the joy and the irony of it. He was lying in the mud with a brute of a horse on top of him, while a woman he cared for more than his own life was in terrible trouble. And yet he was filled with an inexplicable peace

All of a sudden, Ty felt a shudder pass through Quest. The animal groaned as if awaking from a stupor.

Tytus rose up again on one elbow and grinned up at the sky. "Thank—you—Lord!" he shouted. Then turning to the stallion, "Come on boy, you can do it!"

Quest groaned and lifted his great head, then he rocked back and forth trying to stand. Ty grimaced in pain beneath him, until finally; the stallion surged to his feet. Holding the reins in one hand, Ty grabbed the stirrup with the other. He hoped to use Quest strength to help him stand, for his left knee had been badly sprained. The idea might have worked but Ty's weight caused the wet saddle to slip under the horse's belly, dumping Tytus back onto the muddy ground in a heap.

"Easy, boy," he soothed, "eeee-zzyyy now ... "

Quest stilled but he braced all four legs apart, ready to bolt in any direction at the slightest provocation.

"Stand boy, stand..." Ty groaned as he pulled himself closer to the stallion's side.

"I'm trying to help you, partner. Just stand there and let me get that saddle off!"

Rolling up onto his hands and his one good knee, Tytus reached for the buckle on the cinch—and then the very thing he feared most—happened. There was a loud, zip and crackle in the air, as one last renegade bolt of lightning struck nearby. Terrified, Quest pulled away and reared, with the saddle clinging to his belly like an attacking enemy. He yanked the reins from Ty's muddy grip, then the stallion put his head down—and ran!

Chapter 36
Love Your Enemies

"I am sending you out like sheep among wolves. Therefore be as shrewd as snakes and as innocent as doves." Matthew 10:16

Augusta lay in the sand like a forgotten doll. She was unconscious of her peril or even of the storm that stalked from the valley on stilts of lightning. When she finally awoke there was a throbbing in her skull that mimicked a blacksmith striking his hammer on an anvil. Groaning, she peeked out from under her dark lashes, feeling confused. Then suddenly, it all came back to her, and she sat up in a rush.

"Dewey!" she hissed, only to have the world spin around her in nauseating circles.

As things settled, she realized the bay mare was lying beside her with a broken neck.

"Oh—I'm so sorry, girl." she whispered.

Gingerly, she put her hand to her own head, and when she saw the blood covering her fingers, the world took flight again, as an overwhelming feeling of panic gripped her—never had she been so afraid!

But just then, it was if she could hear her father's brogue as distinct as ever it was: "Shake it off A.C.—a bit of a fright ain't gonna kill ya now. Ya've got things to do. So—get on with it."

Augusta drew in a calming breath. "That's right A.C.!" she commanded, "Shake if off!"

With effort she straightened her shoulders and looked all around her.

"I've got to get away from here—I mustn't let Dewey find me!"

Though the throbbing grew worse with every step, Augusta forced herself to walk down the creek bed until the pain became unbearable. Finally, Augusta stared up into the sky and whimpered, "Please don't be angry with me, Papa! I just have to lay down and close my eyes—just for a minute."

Feeling desperate, Augusta spotted a stand of shaggy evergreens. Their heavy branches billowed out and draped down to the ground, like a fine lady's hoop skirt. Trembling, she crawled under the prickly branches, then laid her cheek against the velvety, cool sand. And though she fought to stay awake, her pain and fatigue soon won the battle, and she slept on as if she had nothing to fear.

⚡

Augusta awoke with a scream, as a hand clamped around her ankle and dragged her from her hiding place.

"Well—now—looky what I found!" hissed LeBeau's gravelly voice.

With one quick movement he pulled Augusta to her feet and gave her a hard shake.

"Gal, ya leave a trail like a skunk-bit coyote—a blind man could track ya!"

"No, please!" She winced, feeling as if her head might explode. "Please, Dewey, leave me alone!"

"You little strumpet," he cursed, "yer gonna pay fer fightin' me the way ya done! And ya kilt my bay mare ta boot! Now tear up that petticoat you're wearin', and wrap up this wound!"

Augusta did what she was told, but the moment she finished bandaging his mangled arm, Dewey tied and gagged her, then tossed her onto his saddle, and climbed up behind her. They rode down the creek bed for what seemed like miles and miles, when suddenly there came the loud crack of a rifle fire, and sand and water sprayed up before them like a geyser. The gelding slid to a stop then reared and snorted, just as a familiar voice called out: "Hold it—right there, Dewey—let her go!"

Augusta's terror quickly turned to relief, as she recognized Hitch's voice, then she looked up and thanked God for the sight of him! The foreman of the Bar 61 was looking down from the east ridge of the canyon. He stood tall, his legs braced apart, his rifle trained on Dewey.

"Slide off the back of that horse, LeBeau."

Dewey grinned up at the man, then with a mere flick of the reins, he pivoted the gelding hard to the left, putting Augusta directly in the line of fire.

"Well now, hot shot," LeBeau jeered. "Reckon ya'll have to shoot the gal—if ya want to get to me!"

Dewey spit a stream of tobacco, then made a show of leaning his chin on Augusta's shoulder.

Hitch cursed under his breath, and fought to control his temper—he hated Dewey just now, but he was furious with himself for jumping the man too soon. Still, somehow, he had to save Augusta.

"LeBeau, didn't figure...you was...such a coward! Steal an innocent woman—then hide behind her!"

"That's yer kinda thinkin', cowboy." Dewey mocked. "I treats women and chil'ren just like any other varmint that gets in my way."

Hitch grimaced. He had known Dewey to be a pretty rough character but he'd never caused any real trouble before. Now, however, he pegged the side-winding snake for what he was. Hitch was angry at his own impulsiveness, knowing it was Augusta that would suffer for it. It enraged him to see her treated like this: bound and gagged, clothes muddy, with her golden eyes brimming with tears.

"Tessie's fine!" he assured her quickly. "Joseph and Alvaro too...they'll... take good care of her."

Augusta closed her eyes and drew in a deep breath; slowly she nodded her thanks. He had known the one thing she most needed to hear.

"Well, now ain't that sweet!" Dewey sneered. "All right boy—you delivered your message. Skedaddle on back to the ranch and forget you ever saw us. The boss don't want this vixen. And her foolishness done kilt m' mare back yonder. She ain't been nothin' but trouble her whole life."

Hitch frowned at that, but wanted to keep LeBeau talking.

"How in blazes...would you know...what she's been like...her whole life?"

"Hah—I know a whole passel 'bout this lil' gal—know'd 'bout her fer years!"

Dewey tugged on the reins and the gelding began backing down the creek; he made sure to keep Augusta between himself and Hitch. Soon the cliff's overhang would give him the cover he needed.

"Got nothin' agin' ya, Hitch," he muttered. "But—I'm planning on cashin' in on this gal!" Dewey spit again then added, "Tell the others ya looked but didn't find her."

Hitch's face grew dark. "Dewey—yer talkin' nonsense. The rest of the men...will be here soon. Leave the woman and...I'll let you ride away."

Then Hitch's voice became fierce. "But—if you hurt her—you're a dead man, LeBeau."

"Ya always was stubborn as yer pet mule," Dewey scoffed. "All right, maybe we can work a deal—I'm warnin' ya though—she's bad luck." He grunted and made as if to slide off the back of the gelding.

Though Hitch never took his eyes from LeBeau, the man's next move caught him by surprise.

Still using Augusta as a shield—Dewey drew his left pistol and fired. Augusta sensed a trick and tried to make Dewey miss his shot by digging her heels into the horse's flanks. But she watched as Hitch fell backwards.

Instantly, LeBeau dug his spurs into the horse's sides. They ran flat out for a half a mile when suddenly LeBeau yanked hard on the reins, bringing the gelding to a sliding stop. Cursing, he raised his left arm and curled it around Augusta's throat, pressing so hard against her windpipe that she could barely breathe.

"I said ya was gonna pay for fightin' me, then ya tried to do it again—didn't ya now?"

Augusta shivered as the man's foul breath blew hot against her neck. She trembled as LeBeau reached up and pulled the gag from her mouth.

"Jes' you and me now—gal! None o' them men are comin'. Told 'em—I thought rustlers were gonna make off with the steers in the east pasture. They's all-miles away."

Augusta drew in a breath, "Y-you don't know—that you killed Hitch. And Tytus will come!"

Dewey lowered his head and whispered in Augusta's ear, "Gal, I never miss—Hitch is dead! And ya 'member that loud bolt a' lightnin' jes' before ya went over the cliff? Well, I seen that fancy horse a' your'n and that sorry Southern Unionist—they was both laid out 'n fried up—good and proper."

Augusta told herself not to believe it. But the panic she felt earlier was threatening to return in force.

Lo—rd...pl—ease! Please don't let this be true.

Though she thought it strange, a verse she'd been trying to memorize, suddenly popped into her head. "*God doesn't give us a spirit of fear, but of love and power and a sound mind.*"

Augusta closed her eyes and let the words steady her nerves, knowing that she never would have remembered this verse on her own. God *was* helping her, just when she needed it.

264

For hours, they rode on in silence, winding their way through the towering walls of the canyon. The afternoon sun painted the clouds in shades of copper and rust. And way to the north the last of the angry storm clouds released a brilliant shower of golden rain, as a double rainbow arched in the distance.

Tears pooled in Augusta's eyes and her arms ached to hold her child. Soon it would be Tessie's bedtime, and except for her short daily rides, Augusta had never been separated from her little girl. She prayed for Tessie to be safe and begged God not to let her daughter think that her mama had abandoned her, for she knew just how much that hurt!

Suddenly, she was jolted from her thoughts when she heard a bizarre noise coming from the north. Dewey cursed as the gelding began to crow-hop and blow nervously. Then what began as a distant rumble grew louder and louder, until it sounded as if a run-away locomotive was careening down the center of the ravine.

Dewey listened for a moment, then bellowed, "I KNOW THAT SOUND! IT'S A FLOOD!"

The gelding bolted in panic as Dewey let out a blood-curdling yell, "HAAAAA!" he roared. "THIS THING'S GONNA EAT US ALIVE!"

Augusta had never heard anything so horrendous as the sound of the flood waters as they roared down the canyon. They rode hard—searching for an outlet from the creek bed. Finally, Dewey spotted an antelope trail. The path was nearly straight up and down, but they had to take the chance. Augusta leaned as far forward as she could to help the horse keep his balance, while Dewey clung to her back, cursing and spurring the gelding on. The horse went down on his knees, then righted himself and dug his hooves into the soft, muddy ground, only to lose his footing again as he gasped for air.

The sound of the flood was terrifying, but nothing compared to the sight of it. Augusta screamed when she saw a great wall of brown, foaming water soar nearly twenty feet into the air as mud and debris crashed into the side of the ravine, then broke around the last curve. The angry, churning flood waters were only a few hundred yards away. Uprooted trees and branches were rolling towards them, all in a tangle—like bony fingers—they seemed to be reaching out, intent on taking hold and dragging them away.

As the flood waters came closer, Dewey slipped off the animal's back; he wrapped the gelding's long tail around his left fist, then wedged his shoulder under the horse's hind quarters. Pushing and lifting, LeBeau shrieked like a mad man. He bellowed and cursed and urged the horse to keep moving. Augusta could do nothing but hold on. Finally, with the lighter load and the man's help, the gelding made one last powerful lunge and managed to scramble up over the top of the ravine, dragging Dewey LeBeau, still shouting obscenities with him. Just as they made it to level ground, the tumultuous waters roared past them, devouring great chunks of the canyon walls as it passed.

Groaning, Dewey released the horse's tail and rolled onto his back while the spent gelding sucked in gulps of air, his muscles trembling like an aspen leaf in the wind.

Augusta too was beyond weary, but seeing her captor lying on the ground like a sack of meal gave her a spark of hope! Her thought was to quickly slip from the horse's back, and before Dewey could even think of moving, she would conceal herself in the cover of evening shadows.

Regrettably, she underestimated her own fatigue as well as the strength of her abductor. Stiff and clumsy from her fall, it took her two tries before she could swing her leg over the saddle. And before she had taken a step, Dewey was on his feet. In less than two strides he had grabbed her by the throat.

"If there weren't big plans for ya, gal," he threatened, "I'd toss ya in the river and be done with ya!"

He gave Augusta one hard shake then added, "Now, walk right beside me, or I'll beat ya half to death when we get to the cave!"

Augusta managed to keep up, nearly tripping over the man when he stopped short from time to time.

"This is it!" Dewey finally grumbled.

Too exhausted to care what happened next, Augusta watched as he pulled away branches that concealed the opening to a cave, then he grabbed her bound hands, drug her inside, and pushed her to the ground.

"Sit here and no more a-yer shenanigans! Ya hear me now?"

Trembling from the cold and pain, Augusta nodded mutely and wrapped her arms around herself. Through veiled eyes she watched Dewey strike a match, and was mesmerized by the arc of smoky light as it curved through the darkness. Then, a tiny flame flickered in the dark; it was just bright enough to illuminate the ring of stones neatly surrounding the perfect amount of dry kindling and sticks to start a quick and easy fire. There was even extra wood nearby to nourish it for many days. Augusta's curiosity was sparked along with the tongues of orange-red flames that licked hungrily at the dry wood. She drew close to the fire, then watched as Dewey pulled the bridle off the gelding's head and slapped his rump. The animal moved as if by habit towards the rear of the cave where a large stack of hay awaited him.

Augusta was puzzling it all out, when she realized Dewey was standing over her. She looked up to see him drawing a long knife from the scabbard on his belt.

"Arkansas toothpick," he taunted.

Then he reached down and cut the pigging string binding her hands.

"Tend to my horse and bring me the saddle!" he grunted.

His eyes were red-rimmed slits, and beads of sweat covered his brow as he moved to the opposite side of the fire, wincing as he dropped to his knees.

"Arm hurts like the dickens!"

Augusta watched him warily as she made her way to the gelding: took the saddle from the horse's back, and carried it to Dewey. Then, returning to the gelding, she rubbed his coat with handfuls of dry hay as she took in her surroundings. At first the dancing flames made strange shadows waltz about the cave walls, making it hard to focus. But as she grew more accustomed to the light, she found that Dewey had a wealth of supplies. There was a barrel of flour, another of meal, stacks of food tins and various crates lined up against the walls.

This isn't just shelter where a cowboy might take refuge. This is a robber's den—a hide-out!

When she looked back at Dewey, he was watching her, with cold gray eyes and a sneer on his lips. Augusta quickly turned away but her heart began hammering in her chest.

Lord? I don't know what to do. Please—tell me what to do—just tell me—and I'll do it!

Her promise had no more than left her thoughts when two words popped un-bidden into her head.

Help him!

"WHAT?"

The word burst from her lips before she realized that she'd spoken out loud.

"I didn't say nothin'," Dewey responded with a frown. Then he leered at her and added sarcastically, "But I reckon yer wantin' to know—*what*—could ya be doin' for ol' Dewey? 'Zat right?"

He cursed then shook his thumb towards the back of the cave.

"Got a few jugs a' 'who-hit-john' back thar by the haystack. Fetch me one and be quick 'bout it!"

Augusta hadn't heard of that before but could guess what it was. *Lord, please,* she begged as she spotted the jugs. *Surely, you don't really want me to help this man?* She waited for some sign to tell her what she was to do as she picked up a jug, and gave it a shake.

When she finally found one that was nearly full, the words to her least favorite Bible verse sprang to mind: *'Bless them that curse you, and pray for them which despitefully use you.'* Alvaro had told her to say it to herself every time Ty was especially ornery! She had wrestled with Christ's call to forgive and turn the other cheek for a long time, and now here it was again, like a burr she couldn't shake loose.

Lord, Dewey LeBeau is an evil man. You alone, know all he's done. Please don't ask me to bless—this man—of all men. I'll do anything else! But—please—not this.

Slowly, Augusta sat the jug beside Dewey LeBeau and backed away.

Glaring up at her, he slowly unsheathed his knife. "Got big plans fer ya tonight, little lady."

When Augusta's eyes grew large, Dewey snorted as if he had made a great joke.

The man's insufferable attitude infuriated Augusta but it also gave her courage. She turned her amber eyes to his blood soaked bandages, then said coolly, "LeBeau, if I don't cauterize that wound, the only thing you'll do tonight—is bleed to death."

Dewey sobered at her appraisal. "I'm bleedin' all right—like a stuck hog! Know how to fix it—do ya?"

"It's simple enough," she said, pretending a confidence she didn't feel. "But I'll only do it on one condition." She hesitated a moment, waiting for the Lord to change His mind. But—when a peace washed over her instead—she sighed and continued.

"God wants me to help you—but it's a pure waste to save a man's life physically and then let him die spiritually. So—I'll help you, but first I'll tell you about the gift God has for you."

Shocked by her words Dewey stared up at Augusta. Finally, he muttered, "Well now—if you don't beat all. Sure!" he slurred. "You can talk all ya want—while I get drunk!"

Augusta bit back a sharp retort—while LeBeau drank his fill of whiskey. Then she began to share what she had learned herself—not long ago.

"I knew very little about God—until I met Timothy. I didn't even know who Jesus Christ was! Didn't know that He was God's only Son, or that He was the Savior of the world." Augusta leveled her gaze at Dewey. "God knows everything about you, Dewey LeBeau, and yet—He's giving you this chance to make things right!"

Dewey ran his dirty hand over his prickly gray whiskers and eyed Augusta warily as she picked up the long knife he'd called an Arkansas toothpick. She continued to speak as she splashed whiskey over the long blade, then rolled it slowly back and forth over the flames.

"Since Adam and Eve," she continued, "we've all been born to sin. In a way we all have a price on our heads for the wrongs we've committed, and the penalty for our sins, is death! But God's son, Jesus came to earth as a man. He was the only man to ever live a sinless life! Jesus was perfect, He had no debts to pay, but He loved the rest of us so much that He paid the price for our sins. His death on the cross was Him dying for our sins, not His! He took our place! The miracle is, that no matter how bad we've been, if we confess our sins—if we're truly sorry for them and then ask Him to forgive us—He promises to do just that! We can all be born again into a whole new life here on earth and then He gives us an eternity of life with Him in heaven!"

Augusta's voice shook with her own sense of gratitude. "He makes it so simple. Just ask for His forgiveness and believe in His salvation, Dewey, and you can have a whole new life!"

Augusta saw a tremor in Dewey's hand as he reached for his jug; he hefted it to his shoulder and slurred, "Keep on a talkin', gal—I—uh—I ain't passed out yet."

"Dewey," Augusta said gently, "hell is a very real place! And it's every bit as real and terrifying as those flood waters this afternoon! God may have spared us both for just this moment—don't you see?"

LeBeau slammed the jug down and glared up at Augusta, his glassy eyes growing wild. "Twern't God—that saved ya from the flood! Twas ME. Me 'n my fine horse over yonder—we was the only ones that—ssssaved yer hide!"

Augusta sighed in frustration. "Dewey, a year ago, I was a simple naïve young woman who had been sheltered all her life, but I was still a sinner! And if I had died before asking Christ into my heart, I'd spend eternity in hell! And if you had died in those flood waters, hell is where you'd be, right now!" Augusta stared down at her hands; they were clasped so tight the knuckles were turning white.

"Dewey LeBeau, you are my worst enemy, you *are* my nightmare! But even so—I would not wish hell on you. Only God knows all the evil you've done. Neither you nor anyone else *deserves* God's forgiveness Dewey. But—He offers it to us anyway!"

Augusta gave the man a few moments to chew on her words. Finally, she added softly, "God is offering you an incredible gift—don't throw it away!"

The grimy old cowhand sat still for a long while, staring into the fire. He seemed actually to be pondering her words, but when he glanced up and saw Augusta watching him expectantly, his expression abruptly turned dark.

"Ya think I'm a lop-eared fool?" he cursed. "Think ya can sweet talk me or scare me into gettin' religion? I know ya jes' want me to let ya go."

Dewey sneered defiantly, then pointed his gun in Augusta's face. "You listen to me—you fine—Christian lady, if I die tonight—I'll be takin' ya with me! I'll put a bullet in ya the minute I feel myself slippin'!"

Augusta knew the man *had* been listening—she was sure of it—but whiskey and the devil owned him now. She looked down the barrel of his pistol and said in a soft but firm voice: "If you want me to help you—you'll put that gun away."

Dewey frowned and gave Augusta a puzzled look, as if he'd already forgotten it was in his hand.

"All—right," he agreed, "but leave it be—that un's got a hair trigger! I'll shoot ya iffen I have ta but yer mama'd have my hide if ya shot yerself. I'd sooner dance with a grizzly than tangle with her!"

Augusta froze. "My mama? You couldn't know her—I don't even know if she's still alive."

Dewey leaned back against the saddle. "Hah—she's alive 'n kickin'!"

As the whiskey loosened his tongue, he added arrogantly, "Lav—in—ea Wren—ford O'Brien. Ain't that yer ma?"

Swaying in Augusta's direction he added, "We been partners fer years—'n—I'm sick of it! But Vinny says she'll buy me out—jes' as soon as I bring ya ta Denver."

A sudden shiver ran through Augusta. "Why would my mother want me in Denver? She hates me!"

Dewey nodded his head. "Whew-eee, she hates ya all right! Like a cat hates water! Always complaining how ya ruined her life. But she's kept a bead on ya all these years. Bidin' her time 'til yer pa died. Then she found out ya had a husband that was an bringin' ya right ta—her door!" Dewey made a grab for his jug. "And once I get ya ta Denver, boy howdy—she's gonna make ya pay fer bein' born!"

Fear crowded Augusta's throat. "How is—she going to make me pay?"

"Your mama owns a high-class brothel in Denver—she's always planned for ya to work off yer debt—when ya got old enough. Reckon yer pa suspected such—that's why he married ya off to Grainger. But—he's dead too!" Dewey picked up the jug and belched loudly, then he turned to Augusta, slurring, "Yer bad luck, gal! All the men that ever cared 'bout ya—are dead! Ever—last one of 'em!"

Leaning close he whispered scornfully, "Bet ya think yer gonna get shed of me, 'cause I'm drunk. Well, jes' go ahead on and run, gal. Ya won't get far— and there ain't nobody out there lookin' fer ya—nobody."

Augusta couldn't bear it. With Timothy dead and Ty hating her, she thought things couldn't get much worse. But now, maybe Hitch and Ty were dead too. And then to learn that her mother still hated her—hated her enough to do such an evil thing—it was all too awful to bear. Never had she felt more worthless or more alone.

Dewey suddenly roused himself and grabbed her by the arm. "Hey, ya got me palavering like an ol' woman," he growled. "Stop stallin'—ya got doctorin' to do!"

Augusta nodded numbly, as she picked up the knife.

Dewey glared up at her then down at the blade that was now—white hot. "Stupid woman, don't wait too long." he bellowed. "Do it! Do it now!"

Augusta grabbed the end of the latigo strap and shoved it between his teeth. Quickly, she doused the wound with whiskey, and before she lost her nerve, she pressed the searing hot steal down on LeBeau's open wound.

Through clenched teeth the man let out a guttural howl as the smell of burning flesh enveloped the cave.

Quickly, Augusta slid the gun, and the knife out of Dewey's reach, then splashed more whiskey over his wound.

LeBeau spit the strap from his mouth and glared up at her, his eyes blazing with pain and hatred, as he let loose with a torrent of oaths and threats, and then to Augusta's relief, he passed out.

Though exhausted, Augusta knew she had to keep her wits about her and figure out what to do next! Then she saw the ragged veil of rain covering the entrance to the cave. She had no choice but stay where she was for the night.

"Lord?" she pleaded. "What do I do now?"

She waited but this time there were no words of wisdom, no scripture came to mind—nothing. Still, common sense told her, a strong man like Dewey wouldn't stay unconscious for long. Immediately, she began searching for something to tie the man up with, and then suddenly, her golden-brown eyes fell on a stack of crates in the corner. When she studied the black lettering more closely, a sly smile spread across her youthful face.

"Oh—thank you, Lord!" she whispered. "Maybe I'll get some sleep tonight—after all!

The wall of water picked him up and hurled him down the ravine—his arms and legs were caught up in a tangle of tree branches—he couldn't move, couldn't get free! He was being lifted high on the flood waters and carried straight into the fires of hell. Flaming hands were reaching for him as he cried out, "LORD ALMIGHTY!"

LeBeau awoke in a cold sweat as a fiery pain stabbed through his right arm. His head pounded with the familiar whiskey-induced headache, and the taste in his mouth was akin to dry ashes and muddy boots. Groaning, he tried to move his arms and legs, but when they refused to do so, he assumed he was tangled up in his blanket.

"You best be still," came a woman's soft voice. "If you keep thrashing, you'll only hurt yourself."

Still cocooned in a sleepy haze, Dewey pried his eyes open and took in his surroundings. He was flat on his back, in his own cave. The morning sun was shining through the entrance and bathing him in a golden warmth. All around him were the heady aromas of wood smoke, fresh coffee, biscuits, and bacon—topped off by the fresh scent of a new day after a night of hard rain.

Finally, Dewey's eyes focused with surprise on the dark-haired woman turning bacon over an open fire.

"Figured ya'd run, gal," he grumbled. "But here ya be—fixin' ol' Dewey a nice breakfast."

Augusta watched the man out of the corner of her eye. He yawned then, tried again to stretch. That's when he knew exactly why—she hadn't run.

LeBeau looked down in horror to find his body wrapped tight in a red shroud.

"What in tar-nation? Why—you sorry little—ya got me trussed up like a hog! Untie me *now* 'n be quick 'bout it!"

Augusta nearly laughed. "I'm not likely to undo all my hard work. And you'll stay that way, until I decide what to do with you."

She contemplated the situation while she dropped biscuit dough into the hot bacon grease. When each biscuit was golden brown, she split it open, and filled it with crisp bacon.

Setting a few biscuits beside Dewey she shook her head and glanced around the cave.

"I feel guilty eating stolen food! I know all these supplies came from the freight wagons you robbed." When the grubby man only scowled at her, Augusta gave him a wry smile, adding, "Of course, I'm sure the miner's in Cripple Creek would be pleased if they could see you bound up in the Union Suits that were supposed to keep them warm last winter! You know—if you hadn't stolen them—I never would have been able to tie you up so nicely. I'm sure that's one crime—you're regretting now!"

Dewey grumbled out a string of foul words, while Augusta set a cup of hot coffee beside him. It was no wonder he had awoken in a nightmare—he was bound up like a new ham in an old smoke-house. Still, he figured he'd bide his time until he could fetch the knife hidden in his...

"Hey" he demanded. "Woman, where are my boots?"

Augusta smiled. "I took them off," she muttered, "Thought that knife in them might be uncomfortable."

"Why you little trollup!" Dewey cursed. "The very idea—a lady binding me up in long johns."

Surveying his predicament he realized that his head was stuck through the trap door of one pair, with each arm through the legs of another. His right arm was tied up around his shoulder as if in a sling and knotted tight. He couldn't use his right arm or hand at all. Another pair was somehow looped around his left elbow, so he could just barely lift his hand to feed himself. His legs were bound up in similar fashion, with the sleeves and legs of red long johns tied and knotted this way and that.

"Ya should be ashamed!" he hissed. "Handling manly garments such as these. I say ya ain't no lady!"

Augusta could only roll her eyes at the man's insults. Lady or not she was grateful for those—unmentionables! After Dewey passed out she prayed for help and thought that God hadn't answered. Then her eyes fell on the crate of long johns. If they weren't a blessing, she didn't know what was. Nothing could have worked any better in restraining her captor!

Later, Augusta once again felt God's blessing, as she led the gelding from the cave. She was thrilled by the sight that greeted her. The whole country side was like a sea of sparkling glass, everything from the meadows to the foothills shimmered in the morning sun. Raindrops glistened on every leaf, every blade of grass, and it seemed as if the whole world were coated in diamonds. A pair of meadow larks sang out their distinctive flute-like call, while a dozen antelope grazed on the hillside. A sweet breeze came down from the mountains, brushing the wispy curls from her cheeks. Augusta looked up and found a canopy of sapphire blue with a scattering of cotton ball clouds. It was almost too beautiful! And—so very peaceful.

"Oh, Lord!" she breathed. "Thank You for this! How gracious You are to allow beauty to mix with hardship. It used to make me angry, but now I understand! You send us sights like this, that we might be strengthened for what lies ahead. To remind us, even in the middle of our troubles, that You do still care! I could have been killed a dozen times by now, but You've spared me. Thank You! Please spare Ty and Hitch too! Let them be safe and help us find each other and get back to Tessie!"

Augusta made short work of hobbling the gelding in the grassy meadow. Then she began her search, by walking along the edge of the ravine.

Augusta had Dewey's pistol, but no bullets—she hadn't been able to loosen his gun belt—it seemed to be rusted in place. It didn't matter; she had the pistol, his knife, and his Sharps.

Knowing full well it was a risk, she decided to send up three shots as a call for help. The Sharps was awfully heavy, but thanks to Timothy, she knew how to use it. She loaded it easily enough, but it took a number of tries before she was able to pull the hammer back. Struggling, she finally raised the cumbersome rifle, just barely managing to point the thing to the sky, before squeezing the trigger. The air exploded around her, while the recoil kicked like a bad-tempered mule. Augusta was stunned to find herself lying flat on her back, gasping for breath!

"Ohhh, that hurt!" she moaned as she struggled to sit up.

The jolt plus the ear-shattering noise set her head to throbbing again, but when tears threatened, she hissed, "Get on with it, A.C., it has to be three shots!"

Again, she loaded the gun, then pulled back on the hammer until it clicked into place. This time, however, she braced the stock firmly on the ground, pointed the barrel straight up, leaned away, then—cautiously—squeezed the trigger. The gun bucked violently in her hand and the noise made her head feel like it might just split wide open, but she'd done it!

"One more time," she ordered with a grimace.

Quickly she re-loaded, cocked, then triggered the gun!

The final shot sounded louder than the first two put together, and now her ears rang like church bells. The shots had been a dangerous gamble. They could bring help, or just as easily fetch more trouble. After all, the world was full of rogues, and she was a woman alone, in a land full of woman-hungry men.

Augusta shook off the thought; she knew at least two *good men* who had come looking for her. Now she needed to find them—they might even be in need of her help! Putting her fingers to her lips she whistled loudly. The piercing sound hurt her head, but it also carried for miles, so she'd walk and whistle and then stop and listen. But there was only the faint echo of her own melody as it ricocheted against the canyon walls. Finally, she gave up and turned back to check on the gelding and her prisoner.

Suddenly, in the distance she heard a whinny; at first she thought she'd imagined it. Then it came again. It was a distant but familiar call that wound its way between the spear-shaped pines.

"Oh, Quest..." Augusta breathed, then she let out the loudest whistle she could muster. And there it was again. It was Q's own unique call—it sounded weak—but it was him!

Augusta walked along the ravine until she found her stallion caught between two large boulders and a tangle of prickly scrub oaks growing dangerously close to the raging flood waters.

"Hey, boy," she said calmly, "easy now—I'll get you out of there."

When he heard Augusta's voice Quest lowered his head and began murmuring to his mistress.

The horse was in a pitiable state: he was encrusted with mud—and his saddle, the blanket, and both reins—were all in a jumble around his legs and knotted around a thicket of brambles. He could neither paw at the ground nor raise his head, for the branches as well as his own tack held him captive.

Quickly, she set both guns on the ground. Then using LeBeau's knife she began the arduous task of freeing the horse from all that held him fast. But seeing Quest like this only increased her fears for Ty.

Oh, Lord, if Quest is in this mess—where on earth is Ty? Please protect him and help us find each other!

Once she'd freed Quest, she led him along the ravine and continued to whistle and call for Ty and Hitch. But as the sun began to slide toward the mountains, Augusta suddenly remembered that she left the guns and Ty's saddle back in the bushes. Mortified by her own carelessness she quickly mounted Quest bareback and hurried to retrieve them. But when they finally got near the place where he'd been trapped, Quest grew anxious, he blew loudly, and side-stepped.

"I don't blame you, boy," Augusta soothed, "but we need that saddle, and the guns."

She nudged her stallion forward, but when he had taken only a few steps, a meaty hand suddenly snaked out from behind a boulder and grabbed Quest's reins.

"Augusta screamed in terror as Dewey LeBeau appeared before her like a phantom. He glared up at her, his hate-filled eyes were red rimmed—a mix of pain, and anger, and last night's drunk.

Hello, vixen—have ya missed me?"

Immediately, she pressed her heels against Quests side, and yanked on the reins, intent on getting away. But Dewey's hold was too powerful to break. Then Augusta looked into his blood-red face and saw that a blind rage was fueling his strength.

"So ya thought ya'd leave ol' Dewey as helpless as a new babe—zat what ya thought? Stupid woman, didn't think I'd have more weapons in that cave?"

When LeBeau shook the reins, Quest twisted and tossed his head; as he backed away, with eyes wide and nostrils flaring. The stallion tried to pull free while Augusta could do nothing but tangle her fingers in his mane and hang on. Each time Quest took a step back, it brought them closer to the edge of the ravine and the still rapidly-moving flood waters. Suddenly, a wave splashed high against Quest's flank and the terrorized stallion jumped forward, believing yet another enemy was attacking him.

It was then—without warning—everything changed. The powerful stallion stopped retreating and became the aggressor. He shrieked like a war horse, and with head down and ears flat against his neck, he opened his mouth and charged at LeBeau. Somehow, Dewey moved just in time, but not before he felt the stallion's hot breath and the glance of his teeth against his throat. Clamping down on LeBeau's shirt collar, Quest tossed his head, throwing the man to the ground and ripping the shirt from his back.

Now, it was Dewey's turn to know terror! He scrambled back, fumbling wildly while trying to free his knife from its scabbard. His right arm was useless and his left hand refused to obey. In a panic, he gave up on his knife and picked up a heavy club-like branch. Regaining his feet he swung at Quest, frantically trying to protect himself.

Augusta, seizing that moment to escape—yanked on the reins and kicked hard! But Quest paid her no more mind than if she'd been a fly on his back. At first, Quest had wanted to run from the man he hated. But now, as hot blood raced through his veins, all he wanted to do—all he could do—was *fight*! In a savage fury, Quest lunged once more for LeBeau's throat. Dewey evaded him, but when Quest came at him again, LeBeau stepped back and swung his club as hard as he could, landing a blow full force across the stallion's jaw. Quest squealed in pain, and shied away, momentarily stunned. Dewey dropped the club and unsheathed the long knife hanging from his belt and sprang towards Quest. But the man's last blow made the stallion more guarded. Quest side-stepped and reared when LeBeau's long blade slashed out in a wide arc. Instinctively, the horse rose up on his hind legs, clawing at his enemy with his sharp front hooves.

The clash between man and beast continued with Augusta desperately clinging to Quest's back like a shadow—afraid to jump free lest she get trampled underfoot, or worse yet, allow Dewey the chance to take her again. Tenaciously, she hung on until her hands cramped. Then as her strength ebbed away, she felt her body slipping from Quest's back.

"I've got you!" growled a deep voice.

Augusta felt a strong arm curling around her waist. She turned to see a face she knew so well. It was Timothy's face, and it was Ty's. The man was filthy, his dark features were drawn, and his expression was fierce. And yet to Augusta, Tytus Grainger had never looked more wonderful!

Ty hauled her up against his side, half carrying, half dragging her. She could tell he was limping badly, but somehow, he managed to move her out of harm's way. The moment he settled her on her feet, she gazed up at him.

"Tytus...thank God!" she breathed, and then quickly added, "Wait here—I've got his Sharps in those bushes!"

Without another word she hurried away and brought the rifle to Ty, while the battle between Quest and Dewey raged on. Both man and horse were now mud splattered and bloody. Just then Quest reached out with one powerful hoof and clipped LeBeau's hand, his knife flipping end over end, until it landed at the very edge of the ravine.

Dewey hollered and threw his arms in the air, trying to frighten Quest even as he backed away, then he turned and ran for the knife. He slid to his knees at the water's edge where the blade teetered for a moment, then disappeared into the muddy waters.

Dewey spun around to find Quest bearing down on him. He had only enough time to double his fist and slam it into the stallion's tender muzzle.

Quest shrieked with pain and staggered back.

It was then Ty cocked the rifle. "It's over, Dewey!" he shouted as he leveled the gun at LeBeau's chest.

Augusta hurried to Quest, grabbed the reins with one hand, and placed the other on the horse's withers.

And while she worked to calm her stallion, LeBeau put his hand up and gasped for air.

"All—right, boss—all right," he panted, "jes' keep that devil away from me!"

The man wheezed and coughed as his cold gray eyes watched Augusta leading the dark stallion away.

"Catch your breath, LeBeau!" Ty ordered. "I want to know, what's all this about—why did you do this?"

Before Dewey could speak Augusta called out, "Ty, he has a cave full of supplies! I think he's the one who's been attacking the freight wagons! He's probably the rustler too!"

When Dewey glared at her, Ty growled, "Sounds like you've got a lot to explain, LeBeau. And it had better be the truth or she'll turn that stud loose, and we'll both watch him rip your throat out and toss you into that river!"

Ty took a step closer to Dewey, then added, "But if you talk straight, I'll take you to Denver and you can have a fair trial—before you hang."

Dewey glared at Ty then Augusta—he hated them both! But he had never hated anything like he did that stallion. He could still feel that animal's hot breath and the graze of his teeth against his throat.

"All right," Dewey sneered. "But we ain't in Denver yet. Maybe I will hang—someday—maybe I won't!" Then he glared at Ty, adding, "And—maybe it's 'bout time I set ya straight! Sure, I hit the freight wagons and I've rustled yer beef. Ya never seemed to wonder why I liked to work the cattle in that lonely stretch in the north pasture." Dewey laughed. "Me and m'partner have done jes' fine over the years."

Ty took another step closer, keeping the gun trained on LeBeau. "Who's your partner?" he demanded.

A cynical smile crossed LeBeau's lips as he shook his dirty thumb towards Augusta. "That gal's mama! She's been my partner in all of it—if I hang—I'll make sure she does too!"

Ty's gaze went instantly to Augusta, confused when she didn't deny it but stood with eyes downcast.

Dewey noticed Ty's puzzled expression and wondered if he still might work this to his own advantage.

"Ya know, boss—yer all banged up!" he said smoothly. "Why don't ya ride that fancy stud back to the ranch 'n let the Spaniard doctor ya up? Ya don't want this gal—I'll make sure she don't trouble ya ever again!" He scowled at Augusta then added, "No one'll ever know—tell the men she fell off a cliff 'n broke her neck. I'll make it so ya can be done with her, once 'n for all."

Ty glanced at Augusta once more and saw her shudder at LeBeau's words.

Encouraged by Ty's silence, the grubby man kept talking. "She ain't yer lookout—no how! Ya've hated her—her ma hates her too. Jes' hustle on back to the ranch. No one'll be the wiser!"

LeBeau's words enraged Ty, but he wanted to keep him talking, so he clenched his jaw until it ached.

"I'll think on it." He muttered then asked, "So, how did her mother come to be your partner?"

Dewey scratched the thick growth of beard on his chin, then he eyed Grainger, all the while figuring how he might just talk himself close enough to make a grab for the gun.

"Well now," LeBeau grumbled as he took a step closer to Ty. "Met Vinny back in Georgia. She's a pure wonder—that'un. Knows a thousand ways to make money! She's rich—mostly, from rustled beef and fancy houses. Now all she wants is revenge—and she'll stop at nothin' to get it!"

When Dewey noted Ty glancing towards Augusta, he took another step closer, then jeered, "And that gal ain't no better'n her ma. Ya been right 'bout her all along." Leaning towards Ty, he added slyly, "The sorry truth of it—yer brother'd be alive today—if he hadn't married up with *her*."

Augusta felt thunderstruck. Dewey hadn't said anything about Timothy before, only her mother.

Still inching closer to Grainger, Dewey added, "Lavenia's the kind that needs payback! She hated the Grainger's, so we took Bar 61 beef cause yer family thought they were better'n hers, back in Georgia! She hated her daughter—said she ruined her life. Calls it 'poetic justice', making her girl work off her debt in one of her mama's fancy houses." Dewey snickered scornfully. "Mother's love…ain't it grand?"

Ty pointed his rifle at Dewey's chest and commanded, "Tell me—what did you mean when you said Tim would be alive today, if he hadn't married Augusta?"

Augusta stared at Dewey, not wanting to hear and yet needing to know what she had done.

LeBeau shrugged as he gauged his chances of taking his Sharps from Ty's firm grip. How he'd slam his boot into Ty's swollen knee then turn the gun on him and fire! But then again, Tytus Grainger was a powerful man.

"LeBeau!" Tytus growled, "What did all this have to do with my brother?"

Dewey wiped his sleeve across his face—few men were as quick and agile as Tytus Grainger! He suddenly wasn't so sure of his plan, not to mention the fact that Ty had two good arms to his one.

"Well, twas like this, boss," he groaned. "Vinny got word that her husband had finally died and that this gal had done married a man—by the name o' Grainger. Then she heard they was headed to the Bar 61. Vinny thought it quite a joke! She'd already been rustlin' yer beef. And now yer brother was bringin' her daughter right to her, makin' it all so easy! The plan was to take her jes' before they got to the ranch, figured yer brother'd pay a hefty ransom. But when I went to get that little snippet, that loco stud made a lunge for me and ended up knocking her silly—I couldn't get to her. 'Course after that, with yer brother dead, 'n you hatin' the gal, Vinny had to give up the ransom idea. She told me as soon as the baby was weaned I was to nab the woman, hide out fer a spell, then bring her to Denver."

Tears of shame filled Augusta's eyes.

Timothy, why didn't you listen to me and annul our marriage? You'd be alive—if it weren't for me!

Dewey's cold gray eyes studied Ty closely. He knew Grainger had a temper. If he riled the man up—made him lose control—he'd have a better chance of turning the tables on him.

"Ya know," LeBeau said smoothly, "twas never meant for yer brother to get hurt! Them two fools was supposed to keep him busy while I got the gal. Guess he must have jumped 'em 'n got shot?" Dewey rubbed the back of his neck as he glanced away. "That's the only way I can figure it."

Ty's face grew dark, as he swallowed back the bile rising in his throat. Deeply etched into his memory was the sight of his brother's body and two other men lying dead in the sand. He had always believed that there was a fourth person there who had shot both Timothy and one of the other men. It hadn't made sense that it was Augusta *and yet she was the only other person there, or so he had thought—until now!*

But by his own account, Dewey had admitted to being there while Timothy was still alive. Finally, he knew without a doubt who had killed his brother!

Suddenly, a rage like nothing Tytus had ever known consumed him. His blood grew hot and thick in his veins, and his heart thundered in his chest. Dewey LeBeau had killed his brother and Ty wanted only one thing—and that was to tear this man apart with his bare hands.

Augusta watched the two men. She could plainly see what Dewey was trying to do, just as she saw the violent storm cloud of pain and loathing spread across Ty's face. She had to stop him, but before she could speak, Ty flung his rifle aside and lunged at the man who had killed his brother.

Immediately, LeBeau dropped to one knee and pulled a dagger from his boot. His lips curled in a malicious grin as he swung his blade. Ty jumped back but not before the knife slashed him from belt to shoulder. Before Dewey could attack again, Ty grabbed for the knife. The razor sharp blade sliced a trail across his right palm in the scuffle. He swallowed the pain, then with gritted his teeth, he clamped both hands tightly around Dewey's wrist. They struggled and fought for the knife, until finally Ty was able to slam Dewey's fist against the side of a boulder, knocking the dagger free. An instant later Ty rolled his left hand into a powerful fist, reared back as far as he could, then launched his knuckles into LeBeau's ample nose. The punch came up from the ground, and knocked the man flat on his back.

Grainger looked down on Dewey, his muscles corded and his hands still clenched into brawny fists. "Get up, you devil! Alvaro had you pegged right. I'm not nearly finished with you—get up!"

When Dewey made no effort to stand, Ty yanked him to his feet. Still trembling with rage he brought his fist back again but stopped when he heard Augusta cry out.

"Tytus no—please! He's not worth it. Let the law and the Lord deal with him."

Her gentle voice and wise words broke through his rage—the way light breaks through darkness.

Tytus dropped LeBeau in the dirt; then abruptly turned away, even as a red-hot fury pulsed through his veins. Augusta had stopped him from giving the cur what he deserved. But his powerful hands were still knotted into fists, as he glared down at the loathsome creature who had taken his brother's life.

Augusta looked at Tytus and trembled.

He's the dragon again—full of fire! He has to blame me too—for I'm nearly as guilty as Dewey.

Tytus stood with chest heaving, trying to get himself under control, then he looked at Augusta and saw the fear in her eyes. When he realized that he— not Dewey—was the cause, it shook him to his core.

Forgive me, Lord, revenge is for You, not me. I'll take LeBeau to jail and—I'll leave him to You.

Dewey watched the storm in Grainger's face subside, then he got to his feet, spitting blood and cursing.

"Like I said gal—yer bad luck. Ya've brought folly on every man that's every know'd ya. It's no wonder yer ma hates ya so!"

Augusta listened to the man's vile words, then she dared to glance to-wards Ty. His dark rage seemed to have passed but she could only assume that he was agreeing with Dewey, for he said nothing.

In her misery—Augusta had all but forgotten her horse. And yet—all this while—the dark stallion had not once taken his eyes from the man he hated—hated from the first time he had breathed in his scent With his lungs still burning from their earlier battle, Quest arched his muscular neck and sniffed the air, finding it heavy with the scent of his enemy and the fearful smell of blood. His first instincts had told him to run! But also—beating within the heart of every stallion—was the passion to fight his enemy.

As Dewey strutted about cursing and carrying on; Quest suddenly gave a loud snort and jerked free of Augusta's grasp. With head down and ears flattened against his neck, he charged like a roaring bull, headlong into LeBeau's body. Then with seeming ease, the stallion tossed the man into the sky, as if he were nothing more than a rag doll. It happened so quickly, LeBeau hadn't time to run or even cry out. The only sound was that of air rushing from his lungs as he disappeared over the edge of the ravine.

Stunned, Augusta and Tytus could do nothing but watch, as the flood waters coiled around Dewey's body like a muddy serpent, and then—carried him away.

Chapter 37

The Cave

"Surely it was for my benefit that I suffered such anguish. In your love you kept me from the pit of destruction." Isaiah 38:17

As they led the gelding and Quest back inside the cave, another storm hit the valley with a vengeance.

"I'll tend to the horses," Augusta offered softly. "That knee of yours won't hold you up much longer. And the minute I get back—I am going to dress those wounds!"

Ty grunted and rolled his eyes; he'd already told her he was fine! Then he glanced down at his torn shirt and the bloody handkerchief wrapped around his fist. He knew he must look as if he'd been run over by a herd of buffalo, and that's how he felt. But he'd always been as strong as an ox—and he was determined to make the rest of this miserable encounter easier on Augusta in any way he could.

Earlier, while they were walking to the cave, Ty had covertly taken in her state. She'd had a rough time of it; her clothes were torn and muddy, her gait was stiff, and there were smudges of lavender under her eyes and bruises on her cheek. Her slight body trembled from the cold, yet she tried to hide it all, and made no complaint. Instead, she'd thanked him for coming after her and fretted over his wounds.

Gazing around the cave Ty decided what Augusta needed most, right now, was a good fire! He set right to work and his efforts were rewarded by the expression of pure bliss on Augusta's face when she hurried to the fire, held out her hands, closed her eyes, and breathed in the delicious warmth.

When Augusta turned to thank Ty for the lovely fire, a tenderness twisted in her heart when she watched this big man, who had always radiated such power and agility, stiffly easing his large frame to the cave floor. He tried to hide it but the pain and exhaustion clung to him like a heavy coat.

Quickly, she stepped to his side. "Here now," she chided, "you must let me help you!"

As Ty stretched out his long limbs, Augusta pulled at the rip she saw just over the knee of his buckskins. "You didn't just twist your knee—you've got a nasty gash there!"

Tytus roughly brushed her hand away. "Don't coddle me, Augusta—it's just a scratch," he grumbled.

Augusta's dark eyes suddenly blazed like the flames dancing in the fire. "Tytus Grainger, I may only be half Irish, but I can recognize *blarney* when I hear it! You are exhausted and in pain, and you're only being foolhardy not to let me help you!"

When she stubbornly continued to poke and prod—he tried once more to stop her, but she frowned and slapped his hand away. The slap amused Ty; he was relieved to see this ordeal hadn't broken her spirit. He knew LeBeau's cruel words had hurt her. Then he remembered with shame all the cruel things he had said this past year—and yet, here she was—determined to take care of *him*.

Her concern touched him more than he wanted to admit and he couldn't seem to drag his eyes away from her. Augusta was muddy and bruised, and he couldn't imagine her being any more appealing than she was at this moment. He knew it was partly the relief he felt knowing she was safe. And partly, it was the gentle way she held his large hand, and the way she bit her lip in concentration. Ty fought down the desire to pull her into his arms and hold her close! He wanted to comfort her and be comforted by her! He wanted to promise her that he would never let anything so frightening happen to her—not ever again.

Tytus would always wonder why his brother hadn't told him about Augusta. But it was easy to see how she could have changed Timothy's mind about marriage, for she was *exactly* the kind of woman Tim had always wanted. Of course, it also occurred to Ty that Augusta was the kind of woman he had always wanted too. A sweet feminine woman who would love his ranch, share his excitement over the birth of a spring foal and turn his hacienda into an inviting home. He couldn't deny it any longer—he was in love with…Augusta!

Just then the woman sat back and clucked her tongue. "If I'd seen this *scratch* yesterday, I would have put a few stitches in it!" Then she shook her head. "But now—I think it best to give it a good cleaning and leave it alone."

Tytus grunted his hearty approval, for leaving it alone.

"Honestly, woman!" he grumbled, "I don't want or need *all this fuss!*"

Ty regretted his harsh tone the moment the words left his mouth. He felt even lower when he saw the hurt in Augusta's eyes. As a young southern gent, he had known how to be both tactful and charming. Well, he was obviously out of practice. Still, he knew that even if his words were all wrong, his only desire was for this sweet woman to forget about him and get the rest he knew she needed!

Finally, when nothing either tactful or charming came to his mind, Ty simply muttered: "I, uh, guess all I want…is some rest right now Augusta. And that's what you need too!"

To make his point, he pulled his hat down over his face and folded his arms over his chest.

Augusta struggled to fight back her tears. It wasn't any wonder he didn't want her touching him. Ty had every right to go back to hating her—blaming her for Timothy's death. She blamed herself—why shouldn't he? But she could be just as stubborn! It was her fault that he was wounded—and she was going to help him—*even if she had to tie him up in red long johns to get it done!*

Augusta braced herself, then lifting Ty's hat, she peeked under the brim, and spoke with a stern voice, "You go right on and pretend to sleep if you like. But I'll be hanged if I allow your wounds to grow septic just 'cause you don't like me right now and you feel like being a grumpy old dragon again!"

Then before dropping his hat back into place, she added, "And that's the end of it! Do you hear me?"

Ty's lips lifted slightly and he gave a shrug. "Oh, I hear ya, ma'am. And if you say that's the end of it…" He gave a bit of a chuckle then added, "Then who am I to argue?"

Augusta let out a sigh of relief; his slight smile and chuckle had confused her but at least it seemed he meant to cooperate and that was all that mattered. Quickly, she turned away, flipped her skirt back, then tore up the last of her petticoat for bandages.

When the woman didn't instantly start poking at him, Ty's curiosity got the best of him. He tipped his hat back just enough to catch a fleeting glimpse of velvety skin around a shapely leg before he retreated back under the wide brim of his hat.

After making as many bandages as she could, Augusta reached for Ty's hand, and although she couldn't see his face, she could tell he was clenching and unclenching his jaw. The man had never been easy to read, but from the moment he had pulled her from Quest's back hours earlier, his expressions had ranged from outright disgust to tender compassion! And this silly tension between them was making her crazy.

Shaking off the friction in the air, Augusta reached for the jug of whiskey.

"Tytus," she whispered gently. "I'm sorry—but—this is going to sting."

Ty watched her face as she slowly poured the liquid over his leg wound and outstretched hand. Then she soaked a cloth and cleaned the gash that went across his chest.

If there was pain, he paid it no mind, but his face grew tender when he saw Augusta wincing for him. When she looked up to gauge his discomfort, and noted only his tender smile, she became self-conscious and confused. Quickly, she turned her attention back to his wounded hand but could still feel his gaze upon her. She didn't know what to make of this. Where was the dragon?

Augusta suddenly found herself boldly studying Ty's dark eyes, and for a time neither one was able to look away. Impulsively, she placed her hand lightly against his cheek.

Ty flinched at her touch and sucked in a breath; her hand felt small and cool against his rough beard, and yet he felt like he'd been burned! It was a painfully sweet moment. And like lightning there was a jolt of attraction that raced between them, and they both felt it.

Finally, Augusta blinked and tore her eyes away, then she spoke softly: "Tytus, you don't seem to have a fever but, your eyes—they—well, I think you do have a concussion. It's important for you to stay quiet and rest. It was kind of you to build the fire, but for the time being, you should let me do things like that."

Immediately, she had Ty's full attention; slowly he lifted one eyebrow. "I see! So, you think this ordeal has been harder on me—than it's been on you?"

Knowing men could be prickly about such things she knew she had to put her words just right: "Well? Dewey said you were *struck by lightning*! And—you mentioned on the way here that *Quest fell on you*! You had to have spent last night out in the rain! You've had a fist fight and then a knife fight!"

Augusta shook her head as if to add it all up in her mind then blurted out, "Of course you've had it harder than me! Just look at yourself? I don't know where to put the next bandage. From head to foot, if you aren't scratched and bleeding, you're black and blue. And—I know—it's all my fault!"

Augusta stared down at her hands, feeling horrible for all she'd put this man through.

Ty's heart squeezed. Her sweet outburst of concern touched him more than anything he'd heard in a long time. Very carefully, he curled one finger under her chin then lifted it until she was looking up at him.

"None of this—is your fault! Not what happened to Tim, or to any of us yesterday or today!"

Then a playful twinkle sparked in his dark eyes as he added, "But—by the way you tell it—I must look pretty rough!" Then he added cheerfully, "Of course, you look like you've just arrived at a church social!"

Augusta drew back, then realized he was teasing, just as laughter rumbled from his chest and his grin deepened. She blinked and then blushed—when she saw it—that wonderful Grainger dimple.

She glanced down at her own ragged appearance and then back to Ty's tender smile.

"Papa would have said, 'You two look like you've been rode hard and put up wet!'"

Ty nodded his agreement. "That's an all-too accurate description of what's happened to us!"

Augusta shyly busied herself by adjusting Ty's bandages. When she looked up she found him watching her again. She felt a warmth spread through her— everything between them was going to be all right!

"Tytus?" she asked as her heart filled with wonder. "You've—finally accepted me—haven't you?" Augusta sat back on her heels and studied the man before her. Ty grew serious and nodded his head.

"Why now?" she asked, "You heard the proof today that Timothy might be alive but for me. All this misery was because my mother wanted to punish me. Why don't you hate me? Now that you have good reason!"

Ty's face was a picture of misery and regret as he answered her question.

"Augusta, I've never had any reason to hate you. We know now who's to blame, and it was not you!"

When he took in Augusta's uncertain expression, he added quickly, "But, I've given you reason to hate me! What was it you called me? A grumpy old dragon—that's about right. I've been mean and unfair to you. Still, through it all you've handled yourself so well!"

Ty lowered his head and said softly, "Actually, I thought lately, the two of us had been making progress! And then that scoundrel, Dewey steals you away and feeds you a pack of lies!"

Ty's expression was filled with remorse when he added: "You were under my protection and I should have kept you safe. Listen," he asked gently, "I need to know: did he hurt you? Are you truly all right?"

Augusta suddenly realized that Ty had taken her hand, and she couldn't seem to find her voice.

"Come here..." he whispered, as he pulled her close. Very gently, he cupped her chin in his hand. There were bruises under the dirt on her cheek and dried blood on the back of her head.

Tytus sucked in an angry breath. "Did Dewey do this? Did he? Listen, I want to know what's happened to you since I saw you last?"

Augusta blinked up at Ty, surprised by his protective, even possessive tone. She shook her head. "Dewey LeBeau is—was—a hateful man; he made threats and said a lot of cruel things. He slapped and threatened me, but that's all!" she assured him.

Lifting her hand to the back of her head, she explained, "I got this from Dewey's mare; she kicked me when we fell off the cliff. But—I'm fine now, really!"

Tytus frowned at first and then he couldn't stop a low chuckle from rumbling inside his chest.

"Oh, Augusta, I'm not even half Irish, but even I know blarney when I hear it!" He rolled his eyes heavenward and repeated her matter-of-fact statement: "Oh this, it's nothing—my horse just *kicked* me in the head as we were *falling off a cliff!*"

Augusta stifled a giggle then shrugged her shoulders over Ty's surprising attitude. The dragon himself was smiling and teasing her. Things had gotten better between them but she had never expected this.

"The point I was trying to make," she explained as Ty watched her with eyebrows up and arms crossed, "is that it's over now and I am fine! Even when I was in the cave with Dewey I knew God was helping me! And to be honest, the sooner I forgive and forget Dewey LeBeau—the better!"

"I still think he got off too easy!" Ty grumbled. "But I guess he's already paying for his sins!"

Augusta nodded sadly. "It may sound strange, but last night, God told me to help Dewey. So, while I tended to his wound I told him about Jesus! He scoffed at what I said, and now he's facing God's judgment!"

Augusta shivered then added softly, "Tytus, last year your brother was telling me about Jesus. I was stubborn at first, too! It makes me wonder how things might have turned out if I had kept on rejecting him. It's frightening to realize that when I spoke to Dewey last night, it was his last chance!"

Ty placed his hand lightly over Augusta's then he gave it a squeeze.

"Tim would be very proud of you! And seeing you're strong faith has meant a lot, to me."

The cave grew silent with both of them deep into their own thoughts. Tytus wanted to share with Augusta that God had brought about a change in him. That the thought of her being hurt had reminded him that he had once been a praying man but had turned away from God. He wanted to tell her about the hours he spent in the mud, praying and confessing his sins. But Ty knew it was all too easy to promise devotion in times of crisis, and then forgot when prayers were answered. No, he wanted to walk the Christian walk again, before he spoke of it. Augusta had worried over the soul of her enemy. Her faith humbled him and encouraged him to become a better Christian himself! He was determined that things were going to improve at the Bar 61—and he couldn't wait to begin!

Tytus glanced at Augusta's weary profile and said, "All right lady, you've patched me up—now—it's your turn."

Gently, he placed his hands on either side of Augusta face, carefully tilting her head side to side. His hands were warm and surprisingly gentle for their great size. Augusta's heart started pounding like a shutter on a windy day, and she feared Tytus might hear it too! Surely, his hands could feel the heat rising from her blush. She tried to move away from him but he leaned close and whispered, "You can't hide your secret from me."

"Ss-secret?" she stammered.

"I'm not the *only one* with a concussion, am I?" he asked. "How does your head feel right now?"

Augusta timidly removed Ty's hands, she put a bit more distance between them, then shrugged.

"Oh, kind of like a rowdy blacksmith has been turned loose inside my skull."

Ty squinted his dark eyes. "He's a great big blacksmith with a great big hammer! Right?"

Leaning close, he added with a smile, "But since you and I have two of the hardest heads in the territory, we'll survive! Don't you think?"

A prickly chill ran all through Augusta just then; suddenly, she felt very self-conscious and very aware of this man. Slowly, she got to her feet, gracefully picking up the coffee pot as she stood.

"What I think," she said, sounding calmer than she felt, "is that we could both do with some hot coffee."

Ty nodded and shocked her again when he winked as she stepped past him. Opening a coffee tin, she scooped some grounds into the pot and set it outside to fill with rain water. Immediately, the melody of rain drops began chiming against the tin. She listened to the music for a while, then speaking more to the falling rain than to Ty, she whispered: "I could bear all this—if I knew Tessie was all right. And that I could get back to her soon."

"Tessie's fine!" Ty said sympathetically. "You know the men won't allow anything to happen to her."

Augusta let out a wistful sigh. "My mind knows!" she agreed. "But my heart? I'm afraid she'll think I've abandoned her!" Augusta gave Ty a knowing look. "Timothy told me about your mother and now you know about mine. Thinking your own mother doesn't love you—it's a hurtful thing."

Ty nodded, "Yes—it is! But you listen to me. I promise you that I'll get you home to Tessie, and soon!"

Augusta stiffened, "Mr. Grainger—don't make a promise like that. I know what this rain is doing to that creek out there!"

Just then as if to mock her words, a slashing rod of lightning hit outside, accompanied with the rumble of thunder echoing through the cave. Augusta pointed out towards the storm and glared at Ty.

"Every minute those flood waters are getting higher and higher. And here we sit! On the *wrong* side of that, that—dad-blast-it—river!"

Ty quickly covered his mouth and coughed. Of course, there was not one thing humorous about Augusta's distress. But—he had never heard this very lady-like young woman swear before, mild though it be, and he had to force a frown to keep from grinning. Oh, he understood it well enough. Any female worth her salt becomes a mama bear when separated from her young! Augusta had every right to be upset, and he wouldn't want her any other way.

"Augusta," he began gently, "it is going to be all right! And do you know why? Because we aren't just going to sit here waiting for that water to go down!

Tomorrow, the two of us are going to ride up river until we find a spot where that 'dad-blast-it thing' out there isn't so 'dad-blast-it deep' and then we are gonna cross it—and then, I am going to take you home!"

With a sparkle in his eyes and an impish grin he added, 'Dad-blast it!'"

Augusta put her hands on her hips and gave the man a look that could have easily...boiled potatoes.

But when Ty's roguish grin only grew wider she finally let out a frustrated sigh. Tytus said no more but watched with interest as Augusta glanced impatiently about the cave. She was about to do something that he had come to admire. Biting her lip, a look of determination spread across her youthful face. She wasn't one to waste time on things she could do nothing about; instead, she would focus on something she *could* do! Seeing the coffee pot was full of water, she scooped it up and set it over the fire.

"Well now—that should be ready in a few minutes!" she announced. Then she added with concern, "Tytus—I bet you haven't eaten since yesterday. How do biscuits and bacon sound?"

"That a girl!" Ty grinned. "I'll even slice up the bacon while you make the biscuits."

Later, after they had both had their fill, Ty sighed, "Tell me again about Hitch? Your teeth were chattering so hard as we walked. I'm not sure I got it all."

Augusta nodded and retold the story. "It all happened so fast—I tried to make Dewey miss his shot, and I might have! I just don't know?"

Ty nodded and stared into the fire, his thoughts drifting back to how he and Hitch had been at odds with each other as they searched for Augusta. Hitch had been more than Ty's foreman; he'd been a good friend. The foreman was the first man he'd hired and they'd rarely had a cross word. Ty prayed earnestly for Hitch to be all right, knowing full well that Hitch wanted Augusta for himself. Ty had convinced himself that he didn't need or want a woman. But the thought of Augusta with Hitch or any other man made him feel like the dragon again. Still, he had to face the truth: if he truly cared about Augusta he would want her happiness—even if it meant Hitch taking her away! The thought left him feeling empty.

Augusta broke into Ty's thoughts and whispered, "Listen to me. I know exactly what you're thinking, and I don't want you to give up!"

Ty's eyes went wide. "You don't?"

"No!" she answered gently. "After all, Dewey believed he killed Hitch. But he told me the same thing about you and Quest. I think there's a good chance that Hitch is just stuck on the opposite side of that ... " She stopped and sighed. "...that ornery creek out there!"

Ty nodded to her and gave her a lop sided grin. The woman blamed herself for just about everything, except the havoc she was wreaking in his heart.

As the evening grew late, Tytus drifted off to sleep, but for Augusta it wasn't so easy. She kept awaking to what she thought was Tessie crying or to the threats and taunts of Dewey LeBeau. Finally, just before daybreak she decided to stretch her legs. Quietly, she made a small torch and found herself wandering towards the back of the cave; it was far deeper than she had realized. At the very back she followed a sharp curving corridor that opened out into a larger area. Holding her torch high she was stunned by what she found! Against the cave walls were stacks of neatly organized crates and barrels—surely, here was the remainder of stolen plunder from the freight wagons. If she hadn't already guessed that Dewey was the bandit, there would be no doubt now. There were crates and barrels containing everything from dried and canned foods to dress goods. There was even a new plow—and except for some worn saddlebags that he'd thrown in the corner—it was all brand new!

Ty was just waking up when Augusta returned. When she'd told him of her find, he was sure that most if not all of the stolen supplies had been found. That knowledge took a bit of the sting out of the fact that his knee had swollen up like a cantaloupe overnight. And though it chafed them both to admit it, they agreed it was wiser to stay put another day and rest. Here at least they had shelter from the rain that still fell outside and more than ample supplies to keep them comfortable.

After breakfast Tytus seemed lost in thought until suddenly he turned to Augusta.

"Since we have this time, I have a favor to ask?" he began softly.

"Certainly, what is it?"

Her golden eyes, so soft and unassuming, caught him off guard for a moment, then he swallowed and said, "If it's too painful, I'll understand—but it'd mean a lot to me if you could tell me about my brother."

All this time, he hadn't allowed her to talk about Timothy. But now he said, "You were with him on his last days. Would you mind telling me? Anything—anything at all?"

Augusta stiffened noticeably. "We were married, but I still haven't found our marriage certificate."

Ty hung his head. "Augusta, I know very little about you, but I do believe you are an honorable woman. So, please, tell me about your husband."

Augusta bit her lip and pondered a moment, then began, her voice soft and thoughtful.

"Well—it was about two years ago—Papa told me that a good friend of his, Mister Timothy Grainger, would be arriving soon. He was a lawyer from Boston and he planned to stay in our town through the winter while he prepared to go west with the spring wagon train. Papa told me he wanted me to help the man purchase his stock and supplies. For some reason I pictured an old man: a Boston dude, bookish, pudgy and slightly bald."

Ty frowned at that. "That certainly does not describe my brother!"

"No, it doesn't. I know…" Augusta protested. "I just said that's how I pictured him."

"So, what *did* you think when you finally met him?"

Augusta picked at the frayed hem of her skirt, while she gathered her thoughts.

"Well, for one thing—he arrived hours late for dinner, even though the stage was on time! I was pretty unhappy with Papa's friend when he finally arrived. But when I opened the door, and instead of a dowdy old gentleman, there stood a tall, handsome man, I was quite surprised. I had never seen a man dressed so elegantly—he looked too perfect to be real. He had thick golden hair, sparkling blue eyes, and a very roguish grin! I suddenly forgot that I was mad at him!"

Tytus chuckled and Augusta went on.

"Unfortunately, Papa had pestered me about dinner. I'm sure you can guess what happened."

"I suppose—you ruined something?" Ty asked with a grin.

"No…" Augusta groaned, "I ruined everything! It was the worst dinner of my life. Papa had insisted that everything be *perfect*! And you know what trying too hard does to my cooking skills."

Ty smiled, while Augusta's expression became tender.

"Of course, Timothy was charming! He made light of the disaster, then entertained us with funny stories about his trip from Boston."

Ty stared into the fire, thinking of his brother. "Tim was always a good story teller!"

"He was that!" Augusta agreed. "The three of us ended up having a lovely evening."

Augusta twisted the golden wedding band on her finger, and continued, "But—then, everything fell apart—I was washing up the dinner dishes, when out of the blue, Papa tells me that he sold our livery, and that the stranger I had just met had agreed months ago to marry me and that all three of us would be going west come spring! Timothy had even brought a trunk of wedding clothes made just for me in Boston."

Ty's eyebrows rose at this; if she had told him this story months ago he would not have believed it. "That's incredible..." he muttered.

Ty didn't think that sounded like his brother, but then he asked, "So, what did you do then?"

Augusta rubbed her face with both hands, her voice cracking when she said, "I-I lost my temper! Papa was everything to me. I'd always done what he wanted me to do—ride horses I was terrified of—anything to make him proud. Oh, I was feisty at times, but I had never defied him."

Ty nodded to himself; he could see Augusta being feisty, as she called it.

Sadly, Augusta, continued, "But for the first time in my life, I told Papa— NO! I was furious with him, and Timothy! It felt like Quest and I had both been auctioned off, to the Bar 61. Since Papa had given Echo to your father, I thought the Graingers wanted Quest to carry on the legacy. And—I had just been thrown in—like adding a saddle to a horse trade."

"Wait a minute, Augusta," Ty shook his head, feeling confused. "I did have a stud named Echo. But the man that gave him to my father was a well-known horseman."

Augusta nodded. "Yes—and his name was Bull O'Brien. Papa trained Echo, just as he trained Quest and countless others. Including me—I guess."

As she spoke, Ty's face went blank; he said nothing but leaned back against his saddle while he squinted across the fire. His dark eyes grew even darker as he looked at Augusta in a whole new light.

"Oh, no—" Ty groaned. "Augusta—you've lived under my roof for a year—don't tell me that—you—are—A.C. O'Brien."

Perplexed by Ty's odd expression, Augusta hesitated then answered, "Augusta Colleen—only Papa called me A.C.—how did you know? You said you never got a letter about me."

They both were silent for a while, then Ty rubbed his hands over his unshaven jaw.

"Oh, woman—why didn't you tell me you were A.C. O'Brien?"

Augusta bit her lip, then stammered, "I—I don't know—because I wanted you to accept that I was Mrs. Timothy Grainger. He told me to stand up to you." With a shrug she added, "Besides, Papa did talk him into marrying me. Isn't that what you thought? That Timothy had been coerced into marriage? How would telling you that I was A.C. O'Brien make a difference?"

Ty ran a hand through his dark hair, feeling more ashamed than ever.

"Knowing you were A.C. O'Brien? It would have made all the difference in the world!"

Ty closed his eyes and shook his head. "I told you Timothy said he would never marry. But he often wrote me of a girl. At the time, he thought she was too young for him, but he was fascinated by her just the same! She was the daughter of an old friend of the family and her name was A.C. O'Brien."

Augusta frowned. "But you said he never wrote you about me?"

"Not once did he mention the name Augusta." Ty slowly rubbed his jaw. "But your father wrote him about his daughter A.C. And then Tim wrote me about what a remarkable young woman Miss O'Brien was!"

He gave Augusta an appraising look then added, "He wrote me about a tintype your father sent. I don't think any other woman existed for Tim after he saw that picture. He said it captured the strength, beauty, and spirit of both horse and rider. It had to have been of you and Quest—no doubt."

Ty was surprised by Augusta's fallen countenance; she was grimacing and shaking her head.

The cave fell silent again and Ty sighed. "I can see I've embarrassed you," he whispered. "So, now that your presence in Tim's life makes perfect sense, can you tell me more about how this all came about?"

Augusta couldn't look at Ty; she hugged her knees tightly to her chest as her eyes filled with tears. Tytus was about to tell her that she didn't have to say another word, then abruptly she began to speak.

"Bull O'Brien was part Irish, part Welsh—an extravagant combination as story tellers go." She sniffed and gazed sadly up at the ceiling as she spoke, "I can well imagine how grand Papa made that A.C. girl sound—" Then she shook her head,. "But—she never was. As I was saying—I was furious with Papa that night. And—it was A.C. O'Brien's Irish temper that caused her father to have a heart attack."

Augusta stared into the fire, paying no heed to the silent tear that ran down her cheek. Finally, she swallowed and went on: "It all happened in a matter of hours; we had dinner with Timothy, then later Papa and I quarreled. Suddenly, he was near death and insisting that Timothy and I marry immediately! So the next day, I dressed in all the fancy satin and lace that my *fiancé* brought from Boston. We stood in our parlor and said the words the preacher told us to say. That night, I sat on the floor beside my father's bed, still wearing my wedding gown. By daybreak—Papa was gone."

Ty understood now why Timothy hadn't written that he was thinking of marriage; it was all so precarious. Augusta's pained expression made Ty want to say again that she needn't go on, but she stared into the fire as if she were seeing it all played out before her and continued to speak.

"Looking back, it's as if I stepped inside a dark cloud. I didn't really see or feel for a long time. I honestly don't remember signing any papers, but then I barely remember the wedding!"

Her eyes reflected the golden flames as she spoke softly. "You were right all along—I never was worthy of your brother. I tried to tell him so!"

When Ty started to protest she held up her hand.

"No!" she insisted, "It's true, after the funeral, I wanted him to annul the marriage. Timothy said I could do what I wanted, but that he meant the vows he made before God. I was so confused and angry that for the next two months, I did all I could to make your long-suffering brother—suffer!"

A look of shame and sorrow crossed her face, then she smiled sadly.

"The trouble was, the meaner I was to him, the nicer he was to me! When I was bitter, he was sweet."

Augusta conjured up the memory of her husband's face while Ty watched her gold-brown eyes sparkle in the firelight. Her features grew tender, as if she were seeing Timothy again.

"Your brother had the kindest blue eyes and such a special way of seeing the world. He told me about his father's rejection, his separation from you, and his sickly childhood. And then he told me that it was all a gift! It had made him stronger and made him search for the good. He said most people live their lives dwelling on their hardships instead of appreciating their blessings. Timothy embraced every experience, be it pleasant or harsh. He saw every challenge as an adventure—every moment as precious! He truly dedicated his life to following God's will, in all things."

"His letters to me were about that too!" Ty agreed. "But—I'm afraid I never took his advice to heart."

Augusta nodded. "It's not easy—but his outlook impressed me—it still does! Your brother included a beautiful strand of pearls with my wedding clothes. I wore them begrudgingly—but later he explained that pearls are created from the oyster's suffering. He said pearls were the perfect analogy for Christ's suffering on the cross. He said Christ's death created the pearl of great price that paid for our salvation. Timothy truly believed that in every trial of life, there was a pearl to be found in it! A little treasure buried within the suffering. It's no wonder that the gates of heaven are made from pearls—we can only enter heaven through the gateways created by Christ's suffering."

Ty smiled. "I'd like to see those pearls when we get back. And I have no doubt that you were Timothy's pearl the last year of his life as Tessie is yours and mine too, in a way. Something precious to treasure after losing Tim."

Tytus saw the pain in Augusta's eyes at the mention of Tessie. Wanting to keep her thoughts away from concern for her child, he said softly, "Did you ever fall in love with Tim?"

Augusta smiled sadly as she admitted, "I was stubbornly determined NOT to—" She gave a little sigh adding, "But—it happened anyway. Something tugged at my heart the first time I saw him, but after Papa died I was so confused and bitter. But then—he was so kind and good—that little by little I started softening towards him. Then one day he talked me into going on a picnic. He taught me how to shoot a gun, and after that, we waded in the cold water until our teeth chattered."

Ty smiled; he knew his brother would have reveled in a day like that.

"It was a rare—perfect day!" Augusta sighed, as she remembered it all too well. "Finally, I realized that it was just too exhausting to stay mad at a man as charming as Timothy Grainger. It was easier just to love him! Timothy was always assuring me of his love and of God's. Eventually, I surrendered my heart to both of them." Augusta looked up and met Ty's gaze. "We both were very happy the short time we were together. It was an honor to be his wife and his friend! I will always love him—always."

Augusta's voice trailed off and she pulled her knees to her chest, then wrapped her arms around them and hid her face—she couldn't talk anymore.

Tytus leaned back and stared at the ceiling of the cave; his eyes were clouded over and there was a great lump in his throat. He had felt his brother's passing, just as if he had died himself. Seeing a bit of Tim's last year through Augusta's eyes had been bitter-sweet, and yet somehow he felt like a raw wound he had tormented all year—might now—begin to heal.

His gaze fell gently on Augusta's small form. He had maligned her, and yet now—now that he knew who she was—he felt like he had betrayed not only Timothy but Bull O'Brien, a man he'd admired. What would Timothy think of how he had treated his beloved A.C.?

Suddenly, a thought came to him. "Augusta," Ty said, "this morning didn't you mention there were some old saddle-bags in back of the cave with faded markings? They might be the missing mail bags!"

Augusta looked up and locked eyes with Ty; of course, why hadn't she made the connection?

Tytus started to pull himself up, "The letter from Timothy might be in those bags!"

Augusta stood and waved him back. "Save your leg. I'll go get them."

Quickly, she made another torch then headed back into the recesses of the cave. As she wound her way through the dark cavern, the hair on the back of her neck began to prickle. She'd always been a little afraid of the dark, but she shrugged off the childish idea of returning to Ty empty handed and forced herself to go on.

It hadn't bothered her earlier, but now the torch's jumping flames set her nerves on end. They seemed to fashion outlandish shadows that darted about her like ghosts and phantoms. Quickening her step, she hurried to the rear of the cave, determined to make speedy work of this chore and get back to Ty, where she felt safe.

"There they are!" Augusta breathed with relief. But as she reached down for the saddle bags, her light suddenly reflected on something shining on the cave wall. Looking closer she found a brand new lantern hung on a peg.

"Well, now, if that isn't odd?" she muttered to herself, wondering why on earth she hadn't come across a lantern before. Especially when the inventory in this cave could put most mercantiles to shame, and yet until now, she hadn't found even one lantern to see it all by. It was too high for her to reach but thankfully there was a good-sized rock just below it. She stepped up, then stretched her fingers—she almost had it! Suddenly, the rock tipped sideways and she felt her body sliding down into the darkness.

Augusta screamed out in terror, and rolled onto her stomach, clawing at anything that might stop her fall. But the granite surface beneath her angled downward and was as smooth as glass! She slid until the balls of her feet landed on a small ledge, where she came to an abrupt stop. She watched with wide eyes as her torch flew high into the air. For a brief moment it illuminated her predicament; the toes of her boots were perched on a tiny ledge on the side of what appeared to be a deep chasm. Terrified, she followed the fire as it plummeted down; the flame grew smaller and smaller and smaller still, until finally, she heard a sickening thud and then—everything—went black!

It was then that Augusta really began to scream, "Tytus! TY-TUS, HELP ME!"

Not even in her nightmares had Augusta experienced anything like this— no night in all her life had felt this black. It was as if the darkness were a living thing—it crept towards her from the cavern depths. It reached up for her, then wrapped itself around her like a heavy cloak. Augusta felt for the ledge above her. She hadn't fallen very far and guessed it was only a few feet above her fingertips, but it might as well been a hundred. She didn't dare make a jump for it.

"Breathe—" she told herself. "Just—breathe!"

When she felt herself trembling, she willed her knees not to buckle.

"TY!" She cried. "TYTUS!! TYTUS!! HURRY! I'M IN TROUBLE!"

Ty's heart jumped the moment he heard Augusta scream. Without thinking he bounded to his feet but his swollen knee gave way on him and nearly pitched him into the fire. By shear will, he managed to roll himself over the flames, and regain his feet with the aid of his walking stick. He stopped just long enough to check his gun, fashion a quick torch from a burning branch, and grab his lariat. Then, as quickly as his bad leg would carry him, he raced towards the back of the cave.

"Hang on Augusta—I'm coming!" he roared, his deep voice echoing against the stone walls.

Ty cursed himself as he made his way through the darkness.

"I should have never let her go alone," he lamented. "What in the dickens could have happened to her?"

The terror he heard in her voice tore into him.

Lord, he prayed, *she's been through so much! Please, God, protect her! I can't lose her now!*

Ty hurried past the gelding, then saw that Quest was fighting his tethers and pawing the ground.

Realizing he might need the stallions strength, Tytus started to untie him. "Easy boy," he soothed, "stop fighting. I may need your help!"

But before Grainger could free the animal, he was paralyzed by the ghostly voice coming from the dark.

"Leave that devil be, boss! This ain't over yet."

Instantly, Ty spun around, only to see the man he thought dead and gone! He threw his torch at Dewey, and at the same time, he made a desperate grab for his own gun. LeBeau, however, was already swinging his torch and knocked the revolver from Ty's hand. The gun flew back into the darkness of the cave as Dewey sailed his fist towards Grainger's jaw. Tytus managed to block the punch with his right arm, then rebounded with his left fist smashing into Dewey's already swollen nose. LeBeau stumbled back and let out a string of curses.

Tytus swung again but Dewey blocked it and landed a "cast iron" blow to Ty's jaw. Grainger was thrown back against the cave wall, with his ears ringing. He shook off the pain, then cautiously the men began circling each other. They were both powerful men, but they were also both tired and wounded. Ty was young and athletic, but Dewey was a seasoned fighter and his fists were thick and lightning fast. Tytus blocked LeBeau's first few punches, but still the older man managed to land one blow after another. Finally, Grainger fell back, bruised and bloody against the cave wall. When Dewey stepped in to finish the job, Ty managed to grab his walking stick and ram it into the older man's hard belly. LeBeau doubled over with a grunt, then threw all his weight into a wild kick for Grainger's bad knee. Had he made contact, he would have surely broken Ty's leg. However, LeBeau lost his balance, missing Ty's leg by a hair's width, and the toe of his boot collided full force into the hard granite wall.

A searing pain shot up Dewey's entire body and he bellowed and cursed. Consumed with a blinding rage he ignored his injured right arm, doubled both fists, and began swinging wildly.

Grainger faded back into the shadows, staying out of LeBeau's reach, as the crazed man threw punches, until his bare knuckles connected with the jagged rock walls. Finally, LeBeau stopped, gazing down at his raw and bloody fists, he panted for air.

"I've never had such a time as this—it's that bad luck gal! I've been shot and beat up and drowned!"

Picking up the torch, he forgot all about Ty. Instead, he cursed and headed towards the back of the cave.

"I'll fix her fer ya, Vinny!" he roared. "I'll fix her fer good!"

⁂

Augusta heard men's voices and scuffling in the dark, but she was afraid to call out. Squeezing her eyes shut, she fought down the panic and willed her legs to stop trembling. Gooseflesh spread over her body as a musty smelling breeze rose up from the cavern depths. It brushed lightly against her cheek then seemed to whisper in her ear.

Augusta shook her head. *It's just my fear of the dark, playing tricks on me.* For it sounded like a woman's voice floating on the breeze. *"Augusta Colleen,"* it whispered. *"Don't you see—your dream—has come true. You were never meant to be born—and now—you'll die—die—die. Those you loved—would be alive—but for you. You are a mistake—mistake—mistake!"*

Augusta was finding it hard to breathe. Beads of sweat slid down her back. Her legs trembled as she struggled to maintain her balance on the ledge. Somehow, she had managed to stay strong through all that had befallen her, but—this? This she couldn't fight! This she couldn't stand against!

The voice mocked her in relentless assault—she believed the words that floated like ghosts around her. *"Lean back—Augusta,"* the voice taunted. *"Let the shadows take you, where you can do no more harm."*

It's all true! Augusta reasoned as she felt the icy grip of despair clutching at her heart. *Maybe I should go...where I can do no more harm! I've only a hope and a prayer of getting out of this anyway!*

Suddenly, it was like a blinding light.

"Lord, what is the matter with me? I've called for Ty but not for You! Why haven't I prayed? Oh, Father in heaven," she cried out loud. "I'm so sorry! The last thing I thought to do was pray!" She took a deep breath. "Please, forgive me—and please, please help us! Lord, this *is* my nightmare come true. And—Tytus? Oh Lord, I don't know what's happened to him. Timothy died because of me! I beg You not to let anything happen to Ty. He's here because of me! Please God—protect him!"

Augusta could not explain it: she was still in terrible danger, but the moment she cried out to God, her trembling stopped. An overwhelming peace enfolded her heart like a warm blanket, and she knew there was a new presence in the cave, and with it came that familiar voice, the one from her dreams:

"Don't be afraid," it said in a resounding tone. "I am here—I am here, Augusta."

This was not the malicious voice that rose from the cavern depths. This voice came from within and all around her. It felt like a bubbling spring that lovingly encircled her in a glowing embrace. This was God—she was sure of it!

The shadowy fingers that had reached for her earlier now seemed to slink back into the darkness.

Verses from the Bible—those she thought she'd never remember—filled her thoughts: "Be not dismayed; for I am your God. I will strengthen you; I will uphold you with my righteous right hand."

"Thank you, Lord!" she breathed, filling her lungs, and resting her cheek against the smooth stone.

Suddenly, she heard a garbled muttering and the sounds of footsteps coming closer. A stack of crates clattered to the floor. Looking up, she watched the light above her grow bright.

"TY! I'M DOWN HERE!" she called. "BE CAREFUL! DON'T REACH FOR THE LANTERN!"

The light above her was blinding, then the torch moved to the side, and she was looking into the demented face of—Dewey LeBeau. Augusta shrieked and nearly lost her balance.

"NO!" she cried. "IT CAN'T BE!"

Dewey's laugh sounded almost gleeful as he hissed, "Ya fell right into m' trap—I see! Only one lantern in my cave. The one I leave here as bait." Dewey grinned down at her. "Any fool that finds my plunder jes' naturally wants to get a better look. They make a grab fer the lantern 'n—down they go! Yer the onliest one that ever caught that ledge." Then Dewey scowled at his bloody fist.

"Can't rightly decide if I wanta haul ya up, or see how long it'll takes ya to fall!"

He took a long stick, then carefully lifted the handle of the lantern off its peg, causing it to slide down the stick until it rested on his fist.

"What have you done to Ty?" she demanded.

Dewey lit the lantern and the cave grew bright. Looking down at her again, his face contorted into a malicious grin as he lied: "I dun told ya gal, no one wants ya. Boss said kill or keep ya—didn't matter to him."

Augusta bit her lip. Ty would never say such a thing. But, where was he?

"Dewey please…" she begged. "Pull me out of here. You made a deal with my mother, remember?" She heard the man mutter something then trying to keep her voice calm, she said, "If you deny my mother the revenge she's been planning—you know she'll turn her wrath on you!"

LeBeau leaned over the ledge, his face a mask of hatred. "Vinny better step light around me from now on. This whole deal's gone sour from the first! Never come s'close to being caught before. And I'm plum sick a-ya gal and sick a-yer blame mama!"

Abruptly, the man turned, grumbling to himself; he walked away taking both the lantern and the torch with him. Augusta was plunged back into darkness, and with it, came all her fears, the musty smelling breeze, and that soft malicious voice.

"There's no God. You're a fool, A.C. This is your death, just as you dreamt it would be."

Tears filled Augusta's eyes—she could make no sense of anything anymore. Her legs were trembling; she was exhausted and confused. She had felt God's presence and then Dewey had appeared! Was she fooling herself about God and His love for her?

Again the voice within the breeze came up from the cavern below, its long tentacles twining about her.

"Your own mother didn't care—even if God is real—why should He care—for one such as you?"

"NO!" Augusta cried as she clung to the smooth rock wall. "Lord—help me!"

It was the simplest of pleas, but from it, came bubbling up from within her, the still small voice of God.

Once again it soothed her. "Don't be afraid, Augusta. I am here!"

Timothy had told her that God wages war against the devil for the souls of mankind; every day the battle goes on!

"All right," she cried out. "Maybe this is my death! Lord, I see now that I haven't truly surrendered my whole life to You. I used to think that if I could just help Papa enough or love Timothy enough, I wouldn't lose them. But You

304

say only when a man loses his life will he find it. Well, I give my life to You, Lord, all of it this time! I am Yours, whether I live or die—my trust is in You, Jesus!"

Augusta felt the soothing warmth of God's love spread around her shoulders and she knew that she was not going crazy, nor was she imagining the two opposing forces. She was in the midst of a raging war between good and evil, God and the devil.

⊰⊱

Ty slowly groped along the cave wall, using the darkness for cover. Augusta was in a bad way; he had to get her out of there and soon! But first he had to get the drop on Dewey. The trouble was the man had set the lantern and torch down behind some crates, then stepped away. The cave was full of strange and flickering shadows. Ty stopped and listened, and when he heard nothing, he stepped into the light.

At that very moment, like a crazed beast, LeBeau let out a rebel yell and charged at Grainger like a bull. Soon, both men were in a tangle on the cave floor.

LeBeau, with his greater weight, pinned Ty down, pressing his left elbow into Ty's throat. Ty's arms and shoulders were powerful, and he brought both fists up and slammed his knuckles as hard as he could into LeBeau's temples. He pulled on his ears and clawed at his face, but Ty's best efforts had little effect. Dewey seemed to feel nothing—the man was losing his mind—he laughed and cursed and pressed down all the harder, while Grainger's strength was deserting him. Ty's muscular arms strained to hold Dewey off, but gradually Ty felt himself losing consciousness as he gasped for air, and prayed that his men would arrive before it was too late to help Augusta.

LeBeau felt Ty's life ebbing away. "You're dying, Grainger!" he boasted. "And I want you should know—that gal—she's gonna be next!"

⊰⊱

A wild clatter rushed through the cave and Shep was the first to see LeBeau on top of Tytus. The boy threw himself at Dewey like a hound dog on a grizzly bear. It took three of the hands to pull the boy off the older man while the others went to help Ty.

Choking and struggling to breathe Ty wheezed, "Augusta's in trouble back there! But...WAIT..." he ordered, adding quickly, "she fell into some kind of trap. We've got to be careful!"

"Shep," Tytus said coughing, "Go untie Quest and bring him here!"

Turning to LeBeau he rasped, "Dewey, you'll help us get Augusta out safely or we'll let Quest have you, until there isn't anything left of you to hang!"

Hatred and terror flashed across LeBeau's lined face. "Kid—you leave that stud be!" Dewey grimaced, as two of the men pulled him to his feet. "I'm the onliest one thet—can get her out—alive!"

Muttering obscenities under his breath, LeBeau narrowed his eyes; in all his years as a high binder he had never been caught—not once! But tangling with Lavenia's spawn had ruined him. He could almost feel the noose around his neck as sweat slid down his back. Suddenly, strange thoughts began swirling around in his mind and he began to grumble and shake his head. He turned towards the men. "Ya bunch a lop-eared fools! Jes' had to come save that little vixen, didn't ya now? Don't ya know gal's like that are a dime a dozen? And she's nothin' but bad luck?"

The ranch hands said nothing as they followed him towards the far end of the cave. Glancing sideways at them, his cynical smile grew wide and spread across his face. "Planning on a right full day—ain't ya boys? Think ya can save the gal and hang ol' Dewey? Zat right?"

LeBeau suddenly lowered his shoulder and shoved hard against the men walking closest to him, so hard that the one just behind them staggered back as well.

"Well, yer too late!" he bellowed and took off at a run. "If I die—so does she!" he screamed.

They chased after him but stopped short when he dove off the ledge shrieking, "I'm takin' ya with me, gal!"

"Lord!" Augusta screamed as she flattened her body against the cave wall. Then, as if in a trance, she watched LeBeau's torch light up the cavern. She saw his hands franticly reaching for her, felt the suede of his vest brush against her arm, and felt the movement of air rushing passed her! And yet—miraculously—Augusta remained on her tiny perch! While Dewey LeBeau fell to his death, at the bottom of the dark cavern below.

With a tormented cry, Ty ran to the spot where Dewey had jumped. "Augusta!?" he roared, his heart feeling as if it had just been ripped open.

With lanterns held high all the men cautiously approached the edge of the cave, each one calling her name. The echoing noise throughout the cave was deafening.

"QUIET!" Ty bellowed.

When all was silent, they heard a soft trembling voice: "I'm—I'm still here—I'm standing on a small ledge! Please—get me out of here!"

"Hold on there…lil' darlin! We'll…get ya out!"

Augusta closed her eyes and sighed in relief as Hitch's slow drawl rumbled through the cave.

Ty turned, realizing for the first time that his friend and foreman was standing next to him. He slapped the man on the back, and with a strained voice he said, "If we position ourselves on either side of that rock we can pull her out together!"

After hearing the voices of both Ty and Hitch, Augusta felt like laughing! "Oh Lord—thank You!" she whispered.

Just then she looked up and saw a wonderful light breaking through the darkness around her; and with the light, came two strong hands reaching for her!

Chapter 38
Confusion and Clarity

"A time to weep, and a time to laugh; a time to mourn, and a time to dance." Ecclesiastes 3:4

Augusta gazed out the window, watching Tytus ride away on Quest.

"They suit each other," she mused, "the two mighty stallions of the Bar 61!"

She wished she could stop thinking about that man, whether she thought of him as the mighty stallion, the fire-breathing dragon, or even as Tessie's gentle uncle. He seemed to dominate her waking and even sleeping hours. It had started even before Dewey stole her away, but ever since their time together in the cave, she was constantly aware of his presence, just as he seemed to be aware of hers. It made for an odd tension between them—and she didn't like it.

Augusta had naively believed that the moment they were all safely back at the ranch with Tessie snug in her arms, everything would be fine! Instead, things seemed even more confusing—nothing was *fine*.

Especially Ty—he wasn't the dragon anymore—but who was he? The good news was that he no longer doubted who she was, on the contrary; now that he knew that she was or used to be A.C. O'Brien. He treated her with almost too much respect. Overnight, she'd gone from the shrewish stranger he didn't trust to Timothy's beloved widow. And yet the tension between them was—somehow—worse than before! Some days Ty was friendly and attentive—he seemed almost happy! Then the next day, especially if he saw her speaking with Hitch, he would suddenly become distant and moody.

Glancing out the window, Augusta saw Ty riding back into the yard, she slapped the rolling pin down against the dough, feeling that odd tension once more. The man had only just ridden out—*what could have brought him back so soon?*

Feeling the annoying but familiar blush creeping up her neck, Augusta quickly put her hands to her cheeks to cool them, completely forgetting they were covered with flour, sugar, and cinnamon.

She slid the batch of cookies into the oven, then slowly, she straightened and turned towards the doorway, only to find Tytus standing just inside watching her.

She frowned when he looked at her and chuckled. Then he picked up a dish towel and stepped closer. Augusta's golden eyes sparkled up at him like sunlight on a river. They both held their breath, as he gently took her chin in one hand, then brushed sugar and flour from her cheek with the cloth.

"Are you trying some kind of new beauty treatment?" he teased. "Trust me—you don't need it!

Another wave of warmth rushed over her, and without thinking, she put her hand to her face again.

Ty chuckled. "You're as bad as Tessie!"

But this time he used the back of his hand to brush at her cheek, then licked his knuckle and grinned his teeth showing white against his tanned skin.

"Mmm, now I know it's true—you *are* made of sugar and spice!"

Augusta was spell-bound by the look in Ty's eyes, for it was nothing short of...

"Hungry?" Augusta blurted out. "I-I could fix you something. A sandwich maybe...or..."

When Ty's eyes grew more intense, she stammered, "W-what did you ride back for?"

"Well, I—?" he shrugged. "I was on my way to McGee's when I remembered you were baking today. Figured I'd grab some cookies for the road."

Backing away Ty snatched up a handful; then winked, just as Hitch walked into the kitchen.

"Thought...ya...left...boss!" the foreman drawled as he looked past Ty and smiled at Augusta. "Thought I smelled cookies. Molasses?"

Giving Ty a meaningful look he boasted, "My favorite!"

Augusta opened her mouth but Ty answered for her.

"Nope!" he said arrogantly. "She's baking a big batch of sugar cookies."

Ty strolled to the door, resettling his hat on his head and then leaning towards Hitch he growled, "My favorite!"

⌇⌇

After weeks of planning, cleaning and baking, Augusta could hardly believe that the much anticipated party was only a dozen hours away! And—she couldn't stop worrying—what would Ty think? Would he be pleased? He'd given her a free rein with the planning and the details. And though she'd spent weeks laboring to make sure everything was as perfect as she could make it— would it be good enough for Ty?

After all, this was her first party, her first dance! What did she know? Tytus Grainger, on the other hand, had been weaned on fancy balls and cotillions.

The hour was late and Augusta knew she and Tessie needed their sleep but she wanted everything laid out for the next day. Missus Drew had made her a number of lovely gowns before she left for New York. And Augusta had finally chosen a dress the color of the Colorado sky! Bittersweet memories came to mind as she touched the cream-colored lace that trimmed the neckline and short puff sleeves.

This dress would look lovely with my pearls!

At first she thought them too extravagant; but she quickly decided that Timothy would be pleased if she wore them and so would Ty.

Sitting down on the bed with Tessie, she slowly opened the smooth mahogany box. There was a catch in her throat as she drew the necklace out and reverently held them towards the candle light.

"Look, Tessie, pearls! Aren't they pretty?"

Augusta stood before the mirror, as she held the necklace to her throat, she remembered the man who had taught her to look for the little treasures that often accompany suffering. Tessie, however, was more taken with the pretty box. She stroked the soft velvet lining as if it were a kitten; then with a giggle, she up-ended the box. Along with the velvet lining, two white envelopes flew out across the bed.

"Uh-oh, little girl, what's happened there?"

Augusta kissed Tessie's golden head, then she replaced the lining, and carefully set the pearls inside. With a puzzled look she picked up the first envelope, opened it, then pulled out a paper.

As she read the words she began to tremble. In bold script across the top it stated, "Certificate of Marriage." The other words blurred until she saw Timothy's signature at the bottom of the page—along with hers! She still didn't remember signing anything but that was her signature.

"Oh Tessie, you wonderful girl, you found it! Your papa did put it in a special place, didn't he?"

Suddenly, Augusta couldn't wait to see Tytus! Then she remembered there was another envelope. Carefully, she opened it and a sob caught in her throat as she read:

To my dearest wife, my darling Augusta, my amazing A.C.;

If you are reading this letter then those who have said I would not live to be an old man were right! Forgive me love, I know I sound flippant, but you know my humor and that I have always believed that life and death are part of the same adventure! And I cannot bear your thinking of me and being sad.

I want you to know that in our time together, you made me profoundly happy. A.C., you are my joy! I've considered it a miracle to awaken each morning with a wife I delight in. I had never thought I would father a child, but by God's grace the Graingers shall live on for another generation.

You and Tytus are the two people I have loved more than anyone in the world. Should I be taken from you during our journey west, you must go to Tytus. Should he seem gruff at first, please remember broken hearts mend slowly but are often stronger, and better for the mending. So, I ask of you, extend your gentle touch to Ty, for he is a good man and has been the best of brothers!

One more thing my dearest, do not waste one moment of your life in bitterness or anger towards God. I know you've had your fill of sorrows. But remember to search for the pearl in every hardship. Hold fast to the truths of Jesus Christ and teach them to our child! Nothing is more important!

Now, my love, you are young and beautiful. It is my wish that you marry again. I've asked the Lord, should I die, to send you a man that will love and appreciate the wonderful woman you are! However, you are wealthy in your own right. So marry only when and if you find a man who loves the Lord and who truly loves you and our child! And one that you truly love in return!

I shall not say I am sorry for leaving you. For if you are reading this letter—then I am in heaven! A land where there is no sorrow. A land where we will meet again. God bless you, my love!

Sincerely, your adoring husband,

Timothy Delray Grainger

P.S. Remember, my darling A.C., even in grief it is all right to have a good day!

Augusta stood outside Ty's library door. Still reeling from her discoveries, she drew in a number of deep breaths before lifting her hand to knock on the door. Hearing a grunt she peered inside.

"May I come in, just for a moment?"

Ty was seated at his desk, his thoughts miles away. But hearing her voice he quickly got to his feet.

"Of course, Augusta, please come in! Is this—something about the party tomorrow?"

Augusta stepped into the room, thinking how tired he looked...and how handsome! He was at this late hour in his white shirt and gray trousers. Alvaro had cut his hair, and though he shaved every morning, by evening there was a heavy shadow that both masked and accentuated the ridges and valleys of his face. Once again Augusta was struck by the sense that she knew this man, understood him. That familiar fluttering quivered in her stomach as their eyes met. Feeling warmth come to her cheeks, she lowered her gaze to the huge bear skin rug at her feet.

"Augusta? Ty asked, bringing her mind back into focus, "if there is anything you need—?"

Clutching the envelopes behind her back she pondered if this was the right time to share her discoveries. "Oh—um—no. Everything is done or will be first thing in the morning. I hope you'll be pleased!"

"And my hope is that you're pleased!" He said, grimacing over how overly polite they were lately. "You've certainly worked hard enough!"

Augusta could only smile, while Ty struggled not to stare. The woman was ready for bed; he could see her long white nightgown underneath a very proper lavender robe. She usually wore slippers, but she must be pre-occupied, for he could definitely make out ten pink toes peeking out from under her robe. Her hair was brushed out, just the way he liked it, falling long and loose down her back, save one stray curl draped over her shoulder. It was then he noticed her eyes. Ty's look became tender, his voice concerned: "Augusta, you've been crying—please—tell me what's wrong?"

Biting her lip she walked towards Ty's desk, holding up the first envelope.

"Tytus," she said softly, "Tessie found it! I thought I'd looked everywhere. But never under the lining of my jewelry box. Timothy must have put it there for safe keeping. It's the marriage certificate!"

Ty frowned as he hurried around the desk; then he gently rested one hand on Augusta's shoulder. "I hope you still don't think I needed proof—I can't tell you how sorry I am about the things I've said and—"

Augusta put her hand up to stop him from yet another apology.

"No! Don't feel badly Tytus. I know you've come to believe me—even without the proof. I just wanted you to know. And I wasn't crying about that! It was because along with the certificate, I found a letter—from Timothy. He wrote it, just in case something happened on our journey. I thought you'd like to read it."

Ty's expression was sad as he took the second envelope from Augusta's small hand.

"Thank you, Augusta!" he whispered, then added, "I appreciate your letting me read this."

Augusta sighed, "I'm certain my mother has the last letter Timothy wrote to you. That's how they knew so much about our plans."

Tytus nodded his agreement. "I'm afraid you'll always need to be wary, Augusta—she may still want to hurt you! Lavenia seems to be a very shrewd woman. The Sheriff said she sold her house and left town the very day Dewey took you."

When Augusta nodded and sighed, Ty decided it was time to change the subject and lighten the mood.

"Regarding the party—let the men do the work! I want you to enjoy visiting with the womenfolk. I'll be upset with you if you fail to enjoy your own party! Will you do that?"

Augusta met his gaze with a sleepy tenderness that tugged at his heart.

"I will if you will!" she challenged. "Good night, Tytus."

Chapter 39
The Party

"You have turned for me my mourning into dancing." Psalm 30:11

"Hey there—got a minute?" Hitch asked Augusta as he stood in the kitchen doorway.

"Just need a word with ya—before all the men get here!"

Augusta stared at the foreman of the Bar 61 and laughed as she dried the last breakfast plate. "Hitch?!" she moaned. "I've got things to do, and so do you! Can't it wait?"

He took the towel from Augusta's hands, then gently pulled her towards the door. "Please? This won't take long—got to say my peace—gotta stake my claim."

The man's penetrating hazel eyes were staring down at her with such determination, she had to smile. Hitch took that as an agreement, then quickly led her toward the large elm tree, just behind the hacienda.

"Remember the picnic?" he began. "When I said...don't think of me...as a brother?"

Augusta suddenly felt nervous and self-conscious. "I remember."

"And ya liked that...little valley...didn't ya?"

"Of course," she answered, "it was lovely there!"

Hitch grinned. "It's mine!"

The man nearly burst with pride—when he said it out loud, then added, "That and...six hundred acres. Ever spare minute...I've been cuttin' logs...fer a cabin...and a barn!"

Awkwardly, he took Augusta's hand and said, "You were made fer ranchin'! I saw yer worth, right off. Hard worker...good cook." Hitch squeezed Augusta's hand, and smiled down at her. "Want this settled...before every man...in the territory...comes a courtin'."

When she gave him a questioning look, Hitch blurted out, "I'm...askin' ya...to...marry me!"

Augusta gently pulled her hand away, and stared up at the big man.

"Hitch, I——?"

She wrung her hands as she walked around the man, wondering what she should say?

Hitch is a——good man! I don't mind that he's frugal with words——but you'd think he might have managed at least one word, a woman would want to hear, other than marry me! So, he saw my worth, did he? But——not a word about love or even that he finds me—— appealing as a woman.

Augusta paced around the handsome foreman and asked herself the most important question:

All that aside, A.C. Grainger, how do you feel about Hitch?

Augusta had to shake her head as a tender smile played about her lips.

I love Hitch——I do——but even though he told me not to——I love him like a brother!

Augusta shrugged, then, turning to the man who was waiting for his answer, she let out a little sigh.

"Hitch, thank you for asking me. And——I'm flattered that you think I'd be a——*worthy* wife."

"So...is that a yes?" Hitch asked, wondering why she looked so confused; he'd said it all plain enough.

Augusta wondered if maybe she shouldn't——just say yes, they were good friends. The man had risked his life for her but——if he loved her, wouldn't he have said so? And she didn't think her sisterly love for him would ever change.

Hitch took both of Augusta's hands in his then said, "We'll make a fine couple...have a mess a' kids! You birth 'em so easy. " he drawled. "Won't even have to stop work... to fetch ya a mid-wife. We'll have a house full...of strappin' boys....in no time!"

Augusta's eyebrows rose in shock, then she bit her lip——surely he was jesting. But the look on Hitch's glowing face told her that this naïve man was ready to pass out cigars!

All she could do was shake her head. "Oh, Hitch..." she sighed, "I know we seem like a reasonable match. But——something is telling me, WHOA! Let's get this party behind us and talk again later. And besides, remember——Rusty said some new women have moved to the Rosenquist's. Who knows...perhaps you'll fall madly in love with one of them..before this day is over! Now, let's get back to work!"

Hitch took his hat off and scratched his head, wondering what went wrong as Augusta patted his arm, then scurried back towards the hacienda.

Standing before the mirror, Augusta put the last curl into place. She wanted to concentrate on the party but Hitch and Ty were all tangled up in her mind like a ball of yarn with way too many knots.

"Lord," she prayed, "it's all such a mess, when Ty looks at me he sees a burden, and when Hitch looks at me he sees a bargain! The one that wants me—I don't want. I didn't think I would, but I loved being married to Timothy. Do I dare try it again?"

Finally, as she hummed one of her father's tunes, Augusta decided to stop fretting; she had fought for this party and now that she had gotten her way— she was going to enjoy it! Staring at her reflection, she pulled down a few more curls to frame her face. Most of her dark hair was piled on top of her head, but she'd allowed a few ringlets to fall down her back. Then she added just a few of the wild flowers Shep had picked for her that morning.

Although she knew Emily could have done better, she was pleased just the same. Reverently, she touched the iridescent pearls at her throat. They went perfectly with the creamy lace and the bright liquid blue of her gown.

Gracefully she turned to Tessie. "Now, hold still for mama!" she cooed as she placed two blue bows in Tessie's blonde curls.

Mother and daughter were dressed alike. Augusta had found just enough material left over from her own gown to sew a tiny dress for Tessie. She couldn't help but wish Timothy could see his girls today. Her very next thought turned to Ty—*would he be pleased?*

Augusta shook her head then picked Tessie up and pushed away all her worries and fears.

"Well now—my little love—you just listen to me!" she sang as she danced around the room.

"Mama has a surprise for her girl today!"

Tessie giggled as Augusta twirled her into the air.

"You think the world is just you and me and a land full of dusty men in leather and spurs—don't you? Well, you are in for a treat, my darling. We are going to meet a banquet of ladies today—old and young and even little ladies— just like you! Oh Tessie, we are going to have such fun! We are going to make friends and have a wonderful day!"

Augusta was so happy that the little girl was soon completely caught up in her mother's joy.

Finding the papers the night before and the cry that followed had been cleansing for Augusta. She felt better than she had in ages. She would not grieve or feel guilty—or worry! Nope! Today she would do as Timothy had taught her; she would embrace life! She was going to have a good day!

When Alvaro heard the distinctly feminine trill of laughter coming from Augusta's room, he hurried down the hall. When he peeked through the open door, he let out a long whistle.

"Ahh!" he exclaimed, as he grinned broadly. "La señora and señorita, are so beau-tee-ful today!"

He bowed to Tessie and said with great deplume, "Señorita Tess, may I have this first dance?"

Smiling, he lifted the child into his arms. Her deep blue eyes shone with joy and she giggled gleefully as the old man twirled her around, humming a tune more befitting a wild fiesta than a country dance.

As Alvaro whisked Tessie into the air, he called to Augusta, "Señora, is there anything you wish for me to do?"

Augusta sighed nervously. "Just tell me I haven't forgotten anything!"

"If it was forgotten, señora, it was not needed. The day—is—bright, the sky—is—clear. We will never forget today! Eh?"

"Never!" Augusta agreed. "I want so much for everyone to be happy today. At least I think I know why Hitch and Ty have been so gruff with each other. Hitch told me he's starting up a ranch of his own. I'm sure Ty's upset to be losing his foreman. It's a big loss for the ranch. That must be why they've been short tempered with each other—don't you think?"

Alvaro shrugged his shoulders. "Oh! Señora, it is not for me to say."

Still swaying with Tessie on his hip, he seemed thoughtful, then spoke slowly, "I wish to tell you something—even though—it is none of my business."

Augusta placed her hand gently on Alvaro's sleeve. "You, my amigo, may always feel free to tell me anything. Surely you know that?"

The old man smiled then he spoke very gently, "Since you came to this place you are always trying to earn your way—to be pleasant—to be helpful. But, today my dear, it is very important that you remember to listen to your heart!"

"Alvaro, I'm not sure what you mean?"

"As you dance under the stars tonight, señora, you will."

Feeling truly confused, Augusta looked at Alvaro with a puzzled frown.

The old man simply gave her a wink then said, "Remember, you promised to save a dance for me?"

"I'll remember! If you remember—to guard your toes!"

Alvaro grinned as he placed Tessie back into her mother's arms, then danced his way down the hallway.

Augusta was standing in the parlor, trying to think what that wily old man was up to, when the front door swung open and Tytus Grainger stood there gaping at her. Finally, he said, "Augusta!"

He seemed to be memorizing her from head to toe, his dimple drawing in more deeply with every inch his eyes traversed.

"Uh—" he stammered then said, "Your guests are arriving—this is— your party, if you'll recall!"

"No—it's not—my party!" Augusta panicked as the color left her cheeks. "This is your party. I was only to do the work," she stammered. "This is your home—you're the host!"

Ty smiled as he gently took her by the arm and pulled her outside; "Correct, but this is also your home. I am the host—and you are the *hostess*. Now, just stand here beside me," he whispered in a soothing voice. "I want everyone to meet you, and..." He gave Augusta another long appraisal; her glossy dark hair shone in the sunlight, and the luster of the pearls that encircled her throat were rivaled only by her flawless skin and bright smile. Ty took his time enjoying the vision, as he slowly finished his sentence, "...and to see just how truly lovely their hostess is!"

The look on Ty's face, not to mention his words, left Augusta speechless. Her heart fluttered as he bent towards her, but then he kissed Tessie's cheek, adding, "How fortunate I am, to be a host with two such beautiful hostesses beside me."

Ty caught a flicker of a smile before Augusta turned her attention to the arrival of their first guests.

"Welcome!" Ty called.

The driver of the heavy wagon reined in his team, then jumped from his seat and landed beside them to shake hands with Ty.

"Iver, good to see you!" Ty greeted, lifting his hand to the wagon load of people.

"Augusta, this is the Rosenquist family. These are the folks I should have introduced you to a year ago. You would agree, I'm sure!"

"I certainly would!" she said without hesitation, bringing chuckles all around.

Augusta smiled up at the wagon load of people, all blonde headed and red cheeked. But she was intrigued by Ty! She had never met this Tytus Grainger before, not this sophisticated and amiable gentleman. He was charming and gallant as he helped Iver's wife down from the wagon then gracefully turned to make formal introductions.

"Iver and Agda Rosenquist, it pleases me to introduce to you my lovely sister-in-law and business partner, Missus Augusta Grainger! Augusta is the widow of my late brother, Timothy."

Augusta forced her mouth to close and hid her surprise. She had wondered how he would handle the introductions, but she hadn't expected this. Then he reached for Tessie, who happily went into his arms. "And this little beauty is their daughter, and my niece," he added proudly, "Miss Tessie May Grainger."

Tessie's blue eyes were like round saucers, having never seen a stranger before; she hid her face against Ty's collar, then peeked shyly at all the new faces. A moment later though, Tessie forgot her fear when Ty swung her into the air. Everyone joined in the laughter as she giggled and squealed in delight.

Augusta was suddenly swallowing down happy tears. The party had begun with laughter, and Ty's gracious introduction had been like a precious gift. She couldn't keep herself from stealing sidelong glances at this man. A few times Ty caught her at it and gave her a wink before returning to his guests. There was a kind of masculine beauty about this man, from his perfect features to his tall frame. He was at least a head taller than any other man there, and—by the shy glances the few ladies in attendance were giving him—he was too handsome for any woman's peace of mind.

It was clear that Ty was in his element; he was the proper southern gentlemen, self-assured with the men, chivalrous with the ladies, and playful with the children. Augusta found herself asking—where had the wounded dragon gone? And yet she truly had not seen that dragon in quite some time. She remembered Timothy's words: *a wounded heart takes time to mend, but is better for the mending.*

Augusta forced her attentions back to her guests and smiled graciously as Agda introduced her four children. They stood like stair steps, only a year apart, and they were all golden haired with big blue eyes and bright smiles. Augusta was thrilled to learn that little Filippa was only three months older than

Tessie. When they put the two little girls together, they both stared in wonder, then a moment later, they wrapped their arms around each other in a loving hug. Again, Augusta was fighting her tears, another answer to her prayers, a special friend for her little girl!

Ty tried to be inconspicuous as he watched Augusta. How had he ever thought this creature dowdy and plain? She was incredibly beautiful today. And yet the day before when he'd come upon her while scrubbing the tables, with a smudge of dirt on her cheek and a wayward curl falling over one eye, she had still taken his breath away!

He was so proud of the way she greeted each guest with the same grace and warmth. It didn't seem to matter to Augusta whether it was a prim and proper rancher's wife or a lowly young cowpoke who shook trail dust off his clothes while being introduced. Every guest was made to feel welcome! And even little Tessie gave everyone her adorable one-dimpled grin.

My girls have enchanted everyone they've met! My girls? Tytus mused: *Just when, Tytus Grainger, did these two treasures become your girls? How long did you insult Augusta and ignore Tessie? Now you may very well lose them both to Hitch or even some other man here today.* Ty bit back the pain that twisted inside. *Well, today they feel like "my girls" and I am going to make the most of it!*

He smiled as he watched Augusta's face light up as two young women waved at her as they rode up in a buggy. Ty thought he might be as happy to see them as Augusta, for they looked to be about her age!

Maybe Augusta won't be the only available female at this party!

Agda quickly joined the young women to make the introductions. Her soft Swedish accent, instantly, charmed Augusta.

"Ah, Miss—us Grain—ger," Agda began softly. "These two pretty t'ings are Ruth and Helen And—er—son. They are cousins of my new sister-in-law—Anna."

The two sisters were both petite with auburn hair and violet eyes the color of mountain columbines.

"Anna married my brudder, Nathan. He found Anna from a news—paper! There's too many men—not 'nough vomen—here!"

Agda smiled, as she took Augusta by the arm and lowered her voice: "They are...goot girls. But I von't be keeping 'em fer long. They vill get... snatched up!" With her eyes full of laughter, she added: "I varn these girls...

don't be surprised…yu get a dozen proposals…before this day is over! There might even be a veddin'…ya never know?"

Agda pursed her lips and narrowed her soft gray eyes as she appraised her hostess. "And…yu are a pretty…voman…too! So don't be…offended, vin all the men yu…dance vith…asks yu …to marry."

Augusta flushed but didn't even have time to acknowledge Agda's remarks when suddenly an elderly woman approached her, pinched her cheek, then gave her face a playful little slap!

Agda laughed. "Ah…this is Iver's mama. Ve call her Gra——nny Rose."

Augusta stared with wide eyes at the oldest woman she had ever seen! Her face was round as a pumpkin with lines scoring it like a map of the world, and she couldn't help but think of Aunt Sis. And like her friend from the wagon train, the old woman's deep set eyes twinkled with both wisdom and *mirth*. She wore her hair cut short like a man's and it stuck up like an angry porcupine's, in all directions. And though Augusta enjoyed the rolling cadence in the way the old woman spoke, she couldn't understand a word.

Agda quickly came to the rescue. "She don't speak…too goot. Said she vas vantin' to help yu…deliver yer baby…but yu…cheated her…by having it yerself."

Augusta smiled, but feeling embarrassed, she put her hands to her burning cheeks, then said softly: "Granny Rose, you will never know how much I looked forward to your being with me. And I surely do wish I hadn't *cheated you*—believe me!"

The old woman proved that she understood English well enough, when she let out a peal of laughter.

When Ty came to see what the merriment was all about, Granny Rose grabbed hold of his large hand, and then Augusta's. She brought their hands together then slowly and distinctly said, "Yu…got a goot voman…she make a goot vife…ja?"

For the first time Augusta understood every word the old woman spoke, and she gathered by the humor on Ty's face that he understood as well!

Quickly, Augusta turned to Agda. Already feeling a kinship with the pleasant woman, she whispered, "I'm not sure that Granny understands that Tytus is my brother-in-law, and that I'm a widow."

Agda explained to her mother-in-law in a language that sounded to Augusta like a series of dips and turns. But the old woman's eyes just twinkled even

L. Faulkner-Corzine

more brightly. Turning her face up to Ty, she reached way up so that she could pinch and then slap his cheek just as she had done to Augusta. Nodding her head towards her hostess, she winked at Ty and said quite clearly, "Goot vife...ja?"

A sparkle glimmered in Ty's dark eyes; then he crossed his arms and low-ered one brow, as if to consider Granny Rose's suggestion. His slow appraisal made Augusta's face flush with embarrassment, then it turned pink, and then her eyes flashed a warning.

Ty chuckled at Augusta's discomfort, then bent and whispered something in Granny Rose's ear.

The old woman cackled with delight, and gave Ty a hearty slap then moved on to pester someone else.

Agda smiled, "Her heart is goot...yu vill...get used...to her!" then she added, "Ve almost have!"

Augusta laughed; she felt like she and Agda had gotten off to a good start as friends and Granny Rose was adorable—mischievous to be sure–but—ador-able!

When all the guests had arrived and had made themselves comfortable on the benches that had been set out, Ty came to stand before them; smiling he removed his hat, then said, "I'd like to thank you all for coming today! And— since this is a rare holiday for all of us, it seemed only proper to begin our day with the word of God! Tanner McGee knows the Bible better than anyone I know, so I've asked him to speak to us—Mister McGee!"

Ty hurried to sit down beside Augusta, taking Tessie onto his lap. Hitch glared at him but scooted over to make room. The old Scotsman slowly made his way to the front of the crowd, leaning only slightly on his cane. He wore an old black suit with the McGee plaid across one shoulder. His hair was white with a pinkish hint from a mane that had once been a fiery red. His thick eye-brows almost over shadowed his green eyes, and though he spoke each word with distinction, there was yet a soft burr as he spoke.

"Well now, I bet yer wonderin' what ol' McGee has to say, well—I've been wonderin' that meself."

He smiled good-naturedly as the crowd chuckled then he straightened. "I rose early this morn, and I watched from the bluff that looks down on this bon-nie place as everyone was a-comin' from all directions. And I got ta thinkin', heaven will be like this. Folk's a-comin' from far and wide to gather together. And just look at us. We havena' much in common. I come from one part of the

322

world and ye from another! As children many of us spoke in different tongues. Some came from position and wealth—others from poverty and ruin. And ye know that not one bit of it matters to the Lord Almighty! There is but one thing we must have in common to enter the gates of heaven! And that one thing is Jesus Christ! When we have the Savior in common all else is naught!"

He paused, then with trembling hands, he opened his worn leather Bible and read: "In the book of Hebrews, it says that 'Jesus Christ is the same yesterday, and today, and forever.' And in the book of Romans, it says that 'If ye confess with yer mouth the Lord Jesus, and shall believe in ye heart that God has raised him from the dead, ye will be saved.'"

Tanner held up the Bible and said, "Now that tells us that God is still as powerful and trustworthy today as He ever was! And that all the promises and all the warnings God put down in this book are just as valid today as the day they were writ!"

Holding his Bible high he continued, "Right here are the truths we must all stand upon! If any of ye wish to talk wi' me further...be pleased to know that yer always welcome at the Stubborn Scotsman Ranch. But—" he added with a sheepish smile, "I am an oldish sort o' fella, and I fear I'll not be gettin' any younger, so if ye'd have words wi' me, best to be gettin' to it—sooner rather than later!"

Holding his hands in the air Tanner said: "Now, if ye'll close yer eyes and bow yer heads I'll ask the Lord to bless the festivities of this day."

With a frown he cleared his throat then pointed one fierce eyebrow at a few cowpokes who were not complying. With sheepish sidelong glances they removed their hats and bowed their heads.

"Heavenly Father," he began, "We give Ye our thanks! And ask that Ye bless the food and all here. May we be satisfied with what Ye give us but hungry always fer Yer word! Let the journey's homeward be safe. And Father, may Ye bless each one here, that they may know Yer son Jesus as their Lord and Savior! For it's in His name we pray. Amen."

After a few songs were sung, the short service was over and Ty and Augusta went their separate ways. Ty headed towards the men to set up various competitions—horse shoe toss, calf roping, and horse racing—while Augusta hurried toward the women as they arranged games for the children and set out the food.

Augusta was thoroughly enjoying her conversation with the pretty Helen Anderson when she witnessed something she hadn't really believed in—*love at first sight*! They were speaking of the beautiful mountains, when Helen's unusual violet eyes suddenly became a deeper shade of lavender while a rosy blush flooded her cheeks. When Augusta turned to see what had caused the change in her new friend, she found Hitch slowly approaching. Never before had she seen such tender awe in this man's expression nor had she ever heard his voice sound so reverent.

"Ladies!" he drawled with hat in hand. "I just…hoped…I mean…wondered if you…needed any help?"

The usually confident Hitch looked hesitant and vulnerable in the presence of young Helen. He seemed to look upon her as if she were a mythical creature that might vanish all together should he move too quickly. While Helen gazed up at the tall golden-haired foreman with his bronzed face and tender hazel eyes as if he had just stepped out of her favorite novel. Augusta quickly introduced the pair and beheld something magical happen the moment their hands touched in greeting.

Hitch's gaze went suddenly from Helen to Augusta, his expression revealing his bewilderment. Augusta knew she should probably feel insulted—after all the man had just proposed. But instead she felt greatly relieved. Quickly, she gave Hitch a reassuring smile that she hoped would convey her understanding and said amiably, "Helen was just telling me that she raised a mule colt when she was a little girl. I was just about to take her to see Ezmarelda! But now that you're here, Hitch, would you mind escorting Helen out to see Ezzy? I'd like her to see the other horses as well—she loves to ride! And, I'm afraid I really should excuse myself and check on Tessie and on our other guests!"

Augusta smiled to herself as she left Helen tongue-tied, and Hitch of all people talking a blue streak! The man had certainly changed horses in midstream. But the charmed look that came over both Hitch and Helen's faces was telling! So much so, that Augusta decided it was much more fun to play cupid than figuring out how to turn down an unwanted proposal.

Later in the afternoon, Augusta found Hitch alone and took the opportunity to speak to her ex-suitor.

"Helen Anderson certainly is a lovely young woman, isn't she?" she asked gently.

"Augusta…I? I don't want you to think…and yet I…I—?"

Hitch stammered and then stopped. His pained expression made it clear that he was ashamed and confused by his actions and re-actions to a woman he'd just met.

"It's all right Hitch!" Augusta soothed. "We were meant to be good friends. And my friend, something special happened between you and Helen today. Thank God for it! And don't let her get away!"

Hitch ran his hand down his mustache and shook his head. "She's a delicate little thing...probably not as suited...for ranching...the way you are."

Augusta rolled her eyes and grinned. "Would you take a bit of advice from a friend?"

When the foreman shrugged his shoulders Augusta said in a firm—yet sisterly way. "Do not choose a wife with the same eye as you choose a good horse." With raised eyebrows she added, "Don't look at her teeth or ask if she's sound of wind and limb. Or—will she make a good brood mare?"

Hitch flushed wildly and frowned. "Guess my proposal...wasn't very romantic this morning...was it?"

"Nope!" Augusta raised one eyebrow and shook her head. "But that's all right—you were just practicing. You shouldn't marry for anything but love! People sometimes belittle the notion. But it's love that gives you the strength to endure the hard times. Love is the pearl in the middle of life's hardships!"

Hitch acknowledged Augusta's words with a nod then bent and kissed her on the cheek.

"You're a good woman and...I'm proud to call ya...my friend. And uh—" Hitch smiled and rubbed his jaw. "Thanks...for the advice!"

As she watched the big man walk towards Helen, she felt like a burden had been lifted. Oh, she still had things to worry about but at least Hitch was no longer one of them.

Smiling, Augusta gazed all around and found her guests gathered in small groups here and there. Everyone seemed to be having a wonderful day even if they didn't always understand each other's words. Her neighbors had indeed come from far and wide: England, Germany, Scotland, Spain, Sweden, and France. And yet they had worshiped and prayed together; they had shared laughter, food, and friendship. The Bar 61 had provided food a-plenty; two huge steers were roasted, along with all the trimmings. Nevertheless, every woman had arrived with their own assortments of favorite side dishes and desserts. Everyone seemed to enjoy trying each other's delicacies while their children danced around the food tables and then ran off to the next new game. The men, especially those who were single, Augusta noted, entertained the crowd with their skills at target shooting or trick riding. Much of it done to impress the few single ladies in attendance. However, Tytus also offered to the "best hand", a finely braided horse hair bridle.

As far as Augusta was concerned, this day had already gone beyond perfection! Then when evening approached, they all gathered to watch as dusk settled over the valley like a benediction. As if it wished to give one last hurrah to the day, the copper-colored sun slipped behind the ragged mountains and fanned its brilliant rays across the horizon—like the spokes of a wagon wheel.

Tanner McGee motioned for everyone's attention, "Well now," he began with a playful air, "it is time to bid farewell to the day and call up the moon and the stars!"

Reverently, the old man placed his fiddle under his chin. Those who had never heard Tanner wondered what kind of sounds the Scotsman might conjure up from his scratched and worn violin. But just as muted shades of burnished-gold and crimson spread across the sky, Tanner drew his bow across the strings, and everyone fell silent. The sound was so sweet and pure that even the children stopped their play, and the horses pricked their ears forward and grew still. Every note—every cord—was so pleasing to the ear that when the song ended no one wished to break the spell. And yet—appreciation must be given for a gift so rare—and soon the clapping began, accompanied by words of praise and shouts for more and more.

Tanner smiled in his humble way, then with a wink to Alvaro and Hitch, the men picked up their guitars and all three began to play. They leapt right into a lively tune that soon worked its magic, and even the shyest of them could not keep from tapping their toes, while the bolder ones sprung to their feet in search of bright-eyed partners. And when every willing lady had been claimed, including Granny Rose and even little Tess and Filippa, the rest of the men were left to stand in line or dance with each other.

Augusta had promised Shep the first dance and since neither had any notion of what to do, it was mostly just the two of them holding hands, hopping about and laughing. It wasn't long, however, until a line of men had formed—every one of them, happy to teach the pretty young widow just how to step to the music.

Augusta was quick and light on her feet, and in a whirlwind of music and laughter, she soon discovered that—she loved to dance! Still every time a new song began, she would search the crowd for Tessie. More often than not she'd find that Tytus was dancing with her one minute, and giving her a sip of punch the next. Each time she saw them together something painful and sweet twisted inside her. Augusta knew that Tessie would never remember this evening, and that she would never forget it! She gazed around at all the smiling faces. These hard-working people were making happy memories. It felt good that she and Ty had given these friends this gift and, that they had done it together!

Alvaro strolled up behind Tytus and put his weathered hand on the younger man's broad shoulder.

"Ah, the fiesta, it goes well, amigo!"

Ty narrowed his eyes warily, studying the old Spaniard. "You know—" he said slowly, "when you speak to me in front of the men you call me, El Jefe, the boss! When we're alone you generally call me Tytus or Señor Ty—but when you want to give me advice *or chastise me*—it's always—*amigo.*"

Alvaro gave Ty a broad grin, then he nodded his head, "Sí, you are a most observant man—*AMIGO!*"

Ty chuckled. "All right, out with it—whatever it is," he growled.

"I have for you two questions: first—who would you say is the most beautiful woman here tonight?"

Ty made a show of searching all around then said coolly, "Granny Rose! You'll admit, she's one of a kind!"

"Sí, a—fine choice!" Alvaro agreed, with his dark eyes sparkling. "But—I was thinking of the woman—you have not taken your eyes from all day. And, when you are near her—I see my old amigo Tytus Grainger once again. Ah, I remember him well—he was—a good man! I feared we had lost him forever— but—I have seen him lately. Most especially—today!"

Ty's jaw clenched; he couldn't deny it, for even now he was watching Augusta. A scowl crossed his face as two men argued as to which one could cut in while a third cowboy danced her away.

Alvaro noted Ty's grim expression. Following his gaze with a knowing smile, he said, "I once knew a man who built a beautiful ranchero. He built it to share with the woman that God had chosen for him. A woman did come—but she was not God's choice. Now, the right woman has come! God's ways are a mystery—and yet—I truly believe that—she is the one!"

Ty's dark eyes drank in the woman in the shining blue gown as she twirled in another man's arms.

"I know she is!" he groaned. "But I've ruined everything! How can she ever forgive the way I've treated her? It's too late anyway—Hitch proposed to her this morning."

Alvaro's eyes narrowed. "He told you this?"

"Yes! When the morning service ended, he said: 'I hope you find a wife at the party, boss—but I just asked Augusta to marry me!'"

"Sí, this is so—but—" Alvaro gave a sheepish look, then explained, "It was by chance that...I happened to hear his proposal this morning. But the señora—she did *not* say yes—in fact she said very little."

Ty grabbed Alvaro by the shoulders. "Are you telling me—she didn't accept?"

"She did not!" the old man assured him. "And I tell you this—a woman in love says yes before the man has finished asking the question!" Alvaro grinned then added, "Hitch is a good man, but he did not speak of love. Instead, he praises her hard work and how easily she will give him many children!"

"What?" Ty fumed. "And she wasn't insulted by that?"

"Amigo, she is confused—she believes you are saddened by her presence, that she is a reminder of your loss. But I know this woman; she is young, but proud, and so she watches you, just as you are watching her. And I tell you—she cares. It is time for you both—to speak from your hearts!"

Ty watched Augusta dance as Alvaro's words emboldened him. Then turning to the older man he said,

"Thank you Alvaro! But you said you had two questions. What was the second one?"

The older man's white mustache twitched as he gave Tytus a broad grin. "Ah sí, the second question—amigo. It is for *you* to ask!"

Chapter 40
One Last Proposal

**"Hope deferred makes the heart sick, but a dream fulfilled is a
tree of life." Proverbs 13:12**

Augusta, turned when she felt a strong hand on her shoulder and heard
what was now a familiar request:

"Excuse me, ma'am—may I have the honor of this dance."

Augusta was somewhat stunned when she turned to find the handsome
face of Tytus Grainger. His smile was tentative and unsure, as if there was a possibility that she might refuse him.

"Well?" he asked, holding his arms out to her.

Augusta was suddenly bashful. "You surprised me!" she gasped.

"Come now, Augusta!" Ty urged. "You've danced with every man a dozen
times. Won't you take pity and dance with just one more cowpoke? I'll try not
to step on your toes."

Augusta laughed. "It's your toes that are in danger—not mine!"

Then with a concerned look, she whispered gently, "Are you sure your leg
is well enough for this?"

"My leg is rock steady—in fact—I have to warn you—I like a rambunc-
tious waltz—do you mind?"

His playful mood was infectious, and Augusta's golden eyes sparkled as
she looked up at him.

"I don't mind!"

With a broad grin Ty drew Augusta into his arms, then swirled her into a
waltz with such power and style, she knew immediately that dancing with Tytus
Grainger would be unlike dancing with any other man. They moved together
so gracefully, it was as if they were gliding over ice. And yet Tytus danced with
a kind of joyful abandon that surprised and pleased Augusta—she felt as if she
were flying!

In fact, she was so enthralled by the experience, that she didn't even realize when Ty danced them away from the crowd. Suddenly, he slowed and with

his wide shoulders, he pushed back the heavy branches of the tall lilac bushes, then he twirled them both into a small courtyard beside the hacienda.

Once inside, Ty grinned down at her while she gasped to catch her breath. "My goodness! Where are we?" she asked.

"Not far." Ty chuckled. "Just—alone for a moment."

Augusta spun around, her skirt swirling about her as she explored. No one would have ever expected that this impressive stand of lilacs secreted a tiny oasis.

The courtyard had a stone floor and there were two comfortable rocking chairs. Between the chairs stood a small round table adorned with a beautiful hurricane lamp. Its lemony glow sparkled against two crystal glasses and a tall pitcher filled with punch.

Augusta gave Ty an inquisitive look.

"This is my private hideaway! I come out here to stare at the stars and think. Thought you might like to step away from the crowd, just for a bit. You've been the belle of the ball, and you haven't danced one dance where you weren't jostled from one cowpoke to the next."

Augusta was tempted to ask why would he care. He certainly hadn't asked for a dance, until now. Then she grew wary—had she behaved improperly? Had he brought her here to speak to her about it?

"I thought it was polite to dance with anyone who asked. I didn't want to hurt anyone's feelings!"

Ty groaned with frustration; this wasn't what he wanted to talk about. Rubbing his neck, he said, "No—you did just as any good hostess should do! You've been wonderful to everyone—but..."

"But what? You seem upset with me?"

Ty grimaced and shook his head. "Not upset—well maybe—I might have been—a little jealous—"

"Jealous? You never even tried to get near me until now!"

Ty's expression turned tender as he bent to look into her eyes, "Did you want me to try?"

When Augusta only shrugged, Ty picked up the two glasses from the table and handed one to her.

"To the best hostess in the territory! You did an excellent job on this party—and this punch is delicious—but I'd wager you haven't had much of it yourself!"

Augusta gave him a grateful smile and curtsied. "Thank you," she said, then added: "How did you know I was dying of thirst?"

As she took the sparkling glass, her fingers lightly brushing across Ty's strong hand, there was an instant of awareness, but she assumed he was only teasing when he said he was jealous.

Self-consciously she lowered her eyes and drank from the cup.

"Mmm," she sighed. "I saw Alvaro fill the bowl three times, but haven't had more than a sip all night!"

Without another word Augusta drained the glass then added dreamily, "Ah! Now that's better—thank you—this is the best thing that's happened to me all night!"

Ty grinned. "I think so…"

He quickly drained his glass as well, then before Augusta could respond, Tytus sat both glasses back on the table, and pulled her back into his arms. In answer to her bemused look, he stated simply, "It's still my dance!"

Just beyond their flowery arbor, Tanner begun a poignant ballad. This time Ty danced them in slow circles, while lacy patterns of moonlight sifted through a canopy of leaves.

"Augusta," Ty whispered, "you've been a wonderful hostess, gracious and welcoming. And so beautiful—I know you've heard that a dozen times today— you've taken everyone's breath away."

Augusta suddenly wanted to ask, *You too Ty? Could I take your breath away?* But she could never be so bold. Surely, he was just trying to make up for the harsh way he used to be.

Ty drew her a little closer and admitted, "You were right about this party! You had to fight me for it—but it was a good idea—even if you did cheat to get your way."

Augusta looked up at him sweetly, then shocked the man, when she stuck out her tongue. When he'd gotten over his surprise, a low rumble of laughter came from deep in his chest.

Augusta laughed with him then said, "My papa would have called it a tactical maneuver! Besides, doesn't it make you feel good to have given these people this day as a gift! It's been good for me!"

Tytus smiled his agreement as he looked at Augusta. She was good for him! And the way she fit in his arms was just right. He would truly be content, too, if he could hold her like this forever!

Just then Augusta leaned back and closed her eyes, enjoying the sensation of floating on the music. When Tytus realized he was just about to kiss her, he drew back and cleared his throat.

"You, uh, dance very well," he stammered. "Hard to believe this is your first dance!"

Augusta opened one eye and wrinkled her nose. "Papa didn't think I was old enough to dance."

Ty quirked his brow. "Old enough to marry but not old enough to dance?"

"That was my papa!" Augusta shrugged. "You might say he was a bit protective."

Their eyes met for a moment with neither one able to break the connection.

Finally, Augusta looked away; it was then she realized how close Ty was holding her.

"You know, Papa would've had a thing or two to say about the way you're dancing with his little girl!"

It was true. Ty had been holding Augusta a bit closer with every passing minute. He grinned impishly. "Pardon me, madame," Ty apologized. But instead of stepping away he pulled her even closer. "Quite right—this is much better!"

Augusta gasped, feeling light headed. "This is not what I meant Mister Grainger, and well you know it!"

"I'm not sure that I do," he quipped, then his expression grew very tender and he whispered, "Augusta, something started happening between us long before Dewey stole you away, and I just…"

Augusta could feel his warm breath against her cheek as he spoke. She feared that maybe she was just imagining his words, maybe she liked being in the arms of Tytus Grainger, too much for her own good. It was all too confusing. Pushing against Ty's rock-hard chest, she put him at arm's length and said, "You see—now this is what Papa would consider proper."

Augusta stared up, but Ty's dark eyes were too intent to hold his gaze. Looking away she stammered, "B-both arms should be c-completely extended, elbows locked—like so."

Ty grinned; he liked that she was blushing and flustered, because maybe she was feeling it too!

With great tenderness he moaned, "No Augusta—we aren't good apart. Tell me now, isn't this better?"

Tytus gave up all pretense of dancing and folded the woman he loved into his arms.

Sighing, she rested her head on his shoulder. *Yes—it was better!* Tears threatened as she admitted to herself that she had indeed fallen in love with this big—beautiful—dragon of a man! But dragon or not she knew the man hidden inside. He was a good man: she'd seen his integrity, his loyalty, his courage. She finally had to admit that she fell more in love with Tytus Grainger every day. But was he pretending to have feelings for her? Could he be doing this more for his brother by taking care of his widow and child? Suddenly, she pushed out of Ty's arms and looked up at him.

"Thank you for the dance. I really should check on Tessie now."

But Tytus couldn't bear to let her go.

"No ... Augusta, please stay!" he begged, then he took her hands in his.

"Tessie's safe with Granny and I have some things to tell you."

Augusta fought down the threatening tears, and gracefully nodded her consent.

Lord, don't let him say that he loves me, if he doesn't! He could break my heart— please don't let him.

They stood like two statues for a moment then the keening strains of Tanner's violin filled the air once again.

"That's too pretty to waste—dance with me, Augusta."

She allowed Ty to draw her back into his arms as the beautiful music floated around them like a cloud. Tytus lifted his eyes to the moon trying to gather just the right words. Finally, he began,

"Augusta, I've asked for your forgiveness, but I haven't thanked you."

"Thanked me?" she asked.

"Yes! Even in your grief you've made this ranch a better place for all of us to live! You said a minute ago that this party was a gift. That's what you do, isn't it? You are always giving gifts. Your days are filled making things better for those around you. Whether it's sewing curtains or baking, or bookkeeping. But the gift you gave me is that I want to live again—love again!" he added gently.

Augusta searched his dark eyes and began to speak, but Ty put his fingers to her lips.

"No, please let me finish. Augusta, after how I've treated you, you may find it hard to believe, but you are the first person I think of in the morning and the last one I think of at night."

"What would be more accurate…" Augusta said sadly, "is that I've given you nightmares!"

"No, ma'am—not nightmares—dreams! I'd given up on my dreams but then you started turning my hacienda into the home I had always dreamt it could be. Even before I knew who you were, A.C. O'Brien, you had already earned my respect and my trust."

Augusta raised her head to look into Ty's face as one tear slowly rolled down her cheek.

Ty gently brushed the tear away with his thumb, and said, "You may find it hard to believe but, I love you—have for a while now! But, it was easier to ignore than admit!"

"Tytus," Augusta protested, "I've been a thorn in your side."

"I'm ashamed for making you think that!" Ty admitted. "I watched you—looking for flaws. I looked for an enemy and found a woman to love instead. Then Tessie invaded my library and—I knew my days as a dyed-in-the-wool *curmudgeon* were—over for good!"

Augusta sniffed back her tears and smiled knowingly, "Tessie got to you, didn't she?"

"She's a sweet little bear trap!" Ty growled. "She lights up when I just look at her—who can fight that?"

Augusta understood too well—Ty was gazing at her and she felt like a Christmas tree—lit with a thousand candles.

"We'll never understand all that's happened to us this year, or why. But I do know that when you and Tessie came into my life, it was a blessing from God! You two have made me feel like the man I once was. A better man. I don't know how you'll ever believe me—after the way I've treated you."

Augusta smiled. "I've known all along you weren't really the fire-breathing dragon you seemed to be."

Ty ran the back of his hand gently down Augusta's smooth cheek.

"Oh, I probably have one or two hot coals still burning down deep—but you seem to tame the dragon in me. I love you, Augusta! And I love Tessie—more than I can ever say!"

A sudden warmth spread through Augusta like the first spring day after a hard winter.

"Oh, Tytus, we've both been so miserable. Why did you wait so long to say something?"

"When Hitch and I were looking for you he challenged my arrogance. He said that my being rich didn't always guarantee my having the best of everything, meaning you!"

When Augusta only looked puzzled he explained, "I didn't want to get in the way if you were in love with Hitch. If you are? Then, I'll be the one to go away. I've decided the ranch should be yours and Tessie's. The past few weeks I've realized that I built this place for you, Augusta. And it was always half Tim's! So, that makes the Bar 61 more yours than mine! You're a wealthiest woman in the territory Augusta! You don't have to marry anyone. The Bar 61 is yours—no matter what."

Augusta couldn't believe Ty would give her the ranch he loved so much.

"Tytus, I would never take everything from you!"

"You wouldn't be," he assured her, "knowing you has restored my faith in God! I've seen you go through so much and still trust in God through it all! Just as I should have. No matter how this talk ends tonight I want you to know what you've done for me. I am ashamed of how I've treated you. Ashamed that you thought I wouldn't come for you when Dewey took you."

Gently he put both his hands on Augusta's arms, and taking a deep breath, he went on: "Augusta, I know Hitch proposed to you today and probably so has every man that's danced with you tonight! Now...I want you to marry me—but only if you love me! You have to be truthful about this. If nothing else you can simply add my proposal to your list of love-struck cowpokes that want you for their own!"

Augusta stared up at Tytus in a daze, her golden eyes moist with emotion.

Ty had never felt so vulnerable; he was desperate to hear her speak but didn't know how he would walk away if she said no!

"Augusta," he whispered, "I want you. But what do you want?"

Augusta placed her soft hand on the man's hard jaw and smiled shyly into Ty's fathomless eyes.

"What do I want?" she asked hesitantly. "Well—right now—I—I want you to kiss me, Ty!"

The big man looked stunned for a moment, then he saw the loving, golden sheen in her eyes. Ty's heart bucked inside his chest, and with the passion of the dragon, he took immediate possession of Augusta's soft mouth, while she returned his kiss with a fire of her own.

Augusta had needed to know what Ty's kiss would be like! She was afraid it might be too much like another man's kiss, but it wasn't. Even so, their shared embrace carried them away. As if on wings they flew over the lilac trees, heading for a new adventure. The moment the kiss ended Ty drew in a breath, he chuckled, and then he growled low in his throat, "That sure felt like—yes—to me! Was it?"

"Oh, yes!" Augusta agreed, her smile radiant.

Ty kissed her again just to make sure, then he picked her up, and swung her around the courtyard.

When he set her down his words began tripping over each other: "As for the wedding—ever since you said yes—I've been thinking this over!"

"That long?" Augusta laughed as her brows arched, but her eyes were full of warmth and delight.

"Yes!" Ty grinned, a dimple flirting in his right cheek. "It isn't widely known, but Tanner McGee doesn't just know the Bible, he was once a preacher in a previous life. Like most westerners, he has his secrets, but he can still be persuaded to help a couple tie the knot. Of course, it can be any kind of wedding you like. I'll even take you to New York, to be with your friends!"

Ty pulled her close and whispered, "Or we can have another big party here? I don't care—just so long as we end up together!"

With a sigh he added gently, "Of course, living under the same roof with you now—I wouldn't mind if it were sooner rather than later—but I'll leave it up to you!"

Augusta worried her lower her lip, then suddenly an impish twinkle came into her honey-colored eyes, and with it came a shrewd smile as she brushed at his coat and straightened his black string tie.

"I think I'd rather we get married here—with all our neighbors—under the stars in the moonlight!"

Ty nodded his head. "Sure—sure, we'll order up another night just like this one!"

"Exactly like this one? And soon, don't you think? Like Tanner said, he's not getting any younger." Augusta laughed, then she gave Ty her most beguiling smile. "So—what about, right now?" she asked.

When she looked up and saw Ty's mouth drop open—she became terribly self-conscious. "I'm sorry—that sounded awfully bold, didn't it? It's just that I didn't want to…"

She was about to say she didn't ever want to let him go. Augusta was struggling to hide her embarrassment when Tytus leaned his head back and whooped in delight, while a tremendous dimple creased one side of his handsome face.

"Oh, you sweet girl!" he exclaimed. "I was afraid to hope, but that's exactly what I wanted you to say!"

Augusta relaxed, then laughed as Ty picked her up and carried her out into the yard as he called, "Gather around, friends! How about ending the day with a wedding! And you are all invited!"

Alvaro and Joseph, who were standing by the fire, beamed their broad grins, then with a whoop they threw their hats in the air. Everyone began laughing and applauding their host and hostess. Hitch, with Helen Anderson on his arm, approached the couple with a surprised but sincere smile.

"Congratulations—to you both!" he said with a grin.

Ty reached out and shook his foreman's hand. "Thanks, Hitch, I could use a best man—want the job?"

"And Helen?" Augusta asked.

Augusta suddenly felt terribly bashful, then she whispered into Ty's ear, "You can put me down now."

"Nope!" Ty said boldly. "You can say what you need to from here."

Then, he gave her an intent look and said softly, "You are comfortable in my arms, aren't you?"

Augusta answered him with a kiss, which brought laughter from the crowd.

Then, turning back to the young woman who seemed so at ease beside Hitch, she asked, "Helen, will you stand up with me? I'd be so pleased if you would!"

Helen's eyes sparkled, happy to be included in this honor along with Hitch.

Soon everyone was in place, and Tanner McGee stood before them. In his rich Scottish burr he quoted from the book of Ruth:

"Entreat me not to leave thee nor return from following after thee; for whither thou goest, I will go and whither thou lodgest, I will lodge, thy people shall be my people and thy God, my God!"

After the couple had pledged themselves one to the other, he encircled their hands in his and prayed, "May the Lord bless ye," he began. "Ye have known sorrow, may ye know joy in yer life together! May yer love fer God and each other grow stronger with each day. May He bless ye with a houseful of healthy children and may ye raise them in the nurture and admonition of God! Amen."

Later, as Ty carried his blushing bride over the threshold of his bedroom, he knew a moment of concern, "Augusta, we may have rushed into this a bit. Do you mind very much?"

She wrapped her arms tight around her husband's neck and laughed. "Tytus Grainger, of course we *rushed* into this! An hour ago you didn't mind—are you getting cold feet?"

"Not me!" he assured her. "I just suddenly worried that I'd pushed you a bit. How do you feel?"

"So far—I'm quite happy! And don't you remember? It was me that chose the day."

When Tytus relaxed Augusta grew more serious, adding, "I married your brother the day after we met, and we were very happy together. Tytus, we've been through so much this year, both sorrow and danger! And we've both grown closer to God and learned a lot about ourselves and each other. Without our even realizing it we've become a good team, whether we're training horses or adding sums. We've been in love with each other for quite a while now. We were just too stubborn to admit it—until tonight! I'm sure we'll argue at times—we're too alike not to—but ... " Just then, Augusta playfully smiled up at Ty as she added, "Of course—we could always arm wrestle—if we need to settle our differences!"

Tytus grinned broadly, and just before he bent to kiss her, he growled, "I like the way you think, Missus Grainger! The idea of wrestling to settle our difference—now that idea—has definite possibilities!"

EPILOGUE

"In all these things we are more than conquerors through Him that loved us." Romans 8:37

Sahara Storm's silver coat glistened like a diamond in the morning sun; as Augusta cantered the mare across the meadow scattered with colorful wild flowers.

"How like my dream!" she mused, while the cool breeze teased at her dark curls. She could see it all so plainly now: it was all part of God's plan. Both the nightmare and the dream had been a warning on one hand and a promise on the other.

Augusta reined in and gazed across the valley. And there before her stood the mountain guardian that had visited her dreams. Now she even knew its name, Pike's Peak, that mysterious and benevolent giant, so regally guarding the Colorado plains.

When she heard a familiar hoof beat coming up behind her, she smiled but didn't turn. Quest slid to a stop, a moment later she felt a man's hand tugging gently on her gloved fingers. Her heart quickened in response; the rhythm of her pulse always changed whenever Tytus Grainger was near. She turned her gaze and there he was beside her, so strong, so handsome, sitting tall and straight, a more perfect match for Quest. The two mighty stallions of the Bar 61.

Ty's dark eyes were ablaze with warmth. Augusta still blushed when she caught that roguish twinkle in her husband's flashing eyes. The saddle leather creaked as she tenderly reached out to touch the dimple in his right cheek.

They spoke of Timothy as they sat watching the sun slide behind the Rockies. He had taught them both to treasure the pearls, just like this one, hidden in each day. Ty tightened his hold on Augusta's hand, as the mountains became a black silhouette, while the last rays of the sun cast wild and jagged streaks across the western horizon. Shades of gold and amber melted into rose and crimson. The brilliant colors finally faded, then merged into the deeper and darker blue of the night sky.

Ty bent close and his lips slanted over Augusta's—once, twice—then she turned her face up to his with a satisfied sigh. This was her life! It was not a dream—nor did this place remind her of a nightmare. All that was good had been God's doing. She was here because of His constant provision, His unfailing love. Through it all Augusta had learned that whether she found herself in the pit with evil all around, or in a valley, or on a mountaintop, the true Giant of her dreams would be with her.

She had thought it was the mountain that had beckoned to her; but it was the Savior who had called her name.

God was the Giant in her life; He was higher than the mountains, deeper than the sea. He was the one she had longed to know. God alone could see her over the high places and through the low valleys of life.

The true Giant was Jesus Christ—her Lord and her Savior! He was and always would be her...

Giant in the Valley!

THE END

"Don't be impatient for the Lord to act! Keep traveling steadily along His pathway and in due season He will honor you with every blessing, and you will see the wicked destroyed." Psalm 37:34

Bible verses referred to in Giant in the Valley:

Ephesians 3:20 "Now Glory be to God, for by HIS mighty power at work within us is able to do far more than we would ever dare to ask or even dream of, infinitely beyond our highest prayers, desires thoughts or hopes."

I Kings 4:26 "Solomon had forty thousand stalls of horses for his chariots, and twelve thousand horsemen."

Job 39:19-24 "Did you give the horse his strength or cloth his neck with a flowing mane? Do you make him leap like a locust, striking terror with his proud snorting? He paws fiercely, rejoicing in his strength, and charges into the fray. He laughs at fear, afraid of nothing; he does not shy away from the sword. The quiver rattles against his side along with the flashing spear and lance. In frenzied excitement he eats up the ground; he cannot stand still when the trumpet sounds"

John 3:16 "For God so loved the world, that He gave His only begotten son, that whoever believes in Him should not perish but have everlasting life."

John 14:6 "Jesus said, I am the way, the truth, and the life: no man comes to the Father, but by me."

Isaiah 49:15-16 "Can a woman forget her nursing child, that she should have no compassion on the son of her womb?' Even these may forget! Yet I will never forget you. Behold, I have engraved you on the palms of my hands."

Genesis 2:18 "It's not good for a man to be alone"

Philippians 4:13 "I can do all things with Christ who strengthens me."

II Timothy 1:7 "God doesn't give us a spirit of fear, but of love and power and a sound mind."

Luke 6:28 "Bless them that curse you, and pray for them which despitefully use you."

Isaiah 41:10 "Be not dismayed; for I am your God. I will strengthen you; I will uphold you with my righteous right hand"

Matthew 6:25 "Only when a man loses his life will he find it."

Hebrews 13:8 "Jesus Christ is the same yesterday, and today, and forever."

Romans 10:9 "If you shall confess with your mouth the Lord Jesus, and shall believe in your heart that God has raised him from the dead, you will be saved."

Ruth 1:16 "Entreat me not to leave thee nor return from following after thee; for whither thou goest, I will go and whither thou lodgest, I will lodge, thy people shall be my people and thy God, my God!"

Made in the USA
Charleston, SC
30 December 2013